Legends Lost

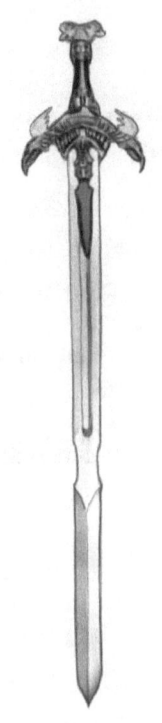

Tesnayr

Nova Rose

Legends Lost Tesnayr

Copyright © 2012 Janet McNulty Cover Illustration by Robert Henry Interior Illustration by Robert Henry Interior Text Design by Janet McNulty Title Page Illustration by Robert Henry

Library of Congress Cataloguing-in-publication data

LCCN: 2012942624

Paperback:
ISBN 13: 978-0615624044
ISBN 10: 0615624049

Printed in the United States of America

—For my mother who let me bounce ideas off of her.

Contents

Book One A Broken Man

Prologue   1

Chapter I A Broken Stranger   7

Chapter II Virnae   28

Chapter III Message for the King   44

Chapter IV New Recruits   68

Chapter V The First Engagement   80

Chapter VI An Ally   93

Chapter VII An Old Metting   100

Chapter VIII Betrayal   117

Chapter IX Rescue   129

Chapter X What Next   145

Chapter XI Winter   163

Chapter XII A Meeting Between Enemies   175

Chapter XIII In the Mountains   185

Book Two Through the Fire

Chapter I Venture   191

Chapter II A Daughter of Kings   196

Chapter III Listening   211

Chapter IV Spring   215

Chapter V Dangerous Road   219

Chapter VI Through the Mountains   235

Chapter VII Strangers in the Mountains   245

Chapter VIII Legend's Road   256

Chapter IX A Cure   278

Chapter X A Captain Made General   284

Chapter XI A Rude Awakening   291

Chapter XII A New Ally   305

Chapter XIII Distcontent   320

Chapter XIV A Dismal Prospect   326

Book Three Five Made One

Chapter I Ride East   329

Chapter II The Council at D'arr   342

Chapter III A Father's Choice   348

Chapter IV Jenel's Decision   351

Chapter V Battle for La'nar   354

Chapter VI Deep in the Orc's Council   365

Chapter VII To Drynelle   368

Chapter VIII A Village Forsaken   370

Chapter IX A Trap   379

Chapter X Illusions   385

Chapter XI The Burning Plains   393

Chapter XII Captured   399

Chapter XIII Revealations in Stone   406

Chapter XIV An End to all Things   417

Chapter XV Amends   431

Chapter XVI Five Lords   436

Chapter XVII High King   441

Epilogue   446

Glossary   450

Coming 2013:

About the Author

If you liked Tesnayr, you'll enjoy:

Other young adult fiction by this writer under Janet McNulty

Get the Latest Trilogy by Janet McNulty

Silvery Seas
Black Mountains
Firey Caves
Le'Dar
Belyndril
Bluhon
Perili Mountains
Changing Woods
Taliny
Amythest River
Azul Plains
Sym'dul
Scales
Rainbow River
Death Valley
Arsa Mountains
Hemil
Esquir Sea
MurDair
Crystal Creek
D'arr
Unsirth Plains
Whispering Canyons
Gangas Pass
Lil' Montes
Swalga
Keep of Ebrel
Castille
Belarnia
Samara

Hill's Valley

Samara

Scales

Rainbow River

Crystal Creek

Death Valley

NurDair

Unsirth Plains

• D'ur

Whispering Canyon

Ganges Pass

Arsa Mountains

Seglis Pass

Lil' Montes

Firey Caves

Swamp Lands

Taling

Scales

Rainbow River

Belyndrii

Silvery Seas

Changing Woods

Death Valley

La Dar

Blubon

Arsh Mountain

Scals Pass

Perili Mountains

Road

Mountains

eglis Pass

Lil' Montes

Ḥamil

Smalya
Keep of Elrei

Castile

Azul P

Belarnia

Sym

Darlui

Esquir Sea

Perili Mountains
Firsche
Flatlands
Amythest River
Azul Plains
Sym'dul
Black Mountains

Book One
A Broken Man

A stranger comes from across the sea
Questions abound: Who is he?
None know and he refuses to tell
his story. He is a broken man.

He is a broken man.
His soul shattered and torn.
He knows not where to turn
for the ache in his spirit.

This man has seen much suffering.
His eyes tell you so.
His face is that of one used to war;
of one used to sorrow and death.

He is a man of few words.
He toils to make a new life for himself,
but everywhere he turns
the horrors of his past return.

War comes in the form of conquest.
The man's new life is ripped from him
as he witnesses the death of one he loves.
So he cries in angst at a past that won't grant release.

Fists clenched, he faces his horrors.
He casts aside his new life
and dons the one he's meant to live.
Sword in hand, he confronts his past, his destiny.

A broken man he may have been
walking a long and lonely road.
His path is hard and full of despair.
Come what may; he will venture it until the end.

Prologue

"Blynak, you never told me that you were going to kill him," yelled Jarown. He grabbed Blynak roughly by the arm and yanked him to a stop. "Selnik is my friend. I can easily get the information from him. You promised me that no one would get hurt."

The aroma of heated steel from the blacksmith's furnace floated in the air. Nothing had gone according plan. If only Jarown had not become jealous he never would have told Blynak that Selnik was captain of the guard and possessed useful information. *Used by greed.* He felt Blynak's steely eyes upon him.

"And no one will be if Selnik cooperates," replied Blynak.

Suspicion clouded Jarown's transparent face. Blynak had broken his word once. What was to stop him from doing it again? "But taking his wife and child prisoner! How—."

"Dare I?" said Blynak coldly. He had met many like Jarown. Disgruntled servants of the king. Easily obtained and easily disposed of. "You came to me. You betrayed your own people, your own friend. And you question me? Perhaps your judgment is clouded by your feelings for his wife. You have been most helpful, Jarown, but I think your usefulness has ended." At a wave of his hand two of Blynak's men pinned Jarown's arms behind him.

"You will regret this, Blynak," exclaimed Jarown, struggling to break free.

"I think not," replied Blynak. "Kill him."

Jarown stumbled as the men pushed him through the encampment. The clinking and grinding of metal filled his ears as soldiers sharpened their swords, repaired their armor, and polished their shields. An enlightening fog settled upon his mind. As they prepared for war, Jarown's heart sank. Blynak had never intended to keep his word. He had been a tool.

When they reached a secluded area, Jarown was thrown to the ground. He acted quickly. He flung himself into the stomach of one man slamming him into a tree. He grabbed the blade of the other's sword, bashing him in the face with the hilt. Afterward, he sliced the other's side. He searched the bodies for weapons he could use finding a sword and a dagger. He wrapped the cloak of one around himself as camouflage.

To reach Selnik, Jarown needed a horse, but they were at the other end of the camp. Jarown crept through the outer edge of the encampment with his head down. His heart stopped. Blynak walked toward him with his two most trusted men. Quickly, Jarown ducked between two soldiers gathered around a fire pretending to warm his hands. The soldiers ignored him. He kept his face down. Once Blynak passed, Jarown stood up naturally so as not to attract attention. Spotting a sack of barley, an idea struck him. He picked it up. The mundane sack allowed him to easily blend in as a stable hand. He hunched his shoulders and stooped low like most of the peons.

Jarown cursed when he saw the guard by the horse pen. There never used to be one stationed there. He wanted to avoid killing him as another body would attract attention. Men's voices passed by him. Strengthening his grip on the sack, Jarown approached the guard devising a plan. "I am to feed the horses," he said meekly, eyes on the ground.

"I am to let no one pass," replied the guard.

"I have my orders, sir."

The guard took a closer look at Jarown, his eyebrows scrunched. "Remain here." He went to another guard several yards away.

While they talked, Jarown seized his moment. The bag of barley thudded in the dirt as he dumped it. The horses flapped their tales and whinnied as Jarown hastily cut one loose. He sped off through the trees followed by clouds of red dust.

Jarown tore through the remaining forest. Branches snagged his cloak in an attempt to stop him. The sting of the wind caused his eyes to water, but he refused to slow down. There was little time. The forest gave way to a valley. The freshness of the air invigorated him to press on even harder.

Smoke filled Jarown's nostrils as he approached Selnik's home. The instant he spotted the men dragging Selnik's wife from the cottage, there was no doubt in his mind. He was too late. One last scream pierced the air as one of her attackers drew his sword and plunged it into her chest.

Jarown pushed his horse harder. Madness ensued as Selnik ran to his wife in a violent rage. He embraced her lifeless body as her attackers advanced. Selnik snatched the blade of one's sword and ripped it from the man's hands. The stunned man doubled over as Selnik jabbed him in the stomach. The remaining four surrounded Selnik. One attacked. Selnik blocked allowing himself to be distracted. The second grabbed him around the neck while a third wrenched his arms behind his back. Selnik struggled forcefully throwing one of the men to the ground. His body went limp as the other two stabbed him in the stomach. Laughter fill the atmosphere as Selnik fell to the ground motionless.

Blynak's men looked up calmly as Jarown galloped toward them and pulled his horse to a halt. "Jarown," said one, "You needn't be here." The man casually moved toward Jarown wiping the blood off of his sword. "Blynak knows he can trust us. Why has he sent you?"

Jarown glanced at the two bodies. Fury engulfed him. The gravel crunched under Jarown's boots as he unsheathed his sword, and lopped off the guy's head. The others watched the head roll across the ground in silence. They looked up at Jarown. His steely expression told them that he was there for his own purpose. Cautiously, they drew near. Jarown stood ready for their attack. One charged him. Jarown sidestepped and swung his sword at the second man. The first man attacked again. Jarown turned in time to block but not before being knocked off his feet. He rolled across the ground to avoid their blows, losing his sword in the process. Panting, he considered his options. He snatched a rock and smashed it in the face of one. Afterward, he dove for his sword, snatched it, swept the feet of another before impaling him. Jarown fought wildly until he had killed them all. He only paused in his fight when he was satisfied they were all dead.

Jarown's victory left a hollow feeling in his gut as he nudged one of the bodies with the toe of his boot. He poked another with his blood stained sword. Jarown carefully checked each corpse making certain they were dead until he noticed Selnik. Emotions slashed his soul as he remembered why this had happened. He ran to his friend. Selnik still breathed, but each breath was shorter than the first. Jarown cradled the man in his arms and leaned close to speak to him. "Selnik," he whispered, "Forgive me. I did not mean—" An unwanted sob choked off his words.

"Nelyn," coughed Selnik, "Promise me you will look after her. Take care of her, Jarown." Selnik breathed his last.

A loud crash burst from the cabin. Warily, Jarown approached. He entered the bungalow and saw that a struggle had taken place minutes before. He walked among the scattered bowls and utensils being careful not to make a sound. A tiny cough vibrated the air. He turned abruptly and discovered a small, blonde haired girl crouched in a corner. She hugged her knees as she looked up at him with frightened eyes. "Where is mummy?" she asked meekly.

Jarown stared down at her impassively. "Your mother is dead," he told her. "You will come with me."

Instead of crying, the girl held her arms toward him. He stood there uncertain of what to do, having never handled children. His mind raced between comforting her and remaining rigid. Awkwardly, Jarown scooped her up and carried her into the daylight. He placed the girl in the saddle. "Stay," he told her.

He then walked over to the woman's body, gently lifted her, and carried her over to Selnik placing her at his side. He set dried brush tenderly around the bodies in the shape of a pyre. His emotions tickled the back of his throat when he lit the torch. Thick, black smoke burst from the licking flames as the pyre burned. A lone tear escaped his eyes.

The girl watched in silence, her cheeks glistened in the sunlight. She never whimpered. Jarown approached the horse and gazed at her for a moment admiring her strength. He had failed to save his friend, a failure that would haunt him the rest of his life. But there was one thing he could do. He could care for Selnik's child. He rode away with her determined to abide by the wish of his deceased friend.

Fifteen years later...

Chapter I
A Broken Stranger

Lightning streaked the night sky. Tumultuous waves tossed the splintered ship as though it were a mere toy. Foaming water crashed onto the deck drenching any unfortunate enough to be on it. More lightning flashed followed by roars of thunder. The ship lurched violently as humungous waves attacked it relentlessly forcing it to dip below the water before shooting back up to the surface once more.

In the cargo hold pounding water thundered against the hull causing the ship to crack and creak with ominous terror. Below deck sat three men chained to the water soaked floor. They paid little heed to the storm. Hinges squeaked as the door opened. Heavy feet stomped down the steps to the men below warning them of trouble.

"That one," snarled a voice. His words were barely audible over the roaring ocean.

Two orcs undid the man's chains. He groaned slightly. They hefted him up callously as he continued to moan from the pain of his injuries. His bare and bruised feet bumped each step as they hauled him through the opening. The bang of the slamming door echoed through the wood only to be drowned by the wrath of the raging storm.

They dragged the man across the slippery deck barely able to keep their balance as the vessel bounced on the agitated water. The man's feet left trails on the soaked wood. One orc stumbled and lost its balance as the ship reeled again.

"Hurry up with that scum," yelled another orc.

BOOM!

More thunder broke the night.

The unusual sound of flapping wings caught the man's attention. He craned his head upward straining his stiff muscles to look. A strange bird rested upon the bow of the ship, staring at him. Its feathers glowed brilliantly despite the harshness of the night. Red and gold.

More giant waves crashed over the ship as the wind howled around it with its pent up fury. Distracted, the man looked away only to find that when he turned back the bird had gone.

An orc screamed and flailed its arms as water swept it overboard into the sea. Crack! The mast snapped as the gale twisted it about its base. Slowly, it tipped over gaining momentum until it slammed onto the deck of the ship snapping lines and tearing the sails.

The man seized his chance and flung the other orc off of him. Summoning what strength he had, he snatched a broken board and bashed it into another's skull.

The ship free-fell as the sea continued to toss it about. Taking a quick sweep of the vessel, the man dove overboard taking his chances with the open ocean. He plunged into the black sea and sank quickly. Kicking with his remaining strength the man burst through the surface of the water inhaling deeply. Seawater trickling down his throat made him cough violently.

He watched as another wave plowed into the ship and overturned it. Fire broke out as the treacherous ocean pulled the ship under and disposed of its horrors. Good riddance, thought the man. A piece of floating debris brushed him. Hastily, he latched onto it not caring if he died or lived. At least the nightmare had finally ended.

*   *   *

Nigilin ignored the damp wind as he walked briskly along the open shore. He momentarily wondered what lay beyond the great waves of the ocean as he stared out across them. "What gifts have you for me today," he whispered to it.

It had become his habit to talk to the ocean each day as he walked along the sand. The sea never answered back, but Nigilin felt that it was alive and deserved to be paid respect. After all, its waters did bring him his means of an income.

Nigilin adjusted the limp bag of twenty or so starfish on his shoulder. Not one of his better days. Hana would pay him for his catch, he knew that. He tried not to think about some of the herbal remedies she put dried starfish in. Though he liked the lamps she sometimes made from them.

Meow.

A black cat did a figure eight around Nigilin's legs. "Hello, cat," he greeted.

The cat ran off stopping suddenly. Its head whipped around. The animal stared at him with its yellow eyes. Ignoring the feline, Nigilin bent down to pick up another starfish that had washed ashore.

"Ouch," he yelled.

The cat pricked his legs with its sharp claws screeching loudly. Aggravated, Nigilin followed the animal with his eyes as it bounded off.

A shadow on the ground caught his eye. The light of the setting sun caressed a facedown body. Dropping his sack, he ran to the still form. Sandy hair was plastered to swollen bruises on the stranger's face. Nigilin checked for any signs of life and felt a faint breath against his cheek. Gently, he heaved the unconscious man onto his shoulders and carried him to his cottage.

Nigilin kicked the wooden door open as he carried the stranger inside and laid him on the only bed in the place. He removed the man's ragged clothes and covered him with blankets to keep him warm. The man shivered violently from fever. Nigilin lit a lamp and took a closer look at the man. He had seen some horrible things in his life, but this made him gasp.

Tangled seaweed littered the stranger's mangy hair. A jagged scar carved his left cheek. His twisted nose had evidently been broken a few times.   Nigilin noted another scar that stretched from the man's right shoulder to the waist.   But it was an old wound from long ago.

Fresh burns marked the man's muscular chest though they barely stood out among all the blackened bruises.   Blood trickled from his cracked lips as the stranger coughed.   Nigilin ran the lamplight over the man's left arm.   His swollen, left arm was caked in more blood.

Carefully, Nigilin removed a piece of cloth that clung to a gash on the stranger's leg.   The foul stench nearly made him retch.   Swollen with infection, Nigilin knew that it had to be treated straight away.

Fresh scrapes and cuts littered the man's body as though he had been trying to escape from some unspeakable terror.   Gingerly, Nigilin lifted the man up.   The stranger's back had clearly been flogged a day or two ago.   He laid the man back down with care.

Sadly, Nigilin shook his head.   *By rights, he should be dead.* Setting the lamp down, Nigilin fetched water from the well and put a kettle in the fire to boil.   He brought steaming water and bandages to the stranger's bedside.

First things first, he thought as he stared at the puss filled wound on the man's thigh.   Nigilin grabbed the knife he had stuck in the fire for sterilization.   He placed leather between the man's teeth.

Taking a deep breath, Nigilin sliced open the scab on the wound cutting deep into the infected area.   A painful groan escaped the stranger's lips.   Nigilin sliced a bit more.   Instantly, white puss oozed from the cut covering the leg with its grotesqueness.   Nigilin wiped it away.   He placed his hands on either side of the gash and squeezed.   Pus burst from the opening hitting the wall behind him.   More groaning escaped the man as he moved a bit.

Nigilin quickly placed a hand on the man's chest forcing him back down. "Steady," he whispered.

He turned back to his task and squeezed some more. Each time he put pressure on the wound pus spilled from it. With each eruption Nigilin wiped the area clean with a cloth soaked in boiling water. After about an hour of forcing the infection from the laceration Nigilin knew he had reached the end. Soon, only blood came forth. To Nigilin, it was a good sign.

He poured warm water over the gash washing it clean. Afterward, Nigilin placed fresh bandages on it covering it completely. He made certain to secure them with enough pressure to stop the bleeding, but not too much where it would cut off the circulation.

With the first task completed, Nigilin began cleaning and dressing the man's remaining wounds working tirelessly throughout the night. If the stranger survived, Nigilin would send for Hana in the morning. As a healer, she had far more knowledge about this than he would ever possess. And so one of the longest nights in Nigilin's life passed.

A knock on the door woke Nigilin. He rubbed sleep from his eyes as a more persistent knock shook the door rattling the hinges. Nigilin opened it to find the boy who regularly delivered goods from the market. "Twenty coins please," said the boy.

Nigilin handed the boy the coins including five more. "I need you to fetch Hana for me. Tell her I have a gravely ill man here."

The boy took the coins and sped off. He returned with Hana within the hour.

The plump woman entered the cottage out of breath. Bits of graying hair fell from her tight bun. She set her basket of herbs by the fire pulling out some dried, foul smelling leaves and handed them to Nigilin.

"Boil these in hot water for one hour," she said.

Hana looked over the sick man while Nigilin set about his task. She carefully examined his wounds and dabbed a cool cloth on his forehead. Upon seeing the dressing on the man's leg, Hana smiled. She lifted it up carefully inspecting it thoroughly.

"You did well on this cut," she said. From Hana that was high praise.

"I learned a few things in the King's army," replied Nigilin.

When the salve was ready she soaked some bandages in it and applied them to the stranger's wounds. "To fight infection," she explained to Nigilin while he watched her work. She placed a hearty amount of the medicine on the man's leg after squeezing out some remnants of pus.

Nigilin helped Hana bandage the rest of the wounds. Mostly, he lifted the man's body so that she could tend to the stripes on his back. Hana's frown told Nigilin that she thought the same thing he did: why would anyone do such a thing?

When they finished bandaging the man, Hana poured water down the stranger's throat. Hana spent the rest of the day tending the strange man while Nigilin went about his chores: chopping wood, tending his garden, mending what needed to be fixed, and collecting starfish. Hana left when evening came.

"I have prepared more medicine," she explained to Nigilin as she prepared to leave. "When it is time to change the bandages soak the new ones in it before applying them. See to it that he drinks plenty of water. I will return in the morning. If his fever does not break by then..." Hana broke off.

There was no need for her to finish her thought. Nigilin knew what she meant.

She paused in the doorway. "Who is this man?"

"I do not know," replied Nigilin. "I found him washed up on shore."

Hana shook her head in thought. "He has suffered much. I only hope that we are doing him a favor by saving his life."

"Should I have left him there to die?" asked Nigilin.

"Of course not," replied Hana. "His physical wounds can be mended easily. It is the ones within his mind that concern me."

Nigilin knew what she referred to. He had shown up on her doorstep one day long ago in the same state as the man on his bed. Broken, Hana tended his wounds. But the last war affected him deeply. That was the year of Rybnik's rebellion. The year they had buried the king's eldest daughter. The bloodiest year of his life, that is how he remembered it. Afterward, Nigilin came here to the shore. He built his little cottage and spent the rest of his days trying to forget. It had been a long ten years since then.

Later that night Nigilin stirred the fire and changed the man's bandages. The stranger's forehead still felt warm. Nigilin wrapped a blanket around himself and fell asleep in a chair. The next morning he awoke to find the stranger staring at him.

"Feeling better?" Nigilin paused unsure of how to address him.

"Tesnayr," said the man in introduction. "I feel tired." Silence ensued until, "Who are you?"

"My name is Nigilin. I found you on the shore. Are you hungry?" The man nodded as Nigilin gave him a bowl of broth. Tesnayr sipped it slowly.

"Tesnayr. That is an unusual name," commented Nigilin.

"No more unusual than Nigilin."

"Duly noted."

A knock at the door interrupted them. Nigilin opened it. Hana waltzed inside handing him more herbs with the same order, "Boil these for one hour."

She walked over to Tesnayr apparently pleased that he had awakened. She beamed as she felt his forehead. "Your fever has broken, but your head is still a bit warm. You will need to rest for the next few days."

Gently, she removed his bandages and examined his wounds. A satisfied expression crossed her face. When Nigilin brought over the boiled herbs, Hana set about dressing Tesnayr's wounds with fresh bandages. Her expertise and years of tending to people's cuts made the task go smoothly.

Morning had passed into afternoon by the time she had finished. Hana prepared a meal for the three of them not wanting to leave her new patient.

"Where are you from?" asked Nigilin while they ate.

"Far away," replied Tesnayr.

"I figured that," said Nigilin. "What is the name of your home world?"

Tesnayr chewed his stew methodically in answer.

"What happened?" asked Hana. "Those wounds did not appear on their own. Are you an escaped prisoner or something?" Her curiosity slipped into her voice.

"Why are you asking all these questions?" asked Tesnayr testily.

"Curiosity mostly," said Hana. "But we've some right to know. You washed up on our shore and are obviously not from around here. Your mannerisms and dialect give it away. And you are quite a mess. This is a quiet village and we've some right to know if we ought to expect trouble."

"Hana," warned Nigilin.

"His arrival is suspicious," said Hana. "The least he can do is tell us how he got here and if anyone is going to come looking for him."

"I was shipwrecked," said Tesnayr, "And yes I was a prisoner on that ship, captured by beasts too terrible to describe. There was a storm and I managed to escape. I never thought I would end up here."

"You mean you hoped to die," said Nigilin matter of factly.

Tesnayr looked away. That was what he had hoped.

"There, that wasn't so hard," said Hana digging into her supper and ignoring Nigilin's comment. "What is the name of your home?"

"It is best left a memory."

"Perhaps we should let the man eat," said Nigilin. "Maybe he will tell us when he has strength enough to do so."

Hana snorted but reined in her questions. Nigilin was right; being too pushy might cause the man to clam up.

The next few days passed without incident. Hana checked on them regularly and remained optimistic about Tesnayr's recovery. Nigilin occasionally asked Tesnayr about his past, but soon learned that such efforts proved useless. Instead he settled on making conversation about menial things so as to break the silence.

Tesnayr kept to himself. He refused to talk about himself, but his demeanor displayed that something bothered him. He had wounds deeper than the ones on his body. He was courteous and polite, always eager to help with whatever chores he could. The least he could do for the man that rescued him.

One night, Nigilin watched as Tesnayr slept fitfully. He easily read the man's character. His manner was that of a soldier, of one used to war and who had fought many battles. Nigilin guessed that Tesnayr had either been betrayed, or like most soldiers, had seen enough of death. He figured it best to just keep the man engaged in the present while he worked things out on his own. Besides, prying into another man's affairs was not Nigilin's priority.

Tesnayr had regained much of his former strength by the second week. The color had returned to his face and he was eager to get outside. Hana stopped by daily, as was now her custom. She brought a staff with her and handed it to him. "You are strong enough to get out of bed. I want you to use this for walking around until your leg has healed completely. You are to spend at least thirty minutes a day walking outside."

Tesnayr regarded the staff coldly. "I do not need that."

Hana shoved the walking stick in his hands and put hers on her hips. Her stern expression unnerved Tesnayr. "I did not ask if you needed it. Nor did I ask if you wanted it."

Relenting, Tesnayr used the staff to help himself to his feet.

Hana beamed triumphantly and helped him out the door. She walked with him outside. "Nigilin tells me that you keep to yourself," she commented.

"Is there something wrong with that?"

"No, but you are a stranger to these parts and the manner of your arrival was unusual." Tesnayr did not say anything and

Hana continued. "I cannot fault you for your silence. However, you must think about your future. If you choose to remain here Nigilin and I can help you find work in town. And I'm sure he will let you stay with him."

"I thank you."

"We are a quiet people, not used to excitement. For the most part we mind our business and allow strangers to pass through without too many questions. Though I must warn you Mrs. Bixby is quite a gossiper. I would avoid her if I were you. If you choose to make a life here it will be a quiet one."

"A quiet life," mused Tesnayr, with a note of longing.

Hana watched him intently. "You were once a soldier." It was a statement, not a question.

Tesnayr gave her a questioning look.

Hana gave him a reassuring pat on the hand. "Do not worry. I will not tell anyone. Nigilin and I guessed it the day we first saw you.

"I had a son once. He was a soldier in the King's army. One year he went off to war a bright, happy young man with a long future ahead of him. Upon his return, I knew he had changed. Of course, that particular war nearly tore this land apart. War changed my son. He got along for a while, but as time wore on he became detached. I buried him six months later. He had the same look in his eyes that you have now."

Tesnayr paused and turned toward her. "How long ago was this?"

"Ten years. You remind me of him. You are still young, Tesnayr. Well, young to me. I am an old woman."

Old woman or not, Tesnayr would not want to be on her bad side. She had a glare that would make even the bravest of men cower.

"Do not follow the same path as my son. It is time to return." Hana steered Tesnayr back to the cottage.

The next few weeks were spent in much the same way. Each day either Hana or Nigilin walked with Tesnayr. He grew stronger every day as his wounds mended. Slowly, his arrival became a distant memory as new activities filled their time.

Hana taught Tesnayr how to mix certain medicines to heal small wounds and cure certain illnesses. He watched eagerly as she ground up herbs and mixed them together carefully.

"You must always measure accurately," she warned him, "Or else these could kill you."

Dismayed, Tesnayr halted what he was doing.

"I'm only kidding about the death part," Hana chuckled. "But you must still be careful as the wrong mixture can make you ill instead of well." She guided his hands demonstrating the proper way to finely grind herbs. "There you go," she said. "Maybe you should be an herbalist like me."

"Don't listen to her," piped up Nigilin as he walked in with kindling.

"Oh, hush, you," snapped Hana. "He is only keeping you for slave labor," she said to Tesnayr.

"And just what do you think you're doing by forcing him to mix your medicines," quipped Nigilin.

"Passing on useful knowledge," said Hana.

Tesnayr continued grinding the already powdered herbs in his bowl not wanting to get involved. He wondered if their playful sparring with words was their way of passing the time.

Having nowhere to go, Tesnayr stayed with Nigilin. The place was small, but he liked it. He also liked the older man's company.

Nigilin was pleased to have an extra pair of hands around the place to help with the chores. He admired Tesnayr's work ethic as it matched his own. He did what needed to be done without complaint. Despite the flawless healing of Tesnayr's wounds, Nigilin sensed that something deeply bothered the man. *If only he would talk about it.*

Scarcely a night passed where he didn't catch Tesnayr weeping silently in an isolated corner, or staring out at the sea with an expression of longing and deep sorrow. Having been a soldier himself, Nigilin had an inkling of what troubled the man. But he never said a word. He thought it best to let the man have his privacy.

"Tesnayr," Nigilin said one day, "Will you come out here."

Tesnayr followed the man outside unsure of what he was up to. His eyes lit up as he realized what lay before him. Nigilin had turned the abandoned shed into a workshop. "I thought you might like this," said Nigilin. "I've noticed you are adept at fixing things and have a fair skill for blacksmithing. I have no use for this shed, but perhaps you do."

"Nigilin, I-" stammered Tesnayr choking up. He squeezed the man in a bear hug, a rare display of emotion.

Nigilin knew he had done something right. Tesnayr's face told him so. He hoped that by giving him his own workspace, he would be able to channel his depression into something useful. Perhaps in time, his emotional wounds would heal.

"Of course, you know that I had an ulterior motive for this," Nigilin chided, "There is much around here that needs fixing."

Tesnayr just smiled. He had never received a greater gift.

As promised, Tesnayr spent his days helping with repairs to the cottage as repayment for Nigilin's kindness. He fixed the roof with such precision that Nigilin said no one could do it better. Tesnayr mended the fireplace with a sturdier stone than what had been originally used. All in all, Tesnayr proved to be a good asset to the older man and the work did him well. Assisting with repairs was not the only thing he did for Nigilin. He made trips to town when needed to pick up supplies and sell the starfish.

Hana usually gave Tesnayr a slice of cake to eat when he stopped by. She never let him leave without one. Tesnayr didn't mind too much. He loved her moist and fluffy cakes.

"Take this," said Hana handing him a wrapped plate with a triple layer cake.

"I couldn't eat any more," said Tesnayr. He had just finished the piece she had given him earlier.

"Who said that it is all for you?" Hana thrust the plate into Tesnayr's hands. "Give some to Nigilin. And I want the plate back."

Tesnayr carefully took the cake. Hana was adept at getting her way.

Word of Tesnayr's arrival spread quickly throughout the town. Many spoke of this stranger whose manner of arrival was somewhat less than ordinary. They admired his willingness to work and many offered him a place to stay. Tesnayr refused their offers saying that Nigilin's hospitality was more than adequate.

He accepted odd jobs from the people making repairs to their homes, wagons, and anything else that needed fixing. They paid him for his services and he used the coins to make enhancements to Nigilin's cottage. Despite the warmth he received from most in the village, there was one person who made his life difficult: Mrs. Bixby. Of course, she made everybody's life difficult.

"Still here," sneered Mrs. Bixby one day. Like clockwork she was once again badgering him with questions.

Tesnayr ignored her as he worked on the axle of a wagon.

"Won't talk to me I see," continued Mrs. Bixby.

"I have work to do," he replied.

"Of course you do. That is all you do is work. Buying our trust aren't you?"

No response.

"Well, aren't you?"

"What do you want?" snapped Tesnayr. He was tired of the old woman's comments.

"I want to know why you are here. Strange things have been happening since you arrived. Strange folk about. People's livestock have gone missing."

"Perhaps, you have a thief," said Tesnayr.

"Except the thieving didn't start until after you arrived. Why are you here?"

"And just what are you accusing me of?"

"Something strange is going on around here and you are connected to it. I know it," said Mrs. Bixby.

"Will you shut up," roared Hana as she came closer. She heard the entire conversation from across the street. Mrs. Bixby had a voice that carried. "Will you quit bothering the man?"

"I only wished—"

"I know what you wanted," snapped Hana, "You just want to learn all the dirty details about this man's life so that you can blab it around town. All you do is spread rumor and hearsay. Never do you bother to consider that perhaps there are some things best left alone. And some things that people do not want known three hundred miles away."

"And what secrets does he have?" asked Mrs. Bixby.

"None of your concern," said Hana. A crowd had gathered around them. "Now you leave this man alone or I will beat you senseless with this stick in my hands."

"You wouldn't dare," said Mrs. Bixby.

Hana took one step toward the woman waving her stick threateningly. Mrs. Bixby shrieked. She grabbed her skirts high and took off down the street to the roaring laughter of the entire town. She never bothered Tesnayr again lest Hana might make good on her threat. Instead, she made up her own story about where he came from and his true reasons for staying. The townsfolk ignored her.

Next day Tesnayr headed into town once again for supplies from Mr. Beasley's store. As he pulled the wagon to a halt a loud clatter drew his attention. Sensing trouble, Tesnayr entered the building and found two men harassing Mr. Beasley.

"Give me some pipe weed, old man," said one of the men.

Mr. Beasley shook slightly as he replied. "You still have not paid me for the bag you bought three weeks ago."

"Did I ask you if you wanted payment?" said the same man grabbing Mr. Beasley around the shirt collar. The second brandished a knife at the store owner.

Tesnayr had heard enough. "Is there a problem, gentlemen?"

"Mind your own business, stranger," said the man with the knife. "We have no quarrel with you."

Tesnayr leaned in close. "Mr. Beasley is an honest man. And I do not like bullies. Therefore, I have a quarrel with you."

The first man laughed. "What do you plan to do?"

"Leave now. If you refuse, you will regret it," Tesnayr said calmly.

The first man dropped Mr. Beasley and swung an axe from the counter at Tesnayr. Tesnayr ducked, smacked the man in the throat and pinned him to the ground. The speed of his movements caught both men by surprise. The man with the knife charged Tesnayr. Just as quickly Tesnayr took the weapon from the thug and threw him across the room. He spun back to the first bully and flung the knife at him, catching the man in the hand as he reached for the axe. Tesnayr dragged one of the hooligans to Mr. Beasley.

"How much do they owe you?" he asked the storeowner.

"Twenty-five gold pieces," replied Mr. Beasley.

"I haven't got any money," blurted the man.

Tesnayr ripped the man's belt off revealing a concealed bag of coins. He took the money, weighed it in his hand before giving it to Mr. Beasley.

"There's over a hundred gold pieces in there," the man protested.

"Consider it payment for the damage you inflicted on this place," said Tesnayr. "Now grab your friend and leave. If I ever hear of you taking advantage of anyone in this town, I will come for you." Tesnayr released him and the two thugs raced outside.

Later that night at the cottage Nigilin found Tesnayr sitting alone in the dark. He called his name several times, but received no answer. Tesnayr sat transfixed by the fire with the poker in his hand. Nigilin placed a calloused hand on the man's shoulder. In an instant Tesnayr had pinned him to the floor with the poker raised to kill. A merciless, blind fury filled his eyes. Nigilin knew that Tesnayr was an inch from killing him.

"Tesnayr!" he yelled.

Tesnayr stared at him breathing heavily as his eyes unglazed. He slowly lowered the poker and dropped it on the floor. Quickly, he helped Nigilin to his feet apologizing profusely for his behavior. "I didn't mean it," he said. "I would never—"

Understanding dawned on Nigilin. He had seen this sort of thing before during his time in the army. "Tesnayr," he said calmly. "I am unharmed. It is all right. Why don't you tell me what is on your mind."

Once again Tesnayr clammed up and stalked outside. He walked to the edge of a sandbank and stared at the moonlit ocean. The peaceful night did little to calm the anxiety churning within him. He plopped on the squishy sand and stared out at the inky blackness that engulfed the ocean.

Something poked him in the hip. He reached into his pocket and pulled out a chess piece. The black knight. He remembered when he first learned the game. He remembered a trust he never should have given. Tesnayr lowered his head into his hands and wept. He thought he had left his past behind him.

The soft meow of a cat brought him back to the present. A black cat sat a few feet away from him. The cat's yellow eyes bored into Tesnayr as though it could see into his inner soul and knew what he felt. He and the cat stared at each other for several minutes. Breaking the hypnotic stare, Tesnayr moved toward the cat, but the black feline ran off disappearing into the night. Mystified, he just stared blankly at where the cat had been. *Strange creatures.*

"Good morning," Nigilin greeted Tesnayr warmly the next morning. "I hope you slept well."

Nigilin didn't mention the night before, as though it never happened. He placed a hot bowl of porridge before Tesnayr.

"Hana has a wall in her house that is beginning to give way. She asked me if you would be willing to take a look at it," he added conversationally. "And you can give this clean and polished plate back to her." He held up the plate that had held Hana's cake from the day before.

"I will stop by there today," replied Tesnayr. "About last night—"

"I should not have startled you," interrupted Nigilin. He continued cleaning the dishes that he used for that morning's breakfast. "I want you to know, Tesnayr, that whatever happens I am your friend."

A black cat jumped on the table and helped itself to Tesnayr's porridge. Its tongue lapped noisily. Nigilin scooped up the cat and put it out the door. "Cat, you know that is not your food. Now, go catch a mouse."

"Is that your cat?" asked Tesnayr.

"He lives around here and pops in and out as he chooses."

"Last night I thought it was following me."

"It's possible. There is a legend about cats that can talk, think, and act like people. It is said that if one were to meet such an animal he should befriend it. To have a talking cat as a friend is a rare gift for they are more loyal than those you have known since childhood. I doubt that that was our little friend."

"Talking cats. I suppose you are going to tell me that there are dragons in this land as well?"

"Dragons rarely visit these parts. They remain mostly in Belyndril. I have heard tales of beasts who live far across the sea that are half human and half horse," said Nigilin.

Tesnayr smiled slightly. "They are not easy to associate with."

"Then perhaps you should not dismiss such tales so readily," said Nigilin. "Every tale has some truth to it even if it is stretched slightly."

Tesnayr finished his meal in silence relieved that Nigilin held no grudge against him from the night before.

MRRRRP.

Tesnayr glanced down. The black cat sat by his feet staring intently at his empty bowl, licking its chops. Tesnayr moved the bowl. The cat's head mirrored his movements. Loud purring filled the room. Reluctantly, Tesnayr placed the empty dish in front of the animal. The soothing purr ceased as satisfied licking ensued.

"I think you made a new friend," said Nigilin.

Tesnayr finished a few chores for the older man before going to Hana's. As he worked, he felt the black cat watching him intently as though it understood everything he did. It had even followed him to Hana's.

"Do you talk?" asked Tesnayr, while he worked.

The cat cocked its head and continued observing him. Tesnayr began to get the feeling that this was no ordinary cat. Eventually common sense overtook him and he ignored the feline as he continued repairing Hana's wall. He's just an animal, he thought to himself.

Snatches of a conversation between Hana and another woman pricked Tesnayr's ears. Even the cat listened closely. He watched them over the wall he worked on. He tried to avoid eavesdropping, but curiosity got the better of him.

"I am telling you something strange is going on," said the woman.

"You know I do not like gossip," said Hana.

"This is not gossip," retorted the woman, "Cedric said that while he was out last night he noticed strange men sneaking through the village. They wore long cloaks and kept their faces covered. The thing is he said that they did not act like men. They acted more primitive, more animal like."

Hana sighed. "Are you certain that Cedric had not been drinking? You know better than anyone his fondness for it."

The woman looked affronted. "He has not been drinking! For the past several weeks strange people have been moving through these parts. Many people have mysteriously disappeared. Some have turned up dead."

"I will not deny that I haven't noticed such things. But I think it's best not to worry about it," said Hana.

The woman snorted and turned to leave.

Hana stopped her. "All the same, it would be best if you carried a knife with you at all times and do not let your children wander far. If these strange creatures prove to be hostile, then you and your husband had best be prepared."

The woman left.

Tesnayr glanced up at Hana a moment before continuing with his work as he mulled over what he had overheard. Their conversation gnawed at him.

At sunset, halfway home, Tesnayr met a girl of about sixteen. She sat in a meadow surrounded by daisies. He watched enthralled as the daisies gently rose into the air and circled lightly around the girl. They floated upwards disappearing into the pink and gold sky. The girl finally noticed him. Startled, she jumped up in fright and ran away. Tesnayr called after her, but she kept running.

He pulled the reins of the horse when something caught his eye. Curious, Tesnayr jumped off the mare. He picked the thing up and almost dropped it immediately. It was a sword with a jagged edged blade. Scraps of material hung from the black hilt. This sword matched the weapon of choice for an enemy he knew well.

Tesnayr wrapped it and put it in his satchel before continuing on his way. Questions and dread darted through his mind. He did not mention the sword to Nigilin. Parts of him wanted it to be nothing more than a dream.

A few days later, Nigilin found Tesnayr sitting at the table holding a dagger in his hands. "We had heard of the orcs before they came to our lands. We had no idea what we were up against," he said unexpectedly.

Carefully Nigilin sat down across from Tesnayr listening intently. He dared not speak.

"We fought and fought and still we could not defeat them. For two years we battled the orcs and to no avail. But during that time we learned their weaknesses. I had a general who understood them. He knew the mind of its leader. With his help the tide of war began to change.

"There is one battle that I will never forget. We were driving them back. But when the time for victory arrived we suddenly found ourselves outmaneuvered and outnumbered. We had been betrayed by the very people we swore to protect. I watched helplessly as the beasts murdered my comrades, my friends.

"After weeks of their filth, those of us left alive were put on a ship. I lost track of the days. One by one we died; tortured to death and forced to work without food and sleep. Before long I was the only one left. They had murdered my brother and I held him as he died. I'll never forget his face.

"So I escaped the brig during a storm intending to jump overboard. I killed any who got in my way. I did not care if I died swimming. At least I would die free.

"I do not remember washing up on your shores." Tesnayr looked up at Nigilin. "You were right when you guessed that I had been a soldier."

"Betrayal has broken many men," said Nigilin. "You are not the first to suffer such a thing, nor will you be the last."

"Comforting words."

Nigilin got up and put his hand on Tesnayr's shoulder. The strength of the man's squeeze surprised Tesnayr. Nigilin sensed there was more to the story, but didn't wish to push it. "You have managed to create a new life here. Do not let the wounds of the past mar your hope for the future."

"What if I cannot escape my past?" Thoughts of the sword he found swam through his mind.

"You cannot escape what is part of you," said Nigilin, "You can learn from it. When your past revisits you, face it. I suggest you decide how you will greet such a meeting. I want you to know that I am glad that I found you on the sand. I value your presence here and not because you are a great help to me. In the short time you have been here I have come to consider you my friend."

The black cat landed in the middle of the table purring loudly. It pushed his head against Tesnayr's hand.

"I think he likes you," said Nigilin.

"Are you certain that he isn't more than just a cat?" asked Tesnayr.

"I'm sure that he is."

The cat meowed in reply. His purr soothed Tesnayr.

Chapter II
Virnae

Nearly two months had passed since Tesnayr had arrived in the village and healed from his wounds. He busied himself with cleaning a stable in town when a woman entered. He had seen her around from time to time, but never paid much attention to her until that day.

"Pardon me," said the woman.

Tesnayr looked up from his work. He wiped the sweat off his brow.

"You are Tesnayr?"

Tesnayr nodded in affirmation to her question. "My father has some work that needs to be done on his farm and would like to know if he could hire your services."

Tesnayr continued raking the muck out of the stable. "Do you have a name?"

"Virnae. He will pay you well for it," she added quickly.

"Why does your father not ask me himself?" asked Tesnayr.

"He is busy and since I was coming into town today, he sent me with the message," replied Virnae. She looked about nervously. "He knows that your work is valued by everyone here. If you have other commitments he will understand."

"I have no other commitments. I shall be there by midmorning."

Virnae seemed pleased. "Our farm is two miles east of here near the big rock. We will see you then."

She left without another word. Tesnayr stared after her. She had seemed apprehensive to be in the stable with him. Not surprising. He had developed a reputation of not only being a reliable work hand, but of also being a man best left alone. Some people had the misfortune of pushing him too far and Tesnayr was certain that Virnae, like everyone else, had heard the stories. No doubt he had Mrs. Bixby to thank for that.

As agreed, Tesnayr arrived on the farm by midmorning. Her father, Firwyk, greeted him warmly. He was a portly man and his skin was dark from years of working in the sun. He showed Tesnayr to the field that he wanted plowed for planting.

"I hope to have a good crop this year," he said, "But am too old to handle the plow these days. I'm afraid my aching joints won't allow it."

"I should have it done within a day," Tesnayr said.

Tesnayr set about the task wholeheartedly. He made fast work of it since Firwyk had a strong ox to help pull the plow. By the end of the day the entire field had been cultivated. Before the sun could set, he, Firwyk, and Virnae planted the seeds for that year's crop.

"Now if it would rain, we could water it," commented Firwyk when they had finished.

"I could build a small irrigation system," suggested Tesnayr. "It won't be big, but could draw water from the river."

"That would be excellent," beamed Firwyk.

Tesnayr impressed Firwyk immensely with his willingness to work that the old man invited him back for more chores. He had Tesnayr help him with repairs to his storehouse in addition to the irrigation ditch. Tesnayr's carpentry skills came into use for mending broken chairs and tables. These jobs kept him busy for several weeks. In that time Virnae forgot about her wariness of Tesnayr and began snatching moments alone with him. Many days she brought him cool water to drink after he had spent several hours in the hot sun. Other times she would bring him things to mend, which he gladly set time aside for, even though he knew that many of these small tasks she could have done on her own. These moments provided them the chance for conversation, moments he began to look forward to.

"I brought you some water," Virnae said as she handed Tesnayr a jug of fresh, cool water.

Tesnayr took the jug and drank deeply. "Thank you," he told her, pausing from his work.

"That cat seems to follow you everywhere."

Tesnayr turned and noticed the small, black cat perched on a ledge watching him intently. It was true that the cat seemed to go wherever he did. He had learned to ignore the feline. "So he does," replied Tesnayr.

"My father thinks highly of you. He said he has never met anyone so willing to work such as you."

"And what do you think?" he asked her.

Virnae smiled shyly in answer which brought a chuckle from Tesnayr.

"Oh look," exclaimed Virnae. She pointed at the trees. Tesnayr glanced in that direction and saw an unusual bird disappear below the tree line. A few moments later it flew upward vanishing into the sky. "I think it was the phoenix."

"Phoenix?" said Tesnayr, puzzled.

Virnae took a deep breath before explaining. "There is a legend in these parts about a bird known as the phoenix. It is no ordinary bird. It can heal people's wounds with its tears, and carry burdens that others find too onerous.

"The phoenix appears to those who need it most or at times of despair to inspire hope. Though the problem with legends is that most people do not realize when they have seen one. Some see the phoenix and attribute it to being just another bird. Others see it and realize that there is none other like it and always hope to see it again. I like to include myself in the latter group. Such beliefs keep me going. What do you believe?"

Tesnayr handed the jug back to Virnae. "I once believed in a great many things."

"So you believe in nothing?"

"The cost of belief was more than I could bear. Men are no different than animals."

"Do you honestly think that?"

Tesnayr tossed his hammer in the dirt. "Men are best left alone."

"A man who believes in nothing is not a man at all. You must believe in something, Tesnayr."

Meow.

"Even the cat agrees with me," said Virnae.

"Virnae—"

"I have to go," she said. Virnae paused a moment. "Many men have asked for my hand in marriage. I turned them all down because they were all arrogant. For you, I might make an exception." Virnae ran off in the direction of her mother.

Inwardly, Virnae scolded herself for her last statement. She didn't know why she had said it. It just came out. But something about Tesnayr caught her interest and she knew that he was the man she wanted to marry.

Weeks passed and Virnae found her original opinions on the man to be flawed. The rumors around town had him painted as a gruff, no nonsense, and unemotional man. Though Tesnayr was stubborn and to the point, he also conveyed a tenderness that others did not. He treated her with respect and never assumed her incapable of anything just because she was a woman.

Virnae was very aware of an emotional barrier that existed and attributed it to the manner in which he arrived to the land. She knew there were things about his past that he did not want to remember and never pushed the issue. With each visit she found herself eagerly awaiting another.

Tesnayr visited Virnae's home often to help her father with the farm. Even when there was no work to be done he stopped by to visit Virnae.

These extra visits had not gone unnoticed by Firwyk. With a childlike giddiness, he observed them while pretending to be otherwise occupied. He may have been old, but he wasn't stupid. He had noticed the change that took place between the two.

Virnae became more welcoming around Tesnayr and Tesnayr seemed more human around her. *Yes, their union would do them both good.* He raised his daughter to be strong willed and knew Tesnayr could handle it. Secretly, Firwyk had hoped the two would decide to marry. Hence why he asked Tesnayr to help on his farm in the first place.

After several hints from Virnae, Tesnayr finally plucked up the courage to ask Firwyk's permission to marry her. Firwyk readily agreed, overjoyed at the prospect of his daughter marrying a hard worker who would more than provide for her. He would be proud to pass the farm onto Tesnayr. He quickly set a date. In his day, people did not waste time planning a wedding and dragging out the festivities. He figured if they could stand each other, and both wanted marriage, the sooner the better. Besides he wasn't growing any younger and wanted to be around when the first grandchild was born.

Far from where Firwyk congratulated himself on his matchmaking skills, sat Tesnayr and Virnae in the field looking at the stars. Virnae hummed a little tune as Tesnayr listened.

"That is a sweet melody," he said.

"It belongs to a song my father used to sing to me," she replied.

"Sing it for me?"

Virnae cleared her throat as she prepared to sing for Tesnayr.

> River of peace, again we meet.
> Along the windy path
> I see your streams.
>
> Take me home; away from where I roam.
> This I ask: guide me
> By your watery dome.
>
> Foolish was I as a young lad.
> Wisdom gained should make me glad.

Will you allow me to follow?
Your noble path
Will cure my sorrow.

Please Gentle River lead me far from here.
I long for peace at long last.
Oh, River, guide me home.

Tesnayr mulled over the lullaby for several moments grasping the meaning behind the words. They reminded him of himself and what he longed for. He noticed Virnae watching him. "That was lovely," he said.

"I've upset you," she cried.

"No." he said calming her. "On the contrary. You have brought me peace."

Virnae snuggled into his arms and stared at the sky hoping that this moment would not end.

"Virnae," said Tesnayr, "Will marry me?"

A small smile escaped Virnae's lips. She was glad the darkness concealed it. Containing her excitement, she said with what dignity she had, "Of course I will."

The day after proposing to Virnae, Tesnayr rode into town for supplies. He pulled on the reins of the draft horses easing the cart to a stop. Children's laughter caught his attention. He noticed a boy tossing something in the air and catching it. Curious, Tesnayr approached them. He snatched the object from the boy's hands. It was a broken spearhead. Tesnayr studied it immediately recognizing the weapon. A mark on the spearhead gave it away.

"Where did you get this?" he demanded.

"Down by the river," said the boy.

Tesnayr ignored the boy's outstretched hand and threw the spearhead into a nearby fire. "Best stay in town." He walked away, unconcerned about the stares that followed him.

Tesnayr arrived back at Nigilin's later that day. He could not find the man anywhere. Tesnayr searched for Nigilin all around the cottage and even outside. Worried, he raced to the beach and noticed a lone figure standing there looking out at the water.

"It's been there all afternoon," said Nigilin as Tesnayr approached.

Tesnayr turned in the direction Nigilin pointed and saw a ship. This ship had black sails. Tesnayr recognized it, but did not betray that recognition. "Has it been still the entire time?"

"Yes," Nigilin said. "At first I ignored it, but when it never moved I paid closer attention. It has remained still for hours. Almost as though it were watching and waiting."

"Strange that it should not move behind those cliffs and conceal itself," pondered Tesnayr. "Unless they feel that we are no threat."

"I thought so too." Nigilin looked at Tesnayr's bewildered expression. "I was not always a farmer. Those rumors about strange beasts wandering through our lands, I believe we have found the source."

The two watched as the ship suddenly began to move. It disappeared around the bend.

"It appears that they have somewhere to be. What do you think it is?"

Tesnayr did not answer immediately. "I have my suspicions. I hope I am wrong. Undoubtedly they had scouting parties mapping the terrain and they have returned to their ship. Those on board will have moved away from shore. Far enough to avoid detection and damage on the rocks. They will return."

"They are getting confident in our lack of alarm to their presence," said Nigilin.

"Maybe so," replied Tesnayr, "Though they have kept to the shadows. Something is headed this way. We'd best be watchful."

"Agreed," said Nigilin. "I have something to show you."

Tesnayr followed the man to another part of the shoreline not far from where they stood. He lit the lamp that he carried with him and pointed it toward a secluded area. Tesnayr recognized the beast lying on the ground immediately.

"When did you find it?" he asked.

"Soon after I noticed the ship," replied Nigilin. "He was dead when I found him."

"Undoubtedly killed by his own," said Tesnayr. "His leg looks like it was broken. Orcs do not believe in saving their sick or wounded. They kill those they deem incapable of going into battle. They never were intelligent when it came to disposing of their dead."

Nigilin lowered the lamp. "I thought you would recognize it."

"Have you told anyone else?"

"I told Derik, the constable. He told to me bury it and not tell anyone else of this. Apparently he is afraid of starting a panic. So much so that he is unwilling to admit that something is terribly wrong and to prepare for it." Nigilin sighed. "All we can do is be aware of this. The scavengers on this beach will take care of the body. It will be gone by morning." He walked back to the cottage.

Tesnayr rubbed his hands over his face. It seemed that his past was returning from the grave despite his efforts to be rid of it. He heard a meow nearby and twisted around to face the black cat. "I have not seen you in a while," he said, turning away.

"But I have been watching you," said a voice.

Tesnayr jerked his head to face to cat. He could have sworn that he heard someone speaking, but the only other thing present was the cat. The cat stared at him, unblinking. Tesnayr shook his head attributing the voice to his imagination. "Cats do not talk," he said to himself as he strolled back to the cottage. The black feline followed him unnoticed.

The next several weeks were spent in much the same way as before. Very few discoveries were made to cause concern and the body of the orc that Nigilin found remained the only one. Any anxieties that were there before waned and people went about their normal activities.

Tesnayr on the other hand, was not convinced that things had returned to normal. He remained uneasy and always carried a dagger with him. He spent hours each day outside manufacturing items, digging trenches, and setting up rope in such a way that could only be taken as a trap. For hours on end he disappeared. Nigilin knew better than to ask Tesnayr what he was up to, but he had an inkling.

One morning Nigilin woke and looked out the window. Then he noticed something peculiar outside. The black cat that frequented his place walked toward the cottage, but not in its usual carefree manner. Instead it wove its way in curved circles as though it were navigating a maze.

Curious, Nigilin went outside heading straight for where the cat was. He cautiously approached what looked like a bed of seaweed on the sand. Carefully, Nigilin lifted it. Just as he thought. Beneath the seaweed was a deep hole with spikes on the bottom. Instantly, Nigilin knew who put it there and why.

He spotted the other piles of seaweed marking death traps. He made a mental note of the line of traps so as to avoid walking into them. He figured that Tesnayr would inform him about them soon enough. Apparently, the discarded body on the beach had rattled him.

The entire town was abuzz for the wedding. Neither Virnae nor Tesnayr could walk anywhere in town without being congratulated on their upcoming marriage. They both set about with wedding preparations. Many of the men gathered together to help Tesnayr build a new home for himself and his bride. The women helped Virnae make things to furnish and decorate the new home. All the excitement about a wedding consumed the town's attention rendering them oblivious to the outside world, including Tesnayr.

Tesnayr and Virnae strolled through town one day planning their wedding feast. They bought supplies so that the women could begin preparing the banquet. The gloomy day threatened rain but did little to diminish the joyous mood of the townspeople. The couple stood in front of an apple display.

"Perhaps we should have apples at the feast," suggested Virnae.

"Just apples? You do not wish to turn them into some elaborate meal," said Tesnayr jokingly. A few droplets of rain dotted his arm. "Earlier you wanted to turn a pumpkin into a cake."

"And why not? I suppose we could make a sauce with the apples or cut them up and eat them with cream." She noticed the quizzical look on Tesnayr's face. "Such a dish is considered a delicacy around here and it tastes better than it sounds."

"Why don't we have strawberries and cream and you can turn the apples into a kind of sauce to go with your pumpkin cake," suggested Tesnayr half joking.

Virnae smiled. "Agreed."

"Virnae," said someone breathlessly as he approached. "You father wishes to speak with you."

Virnae thanked the man for the message. "I will see you tonight. Remember, tonight is the night you must eat with my family."

They embraced each other and Tesnayr promised to be on time for the pre-wedding meal. He watched as Virnae walked down the street to where her father stood waiting. Happiness filled him as he admired her from a distance.

An eerie stillness settled over the market. Tesnayr heard the familiar whooshing of an arrow as it shot past his ear missing him by inches. He dove to the ground instantly. Several people fell as arrows struck them in the chest. No one knew where they came from.

Frantic, people ran in erratic paths as they dodged the onslaught. Tesnayr's only thought was for Virnae. He quickly rose to his feet and ran for her. Her father had pinned her down on the ground taking an arrow in the back. Tesnayr fought his way through the chaos shoving people to the side. Arrows shot past him. Each one missed their mark.

As he neared Virnae, dark figures appeared out of the mist with swords drawn. Desperately, Virnae pulled herself out from underneath her father's limp body. She shook him but he did not move. Tesnayr shouted her name. Virnae stood up looking around for him unaware of the danger that approached from behind. One of the beasts drove its sword into her.

"No!" yelled Tesnayr.

It was too late. Tesnayr caught her as she fell to the ground. Her breaths came in quick gasps. There was nothing he could do except watch helplessly as she died. His name was the last word on her lips.

Tesnayr tenderly held Virnae's body as more rain fell and turned into a downpour. He forgot about the orcs and the commotion around him.

Fearful screams filled the street as people attempted to flee. Swords found their mark with each deathblow. Feet ran frantically through the mud desperate to escape. Death filled the area. A man crashed into the mud beside Tesnayr, his vacant eyes staring at him. He remained detached and motionless with Virnae in his arms.

One of the orcs shouted orders silencing the area, thus bringing Tesnayr back to the present. Arrows ceased their flight.

"We do not wish you harm," shouted the orc in charge. "Our master wishes only to use your land temporarily while we recover our strength. We will leave shortly. If you cooperate, no one will die."

The shouts died as people cowered in fear. Tesnayr noticed more of the beasts approaching. He committed their position to memory. "No harm," said Tesnayr barely containing the anger that boiled within him. "Who is your master?"

The orc in charge walked over to Tesnayr and leered over him. "Galbrok is our master, human."

"Galbrok," Tesnayr whispered to himself. He knew the name. He knew it well. He tenderly laid Virnae's body in the mud.

Enraged, he seized the sword from the orc nearest him and plunged it into the beast. The remaining orcs turned toward him, but Tesnayr's attack caught them off guard. He fought with a skill and ferocity that they were unaccustomed to countering. Never had they met a man who commanded a sword with ease and fought as viciously as them.

The villagers watched horror struck as Tesnayr wielded his weapon as though it knew every move to make. He blocked and attacked with the ease of an experienced swordsman. In a matter of seconds the orcs lay dead on the blood soaked ground.

The growl of a beast sounded behind him. "You fight well for a human," said an orc.

The orc charged from behind. Tesnayr dodged stepping lightly on his feet. He raised his sword high and sliced the orc's arm. The creature howled in rage.

It attacked again. Tesnayr brought his blade up to block. At the last second, the orc changed his maneuver and clipped Tesnayr in the shoulder. Ignoring the burning pain, Tesnayr jabbed the orc with his elbow. Quickly, he jammed his knee into the beast's chest.

Grunting, the orc staggered backward. Without an ounce of mercy, Tesnayr brought his sword down in one swift stroke and cut off the orc's head. He watched emotionless as it rolled on the rain soaked ground.

Tesnayr stood with his sword in his hand, its blade broken from the intensity of the battle. He observed the damage that he had inflicted. Tesnayr dropped the blade from his hand and fell to his knees sinking in the oozing mud. He covered his face with his calloused hands and wept in the pouring rain. His cries of anguish and loss fell on the ears of those present. They kept their feet planted not daring to move. Silently they wept with Tesnayr.

The joy that had filled the day dissipated as grief settled in. The townsfolk spent the remainder of the day disposing of their dead. Tesnayr ordered the bodies of the orcs to be burned. None questioned him.

The next morning funerals were held. Tesnayr placed yellow wildflowers in the hands of Virnae before she was lowered into the ground. After the dirt was thrown over her body, Tesnayr remained. He knelt on the ground by the graveside and sang a traditional lament from his homeland. The wind carried the sorrowful tune to the farthest reaches of the land. All the rest of the morning he never moved.

It was not until Nigilin approached and placed a hand on his shoulder that he finally stirred. "A town meeting has been called," he said, "Your presence is requested."

"Carry on without me," replied Tesnayr.

"I am not going anywhere without you," said Nigilin, sternly.

No response.

"Remaining here will not bring her back," said Nigilin.

Still, Tesnayr refused to move.

"I will carry you to that meeting," Nigilin said with the hint of a threat in his voice.

Tesnayr sighed and rose to his feet. "Are you always this forceful?"

"When necessary."

The two walked in silence as they headed for the meeting. It was clear that it had started without them by the time they arrived.

"We should leave and head for the hills," shouted one angry man. Tesnayr and Nigilin heard his voice through the door as they entered.

"Go ahead and leave you coward," cried another. "I say we stay here and fight if they come again."

"Are you mad? They will kill us! You saw how they cut us down."

"They'll kill us if we do nothing!"

"And what are we to do? We've no army."

"Enough," shouted Derik. The room fell silent. "Those who wish to fight these beasts say 'Aye'".

No one raised their hands.

Tesnayr could stand no more of this nonsense. "In order to fight your enemy you must understand him. You need to know how he thinks, how he acts. You fools would be killed before you ever reached the battlefield."

"And you know these beasts?" asked Derik.

"I know them," answered Tesnayr in a grim tone. "They are orcs: vicious, vile, violent, cruel, and fierce. They are not easily defeated. Orcs kill without conviction. They enjoy it."

"It is curious how you, Tesnayr, know so much about these creatures," said a man.

"Do not forget how he killed them yesterday. I have never seen anyone fight like that," said another.

"Where did you learn to fight like that, son," said an elderly man.

"That is not important," said Nigilin.

"No, Nigilin. They have a right to know," said Tesnayr. "My homeland lies across the sea. Several years ago the orcs invaded it bent on conquest. I joined the ranks of men who chose to fight them. I spent five years at war with these beasts and have seen things the likes of which you will never know.

"Despite our efforts, my home was destroyed. There is nothing left of it but charred remains. But why they have come here I do not know," Tesnayr finished more to himself. "Perhaps all they do is conquer and destroy and once they are through they move on like locusts."

The assembly listened intently to Tesnayr's words. Stillness followed for several minutes before chaos broke out. "You brought them here," shouted one.

"That is foolishness," retorted Nigilin.

"How do you explain their coming here?" asked another.

"Does it matter why they came? What matters is what we do now," shouted a third.

"What do we do now? You saw how they defeated us. Perhaps we should give in to their demands."

"Let them rule us? That is foolishness. They will kill us."

"They will kill us if we fight."

"We cannot just sit here and do nothing."

"And what do you suggest?"

The shouting match continued. Tesnayr and Nigilin glanced at each other and shook their heads. Frustrated, Tesnayr stepped outside and grabbed a fist sized rock. He returned to the room and banged the rock on the table. In seconds the room fell silent.

"I know the orcs," he began, "They will stop at nothing until they have complete control over this land. And then they will move on to the next, and the next, until nothing is left. I suggest that you send messengers to your king. Tell him about the orcs and where they are."

"And who will carry the message?" asked Derik.

"I will go," replied Nigilin.

"You may have fought in the great war of ten years ago, but you are not a soldier anymore, Nigilin," said Derik.

"Since none of you are capable of making a decision I will take the message to the king," said Nigilin. "With luck, I will reach him in time. As a former member of his army, he will have to see me."

"I will join you," Tesnayr said.

"Very well," said Derik, "You two will carry the message to the king about these orcs. Then you will return here."

"I will not be coming back," said Tesnayr. "There is nothing for me here."

"As you wish," said Derik. "I wish you luck."

Tesnayr and Nigilin left the crowded room. They agreed to leave in the morning and spent the night packing. Before they turned in for the night Nigilin asked, "Tesnayr, where will you go?"

"Hunt some orcs."

Chapter III
A Message for the King

The next morning Nigilin awoke to an incessant clanking in Tesnayr's shop. His curiosity piqued, he investigated. There Tesnayr had dressed in thick armor that he had spent the night making. Canteens hung freely from a pack next to him. Nigilin watched as Tesnayr placed a knife in his left boot. "Preparing for a war," he commented.

"War? No. But there is a strong possibility that we will meet some resistance on our way to your king," replied Tesnayr.

Nigilin smiled. "Where did you find all this?"

Tesnayr strapped his traveling pack to his back and sheathed his sword. "I made them all. I began doing so the moment Hana told me about the rumors of strange creatures in these parts. I had hoped that my suspicions were wrong."

Before leaving town the two men paid Hana a visit. Nigilin detested the idea of her being left unprotected from these orcs. He knew that the fortifications Tesnayr had built around his place were strong and would hold until he returned and insisted that she move there.

Hana refused. "I will not leave," she replied to their pleas. "My things are here if people need my help."

"If you stay here and the orcs return you may be one of those they attack," pleaded Nigilin.

"I will not leave. I am no coward."

"You are far braver than most men I know, Hana," said Nigilin, "But you will be of no use to anyone dead and you will be better protected at my cottage."

"What makes you think so?" asked Hana.

"Tesnayr made some modifications," replied Nigilin, "I assure you it is impenetrable."

"We could just carry her there," said Tesnayr growing impatient.

Hana put her hands on her hips and sighed in exasperation as a sign of her accepting defeat. "I have no doubt that you would," she snapped. "Very well. Give me time to pack some things—."

"You have ten minutes," said Tesnayr, "Take only what you need."

Hana packed two bags with herbs and medicines as well as food and supplies.

"There is a sword hidden toward the left of the fireplace," Tesnayr told Hana before parting.

Hana forced a weak smile at Tesnayr's statement. "When you arrive, follow the rocks," Tesnayr finished and departed with Nigilin.

"Tesnayr," Hana grasped Tesnayr's shoulder, "I am sorry about Virnae."

Tesnayr patted her hand appreciating her sympathy. "Stay safe."

Tesnayr and Nigilin left Hana's home taking the main road out of town. A black cat trailed behind them close to the shadows.

Late that afternoon Tesnayr and Nigilin reached the road heading north to Drynelle, the city of the King of Sym'Dul. Tesnayr set a brisk pace to which Nigilin tried desperately to keep up. His panting gave away the raw fact that he was not only older, but unused to this type of physical exertion. Tesnayr ignored it out of respect for the man and slowed slightly.

"Tell me about your king," said Tesnayr.

"There isn't much to tell," said Nigilin. "King Slyamal is a proud man. I fought for his father years ago. But Slyamal is very different from his father. He changed even more after an attempted coup and his eldest daughter died.

"One thing you do not know is that Sym'Dul is one of five kingdoms in this land. The others are Belyndril, Hemíl, MurDair, and Belarnia. We have fought against each other for as long as anyone can remember."

"Constantly?" asked Tesnayr.

"There are times of peace, but they are short lived. Treaties come and go. Currently, Sym'Dul is at war with Belarnia," replied Nigilin

"It doesn't make sense."

"Since when does life ever make sense?" Suddenly, Nigilin pulled Tesnayr to a halt. A woman sauntered toward them: the sorceress, Ernayn.

He stayed Tesnayr's hand when the man moved it to his sword. Nigilin did not despise the sorceress, but he remained wary of her. She only appeared when trouble was near and usually gave cryptic warnings.

Ernayn had sharp features which added to her beauty. Her light brown hair fell neatly around her face accentuating her hypnotizing eyes. Accompanying Ernayn was the same teenage girl that Tesnayr had seen with the daisies. Her midnight black hair swayed gently in the breeze. The girl noticed the two men first and ran to the sorceress.

"Hello travelers," said Ernayn in greeting.

"Watch yourself," whispered Nigilin to Tesnayr, "The sorceress, though good, is not to be trifled with." Nigilin walked ahead a little, "Good day, Ernayn. What brings you here?"

Ernayn moved elegantly toward the two men. "My new protégé," she said, indicating the teenage girl. "This is Quesha du'Adieu. Quesha, this is Nigilin and Tesnayr."

"How do you know my name?" asked Tesnayr, with an edge to his voice.

"I know many things," replied Ernayn. "And Quesha told me that she has met you once before."

"A quick meeting," said Tesnayr, "She never said a word."

Ernayn smiled. "Quesha is a shy child. In time she will overcome that shyness." She turned her attention toward Nigilin. "When was the last time we met?"

"Nearly ten years ago," replied Nigilin.

"You are not here so your student can learn a lesson," said Tesnayr losing patience at this interruption.

Ernayn's expression darkened slightly and Nigilin gave him a warning look. "No I did not. I came because I have heard of you, Tesnayr *Deoraí*. A destination awaits you. You have only just begun the journey."

"How do you know about me?" asked Tesnayr.

Ernayn glanced at Quesha, who busied herself with making flowers bloom and float upwards in the air. "As I said before, I know many things. I know from where you come and where you are headed. And I deliver this message to you: you go to a king you have no loyalty to and will end up serving yourself. A day will come when you will make the choice between yourself, or something far greater. I hope you choose the latter."

Tesnayr eyed Quesha. "Where I come from she would have been killed for that. Such power is considered unnatural."

"Man will murder anyone out of ignorance, vengeance, and jealously. I know the laws of your land. They are why the orcs prevailed there," said Ernayn. "We all have our talents. I, and my protégé, understand nature and the inner workings of the world. The woman, Hana, understands the nature of healing those who are ill; their wounds speak to her in a way others do not comprehend.

"You, Tesnayr, know how to command and to lead because you appreciate people and truly care for them. However, you do not know yourself. A flaw many have.

"We are given certain abilities and gifts which are to be used to benefit others. If we ignore them or use them in a manner that only serves our own desires then we lose those gifts. Is that understood, Quesha?" Ernayn finished turning toward the girl.

"Yes, mistress," replied the girl.

"You came to give us riddles?" demanded Tesnayr.

"Hardly," said Ernayn. "For a man set on forgetting his past, you are well on your way to meeting it. Continue this course and you will have to face yourself."

Ernayn took note of the position of the sun in the sky. "The day is late and we must go," she said. "It was pleasant to see you again, Nigilin. Perhaps we will meet again under more favorable circumstances." She and Quesha disappeared quickly as though they had never been there.

"Mysterious woman isn't she," said a voice.

Tesnayr and Nigilin both turned to find a black cat sitting in the middle of the road, coyly licking its paw. They both gaped slack jawed at the feline.

"I assure you that this is no illusion," said the cat moving closer.

"You are the cat that has been following me since I arrived here," said Tesnayr.

"Yes, and I have been following you for the past few hours," said the cat.

Tesnayr whispered to Nigilin, "We should continue."

"Suffice it to say that I am coming with you."

"No you aren't," said Tesnayr.

"Yes, I am," said the cat.

"You are not coming with us," reiterated Tesnayr.

"Do you have a name, stranger?" asked Nigilin breaking up the argument.

"Turyn," said the cat.

"Well, Turyn, I am afraid that we must take our leave," Nigilin said to the cat.

Nigilin and Tesnayr walked onward leaving the black feline alone in the middle of the dirt road. They travelled in silence unaware of a shadow following them. Two hours later Tesnayr pulled Nigilin to a halt. On a rock directly in front of them sat a black cat with a very smug look on his face. His tail swayed aimlessly.

"There you two are," said the cat, "I've been waiting for you for quite some time." In actuality he had only been waiting for five minutes.

"How did you get here?" asked Tesnayr.

"I followed you of course," replied the cat.

"Well your journey ends here," said Tesnayr.

The two men started to leave, but the cat stopped them. "I would not go that way. There are at least fifty orcs heading this direction. You will need to find another way north."

"How do you—"

"People have a habit of ignoring cats. That provides ample opportunities for me to listen in on their conversations. I know what message you carry and I am willing to help you."

"We don't need a cat tagging along," said Tesnayr.

"Then by all means, carry on," replied Turyn. "But I will follow you anyway and be of further annoyance than if you just allow me to join you."

"We'll just lose you along the way," snapped Tesnayr.

Turyn chuckled to himself. "You know nothing about cats. No one gets rid of us that easily."

"Then lead the way," said Nigilin silencing Tesnayr.

Tesnayr gave Nigilin a piercing stare.

"Have you ever tried arguing with a cat," Nigilin whispered to him. "The cat always wins."

They followed the cat for the rest of the day until the sun sank low in the sky. He trotted at a brisk pace. Turyn took a route that even Nigilin did not know existed. Its rough passage and sharp rocks proved difficult, but not impassable. The cat dashed through them easily with constant reminders to hurry up. Turyn's vocalizations raked Tesnayr's nerves. If it wasn't for Nigilin, he would have skinned that cat alive.

Finally, night fell forcing them to stop. They quickly made camp, forgoing a fire. All three ate in silence before going to sleep.

Tesnayr woke to a start the next morning. He glanced at Nigilin and noticed the black cat curled next to him. *It wasn't a dream?* For a fleeting moment he had hoped that the talking cat was a figment of his imagination. But as memories of the previous two days rushed him, Tesnayr realized that it was all real. *Talking cats. What next?*

A sharp, piercing cry echoed through the small ravine they slept in. Recognizing this as the thing that woke him, he got up. Tesnayr crept in the early morning sunlight examining the terrain as he followed the shriek. Its inhuman sound filled him with apprehension. His pulse throbbed in his neck. Curiosity outweighed his anxiety as Tesnayr headed for the deafening sound.

Mud slurped around his boots as he entered a small marsh that drained into a lake. The strange noises grew louder. Absent mindedly Tesnayr gripped the hilt of his sword. He jumped, startled, at what he saw, and dashed behind a boulder.

Ahead lay a dragon on the sandy lake-side poised in self-defense as a group of orcs circled it. It gasped in great heaving pants. Droplets of blood dotted the ground below the point where a lance protruded from its shoulder painting it red. Unsure of what to do, Tesnayr watched from his hiding place.

Giddily, the orcs danced around the dragon poking and prodding it. One jabbed it again with its spear twisting and grinding it deep within the dragon's flesh. The great beast reared its head releasing another deafening roar. Tesnayr covered his ears from the loud outcry. He peeked around the giant rock. The orcs continued taunting the dragon. One brought its crooked sword upon its snout. The dragon swung its head to the side catching the orc and flinging it in the air. It landed motionless. Angered, the other orcs stabbed it. Many times their blades bounced off the hard scales, but a few did pierce its flesh. Each time the dragon roared in pain.

Tesnayr could stand it no more. He weighed his options. He could not take on an entire group of orcs, nor could he go for

Nigilin. By the time they returned it would be too late. Racking his brains Tesnayr snatched a rock from the ground. He eyed the orcs making certain they were not looking in his direction. With all his might, he flung the rock overhead. It arced over the dragon and the orcs crashing on to the ground with a soft thump.

The orcs stopped their play. One walked over to the sound. Suddenly, the dragon rose on its hind feet howling ferociously. Smoke billowed from its nostrils. Awestruck, Tesnayr watched as fire burst from its mouth engulfing the orcs. The dragon spewed fire until the entire lake and marsh cooked from its heat.

Slowly, the flames died away. Charred remains were all that was left of the orcs. The dragon slumped to the ground. Gingerly, it tried to pull the lance from its shoulder only to fall back into the sand in even greater pain.

Pity moved Tesnayr. Carefully, he left his hiding place. Tesnayr approached the dragon with caution. 'I won't hurt you," he soothed. He pulled his sword from its scabbard and made a show of placing it in the sand.

The dragon eyed him suspiciously.

Step by step he neared the beast. "I'm just going to pull this thing from your shoulder. I wish you could give me some sign of understanding."

The dragon snorted.

Tesnayr gently reached for the lance. His powerful hands grasped it. Quickly, he yanked it out of the dragon's shoulder and jumped back as the beast cried in agony. Tesnayr dropped the orc spear onto the ground. He stood with his back against a rock wall facing the dragon knowing that at any moment it could devour him.

The dragon spread its massive wings and beat them furiously. The pounding of the wind they created swirled around Tesnayr as he crouched low to the ground covering his head. Futilely, Tesnayr tried to protect himself from the pelting sand. It stopped.

"I suppose I should thank you," said a female voice.

Tesnayr looked up at the dragon. He rose to his feet staring at the creature.   "You're...You're welcome," he stammered. Tesnayr moved away from the rocks. "Are you a dragon?" he asked.

"You have never seen one I presume," answered the dragon. "Yes, I am a dragon."

"Dragons do not exist where I come from. What happened? How did the orcs capture you?" Once again Tesnayr's curiosity got the better of him.

"You are not one of them?"

"No."

"I was resting in this ravine when they chanced upon me. Apparently they have never seen a dragon either. What is your name stranger?"

"Tesnayr."

"And I suppose you want a gift for saving me."

Tesnayr's brow furrowed. "Gift? I want nothing. I was just helping someone in need." He managed to catch himself before saying the word animal. Silently, he willed his palms to cease sweating.

The dragon leaned close to Tesnayr staring him in the eyes, studying him. Tesnayr tried not to cough from the putrid breath. The dragon grunted. "You speak the truth."

"Is it that surprising?" Tesnayr almost kicked himself for saying that. That dragon could eat him if she wanted to.

The dragon turned its head toward a pile of marble stone and breathed blue fire on it. Slowly, the stone transformed into a horn.

"My name is Selexia. I am the queen of the dragons. Take this horn and should you ever need my aid its call will bring me or my dragons to you. From this day forward I bind the dragons in service to you and your descendants until such a time as we are released from that service. This is my gift to you. Use it wisely."

Tesnayr gingerly took the horn into his hands and looked at it as he turned it over in awe. "Thank you," he said.

"You are a strange one, Tesnayr. Be certain that your bravery is not a disguise for foolishness."

Selexia eyed him one last time before spreading her giant wings and taking off into the blue sky rapidly becoming little more than a speck. Tesnayr stuffed the horn beneath his cloak and dashed back to the others. He arrived just as Nigilin sat up.

"Good morning," said Nigilin. "Anything interesting happen while we slept?"

"No," replied Tesnayr. He thought it best to keep his encounter with the dragon a secret for the moment. He barely believed it himself. "How much farther?'

"I suspect we will reach Drynelle by the end of the day."

"We best get going then. We'll eat as we walk."

A scuffling noise distracted Tesnayr. Turyn's tail stuck out of his pack. Tesnayr reached down and pulled Turyn out by his tail. "What are you doing?"

"Nothing," replied the cat as he licked his lips.

"Eating our food, I suppose," said Nigilin.

"Was not," said Turyn.

Tesnayr leaned over and picked a crumb off of Turyn's whisker.

"I wonder how that got there," said Turyn. His cloak of innocence did not go unnoticed.

Nigilin knew the land quite well, and as promised they reached Drynelle before sunset. Tesnayr eyed the city, unused to such splendor from his time spent in the simple village by the ocean. The city gleamed from a distance beckoning any to enter. On top of a hill stood the palace where he knew the king must dwell.

They entered the city gates with a throng of merchants getting ready for a day's worth of business. The bustle of the city gave little indication of trouble in the outside world. They wound their way through the crowded cobble stone streets. Various merchants hollered at them to buy their items.

Turyn disappeared. This did not concern Tesnayr as he did not trust the cat. Within an hour, he and Nigilin reached the topmost layer of the city and stood before the palace doors.

"Remember," said Nigilin, "Do not lose your temper."

Tesnayr and Nigilin were admitted into King Slyamal's court without delay. They walked respectfully on the hall's stone floor. Their echoing footsteps bounced off the high ceiling as all eyes rested on them.

"Step forward," commanded the guard leading them to a man seated upon the throne. He motioned for them to stop directly in front of the king. "King Slyamal, I present to you two messengers: Nigilin and Tesnayr," announced the soldier.

"What is your message?" asked the king.

"Your majesty," said Nigilin, kneeling before the king. Tesnayr remained standing. "We bring grave news. Our land has been invaded by conquerors from across the sea. They are vile beasts known as orcs. We believe that they not only intend to conquer Sym'Dul, but its neighboring kingdoms as well."

"You believe," said the king, "And how do you know of their intentions?"

Nigilin eyed the king uncomfortably. "They have already attacked my home and those of my neighbors without remorse. These orcs must be stopped before too much of our land falls to their control."

King Slyamal said nothing at first. He conversed quietly with one of his guards. "I have heard of these orcs, as you call them. The southern lands have already fallen to them. I have dispatched one thousand of my soldiers to stop them. The matter shall be resolved shortly."

The king dismissed them, but Tesnayr stood rooted to the ground aghast at what he just heard. King Slyamal's arrogance stunned him. Pain radiated through his hands as he dug his fingernails into his clenched fists in an effort to control himself. He failed.

"You fool!" said Tesnayr. "One thousand men will not be enough. They will be slaughtered. You have no idea of what you are up against."

"And I suppose you know more on how to fight these orcs," demanded King Slyamal.

"I know them. I understand them," replied Tesnayr, "I have fought the orcs in the past. And I know their leader, Galbrok."

"You are not from Sym'Dul," said the king. "Your speech is different."

"I come from across the sea. The orcs destroyed my homeland and they will do the same to yours."

"My advisors inform me that these orcs are a rabble of beasts, unorganized at best. They will be dealt with. I have more important matters to attend. The king of Belarnia and I are at war. I have been informed that King Edrei intends to form an alliance with him. The orcs are of no consequence and are a problem easily dealt with."

"Of no consequence," sputtered Tesnayr loudly. His voice, tinged with disbelief, echoed throughout the chamber so all could hear. "Are you mad? Do you not care for your own people?"

"Tesnayr," hissed Nigilin.

"You care more about your petty quarrels and expanding the borders of your kingdom," shouted Tesnayr, ignoring Nigilin's warning. "How many men have you sent to their deaths so as to quench your insatiable thirst for more power? In all these years have you ever wondered if all these private wars were worth the cost?"

"Enough," yelled King Slyamal, but Tesnayr continued.

"But now you have a true problem on your hands and you are ill-equipped to deal with it."

"Silence!"

"You are a greedy, arrogant man. You have ruled by selfishness. You and your fellow kings care nothing for the safety of your lands. How much longer will you force your people to suffer until you come to your senses? If you continue this foolishness you will soon be enslaved to the very thing you claim to be a nuisance."

"Silence!" thundered the king for a third time. His face had turned a brilliant shade of purple. "You—insolent—how dare you speak to me in such a manner. I am your king—."

"You are no king of mine," shot Tesnayr. "Nor will you ever be! Go ahead and sit on your throne behind your cloak of kingship. You have not learned the nature of true leadership and you never will while you remain encased in this tomb of stone."

"You, Tesnayr, are to be held here until I decide what is to be done with you. As for you," said King Slyamal to Nigilin, "I am appalled that you would travel with such a man. I am certain that you have learned your lesson."

"Lesson, yes" said Nigilin. King Slyamal's dismissal of his message angered him. "Tesnayr is a better man than you. I wore the crest of Sym'Dul and yet you pay me no more attention than that of a common street beggar. Your father would have bestowed upon me the honor I deserve as a soldier.

"I sacrificed much in the service of your father and that of Sym'Dul. Yet, I was received with no respect. I am saddened to find my service to be in vain and to find the rule of this kingdom taken over by an incompetent fool with the temperament of a mere child. You are not fit to be the son of kings. Your own brother, inept as he was, was a better man than you. At least he died honorably."

"Silence the both of you," raged King Slyamal. "I will teach you to respect your king. Take them away. Let them stew in their disloyalty!"

Tesnayr smiled as he had the last word. "I thank you for such a delicious meal. We will save a bit of our stew for you because you deserve loyalty from no man."

Two guards roughly grabbed Tesnayr and Nigilin and shoved them crudely from the courtroom. They passed a young woman concealed in the shadows. She stared at Tesnayr with a mixture of contempt and wonder.

The guards pushed them down stone steps and deep within the heart of the palace. Water dripped from the walls the deeper they went. The sounds of the castle faded as they descended to the dungeon. Within minutes they reached the bottom.

Flickering torches provided the only light in the musty area. Forcefully, the guards thrust them into a tiny cell and slammed the door shut locking it securely. Tesnayr listened as their footsteps faded.

"I congratulate you in not upsetting the king," said Nigilin jokingly.

"I do apologize," said Tesnayr.

"No need. King Slyamal is a fool. His father would have paid more heed to our message."

"Who was that woman," asked Tesnayr.

"She is the king's daughter," replied Nigilin.

Tesnayr grunted.

"Do not judge her by her father's deeds," said Nigilin. He looked around the cell. Moss grew on the wall. Hay littered the floor, barely enough to use as bedding. "I guess we ought to get comfortable."

Nigilin glanced over at Tesnayr as he tossed in his sleep. *Another nightmare.* Nigilin was familiar with these fitful sleeps of Tesnayr. He had witnessed many of them since the day he brought the man into his cottage. He wished he could do something to help him. But whatever haunted Tesnayr's dreams was buried deep within him.

Nigilin felt the scratches in the stone wall. Since the day they had been locked in the cell, Tesnayr had kept count of the time. One mark for each day. Seven lined the wall.

Tesnayr squirmed some more in his sleep. Quietly, Nigilin went to him. He put his hand on the man's chest like he had done on countless occasions. "It's only a dream, lad," he whispered. "It's just a dream."

Tesnayr turned on his side. His snores filled the cell. Satisfied, Nigilin flopped down on his small pile of hay. He laid on his back stretching. Slowly, he closed his eyes and drifted off to sleep.

Up in the dark shadows of the rafters sat Turyn. He had watched the entire episode. He had disappeared for the past several days. He knew that the two men wouldn't appreciate his absence, but he had a mission.

With Tesnayr and Nigilin locked up, he could begin spreading the stories about a magnificent warrior who could lead the people against the invading orcs. He knew that no one believed Tesnayr about the orcs. And those who did came to the belief too late.

Turyn slipped off the rafters and through the bars of the window. He trotted through the empty streets to the city with ease. His black fur blended in with the surroundings allowing him to remain invisible. Raucous laughter pulled him to a building with light spilling out. Turyn padded over. Three off duty guards busied themselves with telling stories and drinking.

Perfect. Turyn slipped inside and crouched in a corner behind a broom. His yellow eyes remained fixed on the men in the room.

"Do you think there is any truth to that messenger's claim about strange beasts?" asked one man.

"Truth," slurred another, "He is a madman."

"I don't think so," said Turyn.

"Oh you don't," said the second man.

"Don't what?" challenged the first a bit confused.

"Many of the villagers have seen strange folk about," said Turyn throwing his voice.

"Is that so?" piped up a third guard. "I suppose there have been rumors about farms being burned and livestock disappearing."

"So perhaps that messenger was correct."

"But if he was, who knows anything about these beasts? Our king believes it is all fanciful imagination."

"Tesnayr," whispered Turyn. "Seek Tesnayr."

"Tesnayr," mused the first man. "Why does that name sound familiar?"

"It was the messenger's name," said the third guard.

"But he's locked away in the prison," said the first man.

"Bars cannot keep him," said Turyn.

"But what if he is waiting for the opportune time to escape?" asked the second man.

"Opportune?"

"Everything has its time," said Turyn.

"Yes it does," said the first man. "He may be waiting for people to gain some sense."

"If our king does nothing, then Tesnayr will be my commander," said the third man.

"That's treacherous talk," hushed the second man.

"Is it?" said Turyn.

"Is it?" repeated the first man. "Perhaps it's not. If the orcs are real, then I will stand with whoever fights them. I stand for Sym'Dul."

"Then it is settled," said the second man.

"For Sym'Dul," the three said in unison as they clinked their mugs.

Turyn smiled. He stole out of the room and went out into the cool night. He darted down the streets looking for more like the three men he had just left. Tesnayr would need an army to accomplish what he wants. He may not know it yet, but Turyn knew that Tesnayr would not stop until he defeated the orcs.

The next morning Tesnayr and Nigilin were led outside. As they walked, Tesnayr noticed a woman standing on a balcony overlooking the city, the same woman he had seen in the king's court. Captivated by her beauty, he stopped suddenly causing Nigilin to trip over the chains that bound them together and hit the ground hard. Nigilin regained his feet and when he noticed why Tesnayr had stopped he chuckled.

"I am afraid that she is a bit beyond your reach, my friend," he said.

"Keep moving," growled the guard as he pushed them along.

"Who is she?" asked Tesnayr.

The guard laughed when he realized what Tesnayr had been staring at. "Her name is Jenel. Oh, get that idea out of your head, lad, you will never get near the likes of her. She is the king's daughter."

The guard pushed them along.

Turyn easily found the king in a private chamber with one of his advisors. Their heated voices attracted his attention. He snuck in unnoticed and settled himself in a dark corner. Only the glow of his eyes was visible.

King Slyamal paced before the roaring fire in the room. "What do you want me to do, Arnin?"

"Release them. You cannot hold them prisoner. You have no cause to," replied Arnin. He walked over to the only table in the room and filled a goblet with wine. He sipped the refreshing liquid while hoping that his king would see reason.

"You heard what he said in there," stormed King Slyamal.

"You are a king and such insults should mean nothing to you. Unless, of course, he spoke the truth."

"How dare you," snapped the king.

"How dare I?" demanded Arnin. "These orcs that he talked about might be a bigger problem than you realize. There are stories about a distant land from far across the sea that has been conquered by beasts matching the description of these orcs."

"Rumors and hearsay," muttered the king, "You should know better than to listen to it."

"This is more than hearsay. There are reports from other villages of the same nature as those two messengers."

"I sent men."

"They are all dead. A messenger arrived an hour ago."

"Dead?" said the king in disbelief. He sank into a chair. His face had gone ashen. "What are we to do?"

"The man you hold prisoner seems to know an awful lot about these beasts."

"He can rot there!" spat the king. "That man is nothing but talk."

Arnin chucked his goblet into the fire. "For goodness sake man, let go of your pride! Your people are dying! They look to you for help. Who will protect them if not their king?

"We have lost the southern lands! If this man knows how to defeat these creatures we should ask him to join us before he offers his loyalty elsewhere."

"I would prefer the help of a peasant over his," said King Slyamal letting his anger influence his decision.

"You are a fool! If you care nothing for your people, think of your daughter. How safe do you think she will be if these beasts conquer Sym'Dul and reach Drynelle?"

"She's going away. I've made arrangements with the king of Belyndril."

"Belyndril," said Arnin.

"Yes," replied King Slyamal. "I have forged a temporary alliance with him. He has promised to allow Jenel to stay there free from harm."

"And if Belyndril falls?"

King Slyamal sipped his wine and said nothing. The thought had occurred to him, but he pushed the despicable idea away. Belyndril couldn't fall, he thought, not to some unknown army of beasts.

Turyn had heard enough and left as quietly as he came. He slunk through the halls and back to the dungeon. The shadows of the night provided excellent cover, but Turyn wasn't worried about being seen. No one ever paid any attention to a cat.

"Have many people occupied this cell?" Nigilin asked the guard, formulating a plan. He had had enough of Tesnayr's waiting. It was time to leave.

The guard answered lazily as he leaned back in a chair with his feet resting on the table. "No. Normally these cells are empty."

"Has anyone ever escaped from here?" Nigilin inquired when he noticed Turyn entering the prison chamber.

The guard quickly sat up as though an idea had struck him. "It just so happens that a few years ago there were a couple of fellas like yourselves who occupied that very cell."

"How did they escape?" asked Tesnayr catching on to Nigilin's plan.

"No...I shouldn't tell you."

"I suppose if you do not wish to tell us...but there is nothing to do around here and we would enjoy listening to a good tale," said Nigilin encouragingly.

"Very well. I will tell you," said the guard. "One of them had called me over and I set my keys down like this," the guard took the ring of keys from around his belt and placed them on the table before walking over to the cell door, "And approached him. Now, these two knew one of those talking cats and while I was busy talking to them, the cat took the keys from the table."

As the guard talked, Turyn hopped on to the table and snatched the ring of keys. He padded quietly to the cell unnoticed by the guard. Carefully, he slipped the keys through the bars and skittered away.

"And then what happened?" asked Nigilin.

"Well, the cat slipped the keys through the cell bars and I never noticed a thing," said the guard. "He was one of those strange cats."

"Like this?" inquired Tesnayr as he picked up the keys and dangled them in his hand.

"Yes," replied the guard.

"Then what happened?" Nigilin asked again.

"After that," said the guard," I moved over to this suit of armor like this and that cat of theirs was sitting on top of it. After which he knocked the thing on my head. When I came to, the cell was empty and the captain was furious."

"What is that cat doing up there?" asked Tesnayr pointing at the suit of armor.

The guard slowly realized what had happened and glanced up at the armor. On top of it sat Turyn.

"Meow."

The guard mouthed the words "oh no" as Turyn leaped off the armor causing the entire thing to come crashing down on his head. Tesnayr quickly unlocked the cell door. He and Nigilin grabbed their things and placed the keys back on the table.

"Some people never learn," said Turyn as they all left the prison chamber.

Tesnayr's mental map of the palace enabled them to navigate the castle. The three moved swiftly through the stone corridors. Water splashed as their boots crashed into the various puddles. Guided by torchlight, they hurried onward desperate to reach the outside before the alarm was raised. Turyn peeked around corners to make certain that no guards lingered about while following Tesnayr's instruction on which corner to turn next.

Upon reaching the stairs, Tesnayr stopped. He listened intently for sounds of guards. Nothing. Carefully, he and the others crept up the steps clinging to the moist stone wall. Most of the stairwell lay in shadow and provided excellent cover. But that did little to ease Tesnayr's nerves. At any moment they could be discovered.

The three had made it through the castle unchallenged, a feat that made Tesnayr wary. By now someone should have noticed their escape. As they neared the door that led to the outside world, Tesnayr's suspicions were proven correct. Blocking the doorway stood a man in a dark cloak brandishing a sword. Turyn recognized him immediately as the one that had been talking to the king earlier.

"Move aside," commanded Tesnayr.

The man stood his ground.

"We do not wish to fight you," said Tesnayr.

"Strange words for a man who has just escaped the prison chamber," said the man.

"What do you want?" demanded Nigilin.

The man lowered his sword. "I will let you pass on one condition: you take me with you."

"Impossible," snapped Tesnayr.

Nigilin hushed him. "Why do you wish to come? You are finely dressed. Are you not one of the king's advisors?"

"I am," replied the man. "King Slyamal blames his advisors for his foolishness. I wish to join you. I will not remain here."

"I believe him," said Turyn.

"You have a name stranger," said Tesnayr.

"Arnin."

"Well, Arnin," Tesnayr continued, "We need horses."

Arnin smiled. He led them through the door where three horses stood saddled and ready for travel. Arnin tossed them each a cloak that bore the king's crest. "These will allow us to pass through the gates unchecked," he explained.

Tesnayr and Nigilin had little choice but to put them on. They leapt on the stallions and trotted through the city streets. Arnin led the way through Drynelle. Pedestrians jumped out of the way of what they believed to be an envoy of the king.

Upon reaching the city gates a guard halted them. "Who goes there?"

"It is I, Arnin, and two messengers of the king," replied Arnin in an authoritative voice.

The guard approached taking note of the emblem on each of their cloaks. He waved them through.

They galloped through the gates and away into the moonless night. Arnin led them to a place far away from Drynelle well secluded by rocks and trees. They rode for a night and a day without stopping, not even to rest.

"Why were you waiting for us?" Tesnayr finally broke a day's worth of silence as they huddled by a fire.

"I was on my way to free you two, when I noticed that you had done it yourselves," replied Arnin. "What are your plans?"

"I have none," said Tesnayr.

"Might I suggest that we keep moving," said Arnin, "There is a pass a few days' ride from here that leads through the mountains into Belyndril. We could go—"

Nigilin cleared his throat interrupting Arnin. He detested the idea of running. "We should head south."

"I heard some soldiers talking in a nearby town. Belarnia is attempting to mount a defense against them. The orcs have already moved north and have begun to spread eastward," Turyn interjected.

"South?" said Arnin.

"Yes," said Nigilin, "Instead of running or waiting for the orcs to catch us, we should face them. We can gather people along the way who feel as we do."

"Are you insane? We should head to Belyndril and ask the king there for help. Warn him about the orcs," argued Arnin.

"Tell me, Arnin," said Tesnayr, "How do we know that you will not betray us the same way you have betrayed your king?"

"You asked me that question last night."

"I am asking you again!"

Arnin looked into Tesnayr's eyes. Something in Tesnayr's expression forced him to choose his words carefully. "As I have said, King Slyamal is a fool more concerned about his treasury than his people. When a king ceases to put the well-being of his people before himself, when he ceases to lead and govern justly, he no longer deserves to be king, nor does he deserve the loyalty of his people. The people will find another who is wise and just and they would be right to do so. People will only suffer fools for so long."

"Some longer than others," Nigilin chimed in, moving away from his place near the fire.

"And some are just fools," uttered Turyn.

"When I became part of the king's council," Arnin continued, "I swore an oath to serve him. But when he carelessly sent those men to their deaths I knew then that I could no longer abide by that oath. I refuse to serve a man who recklessly does what he wills with little regard of the consequences. If you, Tesnayr, wish to go after these orcs, I will go with you."

"Admirable," said Turyn. No one paid him any attention.

Tesnayr looked at his hand as though he held a sword in it. "I have tried running from my past, but it will not release me," he said to himself before speaking aloud. "The orcs destroyed my home. They murdered the woman I was to marry. They have destroyed any chance of any happiness I might have had. I go after them for one reason: vengeance. I do not ask you to join me."

"Vengeance is a convenient bandage for one's wounds," Turyn said aloud.

Nigilin stepped forward. "Perhaps. I will do what I can to protect my home."

Once again Turyn piped up. "Noble."

"I thought you were a leader of men," said Arnin to Tesnayr.

"I am no leader," replied Tesnayr, "But if you remain with us, you will be given the chance to fight the orcs and protect your people."

"Kill the beasts!" Turyn blurted out. The others ignored him.

"Very well," said Arnin.

"We leave at dawn," Tesnayr told the others.

"Must it be so early?" chimed Turyn.

"Must you always toss in your two pieces of silver," said Nigilin to the cat.

"Cats always do and I am a cat," replied Turyn.

"If you give me that cat business once more, I swear I will filet you alive," grumbled Tesnayr.

Turyn pranced over to Tesnayr and casually stretched as he brushed the man's chin with his tail. "Meow," he said and bounded away.

Arnin and Nigilin unsuccessfully suppressed their smirks as Tesnayr's knuckles turned white from frustration.

Chapter IV
New Recruits

Three identical young men stumbled clumsily through the thicket. The snapping twigs and crunching leaves echoed through the forest. Though well-armed, they walked with vacant expressions on their faces. Drool streamed from their dangling tongues onto their chests. Unaware of the world around them, they followed two beautiful women. The women laughed and giggled childishly relishing in their fun as they galloped through the woods.

Yellow eyes watched them, regarding their prey with interest. Oblivious of the danger, the women trotted merrily leading the confused men. One of the women pulled back some brush revealing a group of hideous beasts. Shocked, the women vanished. Their spell broken, the three men regained their senses while staring at the beasts in bewilderment. Slowly, realization of what had just happened dawned upon them.

They brought their swords up just in time to block an attack. One clonked a creature in the ear and pushed it aside. He dashed away with the other two.

They paused in a small clearing standing back to back and facing their enemy. Orcs chased after them. For a few moments orcs and men just stared at each other. The orcs snarled and growled in anticipation of a kill. The three men linked their arms and swung each other around in a fashion that allowed them to block and strike with precision. Their maneuver prevented the orcs from inflicting any damage while bodies piled up in front of them.

Arrows fell from the sky piercing the remaining beasts with precision. Three older men burst from the trees and surrounded the others. They callously inspected the carcasses of the orcs making certain that they were indeed dead. One of the men grabbed one of the younger ones and dragged him a few feet away. "Just what did you think you were doing?" he growled.

"Nothing...we...we," stammered the man.

"We were following two women," replied one of the remaining two, "Though I think they may have been fairies. To be honest I don't remember much after that first instant we decided to watch them."

"Fairies? You expect me to believe that?" said the older man.

One of the other strangers approached. "Yes, Tesnayr, that would make sense. Fairies are known for putting men under a spell and toying with them until they tire of their fun. And they have obviously been put under one. Let the man go."

Tesnayr released the young man he held in his grasp.

"My name is Nigilin and this here is Arnin and you know Tesnayr," said Nigilin.

"My brothers and I thank you for saving us," said one of the triplets, "I am Nedis, this is Nular, and he is Nylin."

"You are quite welcome," said Tesnayr as he walked away. "Let's move," he said to his companions.

They moved into the thicket followed by the three brothers. "Where are you going?" Tesnayr asked them.

"With you," replied the triplets in unison.

"No, you are not," said Tesnayr.

"Why," said Nedis, "We can—."

"—fight," said Nular, "After all, you need—"

"—help, mate," said Nylin.

"You three let yourselves become dumbfounded by two women and walked right into that company of orcs," argued Tesnayr, "I need people with more—"

"Intelligence?" said the three in unison.

Nylin spoke, "Tesnayr. That name sounds familiar. We've heard about you, mate."

"We do not like these beasts any more than you," said Nular.

"And we might be able to help you," said Nedis.

Nigilin stepped forward. "They have a point," he told Tesnayr, quietly. "Their hearts are in the right place."

"Yet, they walked into a trap," said Tesnayr, "If we hadn't come along—"

"'If' is a word with little to no outcome," interrupted Nigilin. "These three may prove useful."

Tesnayr relented. "If you three choose to join us you must do one thing." The three brothers looked at him curiously. "Wear different colored tunics."

"Why?" they asked in unison.

"Because I cannot tell the three of you apart."

"That is part—," began Nular.

"—of the—," Nedis said.

"—fun, mate," finished Nylin. "What do you say?" he asked his brothers. "Should we oblige him in his request?"

Nedis and Nular looked at each other and smiled. "Why not," they said together in agreement. Tesnayr rolled his eyes in annoyance. Arnin and Nigilin smiled at each other as they tried to keep from laughing.

Nedis, Nular, and Nylin led their new friends back to their camp where a few more men awaited them. From the state of the fire pits, it was clear that they had been there for some time. Men stood up from washing their clothes. Other watched with interest as the triplets led three new faces into their midst. Tesnayr eyed one particular man with a red beard. They glared at each other for a moment before the man broke contact.

The brothers led them to the very center of their camp where everyone could see them. "Everyone gather around," yelled Nedis. "Tesnayr has come to help us."

The triplets eagerly introduced everyone. From what was said, Tesnayr gathered that these men had abandoned their homes and formed their own army after orcs had attacked them. They had camped when possible, but had to always remain vigilant lest the raiding bands of orcs attacked them.

Soon after the introductions had finished, the sentries of the camp ran up to them in alarm. "People are approaching," one reported to Tesnayr.

Tesnayr signaled for everyone to hide. Quickly, men dropped what they were doing and dove behind bushes, trees, even boulders. They watched and waited until those who approached reached the middle of the camp.

A group of twenty to thirty people entered the encampment. They moved cautiously prepared for an attack. One by one, they investigated the smoldering coals of the fires. One man sifted through dirty laundry with the toe of his foot. Tesnayr waited for the precise moment when he gave the signal. The men jumped from their hiding spots and surrounded the newcomers.

"Put your weapons down," said a man.

Tesnayr drew near him. "Who are you? Why are you here?"

"Withdraw your weapons and I will tell you," said the man.

Tesnayr gave the order. Slowly, everyone lowered their arms.

The man did the same. "My name is Jarown. We have traveled here from Belyndril. Word has reached us of your deeds, Tesnayr. Yes, I know who you are.

"There are rumors of beasts who move through the night laying destruction wherever they go. Many of us have already seen these orcs in Belyndril and have decided that it is only a matter of time until more come.

"We have come to offer our services. If we can stop the orcs before they go beyond the borders of Sym'Dul, then perhaps we can save all our homes."

"How did you know I was here?" asked Tesnayr.

"We learned that some had gathered for the same purpose as ours so I led us here in the hope of finding you," answered Jarown.

"That still doesn't explain how you knew exactly where to find me," said Tesnayr with the hint of a threat in his voice.

Jarown eyed him for a moment. He understood Tesnayr's suspicions. He would have felt the same. "Rumors. Stories."

"And why have you come?" Tesnayr asked Nedis.

Nedis took his time answering. "The people you see gathered before you have already had their homes destroyed by the orcs. We know of the king's feeble attempt to fight them and of his failure. Many of our friends and family are already dead. None of us are going to stand idly by while these beasts turn us into slaves. Stories of what you did to the orcs reached us. A few days ago rumors of your coming to these parts reached our village and so we gathered here."

"Rumors," said Tesnayr. "You say that stories warned you of the invasion," he pointed at Jarown.

"Yes," said Jarown. "They told us exactly where to find you. We had no other options so we took a chance and sought you out."

"I'd like to know how the rumor got started in Sym'Dul as well," said Tesnayr.

A black cat appeared out of nowhere and stood by Tesnayr. "I believe I can answer that," he said. "Yes, the cat talks," he added to a few who gawked at him. "It occurred to me that if you are to fight these orcs, then you will need an army behind you. So I visited a few towns and started the rumors."

"That would explain your absence," said Tesnayr. "In the future, consult me before you act on your own."

Turyn stalked off flipping his tail.

"But that does not explain how they reached Belyndril," commented Nigilin.

"A woman showed up four months ago in Belyndril. A rather mysterious woman told us of you," said Jarown, "She is the sort you listen to."

Nigilin leaned in close to Tesnayr. "Sounds like the sorceress knew what was going to happen long before we left for Drynelle."

"Yes," said Jarown, "It may have been her. She warned us of the orcs. She described you in detail, Tesnayr, and told us where to find you should we wish to save our homes. There is little of Belyndril left."

"Ernayn," spat Nigilin. "Leave it to the sorceress to meddle."

Tesnayr hated the situation. He had barely left King Slyamal's prison and had yet to decide on a course of action. And yet, here he stood with a bunch of people who already knew of his existence. They had decided his path for him. But perhaps he could use this to his advantage. If the King of Sym'Dul refused his warnings, and if the kings of the other kingdoms have done the same, he would need an army to call his own. One trained to fight against the invasion of the orcs.

"Listen up," Tesnayr spoke aloud, "As you all seem so keen on following me you will refer to me as your captain. I am in full command of this group and my orders will be obeyed. Nigilin, Arnin, and Jarown are my lieutenants. You will report to them if there are any problems or questions and they will report to me.

"Everyone here is free to leave if he wishes. You are no longer people of Belyndril or Sym'Dul. You are my men."

Tesnayr waited a few minutes for any sign of dissent. Nigilin pointed to Turyn. Evidently, there would be no getting rid of the cat.

"And the cat will be respected as a member of this army," added Tesnayr getting the hint, "Any who treat him otherwise will be dealt with accordingly." Tesnayr dismissed his men and gave orders for sentries to be placed around the camp. Tomorrow, the real work would begin.

The next morning Tesnayr found a rocky cliff face perfect for climbing. His men needed to build their strength. With the help of Nigilin and Jarown he built harnesses to use as safety lines while men tried to scale the 300 foot rock wall.

Many barely made it twenty feet before losing their grip and falling. Tesnayr watched in frustration as man after man failed. Bruised, men grumbled about the stupidity of climbing a rocky cliff face. To them it was just a wall. To Tesnayr, it served as a test of their will, physical strength, and character.

Three more slammed into the ground. They muttered to themselves until they noticed Tesnayr staring at them with a very disapproving look. He watched as a couple more managed to get halfway up before quitting.

"There is no possible way to climb this thing," said one. "And what does it matter if we can climb the side of a cliff?"

Having grown tired of their complaints and lack of will, Tesnayr didn't answer the man's question. Instead, he walked over to the cliff and strapped himself into a harness. He lifted a loaded pack onto his shoulders and tied a sword around his waist.

Tesnayr grasped the rocky mountainside. Expertly, he clamped his hands onto protruding rocks while placing his feet on stable slabs of stone. He slowly, but methodically, hoisted himself upward. When he reached the two men stopped at the halfway mark, Tesnayr ignored them. He concentrated fully on climbing the wall focusing on making it to the top.

His hand slipped. Quickly, Tesnayr grabbed the wall. He paused momentarily to catch his breath and settle his nerves from the fact that he had nearly fallen off. Each time he could, he rubbed his hands in dirt to soak up the sweat that encased them. He pushed himself onward with steady determination aware that all eyes were upon him.

A cool breeze welcomed him when he reached the top. With one last pull, Tesnayr heaved himself onto the ledge. He looked out at the crowd below. "If you are going to allow one rocky cliff stop you, how can you expect to defend your homes? The challenges you will face in this army will be far greater than any cliff."

The men attacked the wall with renewed vigor.

"What was the point of that?' Turyn crawled out of Tesnayr's pack.

"Sometimes you have to show them that it can be done," replied Tesnayr. He rummaged through the bag looking for some jerky that he knew had to be in there. "Where is it?"

A guilty expression crossed the cat's face. "We ran out of jerky."

Annoyed, Tesnayr settled for some water. He opened the canteen and lifted it up to take a drink. Nothing.

"We ran out of water too," said Turyn.

Tesnayr considered chucking the cat off the ledge, but ruled against it. Instead, he grabbed his rope and lowered himself back down to the bottom.

The men had been training for weeks. Tesnayr settled himself on a rock away from the encampment. He pulled the chess piece out of his pocket, the black knight. Twirling it in his fingers, Tesnayr studied it and recalled his distant home across the ocean. The home no longer existed, but he still longed for it. Charred remains were all that was left.

Clang!

Tesnayr turned in the direction of the sound. He watched momentarily as Arnin instructed a group on the proper technique of swordsmanship. Tesnayr knew that eventually he would have to take them into battle. He hoped it didn't happen too soon. A part of him quaked at the thought of facing the orcs again.

He stared at the chess piece. Black, like his mood. A sinking feeling that he was making a mistake plagued him. The last time he fought against Galbrok, he lost everything he cared about. What if he failed again?

A bird chirped beside him. Tesnayr looked at it. The golden creature gazed at him curiously. Once again, Tesnayr had the feeling of being studied. It cocked its head and flew away. Strange place, thought Tesnayr.

Footsteps crunched on the ground as someone approached. "Captain," said Arnin, "You know those horses that you wanted?"

"Do not worry about it," said Tesnayr.

"It isn't that," said Arnin, "It's—"

Thundering hooves interrupted them. Tesnayr stood up to gain a better view at what rode into the camp. A herd of saddled horses galloped into the center of the encampment followed closely by three men whom Tesnayr sometimes wished he had never met. Nedis, Nular, and Nylin pulled the horses to a halt.

"Where did you get these?" asked Tesnayr running up to them.

"From nowhere," answered Nular, "They followed us here."

"Followed," said Tesnayr, skeptically.

"Yes, followed," said Nular.

"The poor things must have been so lonesome," said Nylin.

"And I suppose they came with their own saddles," said Tesnayr.

"Yep," chorused the three brothers.

Not wanting to know how they had really acquired the horses, Tesnayr let the matter drop. He just hoped that the original owners would not come searching for the animals.

"Captain," said a messenger, "There is a group of orcs nearby. They are carrying dispatches."

Perfect. "Where are they?" asked Tesnayr.

"South of here," replied the messenger.

Tesnayr rubbed his beard thinking. It appeared the time for taking his men into battle had arrived. "Arnin, Jarown, Nigilin, choose some men and follow me. We are going after those dispatches."

Tesnayr eyed the small group of orcs in the dim light. Five of the beasts sat around a fire eating and drinking. They talked loudly confident that no one would dare assault them. Their lack of concern would make this easy, thought Tesnayr. Still, he wished to be cautious.

"Nigilin, choose two men and create a diversion while the rest of us move in from behind," said Tesnayr.

A shout drew his attention back to the orcs.

"Drinking again," said a man as he moved into the firelight. He snatched a flask from one of the orcs and threw it to the ground. "You fools! Put the fire out."

One of the orcs reached for his sword, but the man stopped him. He grabbed the weapon saying, "Sit down. You are ordered to follow my commands. Perhaps you have forgotten that."

Growling, the orc relented taking another swig from his flask. "Don't get too comfortable, human."

Arrows swooshed through the night sky. Most of them struck the man killing him instantly. The orcs jumped to their feet, but their drink had slowed their response. Swaying, they looked about them not registering what happened. A hooded figure darted through the night and into the light of the fire. This figure fought the orcs in a manner Tesnayr had never seen. The hooded warrior dodged attacks and deadly blows with ease delivering its own.

One orc bore down on the mysterious warrior. The figure swerved out of the way jabbing its weapon upward. The orc clutched his belly slumping to the ground. Without a moment's hesitation, the stranger swung around. Swords clashed as metal met metal.

"Now," ordered Tesnayr.

His men sprang from the bushes and ran toward the commotion. By the time they reached the fire only one orc remained. Arnin rammed his sword through it and blocked an attack by the stranger. A long moment passed before the hooded warrior lowered her weapon.

"You're a woman," said Arnin astonished.

"Brilliant," said the triplets, smirking.

Tesnayr strode into the center of the crowd. "Find the dispatches they were carrying and put the bodies in the fire," he ordered. "Who are you?" he said directing his attention to the woman.

The woman sheathed her sword. "My name is Nelyn."

"And what is your business here?"

Nelyn did not answer.

"Answer me," demanded Tesnayr.

"Perhaps I would be more forthcoming in providing answers if you told me who you are," said Nelyn, sternly.

"As you wish. I am Tesnayr. We received information that these orcs carried with them a dispatch."

Nelyn eyed him. "The dead you see here I have tracked for a month. I am from Belyndril. These animals arrived in my village. It was my wedding day. They murdered my husband and this man," she pointed at the man on the ground jabbing him with the sharp heel of her boot, "Let his soldiers have their way with me. They killed many of my people. I have spent every day since tracking them. I will not rest until every last one of them is dead."

The others listened in silence.

"They have begun burning Belyndril," said Arnin, "It is worse than we thought."

Tesnayr ignored him for the moment. "I have never met a woman who wielded a sword as you do. Where did you learn—"

"No need to ask, Captain," said Jarown as he entered the conversation, "I taught her. Taught her everything I know. She is more skilled with a sword that most men."

"Jarown?" said Tesnayr, questioningly.

"I have known Nelyn since she was a child." Jarown turned his attention to Nelyn. "I thought I told you to stay put."

"I waited for two months after you left. After that, I chose my own course," said Nelyn.

"How much of Belyndril remains?" asked Jarown.

"Charred remains are all that are left of the eastern edge," replied Nelyn. "You are Tesnayr?"

Tesnayr nodded.

"I have heard of you. I wish to join you."

"It seems everyone has heard of me. No," Tesnayr said to the woman and walked away.

Nelyn seized his arm and spun him around. "I can fight as well as any man!"

Tesnayr yanked his arm from her grasp and looked sternly upon her. "War is the world of men. I thank you for what you have done this night, but you cannot come with us."

"You will not be rid of me so easily," warned Nelyn.

"Move out," ordered Tesnayr. "Young woman, I suggest you return home."

Jarown paused by Nelyn's side. He handed her an extra knife and smiled a knowing smile at her as he bade farewell. Nelyn was left alone in the darkness.

Chapter V
The First Engagement

"How long is he going to sit there?" asked one of the men.

"As long as he deems necessary," replied Nigilin overhearing the man's comment.

"I thought we were to be fighting orcs."

Nigilin stepped closer to the man. "You will get your chance. In the meantime, perhaps you wish to challenge me." The man understood Nigilin's silent message and dropped the matter.

After returning with the orc dispatch, Tesnayr secluded himself to ponder over the orc writing. Though well versed in their language it had been months since he had used those skills. In an hour he had translated the message, however, it soon became apparent that the entire thing was written in code. It took time, but Tesnayr managed to decipher it. What he read deeply worried him.

Tesnayr called a meeting with his officers. "The severity of the situation is worse than we had originally thought," began Tesnayr. "The orcs have attacked the eastern edge of Belarnia. King Shealayr is entrenched there. He and his elves are holding out, but they won't for long. There is a battalion of orcs two days ride from here headed for Belarnia. Reinforcements for the ones that are already there."

"King Shealayr will never be able to defeat that many," Nigilin blurted out.

"King Slyamal sent a second contingent of troops to Belarnia," said Arnin.

Turyn made his presence known. His habit of turning up when he pleased no longer surprised the others. "They are all dead just like the first one he sent."

"Always the bearer of good news," gibed Arnin.

Tesnayr cut them all off. "If that battalion reaches Belarnia, then Galbrok's hold in these parts will be sealed."

"What are you suggesting?" asked Nigilin.

"Those orcs must not reach Belarnia. They are currently in the southern part of Hemil. I think here is the perfect place to set a trap," he said, pointing on the map. "Afterwards, we will ride the two days to Belarnia. There is another matter that concerns me," Tesnayr continued, "Orcs are not known for sending dispatches. What's more, they do not write their messages in code. There is something more behind this."

"You believe they have an ally," suggested Nigilin.

Tesnayr nodded grimly in affirmation.

"The question is: who would align themselves with these orcs and why," said Arnin.

"Turyn," said Tesnayr, "I want you to find some answers to this puzzle." The cat waved his tail as he nodded and bounded off.

"We leave within the hour," said Tesnayr ending all discussion.

Tesnayr crouched behind a boulder with his men as he watched the orcs approaching the ravine. The clatter of their armor echoed around him warning every one of their advance. "I hope they take the bait," he whispered.

"If those three did their job, they will," replied Nigilin.

The orcs began to divert from the path that led to the gulch. Suddenly the creaking and grinding of rubble speeding down a hill filled the area. Dust flew everywhere as the debris came to a rolling halt on the very path that the orcs had begun to take. Orcs dashed out of the way as rocks and trees crashed around them. Yelling and shouting ensued as they argued about what to do next.

"Like the show?" asked Nylin as he approached with his brothers.

Tesnayr silenced him. He studied two orcs as they gestured animatedly. They argued for several minutes before conceding the fact that they must take the road through the gorge. Tesnayr grinned as the beasts filed into the gully. *Perfect.* "Get ready," he said. "Now!"

Nigilin released a flaming arrow into the sky. It shot straight up into the air. Many of the orcs watched from below curious about its meaning. Suddenly, the sky turned dark as arrows rained down upon the orcs from both sides of the ravine. The beasts huddled together locking their shields in an attempt to protect themselves. A series of clattering and clanging noises echoed through the ravine as the arrows pounded their shields. Many squeezed through the cracks and pierced soft flesh.

"It's a trap," yelled the orc commander. "Pull back!"

"Signal the second wave," said Tesnayr.

Nigilin fired another flaming arrow into the sky. Men on both ends of the ravine burst from under mounds of brush and charged the orcs. The beasts braced themselves. Their position put them at a severe disadvantage. Cries filled the gorge as swords clashed. The orcs huddled close together only to realize their mistake too late.

Leading his men into the gorge, Arnin charged. Thunder roared as they stormed the enemy carrying sharpened lances. Debris flew around them as they picked up speed. The impact jarred Arnin's arm as his lance pierced an orc's shield and struck the beast behind it. He quickly pulled out his sword and sliced another.

The orcs attempted retreat back the way they came but found their path cut off by a group of armed archers.

"Fire," yelled Jarown.

Arrows shot straight through the air knocking down the orcs at the front of the line.

"Again," shouted Jarown.

More arrows whistled as they left their bows heading straight for their target. Orcs crumpled to the ground clutching their throats with arrows protruding from them as sticky, black blood poured from the wounds.

"Plow your way through," ordered their commander.

The orcs wavered slightly before charging.

"Now, you scum," screamed their commander.

Releasing a deafening cry, the orcs raced toward the archers. They raised their weapons high for the attack.

"Swords," yelled Jarown.

His men obeyed. They braced themselves for the onslaught. At the right moment, Jarown gave the signal. His men ducked and lurched forward effectively dodging the attack and throwing the orcs off balance. In such a tight space, the orcs found it difficult to maneuver so as to counteract their enemies' defense. But Jarown's men were prepared. They whipped around and attacked from behind. Within moments chaos ensued as the two opposing forces slashed and moved.

Arnin dodged and weaved his way through the mass of fighting orcs with his men heading straight for the group that battled with Jarown's unit. They cut off any chance of escape, pinning the orcs down.

Tesnayr watched from his vantage point. "Let's go," he said. He and those on the hillside dropped ropes down into the ravine. They slid down them with ease. Quickly, they joined the others in battle, but the orcs had already been decimated. Only a few remained.

The orc commander charged from behind as Tesnayr slid off the rope. Tesnayr jumped out of the way using the rope to knock the weapon from the orc's hands. The orc punched Tesnayr knocking him back a few paces. Tesnayr swerved out of the way of another punch. He rammed the heel of his boot in the orc's knee and felt the bone crack. In one swift strike, Tesnayr brought the blade of his sword down severing the orc's head. It rolled across the gravel until it stopped by Nigilin's feet.

Surveying the aftermath, Tesnayr made certain that their goal had been accomplished. He wasted no time in pushing the army onward when it became clear that they had suffered no losses. "Put their armor on and take their weapons," shouted Tesnayr.

Men stripped the dead orcs of their armor and swords. Tesnayr watched unconcerned as the unceremoniously stripped bodies were left to rot. Crows circled above waiting for their chance to feast on the carnage.

"This smells horrible," complained one man as he put a dead orc's helmet on.

"Hold your breath," said Tesnayr. "Mount up. We ride for Belarnia without rest. Nedis, lead the way."

"I'm not Nedis. I'm Nylin."

"I thought you were Nular," said one of the other triplets as he approached.

"I guess I could be," said the first.

The third triplet approached apparently right on cue. "I thought I was Nular."

"If you are, then who am I?" asked the first with a wide smile.

"Nylin I presume," said the third.

"Then I guess that makes me Nedis," commented the second. "Of course, I could just as easily be you as you could be me."

"When you three finish figuring out who you are," said Tesnayr, "Feel free to join us in Belarnia." He rode off. Dust billowed everywhere in heavy clouds as horses pounded the earth on their way to war.

*   *   *

King Shealayr stood underneath a burned skeleton of a tree. Ash rained down upon him as though the sky itself mourned dark tears of torment. He brushed the substance from his shoulders staring at his stained palm. The sweet midmorning air had been replaced by the smell of ashes and smoke. Gingerly, King Shealayr picked at the charred bark of a tree and watched as it crumbled between his fingers. *A dismal end.* Sadness enveloped the elf as he surveyed what was once his home.

For six days the elves had engaged the orcs. Six days the forests burned. What was once a place of song was now the dominion of death. Only a soft weeping filled the air as more trees were lit aflame. The king's heart ached with the departure of their spirits. A single tear escaped his eye as he watched the smoke billowing in the distance. The reverberated cries of the orcs reached his ears. Death approached.

Elves darted from tree to tree in a desperate effort to escape the onslaught. They tripped over their fallen comrades too frightened to show even the slightest measure of respect. King Shealayr let them flee. He understood their fear. The king looked at the sky, now obscured by blackness. "We need help," he whispered. The pit of doubt told him that his pleas would go unanswered.

"My king," said an elf pulling King Shealayr from his reverie.

"Idæas," said the king.

"My lord, the orcs are regrouping. We must fall back. We are vulnerable here."

King Shealayr sighed. "They have broken our backs and now they wish to crush our spirits." He kicked the ground. "Where have these beasts come from?"

"No one knows, my lord."

Shealayr glanced at the burnt tree and scanned the surrounding hills. An idea hit him. "Are you familiar with the ridge of Ninspíríl?"

"Ninspíríl?"

"That place was once a fort was it not?"

"Yes, my lord, but as I recall we elves lost the last battle to take place there."

"Barely. However, if we move there, the ridge would provide cover for our forces and it could buy us some time."

"Time for what?" asked Idæas.

"Time to mobilize our forces. We head for Ninspíríl."

"My lord, this is madness."

"Perhaps, but so is staying." King Shealayr glanced at the destruction around him. "You have your orders, Idæas."

Idæas saluted his king and left. The ridge of Ninspíril lay only two hours away. The elves packed all they could carry and hurried there in the hope of reaching the ridge before the orcs noticed they had left the edges of the forest.

The uphill trek slowed them, but King Shealayr pushed them onward with determination. They marched single file weaving their way among the trees. The elf king did not dare take a path. Such an act would make it all too easy for the orcs to follow.

Deep within Belarnia rested the ridge of Ninspíril. Its enormous structure circled around the forest. Overgrown vines infested the entire ridge giving it the look of abandonment, but also provided great camouflage. Small rectangular holes lined it. Each looked manmade as though the ridge itself had been turned into a kind of fort. A lone path led to the top. A hidden doorway stood at the end of that path with stairs leading down inside to the carved out windows.

King Shealayr studied the structure. Its dismal appearance did little to reassure him, but he had little choice. This was their last defense against the orcs to prevent them from reaching the city.

"Idæas, take thirty elves to the top of the ridge. Sergeant, take your elves and conceal yourselves along the base of the ridge," ordered King Shealayr.

He watched as more elves stationed themselves halfway up the ridge and along the path. "Chop the trees on both sides along the path up the ridge three-quarters of the way through and attach rope to the tops in such a way that when pulled the entire tree will fall."

As much as it pained him to do it, the rigging of the trees was a necessity. Within the hour all preparations were made. Afterward, the elves hid and waited.

The heavy rumble of catapults being pushed across the ground grew closer. Their heavy wheels rumbled through the earth warning the elves of impending doom. The orcs marched confidently, trampling the vegetation of the forest. Espying the path of the fort, they rushed for it. King Shealayr watched breathlessly as the beasts raced up the path waiting for the precise moment. "Now," he yelled.

Elves hacked the ropes. A grinding creak echoed as the tree tops detached from their base. Screams from the orcs filled the air as the trees crushed them while careening down the hill. King Shealayr watched in satisfaction as orcs unsuccessfully attempted to flee the falling logs.

"Fire!" Idæas yelled to the archers.

Arrows rained from the sky as the archers released their bows. They quickly reloaded and shot another set of arrows.

Elves burst from the trees among the orcs surprising their enemy. They jumped upon them knocking them to the ground. Metal against metal rang throughout the forest as the elves and the orcs battled for victory. The orcs roared in frustration at the surprise attack. They fought with only one sword hacking and clawing their way through their enemy. The elves, however, attacked with a double edged weapon in each hand allowing them to block and strike simultaneously.

Explosions surrounded them as boulders crashed into the ridge flinging bits of rock and dirt everywhere. Another set of giant rocks rammed into the ridge taking out an entire section. Steel-tipped arrows whooshed past as they sped from the holes within the ridge.

"Stay your positions," commanded King Shealayr to his elves, "We will fight to the last elf!" He pushed his way through a group of orcs slashing as he went.

A commotion arose on the other side of the battlefield as a battalion of orcs pulled up. "About time you scum arrived," growled the orc commander.

The one at the head of the group leapt off his horse and walked up to the orc commander.

"Get back in line and take your unit to the top of the ridge," ordered the beast. The orc watched in confusion and anger as the one before him pulled out his sword and plunged it into him.

Suddenly, the mysterious orc ripped off his helmet and tore off the orc armor to reveal his own. "Now," Tesnayr yelled.

The newly arrived orcs tore off their armor as well to reveal that of Tesnayr's army. The surrounding orcs watched in disbelief. Kicking their horses, Tesnayr's men plunged into action.

Arnin lead a group of men to the catapults. "Turn these machines around and fire upon the orcs," he ordered.

Straining from the effort, his men shifted the heavy catapults turning them around and aiming them at their enemy. They loaded them up and fired flaming rocks at the horde of beasts.

Arnin whirled around as an orc charged at him with flailing arms. He side-stepped as he raised his sword up and sliced open the beast's stomach. He renewed his focus on the catapults.

While Arnin took care of the catapults, Nedis and his brothers worked their way up the ridge. With the path up the ridge washed out, the three brothers were forced to climb the steep hill. Halfway up, a hailstorm of axes crashed around them. Orcs stood below throwing their hatchets at their new target. The three brothers dove behind some brush and weighed their options.

"I'll sneak up behind them," said Nylin to the other two as another hatchet hit the dirt beside him.

The other two agreed. While Nylin made his way toward the orc ax throwers, Nular and Nedis crawled around the ridge as a distraction. They darted about keeping their movements sudden and unpredictable. Unseen, Nylin reached the orcs. He pulled out his bow and fired a slew of arrows at them.

"Well, done," said Nedis from above.

Nylin smiled in triumph as he and his brothers continued their trek up the ridge.

"Kill the commander," Tesnayr ordered Nigilin.

Nigilin sped off.

Tesnayr spotted one attempting to organize those that had dispersed. He raced toward the beast. His horse's hooves pounded the earth. Tesnayr breathed in tune with the animal, focused on his target.

Something crashed into Tesnayr and knocked him off his horse. Stunned, he lay motionless on the ground. Orcs approached him. Tesnayr reached for his weapon. Nothing. He searched around him for anything he could use. Sensing victory, the orcs smirked as they drew near.

A soldier bearing Tesnayr's insignia stormed through the melee until reaching his side. The unidentified soldier cut the legs off of one orc and the lopped off the head of another in one smooth stroke. The soldier whirled around and clipped another orc in the back. Quickly, he repositioned himself and stabbed the orc in the stomach.

A loud crack sounded above Tesnayr as a boulder split a tree in half. He looked up in time to see half of the tree falling right for him. There was nowhere for him to move. Tesnayr braced himself for the inevitable crushing blow that never came.

Caw!

A giant bird swooped through the air darting and weaving between the branches of the trees. It seized the tree half with its powerful claws and hauled it away. Tesnayr and several others watched awestruck at the spectacle. Their moment of awe was short lived as Tesnayr quickly returned his attention to the battle. "Direct them toward the ridge," he yelled.

King Shealayr watched from his vantage point understanding Tesnayr's maneuver. "Idæas," said King Shealayr, "I don't believe those orcs are orcs. It appears King Slyamal's troops came through after all." King Shealayr looked about him. "Take your elves and move along the left flank down the ridge. I will take the right. Concentrate your arrows on the beasts."

Idæas saluted.

The elves charged down the ridge of Ninspíril, while archers remained on the top. Their unexpected move caused the orcs to stop the attack.   They panicked.   Realizing that they were trapped, the orcs broke ranks and fled.

"Do not let them get away," yelled Tesnayr as the orcs ran. "Kill every last one of them!"

"Captain," said a nearby soldier, "We have won the battle."

"We cannot let them escape and give them a chance to regroup," countered Tesnayr as he led the charge after the fleeing orcs.

His army chased after him. King Shealayr followed suit and ordered his elves to follow after the orcs and to not return until all were dead. He glanced at Idæas and smiled. Belarnia had been saved by the help of a stranger.

Once the orcs had been destroyed, the forest slowly regained its peacefulness, but scars remained. Burnt and misshapen trees remained a testament of the battle. Tesnayr pulled his army away from the center of Belarnia and pitched camp well away from King Shealayr's elves. He had no desire to talk with the king, nor did he wish to become involved in the politics of Belarnia. He had achieved what he set out to do: ensured the survival of Belarnia and dealt a crippling blow to the orcs.

Nigilin and Arnin brought a soldier up to Tesnayr as he sat secluded from the others.

"Here is the man you asked to see," said Nigilin.

"Soldier," Tesnayr said, "I want to thank you for saving my life. You have demonstrated a courage that few men possess. I wish more were like you."

"Thank you, Captain," replied the soldier in a feminine voice.

Tesnayr cocked his head. He knew that voice. He reached out and slowly lifted the helmet off of the soldier before him to reveal Nelyn. "You," he said, "How did you get here?"

Nelyn looked defiantly into Tesnayr's eyes. "Easily," she replied, "I followed you since that night you told me to go home."

"War is no place for a woman," said Tesnayr.

"Who are you to decide that? I will continue to follow you and fight the orcs with or without your consent. You said yourself that I showed courage that few men possess. Do you deny that now because you discovered that I am a woman?"

"I deny nothing," said Tesnayr fuming over her using his words against him. "But know this. We travel hard and fast. We sleep little and eat little. You will not receive any special treatment because you are a woman."

Nelyn answered softly, but firmly. "I have not asked for any."

Arnin opened his mouth and spoke his thoughts before he could contain them. "Captain, you cannot allow her to stay. She will slow us down. She could be killed."

"No more than you and I," said Tesnayr.

"Tesnayr—"

"I dare any here to challenge me," yelled Nelyn losing her temper. She unsheathed her sword.

Arnin pulled out his as well accepting her challenge. They glanced at Tesnayr who nodded in approval. This seemed the only way to solve the matter.

The triplets walked in on the display. "Are we interrupting?" they asked.

"No," said Tesnayr, "What is it you want?"

"It can wait," replied the brothers in unison.

"Very well," said Tesnayr. "Begin," he told Arnin and Nelyn.

"Bets?" asked Nular of his brothers.

"One silver coin on the woman," said Nedis.

"Agreed," said Nylin.

Arnin brought his sword down upon Nelyn. She ducked, twisted around and smacked him in the back. She swiped her sword low knocking Arnin's feet out from under him. He landed hard on his back to find her blade at his throat.

"Any others," yelled Nelyn. No one moved.

"You have proven yourself," said Tesnayr to Nelyn. "I will give you the rank of Lieutenant. After successfully following us, and overcoming today's events you earned it."

"Pay up," said Nedis to Nylin. Nylin dug in his pocket and pulled out a small coin. He tossed it to his smirking brother.

Nelyn sheathed her sword and stalked off, proud of herself.

"That didn't take long," whispered Nigilin to Arnin.

"I let her win," Arnin growled back.

A messenger from the elf king ran up to Tesnayr. "Tesnayr," he said as he approached the firelight, "My name is Idæas. I come with a message from King Shealayr. He requests your presence immediately."

"And if I deny his request," replied Tesnayr.

Idæas stepped closer and grasped the hilt of his sword, but did not draw it. "Then I have orders to bring you by force."

Arnin and Nigilin quickly drew their weapons and placed themselves between the elf and Tesnayr. Tesnayr held out his hand to them. "Stop," he said to them. "There will be no bloodshed here. I will go with you to your king. Nigilin, you are in command until I return."

Tesnayr threw on his cloak and followed Idæas out of the camp and into the night.

Chapter VI
An Ally

Idæas led Tesnayr through the dense forest to a group of trees that had been hollowed out and fashioned in such a way that they formed a small courtroom. For the onlooker, the entire building looked like a mass of gnarled and twisted oaks with a canopy of leaves serving as the roof. Giant, overlapping green leaves swayed gracefully in the wind. Full of life, these ancient trees whispered and wept for the loss of their kin in the forest, a weeping that only the elves heard.

"There dwells the king," said Idæas with a note of pride as they climbed the branches of a tree that fashioned themselves into a staircase.

Casually, Tesnayr tore the glove from his hand and ran it along the rail of the stairs awed by its silkiness. Vines wrapped around each step forming abstract artwork against the brown color. This added to their strength and beauty.

Idæas steered Tesnayr toward the left as the stairs forked. They reached the staircase top and stepped through a wide, arching entranceway into an open room. Fluid markings decorated the walls from floor to ceiling. Sparsely furnished, the room exhibited a majestic presence. Only a table and two cushioned chairs provided some semblance of comfort. King Shealayr stood on the far end of the chamber waiting for them. Awed, Tesnayr glanced up. Leaves parted wide to reveal the stars that twinkled above.

King Shealayr walked toward them when he saw them enter. "Thank you, Idæas," said King Shealayr. "That will be all."

Idæas refused to leave.

"You are dismissed," King Shealayr repeated firmly.

Reluctantly, Idæas saluted his king and exited the chamber.

King Shealayr moved into full view of the torchlight. "I want to thank you for aiding Belarnia in our fight against those creatures. They invaded us unprovoked and if you had not come, we most certainly would have been destroyed."

Tesnayr listened closely to King Shealayr as he gauged the elf's character. "The orcs need no provocation. They attack without warning and they live only to conquer."

"You have encountered them before," said King Shealayr. "I have heard of a man who is not from these lands and seems to know these...orcs, as you call them. I can only assume that this man is you."

Tesnayr said nothing in response.

"Tell me your story, Tesnayr." King Shealayr handed him a cup of mulled cider.

Tesnayr accepted the offer before stepping to the center of the room. *Tell my story?* He sipped his drink knowing that it was not a request, but a command. "It is true what you say. I come from a land far across the sea. The orcs invaded that place. They came in droves with their swords, their torches, and their catapults. I witnessed entire towns and villages as they were destroyed and burned entirely to the ground.

"I buried the bodies of those killed and joined the ranks of the king's army. We fought the orcs but to no avail. They outnumbered us and fought more viciously than anything we had ever encountered. We felt like lambs being sent to the slaughter with each battle. Eventually I was taken captive by the orcs. I managed to escape.

"The orcs destroyed what was once a great and prosperous land. I washed up on your shores only to find that what I had escaped had followed me. Not a day goes by where I do not wish that the sea had swallowed me."

King Shealayr looked curiously at Tesnayr over that last statement. "There are those who are glad the sea placed you on the shores of Sym'Dul. Your action saved Belarnia. And what would have become of those men who follow you had you not come here?"

Silently, Tesnayr regard King Shealayr with suspicion. *What do you know?*

"No, Tesnayr, you are not sorry that you are here. And there is more to your story that you have not told me and understandably so. What you carefully guard deeply wounds you and the very memory of it tears your spirit."

King Shealayr paced the room. "I have a favor to ask of you. The description you just gave me of the orcs tells me that they will return." King Shealayr looked to Tesnayr for affirmation and received it. "You have proven today that you know how to outsmart the orcs and defeat them. I ask that you join me in defending Belarnia from these creatures."

Tesnayr's face hardened and his fists clenched. "I serve no king."

"But surely you cannot continue to go about as you have serving none but yourself."

"And why should I serve a king who busies himself by constantly waging war with the other kingdoms of this land?"

King Shealayr remained calm despite the obvious insult. "If a man does not serve a king he can only serve himself. What is your real reason for turning down my offer?"

"What are your reasons for warring with the other kings? I may be new to these parts, but I am well aware of your feud."

"These are matters that are none of your concern."

"They concern me intensely," said Tesnayr. "I warned King Slyamal about the orcs and he ignored me. The orcs were of little consequence when it came to keeping you from rising above him. You are all selfish men playing your little games."

"And of what of you? Are you not equally selfish as you seek revenge under the cloak of righteousness?"

With great effort, Tesnayr kept his anger under control.

King Shealayr had struck a nerve and he knew it. "Other kings, Tesnayr, will ask you the same as I. You will have to decide if you will abide by their request."

"I will never serve a king," said Tesnayr with finality.

"Indeed," said King Shealayr. "One day, Tesnayr, you will have to determine your real reason for fighting the orcs. Your altruistic motives possess a false echo. In the meantime, I ask another favor of you. I want you to take my captain of the guard with you. He is loyal and will serve you faithfully."

"For what reason?"

"As these orcs are likely to continue their raids, I wish to remain informed of their movements," replied King Shealayr, "And since you have a unique knowledge of them, who better than to send him with you?

"I do not care about your movements, Tesnayr. Our interests are aligned."

"And when they no longer coincide?"

"We will worry about that when the time comes."

"I only accept people who volunteer freely into my army," said Tesnayr in annoyance.

"Do not refuse me. I ask this because I know that we will meet again one day soon. My captain knows parts of these lands that are known to very few. You are going to need the help of the elves and the power they possess.

"Do not scoff at such a notion. There will be a day when you will need the protection of the trees and of nature itself."

Tesnayr let the king's words soak through him. Riddles, he thought. But they were riddles with a hint of truth. He decided that there were worse things than having an elf in his ranks. Besides, Tesnayr had an inkling that King Shealayr would not take "no" for an answer and he was hardly in a position to argue. "Very well, I will abide by your request."

King Shealayr beamed. He strode over to the entrance and called Idæas. The elf walked in promptly. "Idæas, you are going to serve under Tesnayr's command. From this day forward, until

I deem otherwise, you are a member of his army. Serve him as devotedly as you have served me."

Idæas offered no argument. He knew that when his King made a decision, it was not worth protesting. He saluted King Shealayr. "As you wish, my lord."

"You two may go," said the king, "And, Tesnayr, I hope we meet again under more favorable circumstances."

Tesnayr bowed before the Elven king out of respect for his station. A little bit of honey went a long way. He was also keenly aware of the king's guards standing just outside the chamber. Together he and Idæas left the court and made their way back out into the refreshing night air.

As they reached the bottom of the stairwell Tesnayr asked, "You are loyal to your king?"

"I serve my king faithfully. If he ordered me to kill you, I would," replied Idæas. He spoke matter of factly without any implication of a threat. To Idæas it was simple: he did as his king asked, period. "As it is, I have been commanded to aid you and so I shall."

Tesnayr admired such loyalty, a quality rare among men. A part of him decided that this elf may be of some use. "I believe we will get along just fine."

*   *   *

Seething, King Slyamal drummed his fingers against the cold metal of his chair as he listened to the report by one of his advisors. He glared at the dancing flames in the hearth unsure of what to think. The man being described sounded familiar.

"And you are certain of these events?" asked the king.

"Quite, my lord," said the advisor. "He and his men disguised themselves in the armor of the orcs thereby fooling the beasts as they approached. He saved Belarnia that day and King Shealayr is most grateful. He even sent his captain of the guard with him."

"Who is this man?"

The advisor dropped the scroll in his hand and looked at his king. "The man's name is Tesnayr, the same messenger you had imprisoned when he came to warn you about these orcs. The man was right and might even have been a commander in your army had you not treated him so callously."

King Slyamal's face flushed from anger. "You dare impugn me?"

"Your actions have put you in this situation. Even Arnin left because of how you treated this man and failed to heed his warnings. You needlessly sent an entire contingent of soldiers to their deaths.

"This Tesnayr has amassed his own army of people loyal to him. Your own people do not trust your judgment anymore and look to him to save their homes and families from the orcs. It is said that this Tesnayr refuses to serve any king, yet he helps them.

"This man knows these savages. He knows how to fight them and win. Send a messenger to him, my lord. I beseech you. Ask this man for help. Orcs approach our land once again and twice your armies have been defeated by them!"

"Refused a king?"

"Yes," replied the advisor. "King Shealayr offered him a position of honor among the ranks of his elves. Such an offer has never been made to any man. And Tesnayr refused him."

"Where is this Tesnayr now?" asked King Slyamal.

"Scouts have reported that he is headed north as we speak."

"So he is coming to us." King Slyamal stroked his beard in thought. Deep down, he knew his advisor was right; he needed the help of this Tesnayr. But pride stayed his hand.

King Slyamal had suffered two defeats and his people had fared even worse because of his arrogance and stupidity. They grew dissident toward him. Rumors of rebellion spread across the countryside. He needed a victory for his own sake. Orcs approached the eastern border as well as from the north.

Thoughts percolating, King Slyamal conceived of a plan that might solve his predicament.

"Send a messenger to this Tesnayr. Tell him I wish to meet with him."

The advisor shook his head. "My lord, I think it would be best if you rode to him yourself."

"I will not be seen as a beggar!"

"My king, this is not an act of weakness, but one of humility. By going to him yourself, seeking him out, you will be acknowledging his understanding of the situation and it will convey that not only do you need his help, but truly desire it as well."

King Slyamal's features hardened. He disliked the idea of riding out to meet a man, particularly one whom, in his view, was nothing more than a mere peasant that managed to gather followers. He hated the idea of appearing weak and thought that because he was king people should seek his consul at his command. But time was of the essence and he needed this man's help.

"My king, it was not I who locked him in the dungeon," stated the advisor, delicately.

King Slyamal's brows scrunched together. "Very well. Find out where this man is and I will go to him."

"Yes, my lord."

Chapter VII
An Old Meeting

Nelyn placed her foot firmly on the soft earth balancing delicately on one leg, perfectly silhouetted against the backdrop of the Black Mountains. Poised, she held her sword high ready to strike. Within a moment, she attacked the air swinging her weapon with fluidity as she raised it again for another. She placed her other foot on the ground taking a measured step to the left. In one swift strike, Nelyn arched her blade to the left twirling around on her toes.

Clang!

"I am pleased to see that you have heeded my warning about failure to practice," said Jarown.

Nelyn stared at her father a moment annoyed that he had interrupted her practice session. She had thought that she was alone. With ease, she unlocked her sword from Jarown's and rammed it into its sheath. "You taught me that it was wise to stay in practice."

"Yes, and I remember you always groaning about it being less than fun."

"I have need to stay in shape."

"We all do," said Jarown looking upon his daughter with a mixture of pride and sorrow. "Nelyn, perhaps I was wrong to leave you behind, but I wanted to keep you safe."

Nelyn eyed the grass beneath her, head bowed. "I know," she whispered. "Belyndril has changed since you left. Little of it remains. And Blynak has returned."

Jarown's ears perked up at that last statement. He knew the name well. "Blynak?"

"Yes," replied Nelyn. "But, it's different. He was seen with those creatures."

Nelyn knew the story of Blynak and how he had tried to take over Belyndril by overthrowing its king. Rumor had it that the man possessed the desire to conquer the five lands. But the King's army ultimately squashed such a notion and Blynak disappeared. He resurfaced years later in Sym'Dul when a rebellion had sprung up against King Slyamal. Ironic, thought Nelyn, that wherever an uprising took place Blynak was there.

"Aligned with them?"

Jarown's question brought her back to the present. "Yes," said Nelyn. "He led the attack against our village. Inconsequential as we are to him, he seemed very interested in the people there. Why would he care about a remote town in the hills?"

"Does it matter? Blynak has always desired power. He wants to be a king unto himself. I am sure the attack was his method of spreading fear."

Nelyn dropped the matter. Every time Blynak's name was mentioned, her father acted as though he hid something. "They killed Nathan."

"I know, my dear. I know." Jarown stretched out his muscular arms and embraced his daughter. She accepted, but shed not one tear. Inside, he beamed with pride at the strength his daughter portrayed, but he knew that her heart had been broken and he was responsible. "I have something for you."

Nelyn released him anticipating his gift.

Out of his pocket Jarown pulled a piece of a unicorn horn. The pearly white shard of the horn glittered in the sunlight as flecks of gold dotted it. It dangled freely from its silver chain. "This was once your mother's," Jarown told her. "I thought I had lost it years ago, but found it one day and meant to give it to you before I left."

Delicately, Nelyn lifted up her blonde hair allowing Jarown to place the necklace around her neck. "It's beautiful."

"She used to wear it always."

"Did you love my mother?" asked Nelyn.

The corner of Jarown's eye tingled as a tear welled up. Quickly, he blotted it away. "Very much," he replied.

The clomping of horses' hooves charged up from behind them. Nelyn and Jarown turned to find each of the triplets on a stallion. They hung onto the reins with one hand while sword fighting with the other. Dirt and clumps of grass flew everywhere with each movement of the horses.

One pounded toward Nelyn and Jarown. At the last second, the rider yanked the reins pulling the animal to a halt. "Why hello there," greeted Nedis. "Do you wish to spar with us?"

"I spar alone," said Nelyn. She had received many cold looks from the men in the army and had no desire to be made fun of.

"Are you certain?" Nedis hopped down from his mount landing agilely on the grass. "But I suppose if you are unsure of your abilities—"

Without warning, Nelyn snatched Nedis' hand, knocked him flat on his stomach, and wrenched his arm behind his back.

"I didn't mean anything by it," said Nedis, knowing that she could break his collar bone at any moment.

"Nelyn," said Jarown.

Understanding her father's unspoken request, she released Nedis. He rose to his feet rubbing his shoulder. "We've nothing against you being a woman," he said.

By then the other two brothers appeared clearly enjoying Nedis' discomfort. "We could help you tie him up," laughed Nular.

"I think you will find that my daughter is quite capable of taking care of herself," said Jarown. "But a sparring partner is useful."

"Yes, father," said Nelyn, quietly. She hated being chastised even when done gently.

"Did you hear the news?"

Everyone turned to Nylin. "What news?" asked Jarown.

"King Slyamal is headed here," replied Nylin. "He is coming to create a truce with Tesnayr. That is why we have been heading north for the Black Mountains."

"And how do you know all this?" Jarown eyed Nylin accusingly.

"I hear things," replied Nylin with a note of discomfort.

"You hear everything," Nular said.

"I listen," replied Nylin.

"More like eavesdrop," chided Nedis.

The three brothers quickly ensconced themselves into one of their many friendly arguments. Sighing from frustration, Nelyn grabbed her things and left with Jarown close behind.

King Slyamal rubbed his hands to keep them warm from the cold. He sat close to the fire to ward off the chill from the air, along with the two guards riding with him. He scooped some of the loose silt into his palm before flinging it aside. Black, like the mountains' namesake. Why Tesnayr chose the Black Mountains as a place to camp was beyond him. Those mountains proved inhospitable to any who ventured there. Not even the most hardened of men considered going into the Black Mountains. Always cold. Warmth did not exist there.

King Slyamal took out a piece of dried bread and bit off a chunk to chew. He missed the kitchens of the castle. A brush of movement caught his eye. Turning slightly, he found a black cat sitting by the fire staring at him. He took another bite. Slowly, the uneasy feeling that the cat was studying him washed over King Slyamal. He wondered if the feline was judging his character.

"Beat it, cat," said the king.

The cat swept his tail across the ground and continued to stare at him. King Slyamal picked up a rock and threw it at the cat. The rock landed in the dust next to the feline. The cat never flinched. Instead, it began washing its face very delicately as though it had no worries and that King Slyamal's feeble attempt to scare him away meant nothing. The king stood up and swatted at the cat. The cat scurried away into the bushes. Relieved, the king sat back down and continued to eat.

"Meow."

King Slyamal turned abruptly to discover that the cat had returned. He shook his head in annoyance. Never had he seen a cat so determined to sit by a fire or be with people. "Go away." King Slyamal hated cats and wished the pesky animal would leave. Angrily, he picked up a stick and prepared to swing it at the animal.

"Before you do that," the cat said, stopping King Slyamal in mid-swing, "I suggest you listen. Captain Tesnayr has agreed to meet with you. Ride east of here to Diamond Rock. He will meet you there in two hours."

King Slyamal dropped the stick and stared at the cat in disbelief.

"Incidentally," added the cat, "You may want to be friendlier to cats in the future." He bounded off.

King Slyamal turned to his two guards. "You heard him," he growled. "Put out the fire and get the horses ready. We're leaving."

Within minutes the horses had been prepared. They rode quietly through the night making their own trail in the mountains as there were none to follow. Though they moved cautiously, they made good time and within the two hour time limit they had reached a giant diamond shaped, granite rock.

Waiting for the King of Sym'Dul was a group of men and one cat. "I thought you said he was coming," said Arnin to Turyn.

"I delivered the message and am certain he will come. Otherwise, his entire journey has been in vain," replied Turyn.

"Arnin, men approach," said one of the soldiers.

Arnin nodded and motioned for the men to hide. He stepped forward and waited. Out of the shadows three men trotted up on horseback. "Stop right there," ordered Arnin.

"I have come to see Tesnayr," said King Slyamal.

"And you shall," replied Arnin. "Take their weapons." The soldiers obeyed.

This insulted King Slyamal. "I was under the impression that Tesnayr himself would be here. Why does he not come and meet me?" demanded the king as his guards dismounted.

Arnin stepped closer and grabbed hold of the reins. "The last time he came to meet with you, you showed him the hospitality of your prisons. He is returning the favor. You will come with us and meet with him alone. Your guards are to stay here."

"Us?"

"The cat will lead the way." Arnin smiled at Turyn.

Reluctantly, King Slyamal agreed. "Well, you heard him," he barked at his guards, "You will abide by these conditions." He dismounted and followed Arnin and Turyn into the night.

Tesnayr sat in a tent poring over maps. He used his finger to point at various places mulling over strategies in his mind. He snatched a dispatch and read it making a circular motioned on the map with his finger. Frustrated, he threw the dispatch down and rubbed his hands over his face. He leaned back and exhaled a long, deep sigh in an effort to release some stress.

"Captain?"

Tesnayr looked up at the messenger that had just walked in.

"Arnin and Turyn have arrived with the King of Sym'Dul."

"Show them in," said Tesnayr.

Arnin and Turyn entered the tent followed by an irate King Slyamal. Tesnayr greeted Arnin and Turyn warmly and asked them wait outside. The two left Tesnayr and King Slyamal alone. "Well, well, the mighty king of Sym'Dul has left his throne to seek the help of a lowly messenger." Tesnayr's sarcasm was not lost on the king.

King Slyamal glanced around him frowning with each turn of his head. "I see that you have been promoted to the rank of captain. Why not take the title of general? You have your very own army."

"I prefer captain. Generals are like kings: they think too highly of themselves."

"Tesnayr, I know that you and I did not greet the other warmly last time. I am willing to overlook our differences—"

"Cut through the grime and tell me why you have come here," said Tesnayr, impatiently.

"The orcs have invaded Sym'Dul. They approach from both fronts. Each battalion I send to stop the orcs is defeated. None are left alive. My people are suffering and demand that I do something."

"And so you have come to me for help. What makes you so certain that I will be able to provide you with it?"

"Every engagement you have had with the orcs, you came out victorious. I know about your triumph in Belarnia. Your efforts saved the elves, for which I hear King Shealayr is very grateful."

"As I recall, I once came to you for assistance. I warned you about the orcs and what it meant for your kingdom, but you refused to heed my warnings. You repaid my actions with imprisonment."

"Imagine my surprise when I learned of your escape with one of my advisors."

"I offered to help you once, but you refused. Why should I help you now?"

"It is not me you will be helping, but my people. They suffer each day the orcs roam free in these lands—"

"You are right! They are suffering! By your hand! And out of your own arrogance!"

"I did not come here to be insulted!"

"No? I suggest you listen because I have something you need to hear." Tesnayr paced the tent. "Your pride has cost the lives of thousands. I will not be a pawn in your quest to reclaim your dignity."

"I may have made a mistake, but do not let my people suffer for it."

"Your people? You do not care about your people. You care only for yourself! If the people prosper, you prosper. If they suffer, you suffer. Suffer long enough and you might be replaced. They blame you for their losses and you came here to shift that blame on me."

"I came here to ask for your help!"

"You came here not of your own free will, but because you had no other choice! And for once you listened to the advice of one wiser than yourself."

"All right then, I am a fool! And you are right. I did not want to come, but my hands are tied. All my attempts have failed and I need a victory. I do not like you, Tesnayr. You are nothing but a disgruntled man who has managed to muster an army of others like yourself. You are triumphant for now, but that will pass. I am only here because at this moment you are the only man who can assist me."

Exasperated, Tesnayr mulled over his choices. Deep within, he had already decided on a course of action. "I will help you. Your people needn't suffer unnecessarily because of their king's lack of judgment."

"I welcome your assistance." For once, King Slyamal sounded genuine.

"On one condition: your commanders will report to me. They will serve under me and obey my commands. And you will not contradict me. Let me dictate the terms of the battle."

"I will not—"

"Those are the terms, King Slyamal. Either accept them or leave. You have my solemn promise that I will never serve under you."

King Slyamal squeezed his fists until they turned white and sighed. "I agree to your terms."

"Do I have your word on that?"

"Would you prefer that I make it an edict, in writing?"

"If a man is not as good as his word, what difference will the written edict make?"

"I give you my word as king that my soldiers are under your command. But I want to be kept informed of your plans."

"That you shall."

Tesnayr walked to the entrance of the tent and stuck his head outside. He came back in with both Arnin and Turyn. "Take the King of Sym'Dul back to Diamond Rock." Arnin saluted Tesnayr and motioned for King Slyamal to follow him. "Send your men to Diamond Rock within the week," Tesnayr told King Slyamal before he left.

"Understood."   With a sense of uncertainty, King Slyamal followed Arnin outside and into the still night air.

The next morning found Tesnayr seated on a rock overlooking his army's encampment. He watched as Nedis, Nylin, and Nular played jokes on various people. They were always good for a laugh, full of life. The three brothers were inseparable, doing everything together. He liked them. Everybody liked them. The other soldiers tolerated their antics not because they had to, but because such frolics brought a smile to their faces and a moment of enjoyment in baleful times. The world needed people like the triplets. Inwardly, Tesnayr was thankful to have them.

Tesnayr glanced around and spotted Nelyn sitting by herself next to her small tent. For various reasons, she had secluded herself from the rest of the men. The men learned quickly not to venture too close to her tent. She put any who dared in his place. The only men she allowed to come near her was Jarown and occasionally the triplets. Like the others, she found them good for a laugh.

Tesnayr admired her courage. Most women did not have the strength to endure what his army had. Most men would have left by now and many had done so, but Nelyn remained driven by some private need for revenge and something else that he could not fathom. She never slowed them down. When they marched all day Nelyn could be found in the front lines. When they drove themselves knee deep in mud, she trudged right alongside them.

Nelyn slept when they slept. She never complained, nor did she demand any special treatment. Whining was not her nature. She volunteered for the life of a soldier and gladly accepted what such a life offered.

In battle Nelyn proved her worth many times. True to Jarown's word, she was equal to a man in combat. At times, better. She fought fiercely with a courage Tesnayr had only seen once before. Yet, she also possessed the capability of showing mercy. In one skirmish, Nelyn disarmed three soldiers who were no more than fourteen. She broke their swords in half and let them go warning them that if they met again, they would not be so fortunate. To her they were not worth the kill, having been pressed into the service of the orcs. No other in his army would have done what Nelyn had. Tesnayr admired her for it. He knew that his men had been hard on her, but not once did he do anything. Any man who challenged her soon regretted such action.

Tesnayr noticed Arnin walk up to Nelyn. By their actions it became clear that they were engaged in another argument. After several minutes, Arnin stalked away. Tesnayr sighed. He decided to remind his men to treat Nelyn with the same respect that he had shown each of them.

Raised voices drew his attention. Tesnayr saw Jarown shouting at the triplets. Apparently, they had just finished playing a joke on him, one he found anything but funny. He did not know what he thought of the man. Jarown served well and Tesnayr left him in command of the men from Belyndril. He figured that they ought to be directed by one they trusted. But Jarown's haunted eyes always hinted that something in his past gnawed at the man. Such an observation filled Tesnayr with uneasiness. Sometimes a man's past catches up with him and makes him unpredictable. Tesnayr decided to give the man the benefit of the doubt. After all, Jarown did raise Nelyn. His actions displayed the love and respect he had for her.

Krulak strolled by. He waved a greeting at Tesnayr and Tesnayr reciprocated. A dear friend of Jarown's, Krulak had proven himself to be quite valuable. He had demonstrated an aptitude for scouting and leading small raids. Because of him they had been able to destroy many small parties of orcs and to keep the beasts from regrouping for massive invasions. There were moments when he thought Krulak hesitant in fighting the orcs, or that the man hid something, but Tesnayr shrugged it off as something that all men feel when fighting a war.

A weight pressed down on Tesnayr's shoulders as fur rubbed against his cheek, and then hopped down. Turyn stood before him waving his tail. "Arnin, Nigilin, and Jarown are ready to meet with you," said the cat.

"Thank you, Turyn," said Tesnayr. Turyn made a good messenger.

Upon entering the tent where the three men waited for him, Tesnayr relayed the conversation he had had with King Slyamal the night before. He told them everything the king had said to him about the orcs invading Sym'Dul.

"I have agreed to help King Slyamal drive the orcs out of Sym'Dul," Tesnayr finished.

"What of Belarnia?" asked Arnin.

"They are safe for the moment," replied Tesnayr, "Our main concern right now is Sym'Dul. Orcs are arriving on the eastern shores. They are most likely joining up with those at the northern border of Hemíl near the Amythest River."

"Undoubtedly they are going to Belyndril. Orcs had already reached there when I left," said Jarown.

"Or they are planning an invasion of Hemil. The northern border is King Edrei's weakest point as the orcs have been keeping him in the south. We cannot let this happen. Arnin, you are to go to King Edrei and ask him to join us. I have already sent him a message asking him to meet with you. I want him to bring his forces here." Tesnayr pointed at Hemíl's northern part of the map. "There is a unit of orcs there carrying supplies to Galbrok.

"Take half of our forces with you. You are in command."

"How should I convince him to help?" asked Arnin.

"Diplomacy," Tesnayr answered.

"What if King Edrei refuses our request?" asked Arnin.

"Then you and your men will fight alone," replied Tesnayr. "Those supplies must not reach their destination."

"Understood," said Arnin.

"I know what you are thinking, but we cannot attack one before the other. If we were to attack the orcs at the Cym River first, there is a chance that they will send word to the orcs in Hemil before we arrived there. We cannot chance that. We must surprise them at both fronts by attacking them at the same time," said Tesnayr. "Everything depends upon speed and secrecy."

"Krulak is familiar with the territory there in Hemil. You should send him along as well," suggested Jarown.

"Agreed," said Tesnayr.

"King Edrei might not let Arnin command his army even if he agrees to help us," said Nigilin.

"He will, if he wants to be rid of the orcs," replied Tesnayr. "King Slyamal will be accompanying the rest of us to the Cym River. We will stop the orcs there and then meet you in Hemil."

Nigilin rubbed his beard in thought. "Are you sure this is wise? Hemil and Sym'Dul have no love for each other."

"I am hoping that current circumstances will rule over their emotions," said Tesnayr.

"That is asking for a lot," commented Arnin.

"King Slyamal has given me his word that the army of Sym'Dul will obey my command. However, if anything should go wrong, come straight back here to the Black Mountains." Tesnayr looked at each of the men to be sure that they understood his instructions. Satisfied, he ended the meeting. "Arnin, you are to leave in an hour."

"An hour, Captain," said Arnin uneasily. He glanced at Nigilin who shook his head in response. Jarown looked at his feet.

"Is there something I should know, gentlemen?" asked Tesnayr.

"Well, you see, Captain," began Jarown. "You tell him."

Nigilin cleared his throat. "Tesnayr, something happened. And—"

A commotion sounded outside the tent. Tesnayr walked outside followed by the other three. Before him stood a group of men carrying what appeared to be a cake. On top of the cake sat Turyn wearing a collar made of lace and a pink veil. The cat did not look pleased. "Happy Birthday," yelled the crowd.

"Turyn accidentally let it slip," replied Nigilin to Tesnayr's astonishment and unspoken question.

"How did he find out?" asked Tesnayr.

"I am a cat," replied Turyn.

"And a cat knows everything," said the others finishing Turyn's usual statement about cats.

Gradually, Tesnayr paced around the cake and the cat. In his efforts to consider all possibilities of defeating the orcs, he had forgotten about his birthday. A part of him was frustrated at all the fuss, but another part figured that a moment of fun might be warranted. "Turyn, that color really does bring out the color of your eyes," said Tesnayr quietly to Turyn, a small grin tugging at the corners of his mouth.

Turyn looked up at Tesnayr. "You really think so?" Tesnayr nodded still trying hard not to smile. "Then I am sure that you will love the present I left on your cake."

At that moment two women appeared out of thin air. They were both fairies and possessed a beauty most women envy. They each had light brown hair and hazel eyes. "Oh, a festival, Serein. I love festivities," exclaimed one.

"So do I," replied the other, otherwise known as Serein. "Sarwyn, you know what to do."

Sarwyn smiled and threw sparks in the air which turned into confetti. The two women giggled with delight while everyone else observed them with curiosity and uneasiness.

Nedis, Nular, and Nylin looked at each other, recognizing the fairies as the two women whom they had followed on the same day they met Tesnayr. "Aren't they the—," said Nedis without finishing his statement.

"Yes," replied the other two.

"Very well," said Tesnayr, relenting, "Tonight we will celebrate. Tomorrow we have work to do." Cheers went up at the prospect of having a bit of fun. "You two may stay," he told the fairies as he walked past them. Not that it would have mattered. Tesnayr would have been hard pressed to get rid of them.

Tesnayr pulled Arnin aside. "Unfortunately, you and your men will not be allowed to participate. You must head for Hemíl now to reach it in time."

Dismayed, Arnin kept his protests to himself. He knew Tesnayr was right.

"Take some of the food and drink with you," said Tesnayr. "Celebrate when you stop to rest."

"Yes, Captain." Arnin walked away rounding up those who would accompany him.

Music flowed and danced throughout the entire encampment. They feasted well that night and the fairies kept an endless supply of ale flowing, which surprisingly did not have any after affects. Dancing and singing ensued. Even the skies opened revealing a vast array of stars twinkling with delight as everyone enjoyed themselves.

Turyn received numerous compliments on his pink veil, which Nedis, Nular, and Nylin had made him wear the entire night. Fed up with all of the comments, Turyn ripped the veil off. He swiped and slashed at the material. One man laughed at his efforts.

Enraged, the cat snatched the veil in his teeth and shoved it down the man's throat threatening revenge on the three brothers.

Before dawn arrived, Tesnayr sent a messenger to King Slyamal with the news of his request to King Edrei for assistance on the borders of Hemil. Within hours King Slyamal stormed into the camp demanding to speak with him.

"Is it true?" demanded King Slyamal bursting in on Tesnayr. "You sent word to King Edrei of our plans?"

Tesnayr calmly faced the king. He had expected this reaction. "Yes, I did. We will need his help to attack the orcs on the borders of Hemíl. You are not the only king whose people are threatened."

"You had no right to ask his help without my permission!"

"I have every right, lest you forget that you gave me your word that you would not interfere with the battle."

King Slyamal closed the distance between him and Tesnayr. "I will not have King Edrei receiving glory on the battlefield."

"No, because it is you who wants all the glory! If there is any to be had, it will not go to you. You are not even fit to be king."

"I will not have King Edrei fighting in this battle!"

"That is not your choice to make. We need his men. The entire encounter depends on it. What is more important to you, King Slyamal: the protection of your people or the person who is glorified when this is over?"

"You just want your name praised throughout the land," said King Slyamal, spitefully.

Tesnayr glared at the man. "If that were true then I would be king. Renown means nothing to me. I gave you my word that I would help you drive the orcs out of Sym'Dul. I will keep that promise."

"If renown means nothing to you, then why do you fight the orcs?" King Slyamal whirled around and stormed out of the tent.

Tesnayr stared after King Slyamal as he left. He had been asked that question many times and each time he refused to answer.   Whenever Tesnayr thought about why he fought the orcs he told himself that it was to protect those who could not protect themselves.   The real reason frightened him and yet drove him onward.

"Listen up," yelled Tesnayr gathering his men around him as he exited his tent, "We ride for the Cym River. When we succeed there, we will head to Hemíl. Should we lose the battle there, all of you are to return to the Black Mountains where we will regroup."

"Fight alongside those of Hemíl," spat King Slyamal from a distance. Despite his efforts to keep his voice down, it carried through the crowd. "I do not wish to join them in this fight. It's...it's preposterous! For twenty years, Sym'Dul and Hemíl have feuded."

"Tesnayr, do you think King Slyamal will keep his word?" asked Nigilin when he finally had a moment alone with Tesnayr.

Tesnayr chewed his lip before answering. "Whether I think so or not does not matter. It is too late to change the plans now. We ride to war even if we ride alone."

Nigilin gazed at the sky for a moment studying the moon that remained visible even in the sunlight. He released a long sigh. "I hope it is not in vain."

Idæas walked up to them from the shadows. "Captain Tesnayr," he called, "The men are ready."

"Give them the order," said Tesnayr.

Idæas saluted. He looked at the moon, which now seemed to be covered in a dark shadow.   "A shadow covers the moon this day. There is treachery in the air," he said to Tesnayr and walked off.

Nigilin glanced at Tesnayr. "Crazy elves," he said.

Tesnayr clapped his hand on the man's back and urged him along.

The army rode in the deceptively calm morning to what lay ahead. Partly for his reassurance, Tesnayr forced King Slyamal to ride at the front of the line with him. He wanted the king where he could keep an eye on him.

Chapter VIII
Betrayal

A woman sat by the window watching her husband chop wood. She smiled at him and continued to fold her linen. A baby stirred in its nearby cradle. The woman put her linen down and checked on the infant. She brushed the top of the baby's head and sang to him, her voice producing a soothing lullaby. At that instant her husband burst through the door yelling at her to grab the baby and leave. In a panic, he snatched items from shelves stuffing them into a bag refusing her inquiries. He shoved the infant into her arms and slung the bag over her shoulder.

"Go," he ordered.

A pounding noise sounded at the door. The hinges rattled violently with each strike. The woman hugged the baby and kissed her husband as she ran toward the back entrance. The door ruptured as orcs poured into the small interior of the lodge. Throwing himself between them, the man attempted to ward off the beasts. The woman screamed as they killed him. Desperately, she darted through the back exit only to meet the most gruesome creature she had ever seen. It was the last thing she ever saw.

Later that same day Tesnayr and his army passed by the cottage and the carnage that had taken place. Slowly, he steered his horse through the wreckage, his face growing more and more disgusted. "Bury them," he ordered. "And burn the place."

"If we linger here much longer King Edrei will have victory in the battle and be riding to our rescue," argued King Slyamal.

Tesnayr yanked King Slyamal off of his horse and dragged him to where the bodies of a woman and her infant lay. "Look at it! Look at it you pompous fool! This is what remains of your arrogance and selfishness. Look at it! I hope this image burns itself in your memory and haunts your dreams." Tesnayr chucked the king to the ground and stormed off.

King Slyamal seethed with anger. He did not know what he was most enraged about: Tesnayr's actions or his words. He dusted himself off and marched away ignoring the stares of those around him.

*   *   *

Arnin rode into King Edrei's camp alone with his arms outstretched. Purposefully, he ordered his men to stay a certain distance away. The last thing Arnin wanted was to start another war.

Clomp. Clomp.

His horse's hooves plopped on the rocky ground echoing throughout the silent camp as all watched him proceed. Gradually, Arnin made his way to the center of the encampment where the king's tent rested. Shields and flags bearing the crest of Hemíl marked it well.

Arnin dismounted once he reached King Edrei's tent. Immediately, a guard stopped him. "Weapons," he said.

Grudgingly, Arnin handed the man his sword and daggers.

"Proceed." The guard waved him toward the tent flap.

Inhaling slowly to calm himself, Arnin stepped through the entrance and into the well-lit interior. He surveyed the inside noting the table littered with papers, a cot, and a whole array of weapons.

"I suppose I have the honor of addressing Arnin," said a deep voice.

"Yes," replied Arnin.

"I received your captain's message," said King Edrei flinging the piece of paper on the table. "His request seems reasonable. But why should I trust him?"

Arnin frowned. Of all the things I didn't want to be asked, he thought to himself. With little time to waste, Arnin decided not to even try to persuade the king with smooth words of praise. "I can't tell you why."

King Edrei's eyebrows arched upward. "You can't or you won't?"

"A little of both," replied Arnin. "You have no reason to trust a man you've never met and nothing I say will change that. The real question for you is this: do you want to take the risk of trusting Tesnayr? Or would you prefer to keep things as they are and face the orcs on your own?"

"You have an interesting way of persuading people."

Frustrated, Arnin grew tired of this bantering. Time was short. "King Edrei," said Arnin, adopting Tesnayr's candor, "Tesnayr has not lied to you. I have not lied to you. He simply requests your assistance."

"Is that all?"

"No. You have one minute to decide. In that time, I am leaving. The question is: will you be coming with me?"

King Edrei flicked a speck of dirt off the mahogany table mulling over Arnin's words. He certainly has brass, he thought. "Colonel!"

In walked a well-armed soldier.

"Ready the men," ordered King Edrei. "We leave immediately."

The Colonel saluted and left.

"For your sake, you better be telling the truth. Because if you are not, I'll kill you myself," King Edrei warned.

I've no doubt that you would, Arnin thought. He kept his mouth sealed, bowed, and walked out into the sunshine. *Now the real fun begins.*

*   *   *

To Tesnayr's relief the orcs had camped near where the Cym River forked effectively eliminating any avenue of escape. He spilt the troops into two groups planning to attack in two waves. The second group consisted mostly of King Slyamal's soldiers with some of his own mixed throughout and with Nelyn in command.

"Hide on the opposite side of the river," ordered Tesnayr, "Stay out of sight and wait for my signal."

Nelyn saluted and left. Carefully, her group waded across the river making no noise. Once on the other side, they scurried behind the trees and rocks blending in with the background.

Tesnayr waited atop a hill with the first group. He regarded the orcs as they sat around feasting, drinking, and quarreling with each other. *Not even a sentry posted.* Amazed at their lack of concern about a possible attack, Tesnayr had a fleeting thought about how this particular fight may be an easy victory. Mentally, he scolded himself for such foolishness. Tesnayr glanced at the sky. Dark clouds stretched from the mountains over the land. They reminded him of smoke instead of clouds. A foreboding of what was to come.

"Now!" he yelled.

A roar of thunder rose around them enveloping the entire area as his men mounted their horses and galloped toward the orc encampment. Tents and pots rolled in every direction clanging as they were knocked down. Caught off guard, orcs dashed about grabbing their weapons and armor.

Tesnayr swung his sword downward cutting off the head of an orc as he attempted to put on his gear. An axe rushed past him barely missing his temple. Deftly, he turned his steed around, snatched a stake from the ground, and chucked it at the orc that had thrown the axe at him. It skewered the beast pinning him to the earth.

"Drive them to the water," Tesnayr shouted over the melee.

Idæas rode erect on his mount with his double edged sword clasped tightly in his free hand. He held it above his head. Unique from most weapons, the elf's sword had a slit in the center of its steel blade. The hilt curved around the elf's gloved hand providing protection from cuts and scrapes.

Concentrating fully on his target, Idæas twirled his blade severing the arm of an orc while tramping another. Clanging, clashing, and clomping echoed around him. He heard none of it. With expert skill, he steered his horse into a thick group of orcs as they attempted to mount a defense.

He jumped off of his horse crashing into an orc as he prepared his slingshot. They rolled along the gravel twisting and turning until coming to a complete halt. Instantly, Idæas jumped to his feet. He plunged his sword into a charging orc.

Dizzily, the one he had tackled stood up. He shook his head a moment to clear it. Finally noticing Idæas he wobbled toward him. The elf stabbed him in the chest easily.

Pain filled his right shoulder as a blunt object struck the elf from behind. Instantly, he whirled around snatching the club from an orc and bashing the beast's head in. He flung the club at another.

The yell of a different orc alerted him to another oncoming assault. He raised his sword. The orc's blade slipped into the slit in Idæas weapon. With a flick of his wrist, he twisted his sword wrenching the orc's weapon away from his grasp. In the same movement, Idæas pulled the orc blade free with his other hand plunging it into the creature's forehead.

Jab, kick, stab. The elf remained a flurry of movement as he eliminated any who attacked him. Movement flickered in the corner of his eye. One orc charged Tesnayr who remained distracted by another two. Judging the beast's intentions, Idæas snatched the dagger from his boot and flung it at the orc. The knife struck the beast in the back of the neck.

"Idæas," yelled Tesnayr, "The signal!"

The elf rammed his shoulder into an orc knocking him to the ground. He seized a flag. Quickly, he jabbed it into a lone campfire setting it aflame and waved it from side to side.

Nelyn watched from her place across the river. When she saw the signal she rushed back to the men that awaited her orders. "The signal's been given. Mount up," she ordered. The men of Tesnayr's army followed her orders and charged across the river to join in the battle. Those of Sym'Dul stayed put.

"You have been given an order," said Nelyn.

King Slyamal cantered up to her. "We ride to Hemil," he said to his men. He turned to Nelyn. "I will not let King Edrei have any glory for this day."

"You gave Captain Tesnayr your word," countered Nelyn, venomously.

King Slyamal scoffed at that notion. "I am changing the nature of our agreement."

"You know you will never reach Hemil in time."

"I am a king and will go where I think is best."

"Coward," hissed Nelyn.

King Slyamal slapped Nelyn hard leaving a mark on her face. He steered his horse away with his men in pursuit. Nelyn picked up a spear, aimed, and hurled it in King Slyamal's direction. Bits of bark flew everywhere as it plunged into the trunk of a tree missing King Slyamal's face by inches. The king halted eyeing the spear. He glanced back at Nelyn. A deadly expression filled her features and he knew the she could have easily killed him, but had purposely missed. Nelyn kicked her horse charging for the river. A part of King Slyamal regretted his decision as he watched her leave. Ignoring such sentiment, he galloped away with his men.

Air escaped Idæas' lungs as a force rammed into his back knocking him into the dirt. Grit filled his teeth. He spat it out. Quickly, the elf grabbed a stone and threw it at his attacker striking him in the head. Idæas snatched the flagpole and jumped to his feet in time to block an attack. Whap! He struck the orc in the stomach immediately swinging the pole and hitting the beast in the back. Another charged him. Idæas slipped his pole between the orc's legs, lifted him into the air and over his head before slamming the beast into the sharp rocks around him.

Jarown backed away blocking and stabbing. Two orcs had him on the defense and he was unable to get free of their counterattacks. Each step took him closer to the riverbank. He blocked again. At any moment, Jarown knew the orcs would kill him if he did not break free. Suddenly, one orc's eyes widened in shock as it slumped to the ground. Seizing his chance, Jarown used the distraction to jab the other in the stomach. Before him stood Nelyn.

Jarown looked about him. The men she led across the river had shrunk. "Where is everybody?" he asked.

"This is them," she responded, "King Slyamal has left us for Hemíl." She ran off.

Rage coursed through him at such betrayal. Gripping his weapon, Jarown plunged back into the fray determined to kill every last orc.

In the midst of the fight Tesnayr noticed that very few trekked across the river. What Nigilin had feared became a reality. King Slyamal had broken his word. Tesnayr noticed a mass of horsemen galloping away and concluded that they were King Slyamal's. When other soldiers of Sym'Dul detected the same, they fled to follow their king. Apparently, they had been given orders to run away the moment their king gave the signal.

"Idæas! Nigilin! Retreat across the river," ordered Tesnayr, "And head for the Black Mountains."

Having been forced to retreat, Tesnayr hoped the river would slow down the orcs' pursuit giving them time to escape. Instantly, a whirlwind of black dust flared up surrounding them. It circled repeatedly around them as they rode away. Tesnayr's ears ached from the sudden dust storm, a magnitude of which he had never witnessed before. The wind raged ominously as it engulfed the orcs with thick, black dirt.

The further he rode, the more Tesnayr noticed that the storm dissipated.

"Captain," yelled one soldier.

"Just keep riding north," Tesnayr yelled back.

*   *   *

Far away in her keep in Belyndril, Ernayn watched the battle in the Stone of Elya. "Drive the beasts into the ground," she directed the wind storm. It obeyed.

"Why did you help them?" asked Quesha.

"I have my reasons," replied Ernayn. "And, Quesha, be aware of Tesnayr's movements."

"Yes, mistress."

"I have business elsewhere." Ernayn wrapped a heavy cloak about her and disappeared leaving her student alone with the stone.

*   *   *

Not far from the river another fight took place. Arnin had succeeded in gaining King Edrei's support and brought them to where Tesnayr had instructed. An orc encampment rested there loaded with supplies for Galbrok's army. Chaos reigned as the battle there continued.

"Arnin!"

Arnin clonked an orc in the head with the hilt of his sword before turning toward King Edrei. He looked where the king pointed. Odd, thought Arnin, Tesnayr was early. He whirled around as another orc attacked him. With ease, he disarmed the orc and rammed his blade into the creature.

"They are early, aren't they?" asked King Edrei.

"They shouldn't be here at all," muttered Arnin, wondering why the plan changed.

The mass of riders plunged into the battle forging their way to the middle attacking as they went. Finally, Arnin noticed the crest of Sym'Dul. Curses flowed through his mind as he realized what had happened.

"It's King Slyamal," shouted one Hemilian soldier.

At first, King Slyamal's arrival distracted the orcs. Soon, everything went horribly wrong. Old animosities surged within the men from Hemíl and Sym'Dul as they attacked each other.

A man wearing the crest of Sym'Dul hit Arnin from behind. Quickly, he turned around and threw the man off of him. "The orcs are the real enemy, you fool!"

The man from Sym'Dul ignored him. He charged Arnin. Darting out of the way, Arnin rammed his sword into the man's side killing him. Two more men advanced. Arnin dodged. He jumped high slamming his foot into the back of one. Hurriedly, he turned to find King Edrei pulling his bloodied weapon from the second man.

"What is this madness?" demanded the king. "You told me that I could trust your captain. And now Slyamal's soldiers attack us."

"This is King Slyamal's doing, not Tesnayr's."

"We trusted you." King Edrei held the point of his blade at Arnin's throat.

"I never lied to you."

The battle raged around them as King Edrei pondered over what to do. "Then what are your orders?"

"Retreat."

King Edrei pulled out his horn and blew on it. A harsh note escaped from it capturing the Hemilian soldiers' attention. "Pull back!"

"Men of Tesnayr, follow me," yelled Arnin over the chaos.

Instantly, soldiers departed the field in every direction. Those from Hemíl followed their king as others chased after Arnin heading for the Black Mountains leaving Sym'Dul alone to clean their own mess. As Arnin took one final glance at the field, the clashing of metal filled his ears and emptiness filled his heart. They had lost.

*   *   *

"Captain," said Jarown, "It is believed that some of the men fighting in the battle were neither with Hemíl nor Sym'Dul. These men wore the armor of the orcs."

Tesnayr had gathered his counsel far away from the others so as to converse in private. Two days had passed since the dismal failure of the coordinated attacks.

"What would possess them to fight alongside those beasts?" said Nigilin in disbelief.

Tesnayr shook his head. "This does not bode well. There is more happening here than we know."

Dirt crunched. Out of the shadows appeared an exhausted Arnin. "I'm sorry," he said. "I meant to be here earlier, but we had to go around a legion of orcs." Nigilin thrust a flask into Arnin's grubby hands.

"The supply line?" asked Tesnayr, though he guessed the answer.

Arnin shook his head. "I failed you," he said, "King Slyamal arrived with his men and before I knew it the soldiers of Hemíl and Sym'Dul turned on each other."

"How did he cover that distance?" asked Jarown.

"Trained riders can cover the greatest distances in the shortest amount of time," replied Nigilin, "The horses for Sym'Dul's cavalry are bred for speed and endurance. I was once a cavalryman myself."

"Captain Tesnayr," said Krulak interrupting them. "A messenger arrived with a dispatch from King Slyamal."

"Send him in," Tesnayr said.

"He is not here with me. I left him under guard outside the camp. King Slyamal wishes to meet with you near Diamond Rock. What shall I tell him?"

"Tell him to go to—"

"Tesnayr," warned Nigilin. "Perhaps meeting with him would be worthwhile."

Tesnayr clenched his fists before slowly releasing them. "Tell him that I will meet with him," he said to Krulak.

Krulak left.

"Arnin, you will stay with Nigilin and take charge of the men," said Tesnayr, "I want you and Nigilin to move them to another location. Jarown—"

"I am going with you," interrupted Jarown.

"Very well."

Darkness had fallen as Jarown and Tesnayr hiked along the treacherous mountain trail with Krulak. Fuming, Tesnayr pondered the many reasons as to why King Slyamal would request to meet with him. He knew exactly what he wished to tell the man, none of it pleasant.

Silence reigned throughout the mountains. Not even the chirping of crickets greeted them. Wrapped in his thoughts, Tesnayr never noticed.

Soon, Diamond Rock came into view. "Where is he?" asked Tesnayr glancing around. No one was there. The feeling that something was terribly wrong hit him too late.

Within seconds a mixture of orcs and men surrounded them. Tesnayr hands went for his weapon but Krulak pointed a sword at his throat stopping him. Reluctantly, Tesnayr released his weapon raising his hands above his head.

"Krulak," said Jarown surprised at the man's betrayal, "Why are you doing this? I have known you since you were a lad."

Krulak laughed maniacally. "You are a gullible man. All the while I was able to garner your sympathy while I was truly serving someone else. A man you once served years ago."

"But, you saved my life once. I trusted you," said Jarown.

"Which proves your ineptness," replied Krulak.

Tesnayr remained calm. Even though his heart raced, he showed no emotion. "How much is this man paying you?"

Krulak enjoyed his moment of triumph. "Twenty pieces of gold," he bragged.

Tesnayr sighed. "A pittance for a man's soul."

The orcs bound the hands of Jarown and Tesnayr. Suddenly, Turyn dropped from above and landed on Krulak scratching and biting furiously. Krulak threw the cat off of him but not before Tesnayr pushed Jarown down the hill and into the deep forest where he disappeared. Two orcs charged after him. "Stop," shouted Krulak, "We have what we want. Do not waste your time with the other one."

Dismayed, the orcs obeyed. Tesnayr eyed his captor committing every feature to memory before his world went black.

Chapter IX
Rescue

Constant scraping against his raw cheek woke Jarown. Groggily, he sat up in the darkness knocking Turyn off of his chest. Jarown rubbed his aching head. It hurt immensely. Tenderly, Jarown touched his wet cheek and winced a bit from its sting. "Where am I?" he asked.

"Still by Diamond Rock," replied Turyn.

"Tesnayr!" Jarown bolted to his feet as the memory of what had occurred rushed back to him. Instantly, his world spun forcing him to slump back to the ground.

"Gone," said Turyn. "They left over two hours ago. I've been trying to wake you up."

Jarown glanced about him, but the darkness prevented him from being able to make out any detail. And he was far from the path.

"Come," said Turyn. "We must go."

Jarown shook his head still disoriented. "I do not know the way back to the path."

"Follow my voice," said Turyn as he bounded off through the thick forest.

Carefully, Jarown stood up leaning against a tree for support.

"Come on," repeated Turyn, impatiently.

Jarown took a step forward using his foot to feel the solidity of the ground beneath him. He put his weight on the foot. Painfully, Jarown repeated this process of feeling the ground with his feet before taking a step forward. In addition, he held his hands out before him navigating his way through the trees by touch.

Not once did he hear Turyn, except when the cat spoke. Jarown felt so turned around, he wondered if he would ever get out. Snap! Again he broke a twig as he clumsily moved through the forest making so much noise that anybody could hear him.

"This way," said Turyn forcing Jarown to turn to his left.

"OOMPH!" Jarown slammed into the ground as his foot caught on an upturned root causing him to lose his balance.

"Sorry," said Turyn. "There's a root there."

"No kidding," mumbled Jarown.

"There is a bit of an incline here," said Turyn. "Put your hand here."

Jarown placed a hand where Turyn's voice came from.

"Now place your other hand here."

Jarown placed his second hand where Turyn had indicated.

"Now, pull yourself up."

Sweating immensely, Jarown did as ordered. His muscles burned from the effort of hauling himself up the embankment to the solid ground above him. Panting, fresh air hit him in the face as he rolled onto the path and away from the trees.

"You did it," beamed Turyn, brushing against Jarown's leg. "It should be easier from here on out."

Exhausted, Jarown rolled onto his stomach and pushed himself to his feet. He swayed for a moment before taking a step.

"Just go in a straight line," said Turyn. "There are no trees here to worry about."

Each step was harder than the last. His boots plopped on the gravel as he dropped them, his muscles refusing to work. A stabbing prick stung the back of his calf. "Ouch! What did you do that for?"

"Keep moving," said Turyn as he sunk his claws into Jarown's leg for a second time.

Silence ensued as he and the cat made their way back to the camp. Jarown could only guess about the amount of time that had been wasted with him wandering aimlessly. If not for Turyn, he would have gotten lost.

Once more, he faded in and out of consciousness.

Prick.

"Stay awake," said Turyn.

Eyes opening wide, Jarown moved faster with renewed vigor from the cat stabbing him with his claws. The sound of a hammer caught his attention. "You hear that?"

"Yes," replied Turyn, "We're close."

Running down the path with Turyn close behind, Jarown used what reserves of energy he had left to make it to the camp before he passed out. His boots pounded the soft dirt of the narrow trail. Shouts up ahead alerted him that the sentries had spotted him. Before Jarown knew it, arms grabbed him forcing him to a halt.

"What happened? Where is Tesnayr?" demanded Nigilin.

"Betrayed," whispered Jarown. "Krulak betrayed us. The orcs have Tesnayr."

"Krulak," said Nelyn in disbelief. She was well aware of the lifelong friendship between Krulak and her father.

"Where did they take him?" demanded Nigilin.

Jarown shook his head. "I do not know. There was a scuffle. I fell and remember nothing until I came to."

"Turyn, scout down the mountain and report back to me when you have discovered where they are holding Tesnayr."

Turyn bounded away.

"Take him to where he can rest."

A couple of men led Jarown away.

After Jarown had recovered, Nigilin called a meeting. Nelyn, Nedis, Nular, Nylin, Jarown, Arnin, and a few others were all there. "By now, you all know that Tesnayr has been captured. Betrayed by Krulak to the orcs. My question to all of you is: what do we do about it?"

"Rescue him," Nelyn said matter-of-factly, "And those who say otherwise are cowards."

"Now see here," said one of the other men, "Such an attempt would be futile. We cannot blindly attempt a rescue without first knowing where he is and if he is even still alive."

"No one is disputing that," said Nigilin.

"Nelyn is right," said Arnin.

Nelyn looked at him in surprise as it was the first time Arnin had ever agreed and defended her. "We cannot let Tesnayr suffer at the hands of the orcs. He has given us much. Could any of us live the rest of our days knowing that we turned our backs on him?"

"What do you three say?" Nigilin asked the triplets.

The three brothers smiled at one another in agreement. "You tell us what the plan is and we will follow you to the end," said Nylin.

"Even if it's crazy," said Nular.

"Especially if it is crazy," Nedis added.

"What we need is a plan," said Arnin.

"I need a dress," said Nelyn, abruptly.

"Nelyn," said Jarown, "This is hardly the time to act like a woman."

Nelyn glared at him. "Men have aligned themselves with the orcs. A woman's charms have been known to distract them from their duties. And the orcs like to use women for sport."

"Where did you learn all this?" asked Jarown.

"I listen," replied Nelyn.

Nigilin caught on to Nelyn's plan and ordered one of the soldiers outside to find a dress about her size. He remembered Tesnayr speaking to him once about how many men had joined the orcs in exchange for false promises. "Any other ideas for the rescue?"

"I volunteer the triplets to cause a distraction while the rest of us sneak into the camp," said Jarown.

"How very cordial of you, sir," said Nedis.

"Yeah, we love being volunteered," said Nular.

"Do not start this again," interrupted Nigilin. "Will you three do as Jarown has suggested?"

"Of course," the three brothers said in unison.

"What do you plan to do to distract them?"

"That is our trade secret," said Nylin.

"Do we even know the layout of their camp?" Idæas peeled away from the shadows. No one had thought to invite him, but he showed anyway.

Mentally, Nigilin kicked himself for overlooking such a thing. "Turyn should be here by now."

Just then, laborious breathing entered the tent. In crawled Turyn dragging a large, rolled up map on the ground. He hauled it into the lamplight placing it neatly by Nigilin's feet. "I apologize for taking so long," he puffed.

Nigilin scooped up the map and placed it on the table. "Is this—"

"Yes," replied Turyn. "They stupidly made a map of their own encampment. They aren't far from here." The cat splayed out on the floor and laid his head down in exhaustion.

"Very well. Jarown, pick a small group to accompany us on this mission. You," he pointed at another soldier, "Lead the rest of the army to the Perili Mountains. If we succeed, we will meet you all there. Idæas, I am certain that you will be needed on this mission."

The elf nodded reservedly.

Nigilin eyed everyone before dismissing them. "If there are no more suggestions I suggest we get going. We leave in the morning."

*   *   *

Small, razor sharp pebbles burrowed into Tesnayr's palms as he crashed onto the hard earth where the orcs had tossed him. He got to all fours and received a kick in the mouth. Coughing, he spat out globs of blood. "What do you want?" he demanded.

"I am surprised with your usage of their common tongue when there are other speeches more worthy of being spoken," said a familiar voice

Tesnayr looked up as Galbrok leered over him. "I will not dirty myself with your dark speech."

Galbrok smirked. "Dark? You used to speak it. Doesn't matter. Our speech will be heard in this land like it is in yours. I must admit, Tesnayr, that you are unique. You managed to escape my orcs many months ago and now you have become the leader of your very own army."

"What do you want?"

"Information. You know these lands and their leaders. You could also be a valuable asset with an army behind you."

Tesnayr looked defiantly into Galbrok's eyes. "Death is more welcome than life as your slave. I did not betray my people then and I will not now."

"They are not your people," said Galbrok, coldly.

"Neither are you."

"You remember what I do to men who refuse me? Ah, yes, you do. All too well I imagine," said Galbrok.

A man walked into the tent. His curt manner told Tesnayr that he was not to be trifled with. Dressed in red, Tesnayr guessed who he was. *He always wore red so as to hide the blood stains of his victims*, echoed Jarown's voice in his head.

"This is Blynak," Galbrok introduced the man. "He has unique methods for prying information from unwilling lips. You will tell me what I want to know before the end."

Rough hands seized Tesnayr beneath the arms and dragged him away. They did not stop until they reached the far end of the camp. There the orcs stripped Tesnayr of his armor and his tunic. The chill air brushed his skin causing goose bumps to appear. Roughly, his hands were thrust over his head as coarse rope glided over his wrists. The orcs secured him to the tree allowing him to swing with his feet barely touching the ground.

"Tesnayr," said Blynak as he paced around him. "Your name keeps cropping up everywhere I go. No doubt you have heard of me."

"Should I have?" Tesnayr's sarcastic remark earned him a bloody lip.

"Don't play coy with me," spat Blynak. "I know who rides with you. Now, save yourself some pain and just tell me what I want to know."

"What did Galbrok promise you?"

"What I deserve."

Smiling, Tesnayr almost guffawed at the man's statement and its double meaning. No doubt, Blynak thought he would get a parcel of land or some amount of riches. Tesnayr knew better. "You'll get what you deserve, alright. To Galbrok, you are nothing more than the insects that crawl around in the dirt. Once he is done with you, he will leave you for the crows."

Tesnayr's cheek stung profusely as Blynak backhanded him. "Don't be so certain of that," he whispered. "Galbrok may think he is running the show, but I have no intention of coming out on the bottom."

"Do you think you are the first person to try and outsmart Galbrok?" asked Tesnayr. "Do yourself a favor. Walk away, while you still can."

"I tire of this," said Blynak. "Where is your army? How many men do you have?"

"Why would I tell you?"

"You will. I have yet to meet a man I cannot break." Blynak gave a curt nod to someone standing behind Tesnayr.

Instantly, Tesnayr's back burned as a whip lashed across it. Blynak nodded again. A second stripe laced across his bare skin as the whip cracked again. Tears welled in Tesnayr's eyes from the pain. He remained silent.

Angered, Blynak ordered that Tesnayr be whipped until no flesh remained on his back.

Long hours passed as Tesnayr endured the pain of the whip. Still unsatisfied at the results, Blynak ordered that burning embers be placed on his chest. Still, Tesnayr did not speak.

"How goes it?" said Galbrok as he walked into view.

"He still won't speak. We've been at this for eight hours," said Blynak.

"You promised me results," said Galbrok, venomously.

Suddenly feeling the need to placate the leader of the orcs, Blynak decided to reiterate what he had told Galbrok days before. "Belyndril is ready to fall. You should attack quickly, before the king manages to gain an ally. By the time you return, we will have what we need from this scum." Blynak gestured towards Tesnayr as he uttered the word scum.

Tesnayr feigned unconsciousness.

Galbrok grunted. "Giving orders again."

Blynak quickly found the right words to soothe the orc leader. "Merely a suggestion, my lord. There is word that the king of Belyndril has asked King Edrei to form an alliance with him."

"You told me that none of the five kings agreed on anything; that they constantly bickered and quarreled with each other, and fought endless wars. How could this alliance be possible?"

"They do quarrel, my lord, and their alliances usually fall. But there is a change in the air. A change that seems to stem from the man you hold prisoner."

"That will change."

"Perhaps—," Blynak cut off his words upon receiving a stern look from Galbrok. "My apologies. You, of course, know best."

"Remember your place in this world, human," said Galbrok as he stalked off.

A man approached Blynak. "How did it go?" he asked.

Blynak smiled. "Very well. I have that scum eating from my hand. We will let the orcs destroy our enemies. They will make our work easier."

"Should we continue with him?" said the man referring to Tesnayr.

"Leave him be for now," answered Blynak. "We won't get anything from him until he wakes."

A moist cloth pressed against Tesnayr's dry, cracked lips. Wearily, he stuck his tongue out licking whatever liquid he could for his parched mouth. The few drops of water felt blissful to him. Gradually, Tesnayr opened his eyes and saw a young girl of about fifteen lifting a water filled ladle to his lips. She wore a black band around her upper left arm, a symbol of slavery among the orcs. Tesnayr drank what was given him, spilling more than what managed to enter his mouth.

Suddenly, an orc yanked the girl away throwing her to the ground. She gasped as she hit the rocky earth. Covering herself with her arms, she tried desperately to protect herself from the lash.

"You shall receive ten lashes," yelled the orc to the girl.

"Let me take her punishment," said Tesnayr, weakly.

"A noble act. Why would one do such a thing?" inquired Blynak as he approached.

No response.

"I have other plans for you. However, I agree with not scarring her delicate skin when her talents may be better served elsewhere." Blynak stroked the girl's rosy cheek with his forefinger.

She pulled away.

"You have some fight to you as well," said Blynak. "Go!" He kicked at the girl as she scampered away. "Now, where were we?" Blynak held Tesnayr's face up staring into his eyes.

*   *   *

Ernayn walked softly through the trees. She knew the cat was there, but couldn't find him. She hated these games of his. *Why can't he be visible like other animals?*

"A pleasure to see you again, Ernayn," said a voice.

Ernayn turned around and found Turyn seated on a tree stump staring at her. "I was never able to surprise you, Turyn," she greeted.

The cat yawned in boredom. "What is it you want, sorceress? I have important business to tend," said Turyn, impatiently.

"I know what you are all planning," said Ernayn.

Turyn's ears perked up. "Is that so?"

"There are too many of them. You will never succeed with the small number you are taking."

"Why are you telling me this?" question Turyn.

Ernayn paused. "I do not want to see you fail."

"And why is that?" asked Turyn.

"I have my reasons."

"You always have your reasons. Come on, Ernayn. Tell me. Why do you care if we fail?"

"Because the fate of the world depends upon the success of freeing Tesnayr."

"Oh, really? The fate of the world? How noble of you to care about the world."

"Stubborn cat," said Ernayn. "What do you want from me?"

"The truth."

Ernayn let out a long and steady breath. "If the orcs are not stopped, they will destroy the five kingdoms, including my home."

"So now we get to it. You fear death," said Turyn.

"A sorceress may live for centuries, but even she must perish in the end. I have no intention of doing so at the hands of the orcs. Why do you help these people Turyn? A cat who has the gift of speech."

"I help these people because I find Tesnayr interesting."

Ernayn frowned. *Typical feline answer.* "Heed my warning. You are outnumbered."

"That is our concern," said Turyn. "Of course, you could join us. But you won't. You never do. Always playing your games. Always wanting people to abide by your wishes. When will you learn that you cannot manipulate the world? Someday, you will have to make a choice.

"I wish you well, Ernayn, Sorceress of the earth." Turyn bounded off through the underbrush.

"Until we meet again," said Ernayn, annoyed that her warning went unheeded.

*   *   *

Nelyn emerged from her tent. She wore a simple rose pink dress with a white belt. Elegantly, it flowed with every movement she made giving her a delicate feminine disposition. She shoved a dagger under her belt as Arnin stared at her speechless. For the first time in his life he realized that Nelyn truly was a beautiful woman. She possessed a natural beauty that did not require any cosmetic paint to enhance. Her dress accentuated her femininity which usually remained hidden beneath the armor she wore most days.

"How did I do?" asked Arnin finally getting his breath back.

Nelyn sighed. "The dress is perfect in every way, except one. It's pink."

"What is wrong with that?"

"Pink happens to be a girl's color."

"It was the only one I could find and you are a girl."

Nelyn gave Arnin a hard look before knocking him off his feet and walking away. Nigilin approached at that moment doing his best not to laugh. "That is the second time she has kicked you—," Nigilin said before Arnin cut him off.

"I know."

"So what was it this time?" asked Nigilin.

"Nothing." Arnin stalked off.

"I do not know much about human relationships, but I do believe they like each other," said Turyn appearing out of nowhere. Nigilin chuckled and motioned for the cat to follow him.

"Come on," said Nigilin. "It's time to leave."

Poised on a ridge just above the orc encampment, Arnin watched as Tesnayr hung by his wrists from a tree, swinging in the breeze.   His head hung low indicating that he was unconscious.   Orcs marched past him.   One took a rod and slammed it into Tesnayr's stomach getting a yelp of pain.

Arnin surveyed the rest of the camp.   Men guarded the entrance.   More men walked around the camp intermixed with the orcs, but they kept their distance. "Now," Arnin said to Nelyn.

Nelyn strolled down the hill and approached the two guards at the entrance to the camp. She swayed her hips from side to side allowing her curls to flow behind her. With a sly smile, Nelyn glanced at them hoping that her physique would work to her advantage.

The guards blocked her path as she reached them. "Where do you think you're going?"

Nelyn smiled. "Nowhere.   I just thought I would give you some company. It must be lonely sitting out here. Of course, if you want me to leave—" She turned to go.

"No. I did not say that," said one of the guards grabbing her arm. "It does get a bit lonely here."

Nelyn ran her fingers through his hair. "Perhaps, I can keep you both company," she said sweetly placing herself between both of them. She leaned in close pretending to kiss one of them while pulling the dagger from under her belt. Swiftly, Nelyn plunged the knife in the man's stomach and elbowed him in the back of the head. She quickly turned on the other guard disarming and killing him in a matter of seconds. Nelyn whistled. Arnin, Nigilin, Jarown, and a few others appeared.

"Orcs and guards are spread throughout the camp. They've made a protective wall around it. It's not very good construction. Tesnayr is being held at the southern end of the camp. You three patrol this area and keep it clear.   You two take care of the distraction," said Nigilin as Nylin and Nedis smiled at each other. "We will go get Tesnayr."

Idæas motioned for men to surround the perimeter of the camp. They did so, loading their bows and awaiting orders. Once positioned, the elf waited near the entrance with Arnin and Nelyn for the precise moment.

Nedis and Nylin moved stealthily through the camp crawling through the slick mud on their elbows. They scooted forward allowing the muck to cover them. Nedis stopped suddenly. He flicked a pebble at his brother catching him on the top of his head. He pointed at the orc that stood only inches in front of him. Oblivious to their presence, the orc surveyed the landscape around him.

Nylin flung a rock several feet away. Instinctively, the orc jerked his head in that direction. Seizing his chance, Nedis jumped up wrapping his arms around the orc and wrestled the beast to the ground breaking its neck. He scooped some of the black mud over the body in an effort to hide it.

A low whistle caught his attention. Nedis hugged the ground just as a troop of orcs marched past. Gradually, he and his brother inched their way through the encampment. Nedis noticed a row of five catapults lined up neatly in a row, all of them loaded and aimed at the horse pen. He flicked another pebble at his brother's head.

Clearly annoyed, Nylin mouthed, "What?"

Nedis pointed to the catapults. "Excellent," they whispered in unison, reading the other's thoughts.

Changing course, they wormed their way to the catapults. Using some rope they rigged a single trigger to fire all the ballistas with a simple yank. They ducked behind some tents with the long cable in their hands. Smiling at one another, they jerked the rope. A slow grinding filled the air as one by one the catapults fired, hurling giant pieces of stone directly into the horse pen. Frightened, the horses bucked and kicked free of their confinement. Thundering chaotically throughout the camp, the animals stampeded any who barred their way. Satisfied, Nedis and Nylin left to seek the others.

The moment the catapults fired, arrows darkened the sky pelting the earth. Orcs and men ran aimlessly in an effort to dodge the deadly spears. Within minutes, bodies littered the muddy ground soaking it with blood.

On the other end of the camp Nigilin and Jarown watched a group of orcs and men that stood between them and Tesnayr. "Do you think Nedis and Nylin were caught?" asked Jarown.

"No," said Nigilin, "They should act any moment now."

An ear splitting explosion knocked them off balance as the giant boulders pounded the earth leaving craters. Mud and rock flew everywhere raining upon those unfortunate enough to be close by. Distracted, Tesnayr's guards dashed away to see what caused the commotion.

Seizing their chance, Jarown and Nigilin bolted for the barely conscious Tesnayr. Carefully, Jarown cut the rope binding him to the tree and placed him on Nigilin's shoulder. Tesnayr moaned in pain. Gently, Nigilin gripped Tesnayr as he supported him.

"We need to hurry," said Jarown taking Tesnayr's other shoulder.

"Easy, lad," soothed Nigilin when Tesnayr moaned again.

Though barely able to keep his eyes open, Tesnayr noticed the same girl that had helped him earlier. She hunkered behind a bunch of crates and barrels in fright. "Get her," he said.

"What?" asked Nigilin.

"The girl," repeated Tesnayr. "Help the girl."

Jarown noticed the girl for the first time. Instantly, he lunged for her wrapping his arms protectively around her and lifting her off the ground. Together, Jarown and Nigilin dragged them away from the foray.

Back at the camp entrance, Arnin and Nelyn watched as Nigilin and Jarown headed for them. Nelyn spotted a group of armed men and orcs standing between them and the entrance. *They'll never make it.* Nelyn ripped out her sword. She charged into the melee expertly dodging a deadly blow as she rammed her entire body into an orc. Without delay, she plunged her blade into its chest. Quickly, Nelyn turned on the spot raising her weapon in time to block an attack from one of Blynak's men. Her arm tingled from the impact. Straining, Nelyn shoved the man away from her before stabbing him in the side.

Idæas and Arnin appeared beside her. "Hurry," yelled Arnin as he disarmed an orc.

Sluggishly, Jarown and Nigilin heaved the limp body of Tesnayr and the girl to the camp entrance, and their only escape. Their feet slipped in the slick mud with each step. Finally, they pushed past their comrades.

A great weight slammed into Nelyn knocking her into the black slime. She shoved it off of her only to realize that it was Idæas. A quick inspection told her that he had taken an arrow in the arm while pushing her out of its path.

"Help him!" shouted Arnin.

With great effort, Nelyn pulled the elf to his feet.

"I am alright," said Idæas.

"Go!" yelled Arnin.

"What about you?" asked Nelyn.

"GO!" Arnin shoved her away.

Reluctantly, Nelyn followed after Idæas, leaving Arnin alone.

Arnin ducked a deadly blow. Instantly, he righted himself and stabbed his opponent in the back. He quickly whirled around smacking an orc in the mouth with his blade. A man screamed furiously as he ran for Arnin with his weapon raised. Arnin braced himself. Just then, an arrow struck the man in the head. Wasting no time, Arnin dashed for the camp entrance.

A whistle sounded nearby. Nular stood ready with the horses. Nigilin and Jarown placed Tesnayr and the girl on one before mounting their own.

"Hurry," shouted Nigilin as Nelyn, Idæas, and Arnin arrived. "Make for the river!"

Immediately, their horses sped off trampling any who dared to bar their path. Each rider felt the heavy breaths of the horses as they rode. The river lay less than a quarter of a mile away, but to them it felt like a much greater distance.

Nelyn soon found herself at the rear of the group. Water splashed in every direction as they plunged into the river. Carefully, each rider guided their horse through the strong currents holding on tightly so as not to be swept away.

The pursuing orcs halted on the riverbank firing arrows at their escapees. Gradually, they crawled out of the river and onto its soft bank.

"Nedis," screamed Arnin pointing Nelyn out to him as he was closest to her.

Nedis turned around plunging back into the river in an effort to reach her. He was too late. Nelyn struggled fiercely with her horse as it cried in fright. An arrow struck the animal causing it to rear up and throw her into the water. Within seconds, Nelyn and her horse disappeared with the current.

"Nelyn!" yelled Arnin.

Jarown spun around when he heard her name. "Nelyn! Nelyn!" He charged the riverbank only to have Idæas grab hold of his horse forcing him to a sudden stop.

Desperately, Nedis struggled to the riverbank to join the others knowing that he had failed to save his friend. Together, he and Arnin watched helplessly as the river washed away any trace of Nelyn.

"Move out," shouted Nigilin. He smacked Arnin on the shoulder to get his attention. "We have to leave." Reluctantly, Arnin and Jarown followed the others as they headed to safety. They had no choice but to leave Nelyn behind.

Chapter X
What Next?

Groggily, Nelyn awoke on the muddy riverbank under the starlit sky. A dagger lay beside her. She looked about her finding no sign of her horse. Slowly, she stood up. Nelyn staggered forward a few steps and collapsed back on the soft sand exhausted. She sank into the moist earth barely able to hold herself up.

Soft pats in the sand caught her attention. Nelyn twisted around. Behind her stood a unicorn of the most brilliant silver color she had ever seen. Its horn glowed brilliantly providing the only light in the dark expanse. On closer inspection Nelyn noticed that its tip had been broken off. Absentmindedly, Nelyn's hand went to the necklace she wore. *Could it be?*

"Will you take me back?" whispered Nelyn.

The unicorn bowed its head and knelt on the ground beside her.

Mustering what strength she had, Nelyn climbed onto the unicorn's back. "I need to get back to Tesnayr's camp." The unicorn's silence unnerved her. In all the stories she had herd as a child, they spoke, but this one merely bowed its head in response. "Can you not speak?"

"I knew your mother."

The strong male voice of the unicorn surprised her. So did his statement about her mother. "My moth—how—" Nelyn stopped, confused.

"That bit of unicorn horn you wear, I once gave it to your mother."

"What does that—"

"For saving my life. It is powerful. Guard it, like you guard your heart."

Nelyn shook her head. She had no idea what the unicorn was talking about and it made no sense to her. "Is this a dream?" She hoped it was.

"It would be easier if I said yes," replied the unicorn. "But it is not. The horn you wear is a gift. Draw strength from it. Use it to heal."

"I'm confused."

"It will make sense in time," said the unicorn, "Where do you wish to go?"

"Tesnayr's camp," said Nelyn, "In the Perili Mountains."

Nelyn leaned forward accepting the gentle movements of the unicorn's steps before she passed out. She no longer cared if this was a dream or real. The unicorn gently walked through the night taking extra care to not lose his passenger.

Nigilin sat by Tesnayr's bed and mopped the sweat off of his brow. Feverish, Tesnayr shook from alternating chills and delirium. Nigilin shook his head. He had seen Tesnayr like this before and he pulled through, but Nigilin doubted it would happen again. "Hang in there, Tesnayr," he whispered, "The world still needs you."

Arnin walked in. "How is he?"

"The same," replied Nigilin. "Have you found them?"

"No. There has been no sign of Sarwyn or Serein."

"What of Nelyn?"

Arnin shook his head in answer.

"How is Jarown handling the news?"

Arnin sighed. "As well as can be expected. He is helping Turyn search for the two fairies. I didn't dare refuse his offer of assistance."

"Arnin, there is something you should know. I don't know what to do. I have applied everything I can think of. His fever has only increased and his wounds have shown no signs of healing. It is as though he has given up."

"It sounds like we need a miracle," said Arnin.

"Yes, we do." Sadness filled Nigilin's voice. With each passing minute, he felt as though he was losing a son.

Arnin clamped the man on the shoulder and left the tent.

A pop sounded behind Nigilin. He turned to find Sarwyn and Serein standing beside him. "Where have you been?" demanded Nigilin.

"We apologize for our absence, but we have important news. King Telinin of Belyndril has been exiled from his own kingdom by the orcs. He now resides in MurDair and plans to cross the mountains into Hemíl," answered Serein.

Nigilin rose to his feet, doing his best to keep his temper in check. "While you have been gone, Captain Tesnayr was taken prisoner by the orcs. One of our own betrayed him. We managed to rescue him, but for three days now he has lain on that bed unchanged. We needed your help long ago and—," he stopped midsentence and sagged down on the bedside exhausted.

Sarwyn strolled over to Tesnayr and examined him. "Sister," she called and Serein joined her. They conducted a thorough examination with grim expressions. Whispering rapidly to each other in their own language, they ignored all else, much to Nigilin's annoyance as he tried to listen in on their conversation. He cleared his throat to signal that he was still in the tent. The two sisters turned around.

"It is not good," said Sarwyn. "He has been poisoned, but by what I cannot say."

Serein chimed in. "Apparently the orcs were determined to keep him from surviving should he ever escape. By tomorrow's dawn he will be dead."

"Is there anything you can do?" asked Nigilin.

"No," replied the fairies together.

"No?" Nigilin rubbed his hand over his forehead in frustration. "You are fairies. Some of the most powerful creatures on this earth and you can't save him?" His temper rose with the pitch of his voice.

"Even we cannot stave off death," said Sarwyn. "Some things are beyond our powers."

"Then what can I do?" asked Nigilin. The thought of losing Tesnayr tore at his heart. He saved him once, came to view him as a son, and now was forced to watch him die.

"Pray," said Serein.

"Pray?"

"Yes," interjected Sarwyn. "There are two creatures on this earth that can save him. One rarely makes his presence known and is believed to be more myth than real. But the other does exist. But, with the invasion of the orcs, they have disappeared and only come to those of pure heart."

"And it helps if they are female," added Serein.

"You are speaking of the unicorns," said Nigilin. He knew of their existence, but had never seen one. It was said that the beasts spent most of their time deep in the forests of the mountains or in MurDair away from humans.

"There is a third option," said Sarwyn.

"What is that?" asked Nigilin.

"To accept what has come to pass. All men die. Perhaps this is Tesnayr's time."

Nigilin refused to believe that. "No. I saved him once. We need him. If the heavens have an ounce of mercy they will grant him his life." Nigilin stormed out of the tent. He needed some air.

At that moment, a huge commotion arose within the encampment. Murmurs rumbled through the gathering men as many looked on in awe and disbelief. Nigilin pushed his way through the crowd. When he reached the front, he saw a single unicorn with a woman on its back. "Nelyn!"

Arnin burst through the crowd with Jarown beside him, both joyful that she still lived.

The unicorn snorted as he stopped. Ignoring those around them, the magnificent creature knelt down allowing Nelyn to dismount.

"Remember what I told you. That horn will not heal everybody, but sometimes it can heal one who needs it most."

"It doesn't make any sense," said Nelyn.

"It's not supposed to," replied the unicorn. "And remember," the unicorn pointed his horn at Nelyn's heart filling her with his energy and strength, "Stay pure."

The unicorn turned and trotted away. No one attempted to stop the animal. They just stared after the unicorn barely believing what they witnessed.

"How did you," Nigilin began, but stopped. "Are you alright?" asked Nigilin.

Nelyn nodded in answer.

Jarown ran up to Nelyn and enveloped her in a giant hug squeezing the air out of her lungs. "I thought I lost you."

"You nearly did," replied Nelyn. She fiddled with her necklace and a thought occurred to her. "But now is not the time. Where is Captain Tesnayr?"

"Through here," said Nigilin leading her into the tent where Tesnayr still lay unconscious.

Sarwyn and Serein sat by Tesnayr's bedside looking helpless and upset. They looked up as Nelyn entered. Quickly, Nelyn took the necklace from around her neck and placed the bit of unicorn horn in Tesnayr's hand. *I hope I understood him properly*, she thought to herself.

The others watched in intense curiosity. They each wondered what she was doing.

"Please," Nelyn whispered so quietly that no one else heard her words, "If I understood the unicorn correctly, please heal him. We need him."

Nothing happened. Frustrated, Nelyn let her hands fall to her side. *I'm sorry.* Nelyn did not know what she apologized for; the words just entered her mind.

Suddenly, the bit of unicorn horn in Tesnayr's hand glowed. A silver light surrounded him. It grew in intensity and brightness forcing everyone to look away. Slowly, the light faded. The necklace fell from Tesnayr's hand clinking on the ground just as he inhaled deeply. Nelyn scooped it up and put it back around her neck.

"Why are you all standing here?" asked Tesnayr as he opened his eyes. "Don't you all have work to do?"

Beaming, everyone looked from one to another.

"You're back," said Nigilin trying to disguise the delight in his voice.

"Of course I am," said Tesnayr. "Where is the girl?"

It took a moment for Nigilin to remember whom Tesnayr spoke of. "She is safe. We are searching for a place she can stay."

"We know of one," said Sarwyn. "There is a family in these mountains not far from here. They are well protected. Serein and I can take her there."

"Do it," said Tesnayr.

The two fairies left.

Tesnayr began to sit up to which Nigilin immediately placed his hands on the man's shoulders and pushed him back down. "You need to rest," he said. "We are safe for the moment."

Relenting, Tesnayr lay back on the bed and closed his eyes in slumber.

Jarown led Nelyn to another tent away from the center of the camp so that she could rest.

"I'm fine," she argued.

Jarown gave his daughter a piercing glare indicating that he didn't believe her. "Bed."

"But—"

"Now."

Knowing she was not going to win the argument, Nelyn took off her armor and allowed Jarown to tuck her in. Though the bed consisted of a bunch of furs piled together to provide some cushioning, it was comfortable and she instantly fell asleep. Admiring his daughter for a moment, Jarown left her to rest.

When Nelyn awoke fully refreshed she found Jarown sitting beside her. "How long?" she asked.

"A day and a night," replied Jarown. "I had to beg Arnin to let me in here."

"You weren't—"

"Arnin cared for you all night and saw to it that none disturbed you. Not even me."

"And you let him?" exclaimed Nelyn.

"It was no less than what I would have done." A note of admiration filled Jarown's voice.

"You must be getting soft in your old age." Nelyn blocked a playful smack from Jarown and laughed.

"Now, I'll get you some food."

"I will not have special treatment."

"And I'll not have my daughter push herself to the point of death. And neither will Arnin."

"Arnin? He loathes me."

Jarown smiled. "The same way you loathe him? I may be old, but I have not forgotten the ways of the young."

"You could have fooled me."

"When you have eaten there are things that need to be done. I'll see you in about an hour."

"Where did mother get this?" asked Nelyn holding up her necklace.

"I don't rightly know. She came home with it one day saying that a unicorn had given it to her. No one believed her and thought that she had either found it or made it herself.

"But there are stories of unicorns giving certain gifts to humans. There is one tale that tells of a woman that saved a unicorn's life. In return he gave her a piece of his horn. When she needed him most he would appear. Sort of a personal guardian."

"It can't be all true then," said Nelyn.

"What makes you say that?"

"My mother is dead."

"I doubt she is the one in the tale. But you must remember, Nelyn, there are laws that govern us all. Death comes for everyone eventually."

"But this saved Tesnayr." Nelyn pointed to her necklace.

"Don't ask me to explain it, Nelyn," said Jarown. "I don't think there will ever be one. When your mother died she had something more important to think of. You.

"I found this years later. As it was once hers, it is now rightfully yours. Maybe this has some magical power. Maybe you do have a personal guardian. Or perhaps what recently happened was a bit of luck."

"Perhaps," Nelyn mumbled.

"Don't spend much time dwelling on it. It will only drive you insane. Take it from an old man."

Nelyn put her necklace back around her neck. "I miss her."

Jarown nodded his head knowingly and patted her knee. "You take care of yourself."

"You're a good man, father."

The air changed around Jarown as he stared at his feet and a sorrowful expression crossed his features. "No, I'm not," he whispered and left.

Bewildered by his statement, Nelyn climbed out of bed and dressed in her usual attire of men's armor. She had just finished when a voice spoke. "Though it is nice to you see up and about and back to your usual self, I must admit that the dress suited you better. At least, Arnin seemed to think so."

Nelyn turned around. "Turyn! Don't you ever knock?"

Turyn swished his tail and thought for a moment. "No. Knocking wastes precious moments better spent talking."

Nelyn giggled. "What can I do for you?"

"Nothing. I only came to see how you were doing. By the way many of the men have begun singing a song about you and Tesnayr."

"Me?"

Turyn jumped onto a shelf and positioned himself regally and sang the song.

What makes man fight when others run in fright?
It is courage he needs when others flee.
Strength and honor add to his valor.

Two warriors have we who've done marvelous deeds.
They know no fear whether far or near.

Our leader here is named Tesnayr.
He rose above the rest and faced many tests.
With knowledge to defeat our enemy
By his courage we follow today and tomorrow.

Nelyn is the other whose bravery is ne'er tethered.
Tho' a woman she may be, she fights with fierce ferocity.
She is bound by her word and her deeds make her heard.
Her courage and loyalty are true and ne'er brewed.

Tesnayr and Nelyn are ours; we will follow them to the stars.
They know no fear whether far or near.

As soon as Turyn finished the last chorus his foot slipped and he fell off of the shelf crashing clumsily onto the ground. Nelyn roared with laughter.

"I meant to do that," said Turyn, nursing his pride.

"I like you, Turyn."

Turyn bowed. "Thank you. I like me too."

Nelyn placed her foot in her boot only to find something was already in there. Carefully, she tipped it upside down and tapped it against a post. Out fell a half-eaten mouse.

"Turyn," said Nelyn, "What is this doing in my boot?"

"That's where I left my mouse!" Turyn quickly snatched the remains in his mouth and chewed on it greedily. "Want some?"

"No," replied Nelyn, disgusted. "What was that thing doing in my boot?"

"I needed a place to store it," replied the cat through bits of meat, "And your boot was convenient. Besides, you were sleeping and not using it at the time."

"Don't do it again."

"Are you sure you don't want some? It's still fresh."

Nelyn did her best not to retch from Turyn feasting happily on the day old remains of a mouse. "I'm not hungry."

A messenger entered the tent urgently. "I beg your pardon, Lieutenant, but Captain Tesnayr has sent for you."

"I'm on my way."

The messenger left. Nelyn snatched the last of her weapons and stalked out. The sound of men singing greeted her ears as she exited her tent, chanting the same song that Turyn had sung for her. She blushed slightly embarrassed by such praise.

Soon, Nelyn joined Tesnayr, who had recovered fully, and the others: Jarown, Nigilin, Arnin, and of course the triplets. Despite Nigilin's insistence that he get more rest, Tesnayr felt it more necessary to attend to other matters.

Restlessness grew among the men as they had camped for the last week. The cook had suffered some mildly devious pranks and Tesnayr knew who the culprits were. He also wished to convey the disturbing news he learned while he was Galbrok's prisoner.

"I thank you all for what you have done for me," began Tesnayr, "Now there are matters to be discussed. First off, our cook has complained again that some persons keep moving his pots, pans, and food around the camp. Precious time has been lost because he spends it searching for his things."

Nedis smirked. "Quite funny though."

"Usually walks right past it," added Nylin.

"Never finds them he does," chimed Nular.

Everyone, except Tesnayr, smiled. "You three," he addressed the triplets, "Need to stop these antics. This is an army and we have no time for such foolishness. Have you ever had any real responsibility?"

The triplets shook their heads.

"Well, now is your chance. It will sadden me greatly if you fail. I am putting you three in charge of discipline."

"Entertainment would suite them better," commented Nigilin.

"Entertainment," said Nylin.

"I like entertainment," added Nular.

"Much more interesting than discipline," chimed Nedis.

Tesnayr rubbed his temples. "Did anyone tell you that you are most annoying at times?"

The triplets gladly replied to this one after the other. "Often—"

"Even our mother—"

"—chased us with a plank of wood once—"

"—going to spank us she was—"

"—until we hid it from her."

"Ah the memories."

"Discipline," said Tesnayr stopping their bantering. "You three are going to discipline this army and you will do it properly. If I am dissatisfied in any way I will teach the three of you the meaning of that word, *personally*. Dismissed"

Nedis, Nular, and Nylin stopped grinning. The dangerous tone in Tesnayr's voice told them to not argue.

"Think maybe we should tone it down?" whispered Nedis to Nular.

"Yeah," Nular whispered back.

"Galbrok has joined forces with men," continued Tesnayr. "One particular man named Blynak. Their union seems to be a shaky one.

"This disturbs me, gentlemen. Never in all my life have I witnessed Galbrok aligning himself with so many men; especially those who are an obvious threat to him. But it appears the rumors we have been hearing for some time now are true.

"But there is another matter that coincides with this. Krulak was your man, Jarown, and he betrayed us to the orcs. Where does your loyalty lie?"

"How dare you," exclaimed Nelyn. "He helped rescue you! You've no right—."

Jarown cut her off. "He has every right," he told Nelyn. "I know what you are thinking, Tesnayr. You are wondering if I assisted in your capture, if my participation in your rescue was a ploy to earn your trust. The answer to both of those is no. The truth is I know Blynak. He used me like he uses many others."

"How well do you know him?" asked Tesnayr.

"Quite well," said Jarown.

"Tell me everything."

Jarown shifted his feet for a few moments before answering. He had been dreading this moment, but could find no way to avoid it. "Blynak is not a man to be trifled with. I served with him for a time and witnessed his cruelty first hand. In those days a brutal war had taken place in Belyndril.

"Blynak had amassed an army and attempted to overthrow the king of Belyndril. At first I joined the king's army with my friend Selnik. We were like brothers. But, life had other ideas.

"At this time, I fell in love with Nelyn's mother. We loved each other deeply, but her father chose Selnik to be her husband. In accordance with our customs, she married him. Bitterness swept over me and stained my friendship toward Selnik.

"Over the next four years the war dragged on and my resentment grew. Blynak wanted information. Information that Selnik had. Blynak has a unique ability of gathering important data and learned of my falling out with Selnik. So he sought me out and convinced me to tell him where to find Selnik.

"He promised that no one would be harmed, but it was another lie. He sent his men to convince Selnik to talk by holding his wife and child hostage. I tried to save them in the end, but arrived too late. They were both dead when I arrived."

Jarown glanced at Nelyn. "Because of me your parents, your real parents, are dead. I held your father when he breathed his last. Yours was the last name upon his lips.

"I took you in to fulfill a promise to a dying man."

Tears streaked Nelyn's face as it contorted in rage. She had always thought of Jarown as her real father and she never knew the circumstances surrounding her mother's death. "You are not my father?"

"No."

"You killed my mother?"

"Yes."

Nelyn marched up to Jarown and punched him in the face. Blood spurted from his nose running down his chin and dripping onto his shirt. "How could you!" she screamed. Two men seized her arms and held her back as she struggled to be free of their grasp. "You betrayed them! The woman you loved! Your only friend!"

"Get her out of here," ordered Tesnayr.

"I have been living in a prison of guilt since that day," said Jarown as Nelyn was dragged away. He placed his head in his hands.

"I hate you!" Nelyn's shouts continued to be heard as men hauled her to the far end of the encampment.

Tesnayr placed his hand on Jarown's shoulder. "I know this is difficult, but I need you to tell me everything you know about Blynak."

*   *   *

Nelyn wandered the camp in a solitary mood. Several days had passed since Jarown's confession. She attended briefings, but always her mind lay elsewhere. On a few occasions Nelyn lashed out at people for the most minor infractions, some which included not airing their bedding or laughing while performing their duties.

"Nelyn," said Jarown as he approached her.

"Go away," she replied.

"Nelyn, please," pleaded Jarown. "I am still your father."

"My father?" Nelyn closed the distance between them. "You are not my father. You killed him remember?"

"Nelyn."

"Get away from me. You are dead to me."

From beneath a tree Idæas observed their interaction. He watched as Jarown walked away, shoulders slumped in disappointment. His demeanor displayed the hurt Nelyn had caused him. Nelyn snatched a bucket with such force that it swung violently in her hands. She headed for the lake. Idæas followed.

Without warning, he tossed a sword at her and yelled, "Defend yourself!" Idæas charged her forcing her to react. The bucket plopped on the ground as Nelyn dropped it and grabbed the sword thrown at her. They sparred for a bit before the elf disarmed her. "You fight like you have never held a sword before. Try again."

Within moments, Idæas disarmed her again. Enraged, Nelyn picked up her blade and charged. With a flick of his wrist, the elf knocked her weapon from her hands.

"You cannot fight when you are angry," he said.

"It has gotten me this far," Nelyn spat.

Idæas pointed at her sword, which now lay on the ground. "Your emotions make your skills useless. Your anger, your depression, you must detach yourself from them. They have ruined you."

"You elves think you know so much. My anger is my own. It is all I have left."

"You think you are the first to be betrayed by one you love? You are young, Nelyn, and have much to learn. "

"And I suppose you plan to enlighten me?"

"I already have."

"Leave me alone."

"For centuries I have seen how men treat each other. They love. They betray. They commit some of the most heinous acts. But despite their faults, your race is capable of some of the greatest acts of compassion. One being forgiveness. Which act are you capable of?"

"And what would you teach me?"

Idæas held his sword in the air. "How to turn it into something useful. Think about it."

"What do you mean?" asked Nelyn.

"I don't think you're disciplined enough to learn." Idæas' remark had the desired effect.

"I will prove to you that I am disciplined," said Nelyn rising to the challenge.

"Really? Tomorrow. At dawn." Idæas walked away leaving Nelyn alone with her thoughts.

Nelyn stared at the gentle water of the lake. She watched as the light danced on the water's glassy surface.

"You are angered," said a male voice.

Nelyn jerked her head in its direction. The unicorn stood several feet away. "So it wasn't a dream."

"Why would you think it was?"

Nelyn said nothing.

"You are angered."

"Why are you here?" asked Nelyn.

"I appear when you need me most," replied the unicorn. "Such it was with your mother. So it is with you."

"But I never saved your life."

"No."

"Why didn't you save my mother when she needed you most?"

"I was there," said the unicorn. "But no one can save a person who chooses death. Your mother's only thoughts were of you. And so just as I was once your mother's guardian, I am now yours. And so long as you have that necklace I will find you."

Vague memories of her parents' murder filled her mind. Though hazy, the dam that had blocked them broke with Jarown's confession. "Why were you not there when I was alone in the cabin?"

"I told you. I only appear when you need me most. At that time, you had Jarown. Thus far, in all of you troubled times, you have had Jarown."

"And why are you here now?" asked Nelyn.

"I come with a warning," said the unicorn, "Abandon your bitterness before it consumes you." Once again the unicorn pointed his horn at her heart. "Keep it pure."

Confused, Nelyn absorbed his words. "Thank you," she said. "For saving Tesnayr."

"It was decreed that I should."

At that moment the cry of the phoenix sounded. Nelyn did not recognize it and passed it off as the nightly sounds of the mountains. "Decreed? What do you mean?"

"Any other questions?" asked the unicorn refusing to answer her inquiry.

"Do you have a name?"

"Banis."

Nelyn left Banis and returned to the camp with her bucket of water sloshing beside her. Many thoughts plagued her mind and she needed time to think.

Crickets filled the air. They chirped too cheerily for the unicorn's taste. "I know you are there. I can smell you."

Quesha stepped out from behind some brush.

"What are you doing here?"

"My mistress sent me," replied Quesha.

"Your mistress does much for her own ends. One day, you will be a sorceress. Do not neglect your duty to this world, or you will live an eternity of misery."

"Is that all?" asked Quesha.

"I have a message for your mistress. Tell her, to forget about herself."

"I do not understand it."

"That is because the message is not for you," replied the unicorn. "Now go."

Knowing the futility of arguing with a unicorn, Quesha wrapped her cloak around her and disappeared into thin air.

Vapor escaped Banis' nostrils as he snorted into the chill air. Gradually, he trotted away allowing the shadows to consume him.

Jarown sat upon a boulder staring at the stars in the crystal clear night. His heavy heart ached for what he had been forced to tell Nelyn. For years he had avoided it, but fate had another plan. "I have failed you, Selnik," he said to the night air, "I have caused Nelyn unnecessary hurt." All the while, he remained unaware of the phoenix listening to him.

The next morning, Idæas bent down to pick up his saddlebags when a sword crashed into the tree above his head.

"Arm yourself," said Nelyn.

The elf stood up and faced the woman who had already drawn her weapon. Idæas pulled the sword out of the tree bark and held it before him in a defensive posture. He attacked Nelyn. She sidestepped and avoided it easily. Idæas attacked again and Nelyn blocked allowing the steel weapons to clang loudly. They fought like this for several minutes each blocking and attacking with expert skill.

"I see that some of my words have filtered through that brain of yours," said Idæas.

"I am a quick study," Nelyn replied.

Idæas swept his foot at her ankle and knocked her off balance. Nelyn staggered a bit, but quickly recovered. Her hard breathing told Idæas that he had challenged her. Finally, she brought her sword down upon him. He arced his upwards and locked both blades. For several moments they remained in that posture as beads of sweat dotted each of their brows.

"I believe we should call this one a draw," said Idæas.

"Agreed," replied Nelyn.

They unlocked their swords and relaxed. "You are a skilled swordswoman. You are good, but I can teach you to be magnificent."

Nelyn's face darkened. "I've been well trained."

"True, but a wise warrior never stops training, nor does he cease to learn. You have learned the sword. You have yet to learn to use this," Idæas pointed to Nelyn's forehead, "And to control this." Idæas pointed at Nelyn's heart.

"Will you teach me?" asked Nelyn.

"Yes."

Each day for weeks, they sparred whenever they had a spare moment. At times the two attracted spectators within the camp. Even Arnin and Tesnayr enjoyed the show while the triplets took bets.

Chapter XI
Winter

"How long are we to remain here?" demanded Arnin of Tesnayr.

"As long as is necessary," replied Tesnayr, "We will stay here until winter has passed."

"We have been here for two months. A party of orcs passed through these mountains and we did nothing. Since the day you were captured we have not engaged them, even when they were nearby and the odds in our favor."

"What are you implying?" inquired Tesnayr with an edge to his voice.

"It is as though your courage has left you," said Arnin. "You are not the man I freed from King Slyamal's prison."

"How dare you," said Tesnayr, "I have been fighting these beasts—"

"I am not troubled by your past. My only concern is what you plan to do with the present. Orcs are hiding in the mountain. They have been there for nearly three weeks. We should attack them before they are aware of our presence."

"You are dismissed," said Tesnayr ending the conversation.

Arnin stormed out making one last comment. "They would not hesitate to kill you. Why do you hesitate?"

Tesnayr glanced at Nigilin who stood silently in a corner. "You are unusually quiet."

"Arnin is right," said Nigilin in a manner that commanded attention.

Anger flushed Tesnayr's face. "You have never disagreed with me before."

"I understand bedding down for the winter. Even the orcs have been forced to delay their plans because of the fierce winter storms that have ravaged the land. But when the orcs camp so close to us we cannot risk letting them be. Turyn and the fairies bring you reports each day regarding their whereabouts. Yet, you do nothing."

"What are you suggesting?"

"Something is bothering you, Tesnayr. It has imbedded itself in your very soul. I had thought that you had left it behind the day we left for Drynelle. The fear of your past haunts you still."

"I am not a coward!" shouted Tesnayr slamming his fist on the table.

"I am not questioning your courage." Nigilin headed for the tent flap preparing to leave.

"I never left it behind," Tesnayr said so softly that Nigilin barely heard him.

Nigilin stepped closer.

"Being captured by the orcs again, reminded me of my home. I saw men working with the orcs. And I could not decide what disgusted me the most. It is the same story all over again."

"Then, give it a different ending," said Nigilin.

"What do you mean?"

"Some people are here to bring stability to the world. They lead fairly insignificant lives performing the mundane tasks required by us. They raise their families and leave with hardly a mark on the world. But, others are here for a greater purpose. They tread the unmarked paths.

"Your homeland may have been destroyed, but you survived. You, Tesnayr lived. And now the orcs threaten the very land whose very shores you washed up on. Coincidence?

"What beats in that chest of yours, Tesnayr? Is it fear? Or is courage? You must be what others are unable to become."

"I am no leader," said Tesnayr. "Sometimes I sense anger, as though it is locked away and I cannot touch it. For a long time pieces of me have been missing. I am not the man you think I am. I have no courage to attack the orcs in these mountains. I fear losing what bit of humanity I have left. I am plagued by my past. It haunts me even when I sleep."

"My father once told me about man's quest for silent snow: a peacefulness that many search for, but few find. You are searching for that now and yearn for it more than most. Search deep within yourself and discover who you are once again."

"I just want to give up," said Tesnayr.

"I know a thousand people who could give you a thousand reasons why you should leave now and go back where you came from," said Nigilin, "But I can give you one reason to ignore the other thousand."

"What is that?" asked Tesnayr.

"They are nothing more than cowardly fools." Nigilin squeezed Tesnayr's shoulder affectionately. "I will keep the men busy for now."

Fidgety, Tesnayr paced through the camp past the stares, the inquiries, and the people. He hiked further up the snow dusted mountain far away from everyone. He desired solitude.

Anxiety churned his stomach. His mind raced with bits of the previous conversation. A wheel of emotions turned his heart. Inwardly, Tesnayr debated with himself.

Tesnayr stopped. He peered into an ominous cave mouth that he had unknowingly come to. Its mysterious depth drew him in like a magnet. Slowly, Tesnayr took one step toward the cave. And then another. Something waited for him inside. Giving in to his sudden desire to explore the cavern, Tesnayr ignored the warnings within his mind. He took that final step into the hollow opening before the darkness swallowed him.

Tesnayr moved cautiously through the cavern. Water echoed through the tunnel as it dripped from above streaking down the moss covered rock. Pockets of light illuminated the interior as though he were expected. Only the echo of his boots on the hard cave floor filled his ears, blocking out the deafening silence. Suddenly, a dead end appeared.

Disappointed, Tesnayr slumped against the rough wall. As he did so a part of it gave way. Excitement burned through him and he tore at the soft rock with his bare hands amazed at how easily it crumbled. Gradually, a hole formed. Tesnayr pulled out his sword. He dug faster and faster stabbing the rock with such ferocity that the blade broke in half. Undiscouraged by this, Tesnayr continued to pick at it until he had a hole big enough to crawl through.

A huge chamber awaited him on the other side. Once through, a strange bird buzzed him. Tesnayr flung his arms up to protect himself as the bird pecked and screeched. Silence fell. Tesnayr checked himself for wounds but his skin remained unmarked. He looked in front of him. Before him a bright light emanated from the ceiling and fell upon a sword with a bird perched on its hilt.

"Come forward, Tesnayr *Deorai*," said the bird in a deep, resonating voice.

Tesnayr stepped closer confused as to how this bird could not only talk, but knew his name. "Do I know you?"

"No, but I know you."

"Who are you? What are you?"

The brilliantly colored bird spread its wings wide before answering. "I am the phoenix and I have watched you since before you came to be in the five kingdoms. But the real question is: who are you?"

"You said you knew me," replied Tesnayr, boldly.

"I said I know you," said the bird. "Yet you do not know who you are, so how can I know who you are?"

Tesnayr grimaced at the nonsensical statement.

"You are a wanderer, an exile. You are rootless because you are searching for the man you used to be. That man is lost, left behind in what was once your home."

"I left many things behind."

"Except one: your pain. Why do you carry it with you?"

Tesnayr's shoulders sagged as he thought about the question. "It is what makes me who I am."

"And who is that exactly? A man who believes in retribution?"

"No."

"No? Every day you engage the orcs do you not seethe with anger?"

"Yes...but," stammered Tesnayr.

"You wish to give back what they dealt you. You want the orcs to feel what you feel. You want them dead—"

"I—"

"You wish them the same pain that you have carried for so long."

"I—"

"You want to take from them what was taken from you."

"They—"

"You lead these people, but not because you wish to spare them the same fate. You do not care for them, only for yourself. Only for your own—"

Tesnayr contained himself no longer. The phoenix's words had awoken something inside of him that had remained dormant for so long that he had forgotten it still existed. "I do care! I have friends in this fight! Friends whom I love! Every time I see a child lying dead as his mother mourns him I burn from her grief. Each day I see families torn apart by this war my heart bleeds. I cry silently each night because of the havoc these beasts wreak upon people and the suffering they endure. Each passing moment I feel as though I am becoming the thing I hate most.

"Yes, I want the orcs to be punished! I want them stopped! I do not want these people to suffer the same fate that my kin did."

"So you do feel," said the phoenix. "Is it courage or fear in your heart?"

"How do you know—"

"I was there. I am everywhere. For months now you have seen me in the corner of your eye, yet you did not recognize me."

"And who are you? You question my motives, yet you do nothing? Where were you when my people needed you?"

The phoenix released a piercing cry and Tesnayr ceased his ranting. He froze.

"I was there," said the phoenix.

"How can I believe that?"

"Who do you think brought you to the shores of Sym'Dul?"

"The wind and the sea carried me there," said Tesnayr.

"I am the wind. I am the sea."

A memory struck Tesnayr. The very moment he had escaped the ship filled his mind as clearly as though it had just occurred. "It was you on the water. Why here? Why now?"

"I brought you where you are needed most," replied the phoenix sternly, but gently. "You cried out for help. I answered."

Tesnayr threw his broken sword across the chamber and sank to the ground. "What do you want?"

"Galbrok and the orcs are bent on conquest and will stop at nothing to achieve that end. These lands have harbored hatred for each other for decades and are so divided that they will easily be subjugated. You can help them. Prevent them from suffering the fate of your people. In so doing, you may find that which you desire most.

"I can free you, if you let me. But you must make a choice. You have been given a rare gift, Tesnayr. You have been given a second chance. What will you do with it?"

"What about the others? Why do they not get another chance?"

"I cannot answer that. I can only tell you about your life, not the lives of others."

"Why?"

The phoenix chuckled. It expected this question. "A man can only control his own life."

"I have done unexplainable acts. Things—"

"That is the past. Your guilt has made you a prisoner."

"Who am I then?"

"You are Tesnayr."

"I am a man and Tesnayr is just a name, meaningless."

"Not to me."

Tesnayr eyed the phoenix suspiciously. "For months I had only my nightmares for solace."

"Cast off your nightmares."

"I do not know how." Tesnayr crumpled on the ground.

"I can take you to a place where misery does not exist, if you wish it," said the phoenix.

"What will become of these people if I leave?"

"I think you know."

Nigilin's words echoed through Tesnayr's head. What was in his heart? "I won't leave them."

The phoenix smiled.

"But, I cannot do it alone," finished Tesnayr.

"You will not be alone. You have Nigilin. You have Arnin. You even have three aggravating siblings."

Tesnayr grinned wanly at that last bit.

"You have people all around you, Tesnayr."

"People die in the end."

"Death is certain. But how will you meet it? You asked me what I wanted. I offer you a choice."

"At what cost?" asked Tesnayr.

"None," said the phoenix.

"How do I know I can trust you?"

"How do you know you can trust anyone," replied the phoenix. "What made you trust Nigilin or the others?"

Tesnayr hated having a question answered with a question. A part of him wanted to scream at this strange bird, but he thought better of it.

The phoenix pointed at the sword on the pedestal. "This sword is the only one of its kind. It is a powerful weapon and answers to whom it wills. And here is your choice: go on as you have been and you will certainly fail, or take up this sword. But know this, if you do, it comes with a great responsibility. Do not take this sword lightly. You must try to achieve something far greater than Galbrok's death."

"What could be greater?"

"You will know when the time comes."

Tesnayr approached the sword.

"This sword is not yours to keep forever. Should you succeed in vanquishing the orcs, you must give up the power of this weapon."

"Give it up?"

"Yes. That is how it must be. Use it with a pure heart and it will serve you well. Use it for any other means and it will kill you.

"So which do you choose? You can leave now or strive for something far greater than you thought possible."

Tesnayr pinched himself to ensure that he wasn't dreaming. The small bit of pain told him he was definitely awake. Carefully, he lifted the sword off its pedestal and held it, studying it. Its gold sheath depicted the phoenix with other runic designs. Tesnayr freed the blade and found the same markings on the untarnished silver. The weapon was incredibly light and very sharp.

Magical power sizzled up his arm and warmed his body as he held the unique sword. The weapon glowed brightly filling the cavern with its light.

"It has chosen you. Use it wisely," said the phoenix. The bird flew away leaving so quickly that it took several moments for Tesnayr to notice that it had gone. Tesnayr sheathed the sword and tied it around his waist. Warily, he left the cave and reentered the world that he had briefly left behind.

Tesnayr slowly trekked down the mountain and back to camp. He pulled his new sword out of its sheath and looked at it again in the sunlight. Never before had he seen such an exquisite weapon. He swung it left and right swiping the air with its silver blade. It moved smoothly as though the sword itself knew what he meant to do.

Tesnayr spotted a branch hanging limply from a nearby tree. Curiosity took hold of him. He attacked the branch and the blade sliced easily through the wood in much the same way one would cut through cheese. Tesnayr stared at the sword and the branch that now lay on the snow covered ground in disbelief and awe.

"Having fun?"

Tesnayr swung around looking for the source of the voice.

"Up here."

Looking up, Tesnayr saw Turyn seated comfortably in the tree whose branch he had hacked off. "Must you always sneak up on people? Why can't you make some noise?"

"I'm a cat and cats are very silent," said Turyn jumping out of the tree. "Besides, what sort of scout would I be if I went around chopping trees and making whatever noise I could?"

"What are you doing here?"

"Nigilin became worried about you when you did not return and sent me out to search for you."

"Well, you found me."

"Where did you get that sword?" asked Turyn noticing the weapon for the first time.

"From the cave up there," replied Tesnayr. "I found it along with something else." Tesnayr's voice faded. He remained unsure of what it was he discovered in that cave. It seemed like a dream, but it was very real. "Why do you ask?"

Turyn looked at the sword and then back at Tesnayr cocking his head. "It seems familiar. I have never seen such a sword before, but yet it seems familiar. Something Idæas once said. The elves speak of a man, one who will come from far away, a stranger who will save them from a dark shadow. 'And he will carry a sword with a hilt of gold, with an engraved bird, and blade that never dulls.' Odd."

Turyn shook his head and trotted in order to keep up with Tesnayr's long strides. "May I ask you something, Captain?"

Tesnayr nodded his head in answer.

"We've been in these mountains for quite a while now and so have the orcs. Why have we not done anything? Do you have a new strategy?"

Tesnayr stopped walking. He sat down and motioned for Turyn to do the same. "If I tell you, will keep it a secret?"

"You can tell me anything in the utmost of confidence and I shall never reveal it to another."

"The truth is," began Tesnayr, "I have been afraid to. I feel alone."

The cat put his black paw on Tesnayr's knee and looked him straight in the eyes. "You have me," he said, "As little as I am. Besides, ever since I first met you I decided to make it my life's mission to annoy you. So you'll never be rid of me."

Tesnayr smiled unsure of how he should take Turyn's statement. "Thank you," he whispered. "I apologize if I never made you feel welcome."

"No need. It couldn't be worse than what those three hooligans do."

Tesnayr laughed.

"They keep trying to get me to wear that pink tutu again."

Placing a hand over his mouth, Tesnayr stifled a comment.

Together, they walked back to camp conversing freely. Tesnayr made a mental note to talk with the three pranksters about their treatment of Turyn.

Screams rose from the center of the encampment. Tesnayr and Turyn dashed for the source of the commotion charging past the cooking fires, tents, and blacksmiths. The entire area buzzed with excitement as more shouts and shrieks echoed around them.

Tesnayr paused when he reached the source of the chaos. Amidst the crowds of soldiers stood a terrifying creature that had never been seen in the five lands. The thing stood above the heads of every man there. It glared at all of them as it gaged its mode of attack bearing down upon them with its muscles flexing demonstrating its strength. An ominous growl resonated around them filling them with fear.

Suddenly, the creature swiped at a group of men, its long claws tearing through the canvas material of the tents and marking the iron pots. It slashed again. Debris flew everywhere from the force of the beast's movements.

Nelyn charged it with her sword raised high. She had barely taken three steps when the creature's fist rammed into her lifting her off the ground and sending her flying several yards away. Air burst from her lungs as she slammed into a pile of crates.

"Nelyn," yelled Arnin. He ran for the creature with a spear stabbing it square in the chest. No effect. The thick skin of the beast snapped the spear in half. Disbelieving what just happened Arnin hugged the ground in time to avoid a deadly blow. Slimy drool dribbled over him as it escaped the creature's lips. Quickly, Arnin rolled away avoiding the stomping hind feet and their crushing weight.

Another blow from the creature's deadly swing sent men flying in every direction. Others gathered with their weapons raised unsure of how to kill the thing that stood before them.

Noticing a chain around the thing's neck, Idæas raced for it. He snatched a spike and drove it through the chain pinning the creature to the ground. Instantly, the elf ripped out his sword and slashed its leg. No mark.

The creature roared in frustration as it lashed out. Arms swinging and feet pounding the earth it flailed violently in an effort to free itself. Suddenly, it stopped. Teetering precariously, the creature crashed into the snow covered ground unmoving with Tesnayr's new sword protruding from the middle of its back.

Determinedly, Tesnayr marched up to the creature and ripped his sword from its flesh. Sticky blood dripped from the blade. He studied the body a moment not believing that it was there, another element of his past.

"Nelyn," Arnin ran to her and helped her up.

Nelyn sat up slowly trying to get her bearings. "I'm alright," she said. "What was that thing?"

"A niht'anda," said Tesnayr, "Stabbing it in the middle of the back is the only way to kill it."

"Do you think the orcs know we are here?" asked Nigilin.

Tesnayr picked up the chain that hung around the niht'anda's neck. "Not likely. I think this one escaped." He paced around the creature's corpse. "Nigilin, gather everyone. We have work to do."

Chapter XII
A Meeting Among Enemies

King Edrei's boots echoed around him as he paced the great hall of his keep waiting for the four kings to arrive. He had sent messengers to all of them requesting their presence. A horn sounded in the distance and seconds later a messenger burst through the giant doors. "My Lord, King Telinin of Belyndril has arrived."

King Edrei nodded in acknowledgement of the message. The messenger saluted and left. Edrei paced around his throne as he waited for King Telinin. He did not have to wait long. The king of Belyndril marched into the room followed by two of his guards. His muddied boots left deposits of muck on the marble floor and his red and silver cloak billowed behind him. His tunic bore the crest of Belyndril in magnificent gold thread.

"Your guards will wait outside," said King Edrei in greeting.

"Alone in your palace," replied King Telinin, "They will remain with me."

"That was not the nature of our agreement. I assure you that no harm will befall you whilst you are here."

King Telinin's mouth opened to argue the point but snapped shut when he reconsidered his actions. He signaled his guards to wait outside. "Why have you summoned me here, Edrei?"

"That shall be explained when the others arrive."

King Telinin laughed. "Do you really believe they will come?"

"You came."

"Yes, well, I nearly refused your request."

"Then why did you come?" King Edrei turned and faced King Telinin.

King Telinin did not answer immediately. He himself did not know why he had accepted King Edrei's summons. "Curiosity," he replied.

Another horn sounded. "Riders approach the gates," called the watchman. Again, a messenger arrived. "My Lord, the kings of MurDair, Sym'Dul, and Belarnia have arrived."

King Edrei took his place in front of the throne doing his best to command respect. He stared at the chamber doors as he waited hoping that the entire proceeding would prove valuable. King Telinin held his place directly below King Edrei. Three men burst through the massive doors barely giving them time to open. Shouting ensued as two of them argued. The elf remained silent and composed, his eyes darting about.

"Gentlemen," greeted King Edrei.

The arguing ceased and they all gathered near him.

"King Telinin. Punctual as usual," said King Slyamal, coldly.

Telinin remained silent.

"Well, well, well. I see you have managed to get all five of us here on peaceful terms. Tell me, Edrei, are you sore about losing the battle and I taking glory from the field?" chided King Slyamal.

"The only glory you took that day was the crown of stupidity," replied King Edrei. "We lost that battle because of you. Had you listened to Captain Tesnayr we would have won."

King Slyamal reddened. "Are you certain that it was not because of you that we lost?"

"Come now. Your flair for battle has always been lacking, Slyamal," said King Nalim in a mocking tone.

"How dare you," yelled King Slyamal. "I did not come here to be insulted by the likes of you, dwarf king!"

"You have allowed yourself to be insulted by claiming a victory that never occurred." King Shealayr spoke with a serenity that the others did not possess. "A foe in the night."

"Save your philosophy, elf. I heard that the orcs decimated the forests of Belarnia," spat King Slyamal.

"Not entirely," replied King Shealayr. "Tesnayr rescued Belarnia that day. The orcs have not returned. They have found easier prey."

"Prey," said King Nalim, "Is that how you think of us?"

"No, master dwarf. That is how the orcs think of you. Unfit to live, but worthy enough to be their slaves," replied Shealayr, calmly.

"If your kingdom is so well protected why have you not helped the rest of us?" questioned Telinin. "Belyndril is overrun. I am in exile and my people enslaved!"

King Shealayr regarded King Telinin guilelessly. "You never asked for my help."

King Telinin threw his hands in the air. "Oh, I never asked. You make it sound so simple."

"It is that simple," replied Shealayr. "I have my own borders to protect, Telinin. Why should I aide a man who claims that the elves are his sworn enemy?"

Telinin's temper boiled. "Such a well-reasoned argument. Perhaps it never occurred to you that helping the rest of us would ensure the protection of your own borders."

"From the orcs, but not from you," replied Shealayr. "You expect help when you yourself only give aid when it is rewarded. Of course, your antics are not as bad as some." King Shealayr glanced in King Slyamal's direction.

King Slyamal caught the look and went livid. "My antics? How can you expect me to aid you when my own borders are under attack? Until I ensure that they are safe, you will receive nothing from me."

"And you are doing a magnificent job," sneered King Nalim. His sarcasm did not go unnoticed.

"Any gift from you is a curse," said Telinin. "Stay behind your borders. The world is well rid of you."

"Enough," thundered King Edrei. The room fell silent. "I did not summon you to listen to your incessant bickering."

"Then why did you summon us here?" asked King Telinin for the second time that day.

King Edrei moved toward the other four swiftly and smoothly. "I summoned you here to discuss the problem at hand: the orcs. For months we have fought them and have lost time and time again. Each of us has been fighting two wars: the one in here and the one out there.

"You, Telinin, currently have your army split in two fighting MurDair and the orcs. Nalim declared war on Belyndril and Hemil four weeks after the first orcs arrived. I have lost the northern kingdom because I was forced to fight the orcs and Sym'Dul. And you, Slyamal, ignored warnings from your own people!"

Everyone glared at King Slyamal. He glared back.

"Until recently Belarnia was at war with Sym'Dul. Now I ask you: how are we to protect our lands and defeat the orcs if we continue to fight amongst ourselves? Our alliances never last more than a few weeks. The orcs are using our vices against us. They let us kill each other to make us easier to conquer. Our kingdoms have fought for five generations. Does anyone among us even know why?"

The five kings stared blankly at one another refusing to answer. None of them wanted to appear ignorant.

King Shealayr broke the muted silence. "I was there when it first began and ashamed to say that I do not recall the reason." His matter-of-fact voice caught them off guard.

Everyone hung their heads. If the elf did not know how the fighting began, how could they continue it? But though they were all shamed by his words, a lifetime of fighting is hard to shake off.

"This Tesnayr you spoke of earlier," said King Telinin, "I have heard his name before."

"Captain Tesnayr as he prefers to be called. No one knows anything about the man, except that he came from across the seas. He has formed his own army to fight these orcs. He has won every engagement except one. He was betrayed then," said King Shealayr.

"I heard that the orcs captured him," said King Nalim.

"He escaped," commented King Edrei.

"And gone into hiding," said Shealayr.

"He allows any to join his ranks including women," spat Slyamal.

"Nelyn of Belyndril," said Shealayr endearingly. "She is a remarkable woman and I would not wish to confront her in battle."

"How is it that so much is known about him?" asked Telinin, "Even the dwarves know his name."

"The people sing of his deeds," replied King Slyamal.

"Yes, and the wind carries many things. It has long been believed among the elves that a stranger from the sea would unite the five kingdoms. The voice on the wind foretells it," said King Shealayr.

King Slyamal laughed. "Spare us your mysticism," he scoffed. "The wind does not speak and your prophecies are meaningless."

King Shealayr smiled at Slyamal's skepticism. "Yet here we are. Five kings united on common ground discussing a stranger who may be able to assist us."

"Prophecy or not," injected Edrei, "We have a problem and Tesnayr may be the only man who can provide a solution. If he is willing."

"He may not be. Not after Slyamal's betrayal," commented Nalim.

"Must we start on that again?" stormed Slyamal.

"You gave him your word! And you broke it," said King Edrei. "You are a weasel of a man. The orcs have more honor than you."

"I do not have to listen to this." King Slyamal stormed toward the exit prepared to leave.

"Before you walk through those doors," King Edrei stopped him, "Consider this: You will be on your own and may find yourself no longer the King of Sym'Dul."

King Slyamal stood in midstride for several seconds mulling over Edrei's words. He turned and slowly walked back to the others. "And where might we find him?"

"He was last reported to have left the Black Mountains. No one knows where he went," said King Edrei.

"Then why are we discussing this if no one knows where he is?" King Slyamal asked irritably.

"I know where he is," came a silvery, musical voice. The five men turned toward the far corner of the great hall where the sorceress Ernayn stepped out from the shadows.

"How long have you been standing there?" inquired Edrei.

"Long enough," replied Ernayn.

"Then tell us. Where is Tesnayr?" asked Telinin.

Ernayn circled the five kings eyeing them. She kept the hood of her cloak positioned so that only her face showed. "He is encamped deep within the Perili Mountains for the winter, as are the orcs, far north of here. But who among you will go?"

"Go? Go where?" asked King Telinin.

"Go talk to him, of course," replied Ernayn.

"I will go," volunteered King Nalim. "Perhaps a stranger can persuade the man to assist us."

"Perhaps we shall all go," suggested King Telinin.

"That may make him wary of our intentions," said King Edrei.

King Shealayr stepped forward and with a tone of finality said, "I will go. Tesnayr knows me and I believe he trusts me."

"What makes you so certain?" asked King Nalim, suspiciously.

"One of my elves is with him. Has been these many months," replied Shealayr.

"You treacherous elf. Formed a secret alliance with him," accused Nalim.

"None at all. He helped save Belarnia and I merely returned the favor. I knew that one day we would meet again."

"How long will it take you to find him?" asked King Edrei.

"By the next full moon if the sorceress provides me with a more detailed description of his whereabouts. Otherwise, I cannot say."

"I have told you the area. It is for you to discover the exact location. Consider it a test of your resolve," said Ernayn. "I will send my pupil with you. She knows those mountains and will ensure that you reach Tesnayr's camp safely."

"Preposterous," yelled King Slyamal. "Trusting our fate to a man whose origins are unknown. He will bring destruction and—"

"Silence!" roared Ernayn. She moved over to Slyamal and looked him square in the eye. "You are right to fear meeting him again, King Slyamal, for he will not be pleased to see you and remembers your deed well. You will remain here and your fate will be that of this man. Save what honor you have left before you lose that which is most dear!" Ernayn disappeared into thin air as her words echoed through the chamber.

"It is settled then," said King Edrei. "Shealayr, you will find Tesnayr and bring him here. If he agrees he will lead all our armies. We shall await your return."

King Shealayr left. He found his horse outside with Quesha waiting beside it packed and ready to go.

Back in the great hall only King Telinin and King Edrei remained. "Do you really believe he will come?" asked Telinin.

"I don't know," replied Edrei. "I sincerely hope he does, for all our sakes."

King Telinin left the chamber. He marched through the hallways towards his bedchamber hoping to get some rest. Rest was to be put on hold as King Slyamal cornered him. "Slyamal," sighed King Telinin, "I am not in the mood."

"Save your protests. I am here about my daughter."

Understanding King Slyamal's sudden appearance, King Telinin calmed down. Though he did not care for Slyamal, Telinin liked Jenel and had hoped to form a union between her and his son. "She arrived safely in Belyndril. I plan to head back there in the morning."

"But the orcs, have overrun it."

"They have not reached La'nar. I assure you, your daughter is safe."

A messenger arrived interrupting their conversation. "King Telinin, this just arrived for you."

Telinin took the parchment from the man and dismissed him. He broke the seal and read it in the lamplight. "Oh no," he breathed.

"What? What is it?" demanded King Slyamal.

"La'nar is in flames. Your daughter has disappeared."

*   *   *

Deep within the Perili Mountains rested Tesnayr's camp. Tesnayr busied himself with making the daily inspections, unaware that a decision had been made regarding him and his path in life. In fact, at that very instant, he had come across the three people who annoyed him the most. Nedis, Nular, and Nylin hid behind a boulder waving a piece string back and forth. They wore huge smiles on their faces as they tossed out the string and waited. Tesnayr walked behind them and cleared his throat. "Captain," they said in unison.

"What are you doing?" Tesnayr asked calmly.

"Cat fishing," replied Nylin.

"Cat fishing? At this hour?" Tesnayr noticed Turyn approaching the string. Using Tesnayr's distraction the cat picked it up in his mouth and carefully pulled it around the boulder paying extra care so as not to tug it.

"Yes, Captain. This is always the best time to catch a catfish," said Nular.

Tesnayr crossed his arms and a stern look filled his face. "How is it you plan to catch fish when you are on dry land? Isn't it easier to go down to the river?"

"These fish don't swim," said Nylin.

"Fish that do not swim?"

"Well, this particular catfish does not require water," Nedis chimed in.

"Uh huh," said Tesnayr, suspiciously. "Your story has a fishy aroma to it. You three wouldn't happen to be playing a prank on anyone now would you?"

"Of course not, Captain."

"Gave it up we did."

"For the moment."

Tesnayr eyed Turyn. He had just finished his plan and padded away. "You boys might want to be careful when catching catfish. They tend to be tricky. Sometimes you end up being the one on the fish hook. As it is, Arnin requires your presence. Report to him immediately." Tesnayr left the three brothers and slipped behind a tree so he could watch.

Nedis, Nular, and Nylin all stood up immediately only to find that their feet had been tied together with the string causing them to tumble over. They landed on top of one another amidst a series of grunts and groans. "That blasted feline! He used our own string against us," Nedis cried out.

"If you ask me, I'd say that the Captain was in on it," commented Nylin.

The other two agreed with Nylin. They spent several minutes straightening themselves out while removing the string from around their ankles.

Tesnayr chuckled to himself as he watched. The three jokesters got a taste of their own medicine, he thought to himself.

"Having fun?" Sarwyn stood behind Tesnayr with a displeased expression.

"Sarwyn," said Tesnayr. "You have news for me?"

"La'nar burns," said Sarwyn. "It has fallen to Galbrok with the help of Blynak. You seem unsurprised."

"I half expected it," said Tesnayr. "Where is Serein?"

"Watching the orc encampment near here. They have not noticed the missing—"

"Niht'anda." Tesnayr pondered the news. "I need you and your sister to keep a sharp eye on the orcs' movements. One of you must spy on them in Sym'Dul. The other must keep me informed of their movements in Belyndril and MurDair."

"As you wish," said Sarwyn.

"Why are you and your sister here?" asked Tesnayr. "Why did you offer your help?"

"Our queen commanded it."

"Queen?"

"Fairies are not governed by the same laws as the other races. But events in this world do affect us. And I think she is glad to be rid of us."

"Why's that?"

"You have three perfect examples right there." The fair pointed at the triplets who had finally managed to disentangle themselves. "I'll be going now."

"One other thing," said Tesnayr, "I need a way to call you and your sister, should I need you."

Thoughtfully, Sarwyn bent down and scooped up a handful of leaves that had not been buried by the snow. She stood erect and raised her hand above her head releasing the leaves. Delicately, they floated in the breeze. "Duit'angen gachi," she whispered and disappeared.

Tesnayr shook his head committing the words to memory. *Can't they ever give a straight answer?*

Chapter XIII
In the Mountains

Arnin entered the tent where Tesnayr, Turyn, Nigilin and Jarown had gathered. "I thank you all for coming," said Tesnayr. "Turyn informs me that up the mountain, not far from here lies an orc encampment. This report has been validated by Sarwyn. Like us they have bedded down for the winter. These winter storms have made it impossible for them cross the mountain pass into Belyndril. We are going to give them a warm welcome."

"The orcs have camped three hundred feet underneath a precipice covered with icicles and snow. The slightest noise will send it falling on top of them," said Turyn.

"That will make our job easier," commented Arnin.

"Perhaps," said Tesnayr, "The orcs know nothing of snow and ice. They have none of it in their own land and remain unaware of its dangers. But do not underestimate them."

"Nelyn is there now with Nedis and five others," said Nigilin. "They have placed the rocks in position."

"Their presence remains unknown?" asked Tesnayr.

Nigilin nodded in answer.

"She will do her job," said Jarown sensing Tesnayr's doubt. "She has never failed."

Tesnayr drew a map. "Here is the overhang of snow and icicles. Above it Nelyn and Nedis have placed a pile of rocks the size of this tent. They have rigged it so that a person sitting a couple hundred yards below it can release them."

"Won't it kill him?" asked Arnin.

"No," replied Nigilin, "The ensuing avalanche will fall away from him towards the east."

"We will attack the east end of the camp," said Tesnayr, "That puts us in the path of the avalanche. We will draw the orcs there putting them in its path as well and keeping their attention away from Nedis as he releases the rocks. Once he gives the signal, we need to get out of there."

"It does not take long for snow and ice to fall three hundred feet," said Jarown.

"No, it doesn't," replied Tesnayr. He knew that this mission was as much a suicide mission as a strategic one. "If we do not do this, then, when the pass clears, the orcs will enter Belyndril providing reinforcements to the ones already there."

"When do we leave?" asked Nigilin.

"Sundown," replied Tesnayr.

"Where are the two fairies," asked Arnin.

Tesnayr smiled. "I sent Sarwyn to Belyndril and Serein to Sym'Dul. They are gathering information about the situation in both places. They will give weekly reports."

Jarown chuckled at Tesnayr's last statement. He knew that Tesnayr could give them a time limit, but the fairies did not always abide by it. "It is the nature of a fairy to be unpredictable."

"If only they were less so," said Tesnayr.

*   *   *

Nedis paced through the snow awaiting the arrival of Tesnayr's men. Anxiety ate at him. Nedis had never been so anxious before. Perhaps it was because he was to pull the rope releasing the pile of rocks. This was one time in his life where he wished that he had no brothers as they would be in the path of the falling rock and snow.

"If you keep pacing much longer, you will burn through all that ice," said Nelyn. She sat by the weak fire with the other five soldiers. "If you do not wish pull that rope, I can assign another the task," she told him privately.

"Whether I release the rocks or not will not change the fact that my brothers will be in their path," replied Nedis. "We treat life like a joke. Constantly playing pranks on one another. Even in battle we manage to find something to laugh at. But this is one time where it isn't so."

"You will get through this. You all will."

Everyone turned as the crunching of snow hit their ears and people appeared out of the fog. The others had finally arrived.

"It is time," said Nelyn.

"Report," said Tesnayr.

"The orcs are below. They know nothing of our presence," said Nedis.

"Get in position," Tesnayr told him. "The rest of you come with me."

"Look at our brave little brother," said Nylin chiding his brother. "He is whiter than the snow."

"You'd think he met a ghost," added Nular.

"Cheer up, brother, we shall fight valiantly to our deaths," said Nylin.

"Death might not want us. Too much trouble we are," chimed Nular.

Nedis chuckled at his brother's comments. "Just come back."

Tesnayr studied the orcs. Undisturbed by the cold, they moved about performing their duties methodically. Smoke spiraled from unattended fires. Once again, Tesnayr found himself amazed at their lack of concern over being attacked.

He motioned for everyone to file past into the clearing directly below the proposed avalanche. Quickly, yet silently, men crept over the snow hiding among mounds of ice and taking care to not make a sound. Taking one last glance at the orcs, Tesnayr took his place among his men.

Arnin blew his horn capturing the orcs' attention. Immediately, the beasts snatched their weapons and charged toward the noise yelling and screaming as they went. Their heavy boots thumped in the snow warning every one of their approach.

"Brace yourselves," yelled Tesnayr.

The orcs crashed upon them. Clanging steel filled the mountain air. Tesnayr dove out of the way of an approaching orc slamming into the icy ground. He gripped his sword tightly feeling its power. Flipping himself over, Tesnayr rammed his blade through the beast. "Keep them busy," he ordered.

Nelyn swerved and dodged the orcs that came her way. Practicing a move that Idæas had taught her, she cut off the head of one and kneed another in the groin. Nelyn quickly turned sweeping the foot of the orc out from under it before jabbing her sword into the back of its neck.

Pain rocked her as something slammed into her back. Nelyn crashed into the snow. Recovering quickly, she rolled onto her back ready to defend herself. A harsh yell filled her ears. Out of nowhere Jarown appeared charging the orc, swiping his weapon across its stomach.

Jarown helped her up. Nelyn said nothing as she retrieved her sword and dove back into the fight.

Orcs poured over the ridge unaware of the danger looming above them. "Group them together," yelled Nigilin.

Archers released arrows forcing the orcs to mesh together, congregating underneath the overhanging ice and snow.

"Now," shouted Tesnayr.

Instantly, his men darted away. They fled over the snow leaping over obstacles disappearing from view. Confused, the orcs stared after them.

Nedis watched from his vantage point awaiting Tesnayr's signal. Concealed in the snow he rubbed his palms together to warm his stiff fingers. They tingled. Time edged slowly past. He hated waiting. Eagerly, he watched the battle hoping his two brothers remained unharmed. Then he heard it: "Now!"

Quickly, Nedis slipped from his hiding place knife in hand. He sawed through the rope that bound the rocks in place. A slow rumble began as the rocks ground against each other before careening downhill carrying the snow and ice with them. The roar grew to a thundering storm. Instantly, the entire mountainside had fallen away toward the people below.

The orcs looked up in time to see the onslaught of snow, but it was too late. Scrambling in all directions, they scurried out of the way. The wave of rock and snow crashed upon them crushing any in its path. Horrific screams escaped the orc's throats as the avalanche swept them off the ledge and into the abyss below.

Tesnayr watched with a stony face. Hand on sword he waited until certain that his plan had worked. One less group of orcs, he thought. "Let's move," he ordered.

Nedis hurried down the mountainside to where he was to meet the others. Suddenly, his shoulder stung as warm blood oozed from a protruding arrow. He had little time to register the wound as an orc jumped in front of him. Nedis raised his fist blocking the blow just in time. The orc jabbed at his knee. Nedis dodged, but his foot slipped on ice causing him to fall. Leering over him, the orc raised its weapon.

Determined not to die, Nedis gripped his sword and swung it in front of him catching the orc off guard as he sliced its throat. Gripping the black hole in its throat, the orc collapsed.

Nedis lay in the snow breathing hard. As the adrenaline subsided the pain in his shoulder burned violently. He broke the stem of the arrow off and pushed the rest of it through. Nedis rammed some cloth into the wound to control the bleeding. Grunting, he hauled himself to his feet and continued down the mountain to the others.

Nular and Nylin cheered when they saw their brother. Their cheers switched to concern when they noticed the blood pouring from his shoulder. They ran to him. Nigilin shoved them out of the way as he approached Nedis. Carefully, he removed the cloth examining the wound. He snatched a poker from one of the unattended fires. "Hold him."

Nular and Nylin grasped their brother's shoulders as Nigilin placed the red hot poker on the wound. Nedis screamed as the heat penetrated the skin cauterizing the wound.

Once done, Nigilin tossed the poker aside. "That will seal it for now. It appears we will be stuck with your pranks for a while longer," he told Nedis.

"I'll try not to disappoint you," said Nedis through gritted teeth.

"That's our brother," said Nular, ruffling his brother's hair.

"We need to leave," said Tesnayr approaching from behind. "Unfortunately the avalanche has blocked the road out of here. We have to find another."

"I know of one," said Jarown. "It is narrow and dangerous, but we can make our way back."

"Lead the way."

Book Two
Through the Fire

The world breaks and all is bleak.
My shoulders bear a great weight
thrust upon me by unseen forces,
causing me to hunch over.
A man aged before his time.

Through the fire I must tread.
Like steel tested and hardened
until its strength matches no other.

Heavy footfalls fill my ears.
They are mine, signs of exhaustion.
Tired and worn am I.
My years are the prime of youth.
My body aches. I must go onward.

Through the fire I must tread
'Til my courage is steeled
and my strength refuses to yield.

My path forks and a choice remains.
To take the road well-traveled
or take the other wreathed in flame.
Strength isn't forgotten on cobblestone.
My path is hard. I choose the fire.

Through the fire I must tread.
Only then will I pass the test.
There is no other way to strengthen me.

Chapter I
Venture

King Shealayr pulled his horse through the knee deep snow. Quesha walked beside him in silence. Quiet girl, he thought. She had not spoken a word since they had left the Keep of Edrei. Five days they had travelled. Shealayr had attempted to get the girl to speak, but all his efforts met with disappointment. Pulling himself from his thoughts, King Shealayr concentrated on the barely visible path before him as the road narrowed. Snow fell delicately from the clouded sky. A storm brewed. Reading the signs of the weather Shealayr knew that a terrible storm headed their way and could last several days, if not weeks, in these mountains. *Leave it to the Ársa Mountains to test you.*

Quesha walked ahead of him leading the way through the mountains. A slender staff filled her tiny hands as she used it to gage the depth of the snow. She pointed ahead indicating that they should continue forward.

Why can she not speak? Tightening his hand on the reins in an effort to ignore the cold, King Shealayr trudged onward. He wrapped his cloak tighter around him. A gust of wind rose up knocking him off balance. *Not good.* Straightening himself, King Shealayr continued onward listening to the snow under his boots with each step he took.

King Shealayr admired Quesha's ability to ignore the cold. Her cloak hung loosely around her shoulders as she walked lightly in the snow barely leaving any impression. The wind's chill hardly fazed her. Unhindered by the frozen world, she moved quickly, becoming irritated at the elf's slow progress. Her emotions never betrayed her, such was her tight restraint on them.

King Shealayr noticed a clearing up ahead. "We should stop there."

Quesha ignored him.

"I said we should stop and rest," Shealayr shouted over the wind.

"I heard you the first time," quipped Quesha.

"So you do speak," Shealayr said.

Quesha disregarded the comment. "We have little time and need to reach Tesnayr before he decides to move elsewhere."

"He is camped for the winter."

"That could change."

King Shealayr stopped upon reaching the small clearing. "Look," he said, "We won't reach him if we are dead. The horse is exhausted. I am exhausted. And whether you admit it or not, you are tired as well. We should rest for a few hours before continuing."

Relenting, Quesha dropped her pack. She dug through the hard snow until she found a rock. Tossing it between them, the stone burst into flame giving them a fire for warmth. "Rest quickly."

The elf huddled near the fire relishing its warmth. He rubbed his hands quickly by the flames as feeling returned to them making them tingle. Quesha plopped down across from him refusing to enjoy the fire. "You do not feel the cold?"

"I feel everything."

Now she talks. For five days she said nothing, and now she freely engaged in conversation with him. King Shealayr decided to keep it going not knowing when the girl would silence herself again. "You act as though you do not."

"Shivering accomplishes nothing. Therefore I choose to ignore the cold."

"Interesting," said Shealayr, "Are you sure you know where Tesnayr is?"

"Yes," replied Quesha.

"How do you know?"

"The wind tells me what I wish to know, much like it warns you of the weather."

"How much farther?" asked King Shealayr.

"We are almost to the Perili Mountains. Once we reach them, it should not be long before we run into Tesnayr. You should eat. We will be leaving soon."

With that the conversation ended. Quesha pulled out some jerky and nibbled on it. King Shealayr did the same. Perhaps she was right. The faster they moved, the sooner they could accomplish their mission. But finding Tesnayr was the easy part. Convincing him to come to the Keep of Edrei would be far more difficult.

A noise nearby caught their attention. Both King Shealayr and Quesha dropped their jerky and crept toward the sound. Just ahead of them were a group of orcs and two men. Only the small rise of snow protected them from being seen. An orc threw one of the men to the ground. "Filthy scum," it yelled.

Another poked and prodded the man with the point of its sword. The others grunted with glee, their way of laughing. King Shealayr's knuckles turned white as he gripped his sword, but Quesha's firm hand stopped him. She put her finger over her mouth signaling for silence. Gently, she scooped a handful of snow and blew it from her hand letting the crystals gently fall. Gradually, the snow crystals swirled around her picking up momentum with each turn until they went still.

"Kill them," Quesha ordered.

Mounds of snow burst from the ground twisting and turning until they resembled giant snakes. The snow snakes slithered effortlessly through the snow leaving no trail behind them.

Unaware of the danger, the orcs continued their game. The snow snakes slithered toward them with ease. Instantly, one snow snake erupted from the snow and wrapped itself around an orc. The beast shrieked and struggled in the tight grip. The snow snake held on squeezing more tightly until the orc went limp before hauling the beast beneath the snow and disappearing.

The other snow snakes circled the remaining orcs. Bunched together, the orcs stared at their strange, new enemy. They slashed awkwardly with their axes and swords. Bits of snow scattered in the wind as they broke away from the snow snake bodies. The snakes continued to slither through the snow unaffected by the sharp blades. Hissing filled the air as the snow snakes spat ice in the orcs' faces.

An orc charged. A snake whipped its tail catching the orc in the middle and flung it into sharp rocks. The beast lay lifeless across the jagged surface.

King Shealayr watched in shock as the snow snakes tore through the group of orcs, picking them off one by one. Desperate, two of the beasts dropped their weapons and fled. Instantly, snow snakes crashed upon them. Sharp fangs of ice ripped through the leathery flesh of the orcs.

Shealayr leaned forward for a better look. A menacing growl alerted him to an orc sneaking up from behind. He whirled around only to receive a blunt blow to his stomach. The force knocked him to the frozen ground. Winded, King Shealayr rolled across the snow. He reached for his sword tugging at it with all his strength. Nothing happened. He yanked on his sword again, but the cold had made it stick to the sheath. Sensing victory, the orc leered over him. It raised its crooked blade. Suddenly, a snow snake appeared and swallowed the orc whole before bursting into an array of snow and ice and mingling with the ground.

Quesha appeared before King Shealayr. "You should have stayed by me," she said.

"What were those things?"

"It need not concern you."

Brushing himself off, King Shealayr went to the men that huddled in the snow frightened. "It is alright," he soothed, "They are gone."

The men slowly stood up.

"What are your names?"

"I am Felznic and this is Argur," replied the tallest of the two men. "We are in your debt."

"Where are you headed?" asked King Shealayr.

"To the Perili Mountains."

"So are we," said King Shealayr.

"They wish to join Tesnayr," Quesha piped in.

"How did you—we do—," Argur sputtered.

Quesha glanced nonchalantly at him. "I know many things." She surveyed the area studying the sky and falling snow. "You will join us. We will take you to Tesnayr," her statement was a command not a suggestion. Even King Shealayr dared not argue with her.

"Come," he motioned to the two men, "We have a ways to go before nightfall."

The two men gathered their meager belongings and trailed after King Shealayr and Quesha. Quesha took the lead again as she glided over the snow allowing the others to stumble through it.

Chapter II
A Daughter of Kings

Tesnayr looked across the way at the people gathered on the edge of a precipice. They struggled to reach a rope bridge that stretched across the gorge. Snow fell from above them threatening an avalanche. Preoccupied with their predicament, the group remained unaware of Tesnayr and his men.

"They will never make it to that bridge before that avalanche starts and crushes them," said Tesnayr.

"Either that, or they will fall to their deaths," replied Nigilin.

"We need wings," commented Arnin.

Arnin's comment reminded Tesnayr of the Horn of Selexia. He pulled it from under his cloak and held it tightly as he watched the group toil through knee deep snow and against the fierce wind. If he sounded the horn help would come, but it could also start the foreboding avalanche and harm those people.

"Arnin, choose five men and follow me across," ordered Tesnayr. "Nigilin, find a way to stabilize that bridge."

"What of the others?" asked Nigilin.

"Standby for casualties," replied Tesnayr.

Within minutes Arnin had five men ready to cross the bridge. They walked cautiously, well aware of how unstable the sagging bridge was. The bridge swung violently in the wind. Sliding in the snow and ice, they hurried to the other side as the rotted wood cracked beneath them.

"Use your ropes to stabilize this thing," yelled Nigilin. Quickly, men lashed cables around the supports of the bridge hoping that it would hold.

Hurriedly, Tesnayr approached the group that fumbled along the icy trail. A big, burly man confronted him. "We've come to help," he said.

"Let him pass," said a woman.

The man stepped aside.

Tesnayr surveyed the group. It consisted mostly of women and children, some elderly and a few men attempting to help those who had difficulty walking. Frowning, Tesnayr knew they were mostly refugees. "Help get these children across."

Arnin nodded and motioned for the other five to follow. Each of them picked up a child and carried them through the snow to the bridge. "We need to hurry," said Tesnayr to the woman, "That snow won't hold for long." He pointed at the cornice of precariously balanced ice above them. Hastily, he heaved an elderly man onto his shoulders as he headed to the bridge.

With the help of Tesnayr's men, the desperate group of people stumbled slowly through the dense snow. The wind beat against them as the swirling snow made it difficult to see. The narrow path provided little comfort as each had to be careful of their footing. One slip and they all would fall to the unseen bottom of the gorge.

Upon reaching the span, Tesnayr noticed that Nigilin had steadied it as best he could, though it did little to boost his confidence. The rickety structure still hung precariously. "Take the children and cross now," he told Arnin.

Without delay, the other five soldiers heaved the smallest children on their shoulders and carried them across. Arnin then organized the older kids and ushered them onto the bridge himself. Halfway across, one of the ropes frayed. The bridge lurched.

"Quickly," yelled Arnin to the children.

Their feet pounded the rotting wood as they rushed to the other side where Nigilin and others pulled them to solid ground.

Realizing that the structure would not hold all of them at once, Tesnayr directed the people accordingly. "We can only cross two or three at a time," he shouted over the roaring wind.

Crossing in such increments took time for the thirty people to get to the other side. Tesnayr hated the slow progress, but had little choice. He ordered the woman who had spoken earlier and clearly seemed to be in charge to go first. She refused.

"I'll not cross until after the others have." She grabbed the nearest person and pushed him toward the bridge.

One by one they moved warily across the bridge to the other side. The structure swayed under their weight creaking each time a group crossed, threatening to collapse.

"Quickly," Tesnayr urged.

Some refused to budge. Others walked slowly, reining in their fear of plummeting into the abyss. With each passing minute clumps of snow dropped on top of them. The looming avalanche came closer.

After agonizing minutes of waiting, only Tesnayr, the woman, her bodyguard, and three others remained. The three stepped onto the bridge. At the halfway point, a slow roar rumbled.

"Run! Cross! Now!" yelled Tesnayr shoving the woman and her bodyguard onto the rickety bridge. Massive amounts of snow crashed around them. Desperate, the three in the center of the bridge dashed to the other end and reached it just as a rope snapped. Tesnayr paused. When the avalanche hit, it would wipe out the bridge and everyone on it. He noticed the fraying ropes and the bridge lurched as another broke. Gauging his options, he settled on the only one left to him. Tesnayr pulled out his sword. "Hang on," he shouted.

The woman and her bodyguard stopped, looking back. "Are you crazy?" yelled the woman as she wrapped the rope around her wrists.

Holding on with one hand, Tesnayr sliced the cable. The bridge tore apart. Part of it swung toward the precipice Tesnayr had just left, while the half he clung to crashed against the rocky side his men stood on. The avalanche thundered past missing him by inches.

Clinging tightly to the cord, he hung two hundred yards from the top of the cliff. The woman and her bodyguard were only twenty feet above him. Tesnayr climbed steadily taking extra care as bits of the bridge rushed past him. The ropes holding the bridge together continued to fray causing the thing to pitch uncontrollably.

Tesnayr knew they had only minutes until the entire thing fell into the gorge. Lurch! With no other option, he pulled out the Horn of Selexia and blew on it. A deafening cry echoed through the canyon bouncing off the sides causing more snow and ice to tumble downward. He hoped the dragon would keep her oath.

"Hold on," yelled the man to the woman.

Tesnayr glanced upward. The woman's hand slipped. Her bodyguard tried to catch her but she lost her grip and fell. Quickly, Tesnayr reached out and snatched the woman's hand as she rushed past him. He held on tight and she returned the grip. Straining from the effort, Tesnayr lifted her up so she could clutch on to the remains of the bridge. A rope snapped a foot above them. Tesnayr read the fear in the woman's eyes. Another rope snapped and the wood that he held onto crumbled.

Tesnayr and the woman plunged through the clouds and swirling snow toward the bottom of the chasm below. Suddenly, his body jerked as something seized him, stopped his descent and whisked him upward. The rippling noise of flapping wings filled his ears. Tesnayr looked up into the scaly belly of a dragon. Gently, the dragon carried him to the top of the cliff and released him from its claw. Another dragon placed the woman next to him.

"I am pleased that you remembered the horn," said Selexia.

"I am pleased that you kept your promise," breathed Tesnayr trying to settle his nerves.

Selexia growled softly. "A dragon always keeps its oath."

The woman caught her breath. She had lost her initial shock. "Thank you," she said to the dragon and to Tesnayr.

Selexia nodded in approval. "You are a noble woman. A daughter of kings. I am pleased that you have none of your father's arrogance and possess your mother's spirit."

People stared in awe at the two dragons. Fear prevented them from approaching. Satisfied that they were no longer needed, the two beasts spread their wings and took off into the curtain of snow.

Nigilin ran to Tesnayr and embraced him. Never before had he shown such emotion, but he was so glad to see the man that he lost control. Tesnayr gracefully accepted his friend's show of affection and assured Nigilin that it would take more than a fall to kill him.

The woman's bodyguard approached her. He wrapped his cloak around her shoulders and led her to the others that huddled nearby.

Tesnayr approached the group of people. "My name is Tesnayr," he said, "You are welcome to come with us. We will provide you with food and shelter. When you have regained your strength, you may continue on with your journey."

"Tesnayr," said a man from the group. He spat on Tesnayr.

Nelyn strode up to the man and hit him. The force knocked him back. "This man just saved your life and this is how you thank him?"

"He is the reason the orcs have burned our homes," retorted the man. "It is because of you they destroy our lands and slaughter our people." Murmurs of agreement weaved through the crowd.

Arnin stepped forward. "Tesnayr is the one with the courage to fight the orcs. He is doing what you have failed to do."

The man would not be silenced. "They were satisfied with Sym'Dul, but because of him they moved to Belyndril."

"Elsid? Is that you? You almost joined us," said Jarown as he approached the scene. "You once praised Tesnayr. You said that we needed to follow his example."

Elsid calmed himself. "Things have changed. Our people are enslaved. The fortunate ones are dead. They attacked us because you chased them out of Belarnia and they have been unable to conquer all of Sym'Dul."

"They attacked you because that is their way. The orcs make no distinctions between us or our borders. As far as they are concerned, anyone who is not an orc doesn't deserve to live," said Tesnayr.

"They moved to Belyndril for now, but Sym'Dul will end up just the same," said another man.

"Blynak warned us of you, Tesnayr," said a third, "He says that you were sent by the orcs to weaken us and gain our trust."

"Blynak will say anything to gain power! You know this. He is in league with the orcs, using them to further his own interests," countered Jarown.

"Perhaps you are afraid to admit your wrongs," yelled Elsid.

Nelyn silenced the man as she could hold her tongue no longer. "You blame Tesnayr for something that is of your own doing. The orcs attacked you and yet you did nothing. The signs were there. We all saw them. We knew some darkness had entered Belyndril, yet we pretended it wasn't there. Our lack of action invited the orcs to our land. If you want to know who is at fault look at yourselves."

"Jarown's daughter," sneered Elsid. "I am not surprised. You were always difficult to control. It is little wonder that Nathan perished."

A loud pop echoed across the crowd as Nelyn punched the man again. Blood poured from his nose.

Jarown started toward Elsid, but Arnin held him back. "She's right," he said, "You did nothing to protect yourselves. You did nothing when the orcs came and now you are paying the price. You are satisfied to let Sym'Dul and Belarnia burn. As long as your homes are left in peace you do not care about the rest of the world. But the wars of other lands have a way of reaching us all."

"Arnin," said Tesnayr growing weary of the bickering, "Ready the men. We leave in five minutes."

Arnin saluted and walked off.

Tesnayr turned to Elsid. "If you want to blame me for what's happened to you, go ahead. But blaming me will not solve your problem." Tesnayr turned to go.

"Wait," said the woman. "You cannot leave us here."

"Who are you?" asked Tesnayr, "You do not speak like one of them."

"My name is Jenel, daughter of King Slyamal of Sym'Dul."

Taken aback, Tesnayr stared at her. Of all the people to run into, it had to be the daughter of the one man he truly hated. "King Slyamal's daughter. I know your father well. You may come with us."

"And what of these people?"

Tesnayr did not answer.

"I will not go with you," said Jenel stopping Tesnayr in his tracks. "These may not be my people, but they are people none the less. I will not abandon them. And neither can you."

"They made their choice."

Jenel closed the distance between them and spoke so that only he heard her. "The one thing that makes us different from the orcs is our capacity to care for those we do not know, and our ability to help even those who despise us. If you leave them here, you are no different than the orcs."

"We leave in five minutes," said Tesnayr as he left.

Jenel turned to the refugees from Belyndril. "We will go with him. You may not like him, or believe in his methods, but he did save our lives. If it was not for Tesnayr we would be dead. No arguments. We cannot stay here."

Exhausted, the people around her offered no resistance. They gathered themselves and fell in line with Tesnayr's army following them back to camp where food and shelter awaited them.

Within hours of reaching the encampment a heavy blizzard bore down upon them. The snow pelted the skin of any who dared be in its path. Gales of wind howled past the tents threatening to carry them away. The horrible weather did little to negate the already pervasive bad mood of the people. The soldiers grumbled that the refugees refused to work and earn their keep, while in turn the refugees complained about the soldiers' gruff manner and high expectations.

Privately, Tesnayr shared many of the same sentiments as his men as the last thing he wanted was the responsibility of caring for civilians. The biggest thorn in his side was Jenel. A stubborn woman, she repeatedly pleaded with him to help the despondent refugees find a place of safety.

Tesnayr wanted her to go back to Sym'Dul once spring arrived, but Jenel refused to be left stranded with the evacuees. Strong willed like her father she reminded Tesnayr of King Slyamal. A memory best left forgotten. He had hoped that he was rid of the man, but Jenel remained a lingering reminder that one day Tesnayr would meet him again.

Infuriating him even more was the man who constantly stood by her side, Rybnik. Wherever Jenel went, so did he. He was her constant companion. Tesnayr felt outnumbered each time he tried to convince her that he could not take her or those people to safety. He did not wish to fight Rybnik and knew that the man would take Jenel's side. How could he make her understand that there were more important things at stake?

In addition, food ran low. The more people's stomachs remained empty, the more animosity they felt toward each other. Fights broke out between the two groups repeatedly. Faced with the difficulty of calming people's emotions and ensuring their survival through the winter, Tesnayr had a difficult choice to make.

"You called?" said Jenel approaching Tesnayr's command tent.

"Yes," Tesnayr replied, "Another fight broke out this morning. This is a problem that must stop."

"Agreed. I have asked them to be patient and appreciative of what we're given."

"But?"

"It isn't enough," said Jenel. "The people are starving. They are cold. There is barely enough warmth to see them through the rest of winter."

"They are not the only ones making sacrifices," said Tesnayr. "Many of my men have gone without food so that your people can eat. But now is the time for them to earn their keep."

"What do you mean?"

"I have drawn up work schedules," said Tesnayr, "Some of your people will work with my men to clean out the latrines, gather water, hunt, and do laundry. If you have any metal workers they are to report to the blacksmithing tent. In short, princess, the only ones who will eat around here are the ones who work. Furthermore, anything among their possessions that can be used for kindling will be confiscated and used for our fires."

Infuriated, Jenel railed into Tesnayr at what he suggested. "That is all they have left. You cannot take it from them. They are weak, exhausted."

"We are all hungry. I can take their things and I will to ensure the survival of us all."

"We came to you for help."

"Which is what I'm trying to do, but now it is time for you to help yourselves. It is time for all of you to start contributing, or you can leave."

"You can't—"

"I can and I will. There are too many mouths and not enough food. You will choose the most able bodied men for hunting and send them here. Here is a list of what needs to be done. You can decide amongst yourselves who does what, or I will choose for you. Within the next hour I want everyone to report for duty. You're dismissed."

Fuming, Jenel glared at Tesnayr. Never before had she been treated as a common soldier. "You do not order me around."

"You may be the Lady of Sym'Dul, princess, but here you are no better than the rest of us. Here, I am in command."

Jenel snatched the work schedule from Tesnayr's hands and stormed back to where the evacuees waited.

From a distance, Nelyn observed the proceedings between them. She hadn't meant to eavesdrop, but their voices caught her attention. She chuckled to herself when Jenel marched away. *Spoiled princess.*

"Nelyn."

Startled, Nelyn whipped around coming face to face with Jarown, the one person she didn't want to talk to. "Now isn't the time."

"It is never the right time," said Jarown, "How long are you going to keep avoiding me?"

"I'm not avoiding you."

Jarown gave her a piercing glare.

"I do greet you when we meet."

"You know what I mean. We need to talk about your parents."

"There is nothing to talk about," said Nelyn pushing her way past him.

"Nelyn," Jarown grabbed her arm, "I know there isn't anything I can do. But I never meant—I am sorry. I'd undo it if I could."

"You're right," hissed Nelyn, "There is nothing you can do. I can never forgive you for what you did. You killed them and then took me in as though nothing had happened."

"That isn't the truth and you know it."

"But you never told me the truth. All my life I thought you were my father, married to my mother. Then I learn that you are the reason they are both dead and only took me in to alleviate your guilt." Nelyn jerked her arm from Jarown's grasp.

"I have always thought of you as my daughter," he said to her back.

"I've no doubt that you are sorry," Nelyn said, "But don't ask me to forgive you."

*   *   *

"Why do you remain with them?" asked Tesnayr during another argument with Jenel. "They are not your people."

"I will not abandon them. They may not be my own, but they are people none the less. I helped these people escape when their village was attacked and I am staying with them until the end," said Jenel.

"And where are you planning to take them? This land is crawling with orcs," said Tesnayr.

"There are some caves north of here," replied Jenel.

"This is an army, not a bunch of nursemaids."

"You said that you do this to protect the people. Then help us get to safety. Are these people not also a part of this land? This isn't about some noble cause. This is about revenge. I know your story, Tesnayr."

"You know nothing," spat Tesnayr.

"Has your heart become so blackened by hatred that you will refuse these people? Do you not know the meaning of sacrifice? These people have lost everything. Until they are safe, I'll not go home."

"Sacrifice? I do not sleep nights because my men are in constant danger. They have given up their homes, their fortunes, and everything they hold dear for people like you. I gave up a chance for love, for happiness. I know sacrifice and I will not have my actions dictated to me by a woman who has been given all her wishes. Who has spent her life shut away in a castle and thinks that now is a good time to show her humility."

Jenel slapped Tesnayr so hard that it forced his head to one side. His cheek reddened as the sting slowly faded.

"You leave in the morning." Tesnayr walked away.

Jenel started after him when a firm hand gripped her by the arm. Nigilin appeared from nowhere. He pulled her back. "Let him be," he told her.

"Why is he so stubborn?" demanded Jenel.

"Why are you?" replied Nigilin.

"Well...because," Jenel stammered before silencing herself. "These people are sick and starving. There is no way I can lead them anywhere myself."

"You led them this far," said Nigilin.

"Barely. While we made our way here, the orcs picked us off one by one. But meeting you here tells me that we cannot go to Drynelle, which is where we were headed."

"No you cannot go there," mused Nigilin. He felt for the young woman and the responsibility she had taken upon herself. Yet, he also understood Tesnayr's sentiments. They were soldiers. But the heart of the matter remained that Jenel was King Slyamal's daughter and Slyamal's betrayal burned deeply within Tesnayr. "When have you last spoken with your father?"

"Not for many months, why?"

"Are you aware of your father's treatment of Tesnayr?"

"Where is this going? I have not seen my father since you and Tesnayr escaped. He sent me away to Belyndril for safekeeping."

"Your father pleaded with Tesnayr to help him rid Sym'Dul of the orcs. Tesnayr did, but your father did not honor the agreement. When needed most, he turned and fled."

"My father is not a coward," spat Jenel.

"Yet his actions remain the same," said Nigilin. "A coward he may not be, but a fool he is. A prideful fool. We lost the battle that day."

"I cannot believe—"

"But you do," interrupted Nigilin, "Your father was never a man to accept being humiliated especially by someone he views as his lesser. You know this. Tesnayr insulted him when they first met. Then, your father had to ask for his help, but his pride prevented him from following through. I see much the same in you."

"How dare you--" Jenel cut herself off. The stern look from Nigilin silenced her. She knew her father's failings. She knew them well. Much the same were within her.

"You sister Janine was a kind and generous woman who thought only of others, much like you mother. Try to be more like her."

Tears welled up in her eyes. Jenel remembered her sister. Janine died when she was only ten years old but her memory was never far away. "My father is not a bad man," said Jenel, "He loves Sym'Dul and wants to protect the people. He just doesn't—"

"Know how to go about it. I suggest you apologize to Tesnayr." Nigilin waved his hand cutting off any protests. "It will prove how you are different from your father and it will do you good. He will be at the far end of the camp. That is where he goes to calm down when angered."

"You know him well don't you?"

"About as well as anyone. He is a difficult man, but one well worth knowing."

"You served in the king's army," commented Jenel.

"Yes," replied Nigilin. "I gave everything for Sym'Dul and an unappreciative king." Nigilin left.

Jenel brooded over his words. Janine, she thought. How she missed her.

"My lady," said Rybnik as he strode up beside her. "The people are hungry and tired."

"We all are, Rybnik. They will just have to make do with what little we have. We will leave when the pass opens up."

"To Sym'Dul?   You know I am not welcomed there," said Rybnik.

Jenel brooded over that statement and what she had recently learned. If Sym'Dul had fallen, then a journey to Drynelle would be impossible. But where could they go that wasn't far? "The Keep of Edrei is south of here is it not?"

"Yes, my lady."

"Jenel," said Jenel, correcting Rybnik. She hated that title *my lady*. "Then that makes it closer than Drynelle. Perhaps we shall go there. King Edrei has always been a fair man. He will not turn away refugees. Go back to them. I have business to attend."

Tesnayr paced were he stood. *The nerve of that woman!* His blood boiled. What did she expect him to do? Leave everything and take her where she wished? Such a thing was not possible. After winter had passed the orcs would regroup and attack the other lands. Yet, Jenel had a point.

Tesnayr glanced at his sword a moment studying its rare beauty and unique construction. *Only a just man may use this sword.* The words of the phoenix echoed through his mind.

His shoulder strap had worked itself lose and fell away. Frustrated, Tesnayr yanked on it trying to rebuckle it. His meaty fingers refused to work properly and the smooth leather slipped between them.

"Here," said a gentle voice. Jenel reached up with her soft hands and gingerly secured the strap. "I want to apologize for my actions earlier. It was not my place."

Tesnayr pondered her words as his anger abated. "Trying to placate me?"

"No—yes."

"You had every right," Tesnayr reluctantly admitted.

"No I did not. I realize that you have an army to think of and I cannot ask you drop it all for me. I chose to help these people. It is my responsibility. When the pass clears I will take them to the Keep of Edrei."

"No."

"But—"

"You will not go alone," said Tesnayr. "We will take them together."

"But I thought—"

"You were also right," said Tesnayr, "I cannot truly say that I am helping people when I leave a bunch of them to die."

Chapter III
Listening

Drizzling rain formed a mist around Serein as she crept through the orc encampment. Her gown flowed around her blending expertly in with the damp and dreary surroundings. Deftly, her bare feet touched the soggy earth as she walked toward the command tent.

A noise alerted her of approaching danger. Instantly, Serein froze melting into the scenery. Seven orcs marched past oblivious to her presence. Serein slowly rematerialized and continued toward her destination.

A lone lamplight shone in the distance illuminating where she wished to be. She headed for the open marquee as voices spilled from it. Serein hunkered just outside next to a gnarled tree allowing its shadow to conceal her.

"Where is the supply line?" roared the growling voice of an orc.

"It hasn't arrived," answered another orc, squeamishly.

"It hasn't arrived? Did you bother to find out why?"

"No, commander," said the second voice.

"Then find out."

A man dressed in red strode into the meeting, his sword clinking by his side. "You asked for me?"

"Yes," replied the commander, "We have been here for over a month. Explain to me why we have yet to conquer this land."

"The dwarves are not easily found," said the man.

"You may have helped us take over your own kingdom, Blynak, but don't get too secure in thinking you are above reproach."

"I am here only to serve Galbrok," said Blynak.

The commander grunted. "What are you still doing here," he shouted at the other orc. "Get out!"

The lower ranking orc scurried away.

"I have never failed before," said Blynak, "I will find the dwarves' weakness."

"And yet you let Tesnayr escape."

Blynak's face flushed.

"At least there is a plan to deal with that loss. You better succeed, human, or Galbrok may grow tired of you." The orc commander left.

Fuming, Blynak swept his hand across the table sending maps, quills, and other articles flying before storming away.

A piece of parchment caught Serein's eye. Gently, she placed her hand on the slimy trunk of the tree. A leafless branch reached out wrapping itself around the parchment and placed it in the fairy's outstretched palm.

"Thank you," whispered Serein taking the paper. *A map.*

Serein hurried away diving deep within the forest away from the orcs. She released a soft whistle. The note floated upward through the trees carrying her request.

A soft flutter of wings sounded above her. Smiling, Serein put out her hand allowing a cardinal to land upon it. "Hello, my friend," she said.

The cardinal chirped.

Serein held up the folded map. "I need you take this to Tesnayr within the Perili Mountains. Let the wind guide you."

The bird chirped again before taking the map in its beak. It darted away flapping its wings as fast as it could.

*   *   *

Nelyn stood under a canopy watching the snow fall around her in swirls. Occasionally, the wind blew harder causing the snow to move horizontally. She had witnessed harsh winters before but this was the worst she had ever been in. The cold prickled her exposed cheeks. Sighing, Nelyn released a large breath and watched the cloud of vapor that formed before her. Such a thing always fascinated her.

"Thought I'd find you here," said Arnin as he approached.

"I needed to be alone," she replied.

"Here," Arnin handed her a cup of weak tea. "I assure you that Turyn hasn't been in it."

Grinning, Nelyn took the cup and sipped it enjoying the warmth as it moved down her throat and to her stomach.

"Why is it you and Jarown don't talk anymore?"

"I have my reasons."

"Nelyn, you cannot avoid him forever."

"I do not want to talk about it," said Nelyn, ending the subject. "Will this storm ever end?"

"It will eventually," Arnin said, "This is normal for the mountains. It snows for weeks at a time before the weather clears up."

"Belyndril was never like this."

"Well, this is good weather compared to the Ársa Mountains themselves," Arnin indicated the six tallest peaks within the mountain range. "On those it snows from the onset of winter until the beginning of spring and sometimes even in the summer."

"Too much snow for me. I prefer the warmth of summer and the green pastures and flowing trees. Everything is alive then."

"Everything needs its rest," said Arnin, "I like the crispness of winter. It makes me feel alive."

"It's quiet. Too quiet," Nelyn commented.

"It is the silence of man's soul so that you will appreciate the rebirth of spring." Idæas walked up from behind.

"What is it with you elves and speaking in riddles?" asked Arnin. "Always with you it's 'darkness reaches for us' or 'red dawn of treachery'. Can you not speak plainly?"

Idæas closed the distance between him and Arnin. "Not everyone can be as plain as you. You're wanted in the kitchens."

"I think he was being sarcastic," said Arnin after Idæas left.

Alone in the dark, Tesnayr sat on his cot rubbing his face. Tired though he was, he had not been able to sleep. Some time had passed since he and Jenel had come to a truce, one that he was glad of. Ever since, things had gone more smoothly.

Flapping wings caught his attention. A red cardinal entered the tent and landed on his shoulder with parchment in its beak. The bird dropped it into Tesnayr's lap, chirped, and flew away.

Astounded by the manner in which the fairies sent him messages, Tesnayr lit a lamp and picked up the folded parchment. It crinkled as he opened it. Instantly, the writing caught his attention as he realized its importance. It was not just any map, but one that marked every area the orcs had conquered and what they planned to take next.

Chapter IV
Spring

After several weeks the storms and gales of winter dissipated and the snow started to melt. The renewed warmth in the air indicated the impending arrival of spring. With it would come soggy weather and mudslides if they did not leave the mountains soon.

Tesnayr took stock of the current situation and supplies. Dismayed, he realized that everything had run low despite the hunting and gathering they did.

"You wished to see me," said Idæas.

"Yes," replied Tesnayr. "We need to head to Hemíl and reach it quickly. Which is the best route?"

"The best route would be through the Azul Plains, but we cannot go that way."

Slightly irritated by the elf's tendency to answer the exact question asked, despite the fact that he knew what was meant, Tesnayr tried again. "Why not?"

"Orcs have overrun the plains. They control Sym'Dul and Belyndril. Belarnia is safe for the moment and they have not had much luck in MurDair. Hemíl is their next target. If we leave the mountains we will be captured."

"Then, how do you propose we reach Hemíl?"

"We shall have to go through the Ársa Mountains themselves to reach it."

"The Ársa Mountains?"

"Yes. They are the tallest mountains within this range." Idæas pointed the peaks out to Tesnayr. "They are treacherous and it is a long road that goes through them. But there is little chance of the orcs being there."

"Can you be certain?"

"Certainty is impossible," replied Idæas, "But the mountains have claimed many men. They will not allow the orcs to roam freely."

"How long will it take to cross them?"

"Weeks if the weather holds. Maybe months. That I cannot tell."

"If the weather holds?"

"Though the winter storms are over, there will be a few yet and the spring melts will begin soon after. But that is the least of our concern as the road leading south through the mountains may be difficult to find."

"Difficult to find?" asked Tesnayr not liking where this was going.

"There is supposed to be an ancient road that travels along the mountain spine which we can use if we move quickly."

"Do you know where it is?"

"No one does. It is called the Indrev Tharob. It was built long ago, before the elves claimed Belarnia. No one has traveled it for centuries. But Elven lore speaks of it and using that I might be able to guide us to this road."

"So we are to pin our hopes on some Elven tales of some road that no one even believes exists?"

"Well, we could try the orc infested plains," said Idæas.

Tesnayr detested the proposition, but felt there was little choice. The elf had never lied to him before. "Is there no other way?"

"No, Captain."

"Very well. Prepare for departure," said Tesnayr. "We leave immediately for Hemíl."

"Yes, Captain." Idæas saluted and left.

Ordered chaos ensued as tents were torn down and equipment packed. The soldiers helped the refugees prepare for the trek through the mountains tossing anything considered useless or that would weigh them down. Within hours loaded horses and people trudged through the now slushy snow.

"He never leaves your side," commented Tesnayr to Jenel as they walked together.

"Rybnik is a dear friend," replied Jenel, "And he is my cousin."

"Go on," urged Tesnayr. He was curious about the man and wished to know more.

"Rybnik is very loyal."

"And yet he was banished from Sym'Dul. Nigilin told me," added Tesnayr upon receiving a stern look from Jenel.

"I suppose there is a reason you wish to know. Yes, he was banished. Ten years ago, when I was still a child, Rybnik and my sister Janine fell in love. She was only sixteen at the time. My father forbade their union.

"At this same time war broke out between Sym'Dul and MurDair. Rybnik fought but came home discouraged. Thinking my father a fool, he constructed a plot to have him removed from the throne. With my father gone, Janine would have inherited the crown since she was the eldest and my father had no sons."

"He planned to marry her and become king?"

"No," said Jenel. "Rybnik planned to marry Janine, but not to become king. He just wanted Sym'Dul to be great again and felt that my sister would be a far better queen than my father was a king. There were many who felt the same. But the plot was discovered. My father had sentenced Rybnik to death but Janine intervened. She pleaded with my father that Rybnik's life be spared. So, he relented and instead simply banished Rybnik from Sym'Dul.

"Soon after, it was clear that my sister and Rybnik would never be allowed to marry. He was exiled and she refused to leave with him. I think a part of her felt that Rybnik had used her and it gnawed at her. Months later she died of a broken heart. My father was never the same since. My mother had died in childbirth and then my sister was dead.

"I smuggled Rybnik into the city for Janine's funeral. We've stayed in contact ever since. Why do you wish to know?"

"It seems odd that a man who planned to betray his king, is banished, and then risks his life to protect the king's daughter," said Tesnayr.

"Not at all," replied Jenel. "After Janine died, Rybnik regretted his actions. He never forgave himself for her death."

"He cannot enter Hemíl."

Jenel faced Tesnayr, anger flushed her face. "What do you mean? He is with us. I'll not leave him behind."

Tesnayr held up a hand silencing her. "I only meant that if he does enter Hemíl, he may be imprisoned. He is an exile and most kings do not accept exiles."

Calming herself with a slow, deep breath, Jenel realized what Tesnayr meant. "I see. We will meet that challenge when it comes."

Chapter V
Dangerous Road

Quesha stood poised upon a precipice overlooking the mountain range. Her intense gaze studied the immense area, but it wasn't the peaks she saw, but something else. Gingerly, she held her left hand up feeling the chill wind.

Satisfied, Quesha turned back using her staff to steady herself as she climbed down the hill back to the trail where the others awaited her. Her feet glided through the powder snow barely leaving a mark. She stepped lightly on the ground in front of King Shealayr.

"Well?" he asked.

"There is change in the wind. I suspect we will meet Tesnayr sooner than expected," replied Quesha. "We should go."

Felznic moved closer to Quesha. "We need to rest. We're tired."

"You've had plenty of time to rest during the days we were forced to stop for the latest storm. We're leaving." She marched ahead of them not caring if they kept up or not. Readjusting his pack, King Shealayr motioned for the others to follow after her.

*   *   *

High up in the mountains the rag tag group of soldiers and exiles crept single file along the narrow ledge. Pebbles clattered as they rolled down the cliff face. Fierce winds howled around them chilling them to the bone despite the warm sun that shone upon them. The thin atmosphere made the trek difficult as many struggled to breathe from the exertion. Wheezing, they carried onward hoping that the elf knew his way through the mountains and eager for even a small amount of relief. Men carried small children on their backs. Others supported the elderly that had difficulty even walking.

A whistle broke their concentration. Everyone halted. Dismayed, Tesnayr looked out at the gorge below. The path had ended on the escarpment they were all on leading straight to the empty air ahead of him. Five crevices stood silhouetted against the abyss forming a straight line to the other side. *If it's not one thing; it's another.* Tesnayr bit his tongue to prevent himself from screaming in frustration. These people trusted him to lead them to safety, to deliver on his promise. He had led them to their death.

"I am sorry, Captain," said Idæas, "The trail ends here and picks up on the other side."

Of course it does, thought Tesnayr. He trusted Idæas' statement; the elf's eyes could see twice as well as any man. "How are we to cross?"

"We cannot," replied the elf. "We must turn back and find another way."

"We can't turn back. Turning back means we've failed," growled Tesnayr.

"I am sorry, Captain, but there is no going forward."

Tesnayr slammed his fist into his thigh. *All this way for nothing!* He couldn't believe it and detested his options.

Men moved aside as three others in particular inched their way forward. "Captain Tesnayr," said one of the triplets, "We can get you across."

"We have a particularly brilliant idea," said Nedis.

"Or an insane one," commented Nular.

"Yes, but where would the fun be if it wasn't?" smirked Nedis.

"Hear. Hear," said Nylin.

"What is this insanely, brilliant idea of yours?" asked Tesnayr.

Nedis stepped forward. "One of us can jump across this gorge using the crevices here. He'll take a rope with him and tie it on the other side while we tie an end here. Then we use that rope to ferry people across. We'll have to cross one at a time."

"Do you have any idea how long that could take?" asked Tesnayr.

"Well into nightfall," said Idæas. "This sounds like suicide."

"Where is your sense of adventure?" Nular chided.

"And just who would be dumb enough to volunteer for this adventure?" asked Idæas, dryly.

Instantly, the triplets all raised their hands. Figures, thought Tesnayr. He should have known. "Nular, you will go," said Tesnayr, "Where is a rope?"

Idæas pulled a silver rope from his belt and handed it to Nular. "Take this," he said, "It is ten times stronger than any you have and will stretch to any length you wish."

Nular tied both ends of the rope around himself while his brothers looped it around a giant boulder to use as leverage and create a pulley. Tesnayr and Idæas also took hold of the line. Then, Nedis and Nylin formed a sling with their arms and cradled their brother.

"Ready?" they asked.

"Definitely," Nular replied.

Precariously balanced on the ledge, the two flung Nular across the empty space of the first crevice. Nular grunted as he slammed into the ground on the far side. He lay there a moment before picking himself up. Turning to face his brothers, he waved exuberantly before continuing. Breathing deeply to calm his nerves, Nular sprinted two feet and leapt across the next crevice. His boots echoed on the solid rock as he landed. Teetering on the edge, Nular leaned forward and fell to his knees. The wind whipped around him. His hands felt numb from the cold, but he ignored it.

Nular stood up and eyed the third crevice gaging the distance. Rocking back and forth, he stepped and surged forward with all his might crashing into the next narrow precipice and rolled to the far edge. Desperately, Nular scraped his fingernails along the rock to prevent himself from rolling over the edge. Dust poofed as he came to a halt. Quickly, Nular rolled onto his back away from the edge. *Maybe this wasn't a good idea.* Nular cautiously stood up doing his best not to look down.

"Two more to go," he told himself.

He stared at the gap between him and the fourth crevice. It was bigger than the others. Steeling his nerves, Nular leapt with all his might. He flailed his arms violently as he jumped short, missing the far ledge. Fear engulfed him as he began to fall before crashing into a sharp rock that protruded into the air. Hanging on tightly, Nular calmed himself, forcing his rapid breathing to slow down. He glanced down at the wisps of clouds below him. Gradually, he looked up. The ridge lay a few feet above him.

Grunting, Nular pulled himself up. Sweat dripped from his chin as he inched his way to the top. He grasped the rocky side. His muscles burned with exertion. His foot slipped. Gripping the rock more tightly, Nular's hands burned as sharp rocks ripped into his skin. He slowly hauled himself upward. The closer he got to the ledge, the harder his heart pounded. Blood pulsed in his ears. Reach. Grab. Hoist. Nular repeated the process concentrating fully on completing his task.

Air wafted over him as his hand finally reached the top of the ledge. He seized the edge pushing with his legs while simultaneously pulling with his arms. Relief flooded over him as he lay on the flat surface staring at the sky. He still had one more to go before he reached the other cliff.

Nular faced the final crevice. His muscles weakened from climbing the rock face, Nular gauged the distance. Without a moment's thought he thrust himself across the last crevice. Nular landed on his knees. The howling wind reminded him how high up he was. Wasting no time, Nular heaved himself to the final cliff, landing safely. He untied the rope around his waist and wrapped it around a giant stone. Then, he waved his cloak to signal the others on the other side of the gorge.

"He made it," said Idæas.

"Tie more rope around this one forming harnesses," ordered Tesnayr. "We need to cross quickly. We'll send them two at a time."

"The rope may not hold," said Nigilin.

"It will have to," said Tesnayr. "It is midday already and we cannot stay up here past nightfall."

Tesnayr snatched Jenel's arms and pulled her toward a harness. "I'm not going first," she protested.

"No arguments," said Tesnayr as he fastened her in.

Idæas and Nedis pulled the rope that carried Jenel and one other. She gasped as her feet left the ground and she dangled in the air. Creaking, the rope slowly carried the two to the other side. Jenel's knuckles turned white as she gripped the rope. Sluggishly, she passed over the crevices, her feet brushing the tops of each pinnacle. Inch by inch they moved. Relief soothed her as Nular's hands pulled her back onto solid ground. He quickly helped her out of the harness before assisting the other man.

"Help me with the rope," he said to the man. They both grasped the cord and pulled it sending the harnesses back to where more waited to cross.

The day passed quickly as the people gradually made their way across the gorge. Two at a time traveled across the rope in harnesses. The agonizingly slow process wore on Tesnayr's nerves as he wanted to speed up the process. But common sense held him back. He knew that by even putting two on the rope was risky.

Bit by bit people made it to the other side. Nedis led them down the trail to a more level area once he crossed providing room for new arrivals.

Soon, the sun dipped in the sky indicating that there were only a few hours of daylight left. Frowning, Tesnayr motioned people onward until only he and Idæas remained. Tesnayr strapped himself into a harness while the elf did the same. "I hope the rope supports us," he said.

"A bit late to think of that," replied Idæas. "We will have to pull ourselves across."

Tesnayr went first. His stomach lurched as he let himself drop with only the harness holding him. *I hate heights.* Mentally, Tesnayr scolded himself for never getting over that fear. And of all the times to be reminded of it.

Inch by inch he pulled himself across followed closely by Idæas. The rope creaked ominously with each passing second. Sweating profusely, Tesnayr swallowed the lump in his throat. *Past the first crevice.* Already the man felt like he had been hanging in midair for hours, even though only a few minutes had passed.

With each passing second, Tesnayr's anxiety grew. His muscles burned from the effort of tugging the rope just to creep across the chasm. Silently, he vowed to never set foot in the mountains again. The rope lurched. Instantly, Tesnayr was alert. Without warning, gales of wind swarmed around him buffeting the line.

Tesnayr held tightly onto the cable. He stole a quick glance at Idæas marveling at how the elf managed to remain calm despite the bouncing cable. Hand over hand. Pull. *Halfway there.* The cold did little to calm his nerves or prevent his sweat soaked hands from slipping inside his gloves. He pushed himself onward as the thought of touching solid ground motivated him.

A short pop caught his attention. Tesnayr turned in the direction of the sound and noticed his harness fraying. Realizing the predicament he was in he sped up his efforts to cross.

"Do not go so fast," warned Idæas.

"The rope is fraying," Tesnayr yelled. "It won't hold much longer."

They were nearly there if only the rope would hold. It twisted and unwound with each movement Tesnayr made. He continued his efforts to cross concentrating fully on making it to the other side until he felt weightless as the rope snapped and he began to fall.

Tesnayr gripped the cable tightly.   His feet dangled precariously in midair. The rope jerked and bounced as Idæas scrambled to reach him. Tesnayr hands began to slip. Gritting his teeth, he clung even tighter and felt his nails pierce his skin despite the fact that he wore leather gloves.

"Hurry!" yelled Tesnayr.

His finger slipped and before he knew it, Tesnayr had lost his hold on the line. A moment of weightlessness riveted him before he plunged. Just as he started to fall a firm grip snatched his wrist. Idæas had made it. The elf leaned perilously in his harness with one hand on the rope and another holding Tesnayr.

Tesnayr gripped the elf's arm in return, but knew that they could not remain like this for long. Slowly, they moved onward as those on the cliff heaved the pulley. Suddenly, the elf's harness began to fray, unable to support the weight of both of them. They passed the fifth crevice.

Tesnayr felt his grasp failing. "Idæas," he began, "You must drop me, or we will both die."

"I'll not let go," replied the elf. "The rope will hold." He clamped even harder on Tesnayr's arm.

Each jerk of the rope swung Tesnayr as though he were a piece of laundry hung to dry. He glanced up at the elf. Idæas returned the look with determination. He refused to let the man fall and if they were to die that day, so be it. Inch by inch they neared the overhang. They could almost reach it. Small popping sounds escaped the harness as the rope continued to unravel.

"Idæas, you stubborn elf," said Tesnayr, "There is no point in both of us dying."

Idæas gripped even tighter in response. He had faith that the rope would hold. They were almost there. Just a few more feet and once again they would be on solid rock.

The cable creaked with each yank as Nular and others worked speedily to bring the two to safety. Just as the last bit of the harness fell apart, hands snatched both Tesnayr and Idæas before they could plummet into the nothingness below.

Breathing heavily, Tesnayr hugged the side of the cliff grateful that they had made it. "Why didn't you let me go?" he asked the elf.

"Would you rather I had?" replied Idæas.

"No, but we could have both been killed," said Tesnayr. "These people need a leader and you are far better at it than anyone here."

Idæas kept his features unreadable, much to Tesnayr's annoyance. "I knew it was not your day to die."

"And how is that?"

"Because I was holding onto you." The elf rose and moved down the path organizing the onlookers as he went.

Tesnayr stared after him. Sometimes he wondered if the elf was serious, joking, or just arrogant. Either way he was alive and there was still a long way to go. He went to the line that still spanned the expanse. Tesnayr pulled out his knife and started to cut the elven rope when it suddenly went limp in his hands and wound into a tight coil. He stared at it in awe before chuckling to himself. *Figures.* Placing it in his pack, he took one last glance at the abyss.

"That is one hurdle done," he said to himself. The soft cry of the phoenix echoed in response. "Let's move," shouted Tesnayr as he pushed people into a single file line.

One by one, they walked along the narrow path down the mountain. Tesnayr noticed an elderly woman struggling with the steep incline. He took her bag and put her arm around his shoulder as he helped her down. "Nigilin, carry those down that cannot go themselves," he ordered.

Nigilin saluted and mobilized some straggling soldiers.

As the shadows lengthened from the waning daylight, they trooped down the mountain to the small clearing Nedis had discovered. Their feet slipped on the slush and smooth rock. Many times Tesnayr gripped the side of the mountain to balance himself. Eventually, the path widened as they went lower. Walking more easily, the travelers reached Nedis and the others before the sun disappeared.

Tesnayr released the woman allowing her to join the others. Gradually, the refugees settled around the fires and began preparing a light meal. Most just enjoyed the warmth as it soothed their aching muscles.

Tesnayr watched them and sighed inwardly relieved that for now they could relax. "Arnin, Idæas, and you three," he said pointing at a group of men, "Set a perimeter and stand guard. We will do three shifts tonight."

He eyed the twinkling stars in the clear sky as everyone settled in for the night. His brooding mood refused to release him. They had surpassed one obstacle, but what else awaited them the deeper they went into the mountains? A furry mass burrowed into him purring loudly. Tesnayr shoved it away. Undaunted, Turyn forced his way into Tesnayr's lap again purring even more loudly than before. He rubbed against the man's cheek leaning forcefully into him.

Wishing to be left alone with his foul mood Tesnayr lifted the cat off of him and tossed him aside. "Leave me be," he said. A few minutes later he heard licking. Tesnayr glanced over. Turyn chewed greedily on his food. "Hey! That was my supper."

"Not anymore," said Turyn.

"Cat," mumbled Tesnayr. "What am I supposed to eat?"

"Don't know," said Turyn, "But that mutton was tasty."

Tesnayr swatted at Turyn. The cat skittered out of the way laughing. "You owe me supper," said Tesnayr.

"You're right," replied Turyn. "I could bring you some, but you might not like the manner in which I carry things."

Tesnayr glared at the cat. He could well imagine how Turyn would bring him a slab of meat, dripping with cat spit. The prospect did not encourage his appetite. "I'll just get it myself."

"No. No. I will bring you some. And I promise not to drool on it. Though it might have bits of dirt mixed in."

Before Tesnayr could respond, Turyn bounded off toward the cook's fire. Minutes later the scrapping and scratching of metal on rocky ground filled the air. Tesnayr cursed under his breath. *What is that cat up to now?* Slowly, Turyn came into view. He tugged at a metal plate filled with bits of meat and hard bread. Scrape. Inch by inch Turyn moved the plate over the rough ground and placed it in front of Tesnayr.

"Time to feast," said Turyn with a note of pride in his voice. He sat in front of Tesnayr's hand looking at him expectantly.

Tesnayr reached for his supper. A boisterous purr rumbled through him. His hand paused in midair. Turyn took one step closer to it. Tesnayr knew what the cat wanted. Sighing, he rubbed the cat's ears. Turyn purred even more loudly as he leaned into Tesnayr's calloused hand.

"Now, was that so hard?" said Turyn.

Tesnayr grunted. He picked up the piece of mutton and took a bite. Suddenly, Turyn leaped into his lap and curled into a ball.

"How am I supposed to eat with you in my lap?"

"Oh, don't mind me," said Turyn, "I'm just here to keep you company."

Tesnayr took another huge bite of his food. With each movement Turyn's eyes followed. He began to wonder if the cat had an ulterior motive.

"For some strange reason I do not trust you," said Tesnayr.

Turyn started his motor on again purring so loud that people heard it a hundred yards away. He stared at Tesnayr with a most innocent expression.

"If that paw comes anywhere near my plate," said Tesnayr, not buying Turyn's act, "I'll throw you off this mountain."

"As long as you include the mutton," teased Turyn.

Tesnayr ceased arguing with the cat. He ate his food enjoying every bite knowing that there might not be anything to eat for a long while. When he had finished, Turyn's purr had turned to snores.

Tesnayr looked out at the wide expanse below him. He had hoped they were done with narrow trails with sharp drop offs. No such luck. The cloudy day did little to lift his darkening mood. He was beginning to understand why people did not like the Ársa Mountains. Having entered the mountains themselves, the six tallest in the entire range, he hated them. He breathed deeply to make up for the thin air. Feeling slightly light headed, Tesnayr did not know if the group of refugees behind him could handle the crossing. They had no choice. The trail led back into high altitude.

"Everyone hug the cliff face," he ordered. "Take your time. Do not rush."

They looked at him with apprehension. He understood their wariness. He studied the foot-wide path with the sharp drop off. Despite the life lines he had everyone tie around themselves, even he did not want to do this, but had to show that it could be done.

"Idæas," Tesnayr said.

The elf carefully moved ahead of Tesnayr taking the lead. It was he who knew the path to the mythical road. With his back against the side of the mountain, he walked sideways being careful not to look down. Tesnayr followed suit and one by one in a long line, everyone scooted around the mountain face. Step by step they moved. With soldiers dispersed among the refugees, Tesnayr hoped to ease their fears.

The moaning wind swirled and echoed around them enhancing their anxiety. Pebbles dropped from where people placed their feet. The clinking sound of the small rocks as they fell intensified with each bounce. Gradually, the line of people moved along the narrow track to what they hoped would be safer road.

Jenel scrunched against the wall of rock. Her heart thundered in her chest as though it would pop out at any moment. She took comfort in Rybnik being next to her. "Keep going," she told herself. Her feet scraped across the ground as she moved onward. Two cliffs in two days were too much. But it was either move or die. More pebbles fell beneath her boots, a reminder of what would happen to her if she slipped. She glanced at Rybnik. He looked back at her encouragingly.

A man screamed as his foot slid and he fell below taking two more with him. They dangled precariously in the air as the rope pulled taut. Bracing himself for the strain, Rybnik held on. He took out his dagger and sliced the rope connecting him and Jenel. "Keep going," he told her.

"But—"

"Now!" He refused to let her die in case the weight of the dangling men pulled them all down. He looked at the soldier beside him. The man's fearful features told him everything. "On my mark," he said calmly, "We pull."

The rope swung violently as two of the hanging men desperately tried to climb up. Their panic fed the dread of others and made saving them difficult.

"Stop moving," Rybnik yelled at them.

Eventually the rope ceased its swaying.

"Now pull," ordered Rybnik.

His muscles ached as he and the soldier next to him heaved on the rope. With constant movement they hoisted the men up. With each passing second, anxiety grew among those waiting to continue onward as they hugged the mountainside. Rybnik knew that if they took much longer to pull up the men, more could fall over the side simply from fainting.

He reached down and grasped the hand of the first man as he came to the top. The soldier grabbed the second. Finally, they hauled up the third, but his limp body told Rybnik that he was dead. His caved in skull verified that fact. Rybnik masked his expression as he cut the dead man loose and tossed him into the endless abyss.

"How can you toss his body away like that?" asked one shocked refugee.

Rybnik eyed the man. "He is dead and we cannot afford to carry the extra weight. Move on." Rybnik edged his way along the trail taking the lead and striving to narrow the gap between him and Jenel.

Tesnayr glanced behind him when he heard the scream. He watched as Jenel and Rybnik separated and Jenel continued without him. Unable to stay any longer he continued after Idæas. Rybnik was on his own. There was nothing for him to do but hope that the man could handle it.

His foot slipped. Squeezing against the side of the cliff, Tesnayr caught himself and managed to stay on the narrow ledge. Slowly, he released the breath he held and forced himself to breathe steadily and deeply. Inch by inch he crept sideways. A gap greeted him. The elf jumped it with ease. Tesnayr stretched his foot out and leapt across. *Made it.* He reached out and helped the child behind him. *So far so good.*

Tesnayr stole a quick glance back at Rybnik. It appeared that the man had managed to pull those that had fallen back up. Good, he thought. Turning back to the matter at hand, he concentrated fully on following Idæas and remaining on the ledge.

The elf moved swiftly, undeterred by the narrow path and the prospect of death. He scooted smoothly sideways. Not once did his feet slide, nor did he knock any rocks off. He focused on leading the others and shielded his mind from all other thoughts. His steps came more easily. Looking down, Idæas noticed that the narrow precipice began to widen. Keeping his emotions reined in, he pushed onward. They were close. Soon all of them would be on a wider ledge.

There it was. The path they searched for. All they had to do was one final leap across another gap. Idæas jumped, followed by Tesnayr. Together they helped others across and sent them down the small rise to the wider and far safer road. One by one people landed on safe ground and congregated below. After about two hours, the last person reached the new trail.

"I'm glad that's over," said Tesnayr, relieved.

Idæas just looked at him emotionless. "Our journey is only beginning. Over there." The elf pointed down the incline. There rested a paved road wide enough for wagons and sturdy carts. "We have found the road. The Indrev Tharob is before us. It will guide us the rest of the way through the mountains."

A commotion arose below them. Steel rang out. A bedraggled group of people appeared from amongst the trees and attacked those who waited for Tesnayr's orders. Instantly, his soldiers jumped into the fight protecting the defenseless refugees.

Tesnayr raced down the hill plunging himself into the fray. He blocked an attack by a man in ragged clothes. Instantly, Tesnayr pinned him to the ground. He brought his sword down, but stopped in mid swing. Something about the man caught his attention. He knocked the man unconscious. Glancing around Tesnayr immediately understood who these people were. They were not enemy soldiers but desperate individuals.

Something poked him in the side. Feeling in his cloak Tesnayr gripped the horn of Selexia and knew how to stop the skirmish while avoiding casualties. A deafening cry echoed around them as he blew on it. Many dropped their swords just so they could cover their ears.

The cry of a dragon greeted Tesnayr in response. Everyone ducked as the giant beast swooped low. Fear paralyzed the people as two more dragons landed in the small clearing cutting off any chance of escape. A third settled before Tesnayr.

"You called," said the dragon.

"Yes," said Tesnayr, now feeling stupid that he used them to stop a small fight. "I just wanted to stop a battle." Now Tesnayr really felt dumb.

The dragon snorted, but said nothing.

Tesnayr observed those around him. Mothers huddled to the ground clutching their children while many stood frozen with terror. "Who are you? Who speaks for you?"

One man stood forward. "I will speak for them."

"What are you all doing here?" asked Tesnayr.

"We had nowhere else to go," replied the man. "Strange beasts attacked our homes and we escaped to the mountains. They followed us so we climbed higher until they pursued us no more. We have been here for four months."

"Why did you attack us?"

"Our food ran out. We saw some people gathering here. They looked well fed and we are starving."

Pitying the man, Tesnayr found it difficult to be angry. Many were mere bones. He understood their plight, but could not allow such actions to go unanswered. "These people have also escaped attacks by the same creatures that overran your home. They are in the same situation as you. Instead of murdering and stealing from them, why not ask for their help?"

"No one helps us," said the man eyeing the dragons around him.

"I am helping you," countered Tesnayr, "We are going to Hemíl. Come with us and you will receive food and shelter."

"Who are you?"

"My name is Tesnayr."

Whispers soared through the crowd. Once again Tesnayr's reputation had preceded him. He wondered if he could go anywhere without people knowing his name.

"I've heard of you," said the man.

Surprise, thought Tesnayr. He kept his face impassive.

"Our camp is this way. Follow me."

Tesnayr sent the others after the man. He then turned to the dragons. "Thank you," he said, "We need warmth and food for the night. Can you help us?"

"Selexia has vowed that we serve you, so serve we will," said one of the dragons, "We will return within the hour."

The beat of the dragons' wings nearly knocked Tesnayr to the ground as they took off. He watched them go before trekking down the hill and toward the others' camp. Upon entering, it was clear that these people had been through a lot. A pregnant lady approached him and kissed his hand. Unsure of what to do, Tesnayr just stood there.

"Thank you," she said, meekly.

"You need to rest." Nelyn pulled the woman away from Tesnayr and set her on some blankets.

Tesnayr remained where he was awed that these people managed to survive. Immediately, he took stock of what they had and how they were going to travel down the mountain. The beating of wings disturbed his mental note taking. The dragons had reappeared with fresh kill and wood. They placed the wood in the center and the food elsewhere. Afterward, one of the beasts set the wood on fire producing a warm blaze that everyone gathered around.

"Anything else?" one of the dragons asked.

"No. Thank you," replied Tesnayr.

The dragon bowed and flew off with the other two. Tesnayr glanced about him once before settling in for the night. They still had a long way to go and things just got more complicated.

Chapter VI
Through the Mountains

"What's on your mind?" asked Nigilin as he and Tesnayr walked together.

Now that they had reached the ancient road of Elven lore, the trek was easier, but Tesnayr wondered how long that would last. "Nothing."

"Nothing is never on your mind," said Nigilin.

Tesnayr eyed his friend for a moment. "I could never fool you," he replied, "It's the dragons. Ever since Selexia bound them to my service, I have not been able to figure out how best to use them. And I feel foolish for calling them a few days ago."

"Don't," said Nigilin, "You stopped a lot of people from being killed."

"I've been thinking. Perhaps we can use the dragons to fly to Hemíl."

"I wouldn't recommend it. These people are frightened. I doubt that they could handle being carried by a dragon. Besides, can you imagine how Hemíl would react to see a bunch of dragons coming for them?"

"I hadn't thought of that," admitted Tesnayr.

"Using them is a nice idea, but might not work in this case. We'll get there just as easily on foot."

"There has to be some way to utilize them."

"I'm sure you'll find it. Just think it through carefully before you use the power that the dragons have given you. The chance of abusing it is too great."

Silently, Tesnayr agreed with Nigilin which was why he rarely thought to use the horn. Most times he forgot he had it.

The mass of people came to a sudden halt. Tesnayr pushed his way through the crowd to see what had stopped them. A massive sheet of ice greeted him.

Tesnayr and the others looked out at the frozen lake with disappointment. It stretched before them as the road they were on ended. Deep within the valley, the prospect of turning back wearied them. Halfway to Hemíl, they had to push forward.

"Where is the road?" asked Arnin.

"Under the lake," replied Tesnayr with dismay. He was afraid something like this might happen. The road they had searched for and spent the better part of the trip traveling on was thousands of years old. It was a miracle that bits of it still existed.

"Is there a way around?"

"No," said Tesnayr. "Even if there was, it would take too long."

"Scouts report that this entire valley is under water," said Idæas. "It is still frozen so we can cross, but we must do so quickly. It has already begun to thaw in this early spring weather."

"I am really beginning to hate this trip," commented Arnin.

"Beginning to," said Tesnayr, "I reached that point when we first started."

Turyn charged onto the frozen water. He hopped around scratching and jumping with ease. The cat darted from point to point on the ice stopping at various places to sniff.

"Turyn, what are you doing?" yelled Tesnayr.

Turyn trotted up to the man with pride. "Testing the ice. As I am the smallest it made sense for me to do it. It seems solid enough but there are places where it is thin."

"Crazy feline," said Tesnayr, "I appreciate the effort, but next time check with me first. We cannot cross in a group. We will spread out across the ice forming three lines. The horses will make up the rear. Send the women and children first."

Soon, the soldiers had everyone ready to cross. Tesnayr gave the signal and the first line of people stepped onto the ice. It creaked and groaned under their weight despite the fact that they were the lightest group. Many jumped back to land.

"You either cross or freeze to death here," said Tesnayr to them.

Tentatively, they stepped back onto the ice and hurried forward to the other side.

From his vantage point, Tesnayr watched their progress, gauging the distance. "Send the second group," he said.

With more courage than the first, the second group walked onto the ice barely registering the erupting pockets of air. It groaned even more and cracked in places. Steeling their will, they moved forward. Guided by Tesnayr's men, the refugees strode slowly across careful not to cause any breakage.

Finally, the third and final group walked onto the ice with the horses. Sensing the danger ahead, the horses whinnied and snorted afraid of going forward. The men whispered soothingly to the beasts in an effort to calm them, leading them onto the frozen lake. Gradually, the horses trotted across the ice toward the other two groups.

Tesnayr glanced around them studying the surroundings as they moved. *It's too quiet.* He hated the silence. It told him one thing, danger wasn't far behind.

Steadily, the three groups of people moved over the frozen expanse with Turyn in the lead. His keen senses alerted them to hazards allowing them to pass unharmed. But he could not foresee it all. The sound of their footsteps eerily echoed as they squeaked on the ice while they crept across.

A horse whinnied fearfully. "Whoa boy," said Arnin stroking the beast's mane.

The horse whinnied again jerking its head violently as it reared up on its hind legs ripping the reins from Arnin's hands. It kicked and snorted swinging its head at any who tried to control it. With one last jerk, the horse galloped across the ice in the opposite direction.

"Let it go," said Tesnayr stopping Arnin in his tracks. "We cannot afford to go chasing after it. Just let it go. Keep moving all of you."

The refugees pushed forward with unease. The horse's actions filled them with dread.

Crack!

The sound echoed through the valley stopping everyone. People looked around warily. They stood their ground unsure of what to do and not wanting to move forward.

"Keep moving," shouted Tesnayr. He detested this delay. Though the sound unsettled him, he knew the longer they stayed on the ice, the better chance there was of them drowning.

Following his lead, Jenel looked around at the first group of people. "Come on, all of you," she said, "You have faced snow storms, and an abyss. We've faced starvation and not once has death claimed us. Now keep moving, or we will all surely die."

She walked proudly across the ice after Turyn hoping her display of courage would motivate the scared group behind her. Inwardly, she wanted to curl up in a ball. One by one, people followed.

Slowly, they reached the center of the lake. Many slipped as water formed on top of the ice. Some had to be carried because fear froze them on the spot. Onward they went despite the increase of the creaking and groaning. Growing used to the sounds, Tesnayr pushed them harder. He wanted across the expanse quickly. *Almost there.* As though reading his thoughts, another loud crack sounded. It resonated in people's ears as they all knew that it did not bode well.

Water spurted from beneath the ice as a section broke off. Poppings and bangs moved beneath their feet and cracks streaked across the ice. A section of ice flipped over flinging those upon it into the icy water. Screams escaped their mouths as they landed in the water scrambling to get out. Soaked, their efforts proved useless as they slipped on the ice only to be buried by it as the ice closed over them cutting off their pleas for help. The others watched helplessly as they drowned.

Panic swept through the crowd. Breaking ranks, they darted across the lake making a mad dash to the other side. Ice broke away beneath one unsuspecting woman. She fell into the darkness below and disappeared. Going in every direction people ran across the ice unaware that their actions increased their chances of drowning.

"Make for the other side," yelled Tesnayr.

He didn't bother trying to control the panicking refugees. It would waste valuable time. All he could do was guide them in the right direction. He snatched the reins of a fleeing horse pulling it to a stop. He jumped into the saddle and charged across the ice screaming to get people's attention hoping that they would follow him.

Water gushed over the ice increasing people's fears. Frantically, they screamed with each step they took and trampled each other.

Nelyn herded a group of children toward the shore. A chunk of ice fell away beneath her feet plunging her and a boy into the water. She dove to catch the boy around his waist and kicked for the surface. Nelyn grabbed onto the slush while keeping her hold on the boy. She desperately tried to pull them onto the frozen surface but the slickness of the water and ice made it impossible.

Arnin charged for Nelyn. He pushed his way past everyone. His feet pounded on the ice as he ignored the danger before him. Nelyn struggled to keep her hold on the frozen sheet and the boy. Unable to maintain her grip, she started to disappear below the surface of the water.

Arnin dove for her sliding in his stomach until he reached her. He pulled himself to a screeching halt to avoid diving in the water. Wasting no time, he grabbed her free hand and hauled her and the boy onto the ice. Panting, Nelyn breathed deeply. She had little time to catch her breath as Arnin pulled her and the boy to their feet and pushed them towards safety.

Jenel stood on the shore of the lake helping others off the ice. "This way," she yelled. She watched despondently as people fell beneath the cold barrier and drowned. She held back the impulse to run out and help them knowing that it was too late and she would only endanger herself.

Tesnayr pulled his horse to a halt. Only a few remained. "Don't waste time with your possessions," he shouted.

People dropped their bundles and dashed to the shore. The soldiers gripped many who had fallen and refused to move. They dragged them to land as the ice wobbled beneath their feet. Many lost their balance and tumbled rolling across the frozen expanse only to get up awkwardly and continue onward.

"Hurry," yelled Tesnayr to five of his men as they scrambled to safety.

A large chunk of ice flipped them in the lake and trapped them underneath it. Tesnayr saw the pregnant woman struggling to walk to the other side. Kicking his horse, he raced toward her. He leaned over with his outstretched hand and snatched the woman up and onto the horse. The horse's pounding hooves broke the ice as Tesnayr barely made it safely to the shoreline. He handed the woman to others and dismounted. "Count them," he said to Nigilin.

He wandered around the rag tag mass of people. Soaked and many of them nursing injuries, they ignored him. Tesnayr felt for them. Anger ebbed beneath the surface at their suffering. The elf was right when he called the mountains deadly. He kicked himself as he began to second guess the decision to travel down the spine of the mountain range.

"Tesnayr," said Nigilin.

"How many?"

"Twenty," replied Nigilin, "Five soldiers and the rest refugees. Believe it or not, we were lucky. It could have been worse."

"Indeed," said Tesnayr.

"Follow me," said Nigilin, "There is something you need to see."

Tesnayr trailed after Nigilin up a hill and to a flat area. Before them was a path of the same stone as the one on the other end of the lake. "Idæas' road," Tesnayr whispered.

"The elf was right," said Nigilin. "I hope the going is easier from now on."

"I wouldn't count on it."

A sharp scream pierced the air. The two men headed for the scream and found the pregnant woman crouched on the ground with a group around her. She screamed again.

"What's happening," demanded Tesnayr.

"She's going into labor," said Jenel.

"She can't," snapped Tesnayr. He immediately regretted saying it.

"Like it or not she is," said Jenel. "Nelyn you're with me. Nigilin, if there is a midwife among us, find her. Now help me carry her to a more secluded place."

"It's too early," moaned the woman.

Two men carried her to a tent. They placed her on blankets and then set out to gather water and start it boiling. Others dropped off more blankets and cloth. Nigilin ran up with an elderly woman. She took one look at the situation and took charge.

"Keep the men away from here," she ordered, "The moment that water boils bring it here. We need more blankets."

People cleared away from the area.

"You two," the midwife pointed at Nelyn and Jenel, "Hold her down. I may need to turn this baby around."

Tesnayr paced the ground with unease. His anxiety rubbed off on the others. Back and forth. The ice wore through where he walked unceasingly. Even the bitter cold did little to calm his nerves. He didn't know why, but the fact that the woman had gone into labor rattled his nerves. It wasn't even his baby, but he felt responsible for it.

A part of him thought that his efforts to save her caused the baby to come. He hoped all would go well. For a day and a night he paced. He never knew such things could take so long.

"One would think you were the father," commented Nigilin. He handed Tesnayr a cup of hot tea.

"Where is the father?" asked Tesnayr.

"Dead," replied Nigilin, "Calm yourself. You're making the men nervous."

Tesnayr stopped his pacing and sipped his tea. He knew his anxiety was unwarranted. He hoped they were doing the child a favor by bringing it into a world as harsh and cruel as this one. Though a part of him knew the chances of survival were slim.

The tent flap flung open. The midwife stepped out with Nelyn, their expressions grim. A bad feeling welled in the pit of Tesnayr's stomach. "What happened?" he asked.

"The child is dead," said the midwife. "It was never alive in the womb." The elderly woman walked off disheartened. She had seen this many times, but each time it ate at her heart.

Tesnayr went to the tent to console the woman. He felt partially responsible. Inside, he saw the woman clutching her stillborn child, tears streaming from her eyes. Jenel consoled her, but nothing could take away from this loss.

"I am sorry," said Tesnayr. He didn't know what else to say.

The woman looked up at him. She forced a small smile. "It's not your fault, Captain. It was too early. Perhaps it's for the best," she broke down in another bout of sobs.

Tesnayr left the tent. He slammed his fist into his thigh. *Why?* What was he fighting for when things like this happened? A child born was a chance to hope. Now even that had been ripped away from him. *Curse this world.*

The sharp cry of a bird punctured the air. Tesnayr looked into the star studded sky and noticed a dark shape swoop toward him and into the tent. Quickly, he wrenched the flap back. Inside a magnificent bird sat before the dead infant. Tesnayr recognized it immediately. The phoenix. Silence ensued as everyone stared at the bird. The phoenix eyed the child sadly. Tears fell from its feathered face. The woman held her baby before the phoenix. "Please," she pleaded.

The phoenix tapped the forehead of the baby three times. It spread its massive wings and flew away. Suddenly a loud cry filled the area as the baby wailed. Its strong cries drew a crowd around the tent. Onlookers watched in amazement as a once lifeless baby now cried with the strength of one brought to term. The mother wept and laughed with joy. Even Jenel joined in the merriment. She grabbed another blanket and wrapped the infant in it to keep him warm.

"What will you name him?" asked Jenel.

Wiping her tears the mother replied, "His father's name was Zolo. That shall be his."

Tesnayr left the woman alone with her baby. "Clear out of here all of you," he said to the gathered crowd. "Give the woman some privacy."

Slowly, the crowd dispersed murmuring among themselves at the miracle. The soft cry of the phoenix caught his attention. Tesnayr watched the bird as it flew in front of the moon. *So you've proven me wrong once again.* He went in search of food. Perhaps there was some hope left in the world.

Jenel hugged a blanket around her as she stared into the fire. Never before had she witnessed someone give birth to a stillborn child. The thought of it shook her.

"Drink this." Rybnik held a cup of tea out for her.

Jenel took it. She sipped it slowly appreciating the warmth, even if the drink tasted bitter.

"You did well," said Rybnik.

"You always say that," replied Jenel.

"Because you always do." Rybnik looked at the stars with an unreadable expression. Bits of sadness snuck through.

"Why do you do that?" asked Jenel.

Rybnik glanced at her questioningly.

"Why do you go silent like that and stare longingly at the stars?"

"No reason."

"Yes, there is. You just don't wish to tell me," said Jenel. "In all the years we have known each other, my father never suspected. He forbade our contact."

"Your father is a wise man," said Rybnik.

"Some think him a fool," Jenel said.

"He is a fool."

"You just said that he was wise."

"A man can be wise and a fool," said Rybnik.

"What aren't you telling me?"

Rybnik remained silent.

"Sometimes I think you wish I had died instead of my sister."

"That's not it at all."

"I don't blame you if you do. I miss her as well. I know my father does too. He does his best not to show it, but there are times I catch him holding one of her things with tears in his eyes. He's never been the same since her death. None of us have."

"Death is a part of life," said Rybnik. "And your father was right to forbid us staying in contact."

"How can you say that?"

Rybnik breathed out loudly. "Sometimes I wish I could do things differently." He jumped to his feet and left.

Jenel gazed at him as he disappeared. His manner puzzled her. She brushed it off. It wasn't the first time he acted like this.

Chapter VII
Strangers in the Mountains

Tesnayr stood on a precipice overlooking the dark valley below as hoards of orcs filled it. Galbrok was there this time. He knew it. If only he could kill him then the war would be ended and his people saved. The chanting started again as the beasts beat their swords against their chests yelling words to frighten those under his command. The men around him shifted and squirmed from the building fear.

"Courage, men," he yelled. "We will win this day. On this day Galbrok will be dead and the orcs shall be a memory!" That did it, thought Tesnayr. His men steeled themselves and faced their opponent with renewed fervor. "Charge!"

Thunder rose as thousands of horse's hooves stampeded the earth while Tesnayr led the charge into the midst of the orcs. The horse beneath him breathed heavily with each gallop it took. Concentrating on the movements of the animal, he planted his feet firmly in the stirrups and gripped his sword tightly. Instantly he was upon the orcs. His arm jostled as it absorbed the impact of slicing through the beasts. He steered his horse through the mass of orcs cutting down any he came upon.

Quickly, Tesnayr turned his steed around and looked back as his men followed his lead. He charged through the orcs again swinging his blade mercilessly. The more dead, the better, he thought. His horse snorted from the exertion. Ignoring the animal, Tesnayr continued his onslaught.

Then, he spotted Galbrok. *If I kill him, it is over.* Kicking his horse hard, he charged toward the leader of the orcs. Bending low so that friction would not slow him down, he sped off toward the one that started it all.

Almost there.

A few more yards and he would be upon Galbrok. A sudden jolt gripped him as air left his lungs. Tesnayr found himself lifted from his horse and crashed hard upon the ground. *Niht'anda!* He couldn't believe it. Tesnayr stared at the grotesque beast in terror. They had destroyed them, how could Galbrok have them under his command?

Scrambling across the black ground, Tesnayr snatched his sword and brought it up in time to block an attack by its massive claws. He rolled on the ground avoiding the crushing weight of the niht'anda's massive feet. Tesnayr jumped to his feet and stopped. All around him more niht'anda swarmed the field picking off his men with ease. Time ceased for him as he watched with horror at what he had done. He had led his men to their deaths.

Instantly, the niht'anda grasped Tesnayr in its iron grip. It held him firmly, but did not kill him.

Galbrok chuckled as he rode up, "Did you like my little trap? Did you humans really think I would show myself on the battlefield unless I was certain I would win?"

"Coward," spat Tesnayr.

"Winning is not cowardice," replied Galbrok, "You will never beat me on the field of battle. Do you like my new allies? They are quite useful. Take them all away."

Tesnayr struggled against the beast that held him but his efforts proved useless. Then, his world went black.

Violent spasms woke Tesnayr from another of his nightmares. He glanced about him reassuring himself that the dream was only a dream. Chills gripped him as he wrapped a blanket more tightly around himself. Morning had not yet arrived. One day, he assured himself, he will have Galbrok's head.

"Tesnayr," said Nigilin as he poked his head in the tent, "We have visitors."

Tesnayr picked up his sword and rushed out into the cold night air. He could barely make them out in the dark, but people did approach with one horse. He thought he recognized two of the group as they drew near.

"Tesnayr," said one as he held out his hand.

Idæas' sword sprung into his hand. He stood poised, ready to defend Tesnayr if necessary. Just as quickly, he lowered his blade. "Forgive me, my king, I did not know it was you."

"It is perfectly alright," said King Shealayr. "You have done well, and were only following my orders."

"King Shealayr," said Tesnayr, "What are you doing here?"

"Looking for you," replied the king. "And it appears I've found you. Might we speak in private?"

"Would you rather not rest?" asked Tesnayr.

"What I have to say is of great importance."

Tesnayr led King Shealayr to a secluded area of the camp while Idæas fed the ragged group that had accompanied him. Quesha, naturally, followed King Shealayr remaining in the shadows as her mistress had taught her.

"What brings you here?" asked Tesnayr.

"The other kings and I have had a meeting at the Keep of Edrei. We wish to speak with you there," replied King Shealayr.

"Really? What for?"

"We are losing this war, Tesnayr, and you know it. While the five of us continue to argue among ourselves we cannot hope to win. But there is one area in which we are agreed: we will give you leadership of our armies."

"Me?"

"Yes, you," replied King Shealayr, "In every skirmish you have had with the orcs, you have won. People flee our lands to join you; a man who has no allegiance to any part of this world. You are a stranger here and yet you have accomplished what most only hope for. You have unified people from the five lands in a way we never could."

"That is because I am not busy trying to gain more land for my kingdom."

"Fair enough. We need you Tesnayr. I've come to bring you to the Keep of Edrei deep within Hemíl."

"Why should I go there?" demanded Tesnayr, "The last time I made a pact with one of you, I was betrayed. How do I know you will all keep your word?"

"Have I broken mine?"

Tesnayr thought for a moment. King Shealayr had him there. "No. You promised me the service of you elf and he has done well."

"Yes, he has. Even to the point of killing his king should I bring harm to you. The elves have not harmed you in any way," said King Shealayr.

"They have not done much to help me either, save one."

"Would you have welcomed it? Come now, Tesnayr, we need your help," King Shealayr pleaded, "Yes, King Slyamal will be there. Put the past behind you. He will not renege on this promise. You have my word that I will never betray you."

"And the others?" asked Tesnayr.

"King Edrei is an honorable man. When he gives his word he keeps it even if it means his death. The others are that way as well. They care for their people and as long as the orcs roam free among these lands, their people will remain in grave danger."

Tesnayr mused over the king's words. He did not want to go, but yet he was already headed for Hemíl.

"We are desperate, Tesnayr. We need your help," said King Shealayr.

"Of course I could bring you by force," said Quesha stepping from her hiding place.

Tesnayr turned toward her. "You are just like your mistress. She should be proud that you just barge into conversations that do not concern you."

"But this does concern me," snapped Quesha, "The fate of the orcs concern us all. I do not know why you fight going with King

Shealayr. You were already headed for Hemíl. A detour to the Keep of Edrei is of little consequence."

"How do you know so much?" asked Tesnayr.

"It is my nature. And I have my ways," replied Quesha.

"You brought refugees with you," said Tesnayr.

"Yes, we found them on our way here," said King Shealayr. "Mostly poor folk fleeing the orcs after their homes were destroyed. I could not leave them behind. As I'm sure you understand."

Tesnayr understood. He had been picking up refugees since he started his campaign in the mountains. "I would not have expected less. Very well, I will meet with your kings. Will King Edrei provide shelter for these people?"

"I'm certain he will," replied King Shealayr. "There is more than enough room for them at the keep."

"It is decided then," said Tesnayr, "We will go with you to the Keep of Edrei.

"I am glad you decided to come," said Quesha.

"It's not as though I had much choice," Tesnayr replied.

He went back to his tent and dressed fully, unable to go back to sleep. Afterward, Tesnayr checked their supplies and the horses they had left. With the influx of people, they had gained a wagon so he decided to let it remain as it could carry a lot of provisions.

At dawn the trip down the mountain spine continued. Though the road had widened, it was still slow going. Many limped along with barely the strength to stand and after four straight weeks of climbing and descending it was a miracle they still moved. Others slumped as they walked carrying what few possessions they had left. The wheels of the wagon creaked as they rolled down the bumpy road. Four soldiers controlled its speed so that it would not run away.

The ancient road made walking a little easier despite its crumbling brick. Potholes littered the cobblestone road with its faded and cracked bricks. Much of it matched the surrounding dirt.

Nelyn and Arnin walked together engaged in conversation. Tesnayr watched the two. A few months ago they would have killed each other, he mused. Now they seemed to be good friends, or more than that. He wished them well.

Tesnayr thought back to the day Nelyn had joined them. He had tried to send her home, but her stubbornness refused to let him win. He was glad now that she had stayed having proven to be a valuable addition to his army.

"It is nice to see them talking instead of arguing," commented Jenel as she walked up.

Tesnayr chuckled inwardly. "Yes, it is," he replied.

"I think he loves her," Jenel said.

"What makes you say that?"

"He said as much. And Turyn might have overheard him privately conveying his love for her."

"Is there a time when that cat doesn't eavesdrop?" Tesnayr said to himself. "Still, at least they no longer fight. It has been more peaceful."

"Imagine that," said Nigilin from behind, "It is amazing what can happen when two people stop trying to kill each other." He pushed past them and up ahead to check on the line of migrants.

Tesnayr and Jenel eyed each other awkwardly. "Do you think that was a hint?" she asked.

"I know it was," said Turyn appearing from nowhere.

"You shouldn't snoop," said Tesnayr, annoyed.

"I'm a cat. It's what I do," replied Turyn. "Besides, I thought you would like to know that the path is clear up ahead."

Tesnayr paced the camp later that night when they all bedded down after a hard day of hiking. It was his turn to stand sentry. He always performed some of the menial tasks himself; it let his men know that he was one of them. He always hated ranking officers that put themselves upon a pedestal and refused to get their hands dirty.

Nothing stirred. Not even the wind. He detested these still nights. They always made him feel as though something bad was about to happen. It never helped that something usually did happen. The vast expanse before shone brilliantly in the silver light of the full moon. Beautiful, he momentarily thought to himself.

The crunching of twigs disturbed him. Tesnayr turned around pulling himself back to the present.

"Captain," said Nelyn. "We have a problem. A sickness has cropped up among the people."

"Sickness?"

"Follow me."

Tesnayr raced after Nelyn as she walked quickly through the camp swerving between tents and groups of people. She sped past the warm fires heading straight for a secluded area. The smell struck Tesnayr immediately; the smell of disease. His heart dropped as he noticed the people there. Already weak from weeks of travel and little food, they had now caught a disease.

"What is this?" he asked.

"It's the Maladi," replied Nelyn. "A terrible disease that crops up anywhere, unannounced. There is no way for us to predict when or where it will appear. It is very contagious. We could all have it."

"Calm down," said Tesnayr. "Explain it to me."

"It begins with a persistent cough. Usually the person coughs up blood. Later a fever develops along with red welts on the neck. These welts can burst or ooze. It is very painful and almost always fatal."

"Almost fatal?"

"Sometimes a person can contract the disease as a child and survive. If that happens they become immune to it. Such was the case with me."

"Is there a cure?" asked Tesnayr as concern crept into his voice.

"No."

"How quickly will the illness spread?"

"We could all be stricken with it by morning. We must segregate the sick from the rest. We may have to leave them behind."

The last statement tore at Tesnayr. He had lost enough people on this venture and refused to lose more by leaving them behind to some fatal disease. There had to be a cure. Tesnayr meandered among the sick. Each of them ripped his heart in two. Their forlorn faces reflected his inner feelings.

"Are we all susceptible to this?" he asked.

"The Elves aren't," said King Shealayr. He rose from the side of a sick patient.

"No they aren't," said Nelyn.

"There might be a cure," King Shealayr said.

"There is no cure," piped in Nelyn.

"None that men might know of, but we Elves have stories of a mystical place in these mountains that can cure any illness."

"You Elves always have stories about something," said Nelyn, "But mysticism and legends will not solve our problem. And if this place existed, do you know where it is?"

"Sadly, I do not, but the fairies might," replied King Shealayr.

"Quarantine this area," ordered Tesnayr. "King Shealayr, you, Idæas, Nelyn, and anyone else who is immune to this will minister to these people. Separate the healthy from the sick. Soldier, tell Arnin to take the rest of the refugees a good two miles away from here."

A soldier saluted and sped off.

Tesnayr bent low scooping up a handful of dried leaves. He let them fall in the newly arrived breeze. "Duit'angen gachi," he whispered.

The wind carried the leaves from his hands taking them through the mountains and away into the night. Nelyn watched him in astonishment. He knew what she was thinking. The only one smiling was King Shealayr.

"So they told you how to summon them," said the king.

Instantly a white light pierced the darkness and dissipated leaving two women in its wake. They walked toward him gracefully. "You summoned us," said one.

"Yes, Serein," replied Tesnayr, "We have need of your assistance."

The fairy held up her hand and silenced him. She glanced about her knowing immediately what troubled the man. She walked among the sick taking in every detail. "You have been busy since we left."

"King Shealayr says that you and your sister might know of a cure for this."

Serein touched the forehead of one as he shook from feverish chills. She had seen this disease before. Yet, she could not remember if a cure existed. "Sarwyn, do you know if the elf is correct?"

"There is a cure, but it is difficult to get to. Deep within these mountains is a giant waterfall. The waters there are said to be so pure that they will cure any sickness. However, if you drink from it for selfish reasons you will die," said Sarwyn.

"Will you take me there?" asked Tesnayr.

"We cannot," replied Sarwyn. "Fairies are barred from there. And so are the elves. Only mortal beings are allowed there, but few seek it out."

"How do I get there?"

"That gets tricky," said Serein. "All we have are legends."

"Legends," spat Tesnayr, "I am tired of legends being the only way to get anything done around here! I followed a legend to get us through the mountains and now must rely on another one to save these people. I—" Tesnayr cut himself off as he realized that his burst of anger affected those around him. "Forgive me. What do these legends say?"

"In the heart of the tallest mountain lies a waterfall of the purest water. To get there you must follow the ancient path and let your heart guide you. If what you seek is noble, you shall find it. If it is otherwise, you will wander endlessly until death takes you," Sarwyn said.

You got to be kidding me! More Riddles. Tesnayr clenched his fist in frustration but kept his voice even as he spoke. "If I do not seek this cure, then we are all dead?"

"Yes," replied Nelyn. "It struck my village once and killed half of the people. We could all be infected and cannot risk taking it to Hemíl."

Tesnayr rubbed his beard. There was only one choice. He had to seek this mystical cure on the off chance that it existed, or they all would die. "I will go."

"You cannot go alone," countered Nelyn.

"I won't be. Turyn," Tesnayr said aloud.

Startled, the black cat dropped to the stony ground from the branch he had hidden on. "Since you are so keen to know everything, you can come with me."

Turyn huffed. "I always get talked into these things."

*   *   *

The assassin paced the shadowed area he concealed himself in. *Almost had him.* If only that stupid woman hadn't shown up. It was the perfect time to murder Tesnayr. He was alone and the night provided good cover. If only he had taken his chance. Now he must wait for another time to kill Tesnayr. His master would not be pleased, but what choice was there? Another chance would arise. The assassin was certain of it. And this time, he would not miss it.

The assassin looked up. Idæas stared at him. Quickly, the man walked away as though he had been walking the entire time. *Stupid elf.* Always watching him. He would have to careful from now on.

*   *   *

"Tesnayr?" Jenel poked her head into Tesnayr's tent as he stuffed supplies into an already bursting pack.

"Jenel, you shouldn't be here," said Tesnayr, looking up.

"I had to see you." Jenel stepped toward him placing a small item in his hand.

"What is this?" he asked. He studied the small star shaped pendant.

"It is the star of Kylon," Jenel replied. "It is our guiding star. This belonged to my sister before me. I want you to take it with you for luck."

"I cannot accept this." Tesnayr handed the necklace back to Jenel.

"Take it," she insisted. "Please. For me."

Her pleading eyes melted his resolve. Gently, he placed it around his neck.

Jenel straightened it admiring it on him. She placed a tender kiss on his cheek. "It will protect you."

Chapter VIII
Legend's Road

Tesnayr's pack weighed heavily on his shoulders. It wasn't just the supplies that he brought, but the responsibility of finding a cure for the sick within the camp. All rested upon him. If he failed, they would die. If they continued traveling, they would die or risk spreading the sickness. No, he had to search for this mythical waterfall in the hope that it existed. The slight chance of success meant life.

The sun felt unusually warm upon him as he trekked an obscure trail through the mountains. He shifted his pack to ease the weight on his shoulders. Turyn trotted beside him humming merrily to himself. Tesnayr shook his head. Nothing seemed to dampen that cat's spirits. He thought about what the fairies had told him about the waterfall.

"You must follow this trail until you see a rock that looks like a bird," Sarwyn had told him.

"After that it gets more difficult," added Serein.

"Once you find the rock, the path will only be visible at night. You can travel only then and must stop before dawn or it will disappear forever and you will never find your way back.

"You will know you are close to the falls when you hear the sound of a horn. It will be unlike any other you have heard. The second sign will be when you enter the place of eternal spring.

"I must warn you, Turyn will be tested as well. As your companion he must prove his faithfulness to you just as you must prove your pure intentions. If either one of you fail, you both risk wandering endlessly in the mountains until death."

Tesnayr brooded over the last statement by Sarwyn. The thought of being forced to wander unceasingly because they failed some test worried him. *What is it with these tests?* A part of Tesnayr wanted to walk away. But he could not. He shifted his pack again as Turyn started another bout of humming.

"Why did you decide to follow me back in the village?" asked Tesnayr.

Turyn mulled over the question before lazily replying, "You were interesting."

"How is it cats talk in this place?" The question had plagued Tesnayr for some time and he finally had the gumption to ask it.

"Not all cats do," replied Turyn, "In fact most cats don't. But occasionally a cat is born with the ability of speech. Those that talk live longer than the average house cat. I have always had the ability to speak. Though there have been a few instances of people being turned into cats, but that is not the case with me. Such incidents are rare. Those cats give the rest of us a bad name. I have walked this earth many decades and have always been coated in fur."

The trail sloped upward. Tesnayr's breathing increased as he trudged up the steep incline. He would never get used to the high altitude. His boots scraped the ground with each step. Leaning forward for balance, he made his way to the top knowing that the other side meant the easiness of going downhill. He wiped the sweat from his brow and paused.

The sight of the mountains nearly took his breath away. Majestic in their beauty, he never knew anything could look like this. Then, he saw it. The rock that looked like a bird rested straight across from him. So the stories were true, he thought. Maybe this journey would not be so difficult after all.

"Turyn," said Tesnayr, "We found the rock. Now we must wait for nightfall."

*   *   *

Sighing, Nelyn stepped into the blacksmithing tent. Ever since the blacksmith had fallen ill she had been charged with keeping the weapons sharpened. She dumped her bundle and paused. A single white iris rested upon the whetstone.

Smiling slightly, she picked it up and put it under her nose enjoying the scent. Arnin, she thought, affectionately. She wondered how he knew that irises were her favorite flower and how he came by one.

In a moment of femininity, Nelyn placed the flower in her golden hair using a shield as a mirror to admire herself. When satisfied, she picked up a knife and began sharpening it. The stone whirred making a distinct grating noise as she expertly honed the blade.

"Nelyn?" Jarown entered with a tray of food. "I thought you might be hungry."

"Put it there," she said, not looking up from her work.

Disheartened, Jarown set the tray down and headed for the opening. All of his efforts to earn Nelyn's forgiveness had failed. He missed his daughter and wished she would speak to him again like she used to. "Nelyn, you need to eat."

Annoyed, Nelyn faced her father. "I'll eat when I'm finished."

Frowning, Jarown walked away.

Nelyn focused on the whetstone as it whirled around against the steel blade of the knife. A soft thump caught her attention. She jerked her head in the direction of the sound. Jarown lay in the mud facedown.

Nelyn released her grip on the knife allowing it to clink on the ground as she ran for him. "Father!" Worried, she gently rolled Jarown onto his back. His hot skin burned her. Knowing what she would find, Nelyn pulled back the collar of his shirt. Three red welts dotted his neck.

"Help me!"

Rushed footsteps hurried towards her.

"What's wrong?" asked Nedis.

"He has it," replied Nelyn.

Nedis didn't need Nelyn to clarify her meaning. He bent down and heaved Jarown onto his shoulders carrying him to where the other sick patients were with Nelyn close behind.

*   *   *

A soft, damp paw patted Tesnayr's cheek. He batted it away. Again the paw patted his cheek more insistent than before. Tesnayr swiped it away wanting to sleep. Moments later, a great weight rammed into his stomach forcing the air out of his lungs. Tesnayr sat bolt upright gasping for air. He looked about him for the source of his disturbance and found Turyn staring pointedly at him.

"I thought that would wake you," said the cat.

Breathing steadily now, Tesnayr glared at him. "Did you have to jump on my stomach?"

"I tried to be gentle, but you are a sound sleeper," replied Turyn, "So I chose a more direct approach. The moon has risen. We should be going."

Grudgingly, Tesnayr snatched his pack and sword. He stood up and glanced at the moon. It was beautiful, but he hadn't time to admire it. He had to find the hidden road that only moonlight revealed. He took a step and crashed into a low hanging branch. Tesnayr cursed.

"Shh," came Turyn's voice.

Cursed assignment. He hated traveling the mountains at night. Not only was such a task dangerous, but Tesnayr couldn't see a thing despite the moon's light. "Turyn, do you see the road?"

"Perfectly."

Tesnayr's toe throbbed as his foot crashed into a rock. Hopping on one foot he tripped over an upturned root and crashed into the ground. "I can't see a thing."

Turyn brushed against Tesnayr's leg. "How did you people ever manage to survive for so long?" he asked jokingly. "Follow my directions, I'll lead you. The path is just up ahead."

Turyn trotted through the night guiding Tesnayr's footsteps. His boots crunched the gravel noisily as he stumbled awkwardly through the woods. He hoped the cat knew where he was headed.

"Rock," said Turyn.

Tesnayr took an extra-long stride to avoid it.

"Branch."

Just in time, Tesnayr ducked to dodge another low hanging branch. Brush snatched his cloak as he walked causing him to wobble. Clumsily, he regained his balance only to alert the entire forest of his presence.

Turyn sighed impatiently. "Root."

Tesnayr's boot bumped the giant root just as the cat told him about it. Grunting, he stepped over it. "How much farther?"

"Not far."

Tesnayr crashed into a tree. Groaning, he rubbed his sore nose.

"There's a tree there," said Turyn, sheepishly.

"I think I found it," muttered Tesnayr.

A blue light shone up ahead piercing the darkness around them. The secret road lay just ahead. With the extra light, Tesnayr moved more quickly and easily. He headed straight for it following Turyn's faint outline. The narrow road widened. Hurriedly, Tesnayr headed straight for the bluish glow until it was upon him.

Astonished, he stared at the blue path. It glowed brilliantly with specks of light darting about. Mist swirled above the ground following the road he was to take. He placed his hand in the blue mist. It danced around his skin tickling him, welcoming him.

If the fairies' directions were correct, this should be the legendary road to the waterfall. But which way should he go?

Tesnayr studied the two directions that the road split into. No one warned him that this might happen.

"Which way?" he asked.

Turn flipped his tail. He sniffed the chill air for several moments before darting off.

"Turyn," called Tesnayr.

"This way," said the cat as he disappeared down the blue path.

"How do you know?"

"I trust my nose."

Tesnayr chased after the black cat. Though the road was flat, he still stumbled in his efforts to keep pace with Turyn. "Slow down," he said. "I cannot run in the dark." Tesnayr stopped and searched the area around him. No sign of Turyn. "Where are you?"

"Right here," said Turyn sitting next to Tesnayr's foot.

"Don't do that."

"Then keep up." Turyn bounded off. His tail poked through the top of the mist as a flag for Tesnayr to follow. Frustrated, Tesnayr trailed behind the cat with relative ease. The glowing road allowed him some light to see by.

They traveled through the night nonstop. Despite the onset of early spring, cold air seeped through Tesnayr's cloak chilling him to the bone. Only the repetitive movements of walking kept him warm. Sounds of dripping water filled the still air. He listened for wildlife but heard nothing. They were alone.

Up ahead, Tesnayr noticed a golden glow in the sky. Dawn approached. It seemed as though they had just found the mystical road only to be forced to stop. Heeding the fairies' warning about traveling after daybreak, Tesnayr picked a place on the side of the road to camp.

"We should rest here," he said. "Dawn approaches and I won't risk losing our way."

Tesnayr cleared away the slushy snow and piled some dry brush on the spot forming a bed. Exhausted, he dropped his things and slumped to the ground. A small lump forced him to jump back up.

"Turyn!"

The cat had curled up in Tesnayr's makeshift bed purring contentedly.

"Where am I supposed to sleep?"

"Not here," replied Turyn.

Too tired to argue, Tesnayr cleared another spot of snow and flopped to the ground. He rested his head on his pack and fell fast asleep hoping they could cover more ground the next night.

*   *   *

Nigilin dipped the flask into the frigid water and watched as bubbles escaped the open hole until the container had filled completely. At least they had a water source nearby. But food was running low. He stoppered the flask and placed another into the water. His thoughts dwelled on Tesnayr.

The disease continued to spread. Five more had fallen ill and had to be taken to the quarantined area. Each day Nigilin and Arnin took water and food to the sick. Each day they made the four mile round trip. It wore on him. He did not know how much longer they could keep this up.

Grumblings moved among the people. Discontent rose as more fell sick. Tempers flared as supplies dwindled. He had placed soldiers throughout the camp to keep the peace, but even they were stretched thin.

Nigilin placed the third flask into the water. Ten days Tesnayr had been gone. Wearily he lifted the flasks of water and headed back to camp. Something caught his attention. Nigilin walked toward it. Rybnik strode from the trees toward the camp with a deer over his shoulders.

"Rybnik," called Nigilin.

The man stopped and looked at him. "Nigilin," he said, "Pardon my not telling you. Food has been running low so I set out early this morning to hunt. Luck must have been with me today."

"Good thinking."

"Here, let me take those," Rybnik grabbed the heavy flasks and wrapped them over his free shoulder. "You should rest."

Nigilin didn't argue. He knew he had been working himself nonstop to keep order. "Perhaps I will. But who will ensure the sick get those and—"

"I will do it," said Rybnik. "Arnin and I can handle the cooking of this deer and we will ensure some is sent to the sick."

"Nigilin clasped Rybnik's arm in appreciation. "You have proven quite useful. Thank you, Rybnik. How is Jenel?"

Rybnik's expression fell. "No improvements." He stalked off with his burdens.

Nigilin watched him go. Absentmindedly he glanced in the direction Tesnayr had left. Hurry back, Tesnayr, he prayed silently. He feared they would not last much longer.

A commotion arose within the encampment. Nigilin dashed toward it. Two men wrestled in the mud rolling around like animals. They beat at each other relentlessly.

"Break it up," yelled Nigilin as he wrenched them apart.

Rybnik stepped forward and helped hold one of the men.

"What is going on here," demanded Nigilin.

"He stole from me," yelled one.

"I did not," retorted the other.

"Yes you did." The first man charged for the second one. Instantly, Rybnik grasped his arm and wrenched him back.

"Enough," said Nigilin. "We cannot afford to fight amongst ourselves despite the reasons. Now stop this."

Grudgingly, the men walked away.

"You know it will only get worse," said Rybnik.

"We just need to keep order until Tesnayr returns." Nigilin began coughing violently. Blood tainted his chin. Quickly, Rybnik caught the man before he collapsed. "I'll be fine," said Nigilin.

"You're ill," said Rybnik.

"I said I'll be fine."

"You're coming with me." Despite Nigilin's weak protests, Rybnik held tightly to him and led him to the quarantined area where all those who had contracted the disease were.

*   *   *

Thunder roared above Tesnayr and Turyn. Lightning flashed everywhere. Tesnayr bent low as rain beat upon him until his soaked clothes weighed him down making it difficult to move. Mud oozed over his feet forming a suction with each step he took. The wind howled around him threatening to throw him off the mountain.

The night had started out calm like any other. Unexpectedly, the storm sprung up enveloping them. Torrential rain drenched the mountain as more lightning crackled around him and thunder bellowed. Tesnayr crawled through the muddy path on all fours. The slippery muck made progress difficult and agonizingly slow. Amazingly, the secret road cast its glow brightly despite the weather.

Tesnayr halted. A steep incline blocked his path. He eyed it in the lightening but could see no discernible way up. Turyn hunkered under a shelf of rock shivering in his wet fur.

"We need to find shelter," yelled Turyn over the deafening thunder.

"There is no shelter," shouted Tesnayr. "We've no choice but to go on." Tesnayr studied the steep slope. Rocks dotted it, but with the rain, climbing would be near impossible. He pulled a rope from his pack and handed an end to Turyn. "Do you think you can climb up this?"

Turyn nodded.

"Take an end of this rope," said Tesnayr, "When you reach the top, tie it around a tree or something so I can use it to pull myself up."

Turyn snatched the rope end in his jaws. He ignored the taste of the rough fibers as drool dribbled from the corners of his mouth. With a great leap, the cat sprang onto the slick rise. His four paws sank into the sludge oozing down the incline. Carefully, Turyn crawled to the top. It wasn't far, but the rain made progress challenging.

Turyn dug his claws into the earthy goo. Using exposed roots and rocks, he braced himself as he ascended. Lightning flashed. The cat clamped his jaws tighter on the rope determined not to drop it. His muscles twinged with each passing minute.

Finally, he reached the top. Quickly, Turyn spotted a tree trunk and looped the rope around it tying it securely. He pulled on it signaling Tesnayr that he had made it.

The roped pulled taut as Tesnayr grabbed hold of it and lifted himself up. Bracing his feet on anything he could find, he heaved his way up the slope. Tesnayr set his foot on a relatively flat stone. His foot slipped. Instantly, he fell into the sludge around him clinging to the rope for support. Tesnayr sat up coughing as he spat mud from his mouth. He wiped the slime from his face, but only succeeded in spreading more on himself. Carefully, he stood up.

Tesnayr used his arms to haul himself to the top. His feet skated on the grime unable to support his weight. His hands stung terribly from the effort of holding onto the slick rope. The edge drew nearer. Almost there, he thought. With one last pull, Tesnayr rolled onto the top of the hill and lay there in the pouring rain. His chest heaved from the exertion. He turned on his side and noticed the same bluish glow that he and Turyn had followed for over a week.

A strange sound echoed around him drowning out the thunder and rain. His head perked up. He listened again. The sound echoed once more. "Turyn," said Tesnayr, "Do you hear that?"

Turyn turned his ears in the direction of the noise. "What is that?"

"I think it's the horn that Sarwyn told us about. We found it Turyn!"

It echoed a third time filling Tesnayr with warmth.

"It is the horn. We must be getting close."

Tesnayr jumped in excitement. A low grumble rose beneath his feet. Suddenly, the ledge fell apart. Tesnayr leapt away from it landing on solid ground. "Turyn," he called looking for the cat.

No response.

"Turyn?" Fear gripped Tesnayr as he realized that the cat was nowhere to be found. He peered over the edge of the slope and saw nothing in the darkness. "Turyn!"

Nothing. Turyn had disappeared with the falling rock and slime. Disheartened, Tesnayr curled up on the ledge. He buried his face in his hands and wept for the loss of his only companion while the wind wailed cruelly, as though it laughed at his misfortune.

*   *   *

Nelyn gently lifted Jarown's head to allow him to sip water. His skin burned and the welts oozed relentlessly.

"Here," said Rybnik as he handed her a cloth.

"Thank you," she said. "You should not be here."

"Illness does not worry me," replied Rybnik. "Besides, my place is by my lady."

Nelyn glanced over to Jenel who had also caught the disease. The sickness was spreading rapidly. Soon the number of sick would outweigh those that were well.

"You will need this then." Nelyn handed the cloth back to Rybnik.

"Keep it." Rybnik went over to Jenel kneeling by her side. He pulled his cloak off and wrapped it around the princess with great care.

"Nelyn," croaked Jarown.

"Father," cried Nelyn, "You're awake."

Jarown coughed violently. Blood spotted his lips. Gently, Nelyn wiped them. "I'm not going anywhere before I have a chance to say good-bye," said Jarown.

"No, do not speak like that. You will get well again I promise."

Jarown smiled weakly.

"I am so sorry," said Nelyn. "I should not have treated you so badly. Of course I forgive you. How can I not?"

"Your father would be proud of you."

"You are my father," Nelyn choked back tears.

"I am merely the man that raised you," said Jarown, feebly.

"That makes you my father," replied Nelyn. "You are the only one I've known. You taught me the sword. You cared for me when I was ill. You took me in when no one else would. I no longer care about your past deeds, only about todays. You will get well, and together we will bring honor to Belyndril."

Jarown cupped his hands around Nelyn's face. "You look so like your mother. And you have your father's heart."

"I know."

"I love you, Nelyn, and am proud to call you my daughter." Jarown's hands dropped to his side.

Instantly, Nelyn placed her cheek by his mouth. He still breathed. She sat up relieved, but saddened at the prospect that he might not live for much longer.

*   *   *

Turyn awoke to a horrible pain in his left, front paw. He tried to stand. Pain ripped through him as he fell to the ground. He glanced at his paw and noticed the swelling, which meant that it had broken. Looking up, Turyn remembered the events of the night before. He had fallen with the rubble.

Turyn stood up holding his hurt paw up to avoid putting weight on it. He studied the slope and noticed that since the rain had stopped, it was not as slick as before. Turyn tried to climb up. Instantly, his paw gave out and he dropped to the ground. He tried again with the same result. Turyn lay in the wet dirt unsure of what to do. How would he ever find Tesnayr if he couldn't walk?

A vine tickled his nose. Turyn eyed it, thinking. He grasped the vine in his teeth and hauled himself to his feet. Gradually, he hopped up the hill using the vine to steady himself. His paw throbbed, but he managed to remain standing. Shifting himself, Turyn took another hop up the hill.

So far, so good.

Using a series of movements he continued to hobble up the incline while maintaining his hold on the vine. Slowly, he inched his way upward until he reached the top. Turyn collapsed on the top of the hill breathless. He looked around for Tesnayr. Nothing.

Turyn hadn't expected the man to hang about. Figuring that he had continued on, the cat limped down the trail. He sniffed the air for Tesnayr's scent. Something familiar prickled his nostrils. Taking a chance, the cat moved on hoping that he would find the man. He'd have to use scent by day and the trail by night, if possible.

*   *   *

Rybnik watched Jenel as she slept fitfully. Sweat lined her face as her fever burned. Gently, he placed a cool, damp rag on the welts that covered her arm. One burst. He wiped the pus away.

Memories flooded his brain. A picture of Janine smiled at him before turning into an irate King Slyamal issuing his banishment. Sorrowfully, he remembered the lonely trek through Knot's Pass as he sought sanctuary in Belyndril.

"Still here?"

Pulled from his musings, Rybnik glanced at Jenel who had just woken up. "Always."

"You should rest," said Jenel.

"I'm not the one who is ill."

Jenel eyed him a moment. She tried to smile, but a series of violent coughs racked her body.

Rybnik pushed a cup of water against her lips forcing her to drink.

"I'm so tired," whispered Jenel.

"You should sleep."

"I knew you'd be here when I woke. If only my father knew how you've changed."

"You shouldn't trust me so blindly," said Rybnik.

"You have that faraway look again." Jenel brushed his check with the tips of her fingers.

"Sleep." Gingerly, Rybnik pulled the blanket to Jenel's chin to ward of the cold breeze. He looked out at all of the sick people who now littered the area with a mixture of emotions reeling within him.

*   *   *

Wearily, Tesnayr trudged down the blue path. Only the stars provided light. His shoulder sagged with each step he took mimicking his mood. An owl hooted in the distance. Tesnayr ignored it.

Alone.

Darkness surrounded him mirroring his gloomy mood. Yet, he continued.

Turyn gone.

A part of Tesnayr felt that he should have waited for the cat, but his rationale kicked in. He chose not to wait knowing that such a fall would kill a man let alone a cat. He had to go on. Every minute he delayed brought those waiting for him closer to death.

Figures darted in the night. He disregarded them. Shadows plagued him, taunting him. Dark spirits his people called them. They intruded on his thoughts.

"You killed him," said one thought.

Tesnayr shoved it away unsuccessfully. He felt responsible for Turyn's absence. If only he hadn't brought him. His heart yearned for the cat's humming once more as it did provide company. Only now did Tesnayr realize how much he liked Turyn's presence.

Tesnayr walked in a fog unaware of everything around him. A chill breeze brushed his cheeks barely penetrating his senses. His feet dragged on the dirt grating the pebbles. Tesnayr didn't care if he fell. Surrounded by "if onlys", Tesnayr never noticed the light appearing in the sky.

Head hung low, he continued walking consumed with his loss. A sharp pain stung the back of his head as a tiny stone bounced off it. Suddenly alert, Tesnayr's head shot up. The sky grew brighter. All thoughts of Turyn and the night before vanished. Fearing that he may have traveled too long, Tesnayr rushed to the trees and hunkered low to the ground. The sun came into full view and the path vanished. He hoped he hadn't lost it forever.

Turyn hobbled through the trees trying not to irritate his already damaged paw. It had doubled in size making the slightest movement difficult. The constant throbbing wore on Turyn. He just wanted to stop and rest, but he couldn't. Tesnayr needed him.

The slushy snow made walking difficult, though its cold felt good on his swollen paw. Turyn hopped three legged and fell over. Gritting his teeth, he endured the pain as he forced himself back on his feet.

Something scurried past under the brush. Turyn stopped, ears alert and listening for more. He hoped that an animal had not decided to make a meal out of him. Another rustle raced through the uncovered leaves on the ground. On edge, Turyn braced himself for the inevitable. He stood his ground waiting for the thing to show itself. The leaves moved about as something glided under them coming closer. Turyn hunkered low waiting for the thing to appear. Closer the sound came. Bracing himself, Turyn was ready to spring into action when out popped a squirrel.

Relaxing his tense muscles, Turyn breathed a sigh of relief. "You startled me," he said.

The squirrel eyed him curiously. *You startled me.*

"I apologize," said Turyn. "I am looking for a man. He travels alone by night. Have you seen him?"

The squirrel thought for a moment. *I have seen a man. Strange that he travels here.*

"Where did he go?"

What do you want with him?

Turyn hadn't time to explain anything to this squirrel. He was wasting valuable time. "It needn't concern you. Please, tell me where he went."

Strange that a cat would pursue a man who travels the mountains by night.

Irritated, Turyn reined in his anger. If his paw wasn't mangled he would rip this squirrel to shreds. Forming his words carefully Turyn tried one last time. "I haven't time to explain. The man is my friend and without me he will get lost in this forest. We were separated during the storm and I must find him."

Again the squirrel cocked its head and thought for a moment. *A man did come through here following a strange road. He went that way.* The squirrel pointed its bushy tail in a direction that led through more trees and fallen brush.

"Thank you," said Turyn.

You should hurry.

"Why?" asked Turyn.

A bear roams this forest. It has woken from its sleep and is hungry. It has caught your friend's scent.

Turyn's ears fell. He did not like the sound of this. With spring approaching many animals had woken from their winter slumber. He had to find Tesnayr and help him resume the search for the waterfall. Turyn darted off and collapsed as his hurt paw gave out under his weight. Cursing, he stood up.

I know a short cut.

Turyn turned to the squirrel. "What?"

I know a short cut to your friend. He takes the long way through this forest on that shiny road. But I know a short cut through here.

The squirrel ran off. Struggling on his three good legs, Turyn followed. The squirrel sped ahead through the soft snow and wet underbrush. It would hurry back and thump its tail impatiently as the cat limped behind. The sun rose high into the sky and then dipped lower as the two moved through the forest floor. Turyn hoped the squirrel led him in the right direction.

The squirrel stopped. *This is as far as I go. Your friend should be down there. And so is the bear.*

Turyn sniffed the air. He smelled it too. His heart leaped at the prospect of finding Tesnayr, but fell with the knowledge of the bear being there. "Than—," Turyn started to say, but stopped when he noticed the squirrel had gone. Squirrels, he thought. He dragged himself down the small hill and continued in the direction of Tesnayr. Sniffing the air a few more times, he picked up the man's scent. *He was here.* Hope drove him forward helping him to ignore the pain in his paw.

*   *   *

Shouts resounded around them. Looking up, Rybnik watched as a mob of people dressed in rags approached dragging a wounded Arnin behind. They threw the man to the ground.

"We want these people out of here," screamed one man indicating those stricken with the disease.

"And we want more food," yelled a woman waving her fist.

Cautiously, Rybnik unsheathed his sword and stepped away from the sick. He approached the mob holding tightly to his blade.

"Tesnayr gave us orders and you will follow them," said Arnin through a fattened lip.

"Shut up," said the man kicking Arnin in the stomach.

Instantly, Rybnik grabbed the man by the arm, breaking it at the elbow, and shoved him back into the crowd. "What goes on here?" he yelled.

"We're tired of waiting here while more people fall sick," replied the woman.

"That doesn't matter," replied Rybnik, "We have our orders from Tesnayr to wait here."

"Where is he?" asked a voice in the crowd.

"He abandoned us," said another.

Agreements rose up all around.

Another man charged Rybnik. He rammed the hilt of his sword into the man's chest before knocking him on the back of the head with the flat part of the blade. The man doubled over allowing Rybnik to push him back into the mob. "I'll kill any who dare cross this line!" Rybnik scraped his foot across the dirt.

"As will I," said Idæas, walking up from the side.

One by one, the crowd turned back. Something in Rybnik's voice motivated them to leave.

"Here," said Nelyn, helping Arnin to his feet.

"Oh, I'll be alright," Arnin waved her away. "They jumped me when I least expected it."

"Take him to the others," said Rybnik. He started to leave.

"Where are you going?" asked Idæas.

"Unrest is brewing. I intend to put it down."

Idæas snatched his bow, "I'm coming with you."

*   *   *

Tesnayr woke to a rustling sound near him. Slowly, he sat up blinking in the sunlight. He glanced at it. It hung low in the sky. Good, he thought. Soon night would come and he could continue. He hoped that he was near the place of constant spring, the second and final sign that he was near the falls. A soft growl drew his attention.

Slowly, Tesnayr turned toward it. Standing before him was a grizzly bear. They stared at each other for several seconds. Tesnayr knew he couldn't outrun it, nor did he have any hope of killing it. He sat still, watching the beast and hoping it would ignore him.

Suddenly, the bear charged. Tesnayr jumped to his feet and ripped his sword from its scabbard. He swung the blade at the bear as it plowed into him. The air was knocked from his lungs as he crashed into the soft earth. His sword flew from his grasp and landed several feet away.

Tesnayr scrambled to his feet only to have the grizzly's massive paw ram into his chest flinging him through the air. Dazed, Tesnayr lay on the ground. Before he could move, the bear was upon him. Its massive claws tore into his flesh.

Tesnayr cried out in agony as he felt his flesh rip from his bones. Desperately, he tried to get away. The bear's jaw clamped on his ankle and dragged him back. A loud crunch told him it broke the bone. Stabbing knives shot though his leg as the bear swiped its razor claws down it.

The atmosphere filled with Tesnayr's screams of terror and pain. *Make it stop!* Another swing of the bear's claw hit him.

Out of nowhere, a black blur raced across the ground and leapt at the bear landing on the beast's face. The screeching of a cat and the roars of the bear filled the air.

Reprieved, Tesnayr reached from his sword with his one good arm. His hand curled around the hilt. Power shot through his arm filling him the strength necessary to lift it.

The bear flung the cat from its face. Blood poured from its eyes. It wandered blind, sniffing the ground. Instantly, Tesnayr raised his weapon and sank it deep into the bear's throat. He held it there as sticky blood spurted over his hand and pooled on the ground. The bear fell, unmoving. Tesnayr pulled his sword free. He wobbled for a moment. As the adrenaline of the fight wore off, his torn body felt every ounce of pain. The impulses flooded his brain and Tesnayr collapsed.

A wet, rough tongue licked Tesnayr's face bringing him back to reality, and the pain. He moaned. The licking became more insistent. Weakly, Tesnayr brushed it away.

"Tesnayr, get up," said Turyn. "The sun has set and we must get going."

"Turyn," mumbled Tesnayr. "Is it you? I thought you died."

"Not yet, but you will if we don't find that waterfall. We have to be close. We already passed the place where the horn blows. Now, get up."

Tesnayr rolled onto his side. Agony shot through him forcing him back onto his back.

"Come on," urged Turyn.

Again Tesnayr rolled onto his side. This time, he was able to overcome the pain. He set his sword blade down in the ground and used it to haul himself to his feet. Balancing on his one good leg, Tesnayr checked his injuries. Blood soaked his useless arm, chest, and back. His left foot dangled precariously. Dizziness overtook him and Tesnayr swayed. Sharp pin pricks from Turyn brought him back to consciousness.

Putting his weight on his sword, Tesnayr hobbled to the blue glow that once again revealed the secret path to the healing waterfall. Turyn followed. His broken paw felt worse than before. He didn't know how he managed to leap on the bear, but his paw wished he hadn't.

Tesnayr rested when he reached the road. His breath came in ragged gasps. He was dying; he knew that. Soaked in blood, the cold air froze his clothes to his skin making it more difficult to move. Inch by inch he hobbled.

Wolves howled in the distance. Of course, thought Tesnayr, they smell easy prey. He hopped again, teeth clenched tight in an effort to endure the pain. Warm air sailed past him. Tesnayr wavered a moment before the unusual warmth caught his attention. Trying desperately to focus, he peered ahead.

"Turyn," he said, "Do you see anything."

"Nothing unusual," replied the cat. "The air smells different. It tastes fresh and renewed, like spring."

Tesnayr's sword grated across the ground as he hobbled as fast as he could. They had to be close. He didn't care if he died on the road that night. He wanted to find the falls. Turyn hurried after him. They paused in awe at what greeted them as they rounded a curve in the road.

The blue path ended in a bed a vivid green grass overgrown with wildflowers. Bees buzzed from flower to flower ignoring the new arrivals. Chirping birds sang their melody of joyfulness unaware of the dangers outside. The distant sound of falling water reached their ears. They had found it: the place of everlasting spring.

Tesnayr's strength gave out as he collapsed on the soft grass. Turyn limped over to him. "Tesnayr, get up, please," he pleaded. "We're almost there. The water is just ahead."

Tesnayr didn't move.

Turyn raised his paw and smacked Tesnayr in the face. He didn't want to do it, but he had to wake the man up.

Tesnayr's eyes fluttered open. His swollen tongue hung out of his mouth. "Water," he whispered.

"Yes, water," said Turyn, "Follow me."

Tesnayr tried to stand but sank back to the ground.

"Just crawl," said Turyn, "It's not far."

Tesnayr reached his only good hand out and gripped the grass. With immense effort he pulled himself across it. He repeated the process. Sounds of falling water prickled his ears, but never registered in his brain.

"That's it," coaxed Turyn. "Almost there."

Tesnayr blinked. His vision blurred as he went in and out of consciousness. He just knew he had to follow the voice that kept speaking to him. He pulled himself forward a few more inches. The ground sloped slightly. Another great heave sent pulses of pain through him.

"Two more feet," said Turyn as he staggered beside Tesnayr. "You can do it. Just a little bit more."

Tesnayr's brain no longer worked. His body acted automatically and hauled him closer to the water. His muscles went limp as he rolled the rest of the way spilling over the bank and into the crisp water, taking Turyn with him.

Chapter IX
A Cure

High up in the trees sat the phoenix. The great bird watched as a man and a cat entered its domain and crawled to the water's edge. It remained where it was until the man and cat disappeared under the water. Spreading its massive wings, the phoenix sprang from its position and swooped down upon the pond. With great speed and agility its talons penetrated the water's surface snatching the two and carried them to the shore. It gently placed them on the soft, emerald grass and waited.

Slowly, Tesnayr opened his eyes. The pain had vanished and his mind had incredible clarity compared to just hours before. He sat up. Moving his arms, Tesnayr was amazed that they were both useful. He glanced at his foot wondering how it had healed.

The chirrup of a bird broke his musing. Tesnayr turned to the pond with its massive waterfall and noticed a magnificent bird. He recognized the phoenix. He sat silently as he watched the bird bend down to the water's edge. A single tear escaped down its cheek and landed in the crystal blue water. Suddenly, Tesnayr remembered where he was, how he got there, and why he was there.

"The bear," Tesnayr shouted.

"Is dead," said Turyn flexing his paw that, until recently, had been broken.

"Well, yes, but, where am I?" asked Tesnayr. "I mean, what is this place?"

"My home," replied the phoenix. "You are the first to enter here."

"So the legend is true," said Tesnayr.

"Are you surprised?" asked the phoenix.

"Considering that most legends are too fantastical to be true," began Turyn, "Well, a part of me doubted." He lowered his head meekly.

"I would have been surprised if you hadn't doubted," said the phoenix. "You have used that sword well, but remember, when this task is over you will have to let it go."

"Let it go? Where? How?"

"Again, you will know when the time comes."

Tesnayr stood up and flexed his healed ankle.

"You have a sickness among you," said the phoenix.

Inwardly, Tesnayr scolded himself for momentarily forgetting about the people who waited for his return. "The cure...we need it. I was told that only this water can cure the disease."

"You sought this place for the sake of others. You continued your search even when death was upon you. And you, Turyn, remained by his side despite your own injuries. The two of you have proven your purity of heart and shall have the cure. Take your flasks and fill them in the pond."

Tesnayr lifted the jumble of canteens. One by one he filled them with the cool, crisp water. He glanced at his reflection and marveled at what he saw. Gingerly, he lifted a hand to his face. The scar had gone.

"My scars," he gasped, "They disappeared."

"The water heals all," said the phoenix.

Turyn studied Tesnayr's face wondering why he hadn't noticed it before.

"The water will cure the illness and give you what strength you need to reach your destination. But remember this, once that last person is cured, the water will lose what power it has."

"Why?" asked Turyn.

"That is the way it must be," replied the phoenix. "There cannot be something left idly in the world that solves every ill."

"Otherwise we would never solve our own problems," voiced Tesnayr.

The phoenix nodded his head in affirmation, pleased that at least one man understood. It plucked a gold feather from its body and placed it in the palm of Tesnayr's hand.

"What's this?" asked Tesnayr.

"Keep this feather safe. At some point, you must give it to another to keep it safe until the one who needs it claims it."

"When will that be?"

"That is not for you know. Just like with the sword I gave you, one will search for this feather and it will serve them well." The phoenix stretched its wings and glanced at the sky. "It is time for you to return."

"Return," Tesnayr slapped his forehead. "How will we find our way back? Turyn, how long have we been gone?"

Turyn thought for a moment. "At least fourteen days, maybe twenty."

Tesnayr's heart fell. Over half the camp could be dead by now. "We will have to hurry and travel twice as fast."

"No need," said the phoenix.

"No need?" questioned Turyn. "What do you mean no need?"

"I will carry you," said the phoenix.

Tesnayr finished fastening his pack and the flasks to his back. He and Turyn looked at each other puzzled.

"Just what do you mean by—" Turyn's words broke off as the phoenix snatched him and Tesnayr from the ground. Its gigantic wings lifted them high into the air.

Tesnayr allowed himself to hang limply in the bird's claws. Eagerly, he looked all about him taking in the aerial view of the world. He watched in awe as the falls faded from view concealed by the trees of the mountains. The giant mountains gave him a new perspective at the trip he and the refugees had embarked upon. He stared at them in amazement.

He noticed a great valley nestled into one of the mountains. The sun's golden glow made it shine like a beacon beckoning him to come. He wondered what land that was.

"Hemíl is just there," said the phoenix as though it had read his thoughts.

Hemíl, thought Tesnayr. They were close.

Soon after their trip began, the phoenix lowered in altitude. The ground rushed toward them. With incredible ease, the majestic bird set them on the rocky surface.

"Thank you," said Tesnayr.

The bird bowed. "You haven't far to go before you reach Hemíl, but your journey is far from over. And know this: though you found my domain, you will never enter there again. Nor will you ever be granted its healing waters."

"Never," said Turyn.

"Such is the way it must be," replied the phoenix. "You were the first to find it, but all who find it never do so again. Now, you must go. Your people await you." The phoenix took off, disappearing over the horizon.

Sadly, they watched it leave.

"Too bad we will never see it again," said Turyn.

"Can you imagine if such a power were available for the entire world?" asked Tesnayr.

"I suppose, but I will never be in a place more beautiful, or more peaceful than that."

"Let's go."

Tesnayr walked toward the camp with Turyn bounding before him like a kitten. He hoped they made it back in time.

Tesnayr smelled the odor of lingering death the moment he entered the area where the sick had been quarantined. The grey pallor of the people made his heart ache. He walked among those lying on the ground shocked at how quickly the sickness had spread.

"Captain," said one soldier.

Heads turned in his direction as word of his arrival spread. Sarwyn wormed her way through the mass of people stopping inches in front of Tesnayr. "So you found it."

Tesnayr handed her the flasks of water. "Take these and give each person one drink of the water."

Sarwyn took the canteens and handed them to those who tended the ill.

A harsh cough caught Tesnayr's attention. He turned toward it and found Nigilin lying on a ragged blanket. "Nigilin!" Tesnayr rushed to the man.

"Tesnayr," whispered Nigilin. "I knew you would make it." A series of coughs beset him as blood spurted from his mouth.

Quickly, Tesnayr took a flask from his pocket. He pulled the cork out and put it to Nigilin's lips. "Drink."

Water ran down Nigilin's cheeks as he sipped the cool and refreshing water. Gradually, color returned to his gray cheeks. Nigilin's erratic breathing steadied. "Tesnayr," said Nigilin, "Am I dead?"

Tesnayr smiled. "Not yet. You didn't think I would let you go so easily did you?"

Nigilin took the flask of water and studied it. "What was it like?"

"Like no place I've seen before, and will never see again," replied Tesnayr. He let Nigilin rest while he gave the water to others.

Arnin passed the line of supplies that were to be packed onto the horses with quill in hand and a handful of paper. Though well-aware of what they had, Tesnayr wanted another inventory taken before they restarted their journey.

It had been a few days since Tesnayr's return with the magical cure. He had decided to give everyone a few extra days of rest. No doubt he wanted to rest some himself, thought Arnin. He didn't mind. The extra time gave him a chance to be with Nelyn.

"Arnin," said Jarown, "A word, if I may."

Arnin put his quill down and looked at Nelyn's father.

"You and Nelyn seem rather close."

Close, put it mildly. Arnin wanted to marry Nelyn, but hadn't figured out how to ask her. "Yes," he said.

"I suppose you wish to marry her."

Jarown's statement caught Arnin by surprise. "How did—"

"I was not born yesterday," interrupted Jarown, "Besides, I was young once myself. She loves you. I can tell. So again I ask you, do you wish to marry her?"

"Yes," said Arnin, "I just haven't figured out how to ask her."

"Meaning you hadn't figured out how to talk to me."

Arnin squirmed slightly. Jarown's statement was true, but he didn't want to admit it.

"I will make it simple for you," said Jarown, "Nelyn is strong willed and has always done what she wanted. If she chooses you, you have my blessing."

Relieved, Arnin grinned. "Thank you, sir." He started to run off to tell Nelyn the news.

"One other thing," Jarown stopped him, "You see this knife?" He pulled out a long knife with a very sharp blade and flashed it before Arnin. "Should you hurt her, this has your name on it."

Arnin gulped. "I would never—"

"Buck up, boy," Jarown clapped him on the shoulder, "You're about to get married. Smile." He left with a satisfied expression.

Arnin stood alone wondering if he had made a good decision, but knowing there was no going back.

Chapter X
A Captain Made General

The mass of people paused high up on the mountain ridge looking down upon the canyon below. After their arduous journey they had finally reached the edges of Hemíl. Tesnayr stared down at the stone keep nestled into the mountain. The fortified walls had been completed but the watch towers were obviously still under construction. Rubble littered the inside levels of the keep.

"The Keep of Edrei," said King Shealayr as though he had read Tesnayr's mind.

"A keep," replied Tesnayr. "It looks more like a construction project."

"In this case it is," said King Shealayr, "King Edrei began construction on it five years ago. The outer walls are complete and so is the throne room, but much of the inside has yet to be built. And as you can see the two watch towers are only halfway done.

"He hopes to have it completed in the next few years. It will be a great asset to his kingdom and his people. This will provide a place for them to hide should they be attacked."

"It seems to be in a horrible location," said Tesnayr as he eyed the layout of the fort. "Sitting at the edge of this ravine he has embraced a trap."

"King Edrei does not think so," said King Shealayr.

"Why's that?" asked Tesnayr.

"He said that he found an invaluable advantage provided by the mountains."

Tesnayr thought about it, but could not determine what would be so advantageous about the end of a ravine. He shook his head figuring that that would be the problem of the king and not his.

"Move out!"

Slowly, the line of migrants wormed their way down the path and into the canyon below heading directly for the unfinished keep.

Tesnayr and Jenel marched into the great hall of the keep to meet with the five kings. Torches lit their way as they wound through the maze of corridors.

"Halt," said one of the guards outside the double doors leading to the great hall.

"We're expected," said Tesnayr.

"You are," said the guard, "But she will have to wait outside."

"I will not," Jenel said.

"My lady, my orders are to only allow him entrance."

"My father is the King Slyamal and I will not be denied entrance!" Jenel shoved past the guard and burst through the doors into the great hall with Tesnayr and the guard close behind.

"My lady, please," pleaded the guard.

"It is all right, Gambin," said King Edrei. "She can stay." The guard bowed and left the chamber. "Jenel, always a pleasure." King Edrei gave her a curt nod. "Tesnayr," he said redirecting his attention, "We finally meet. You already know King Shealayr. Here are King Telinin and Nalim. And I believe you've also met King Slyamal."

With one look at King Slyamal, Tesnayr strode over and punched him square in the face. The impact knocked the man to the ground.

King Slyamal glared at Tesnayr. "You see what he just did! I'll—"

"Be quiet," said King Nalim.

"I should do more than strike you for what you did," said Tesnayr.

"I—"

"Save it, father," said Jenel who had watched impassively. "From what I hear you deserve it for what you did."

"Jenel, you would insult your own father?"

"You are not my father. My father was the honorable King of Sym'Dul who would never betray a man. But you did."

"We have business to discuss," said King Telinin.

"Indeed," replied King Edrei. "Tesnayr, word of your exploits has reached us. Only you seem to understand the orcs and the devastation they have wrought. Separate, our forces are inadequate. But united, we could defeat them."

"Then why don't you?" asked Tesnayr.

"I am certain that King Shealayr explained the situation," said King Edrei.

"He explained enough," said Tesnayr.

"Enough of these word games," King Nalim blurted out. "Tesnayr, we need a general to lead our armies. Not one of us can do it as we do not trust each other. So we are asking you. You have won the trust of many across the five lands. I've heard how men have trekked the Ársa Mountains to join your army. Will you help us?"

"You certainly do not mince words," said Tesnayr. "The last time I assisted one of you, I was betrayed. We lost the battle. I cannot help men who wish only to glorify themselves."

"We dwarves care nothing for glory," said King Nalim. "Only one among us is fool enough to put glory before all else."

King Shealayr stepped forward and drew everyone's attention. "Tesnayr, the elves of Belarnia owe you a great debt of gratitude. You saved us, and we will repay that."

"What do you have in mind?" asked Tesnayr.

"It is as Nalim has said," replied King Edrei, "We have been unable to defeat the orcs by ourselves. They have invaded each of our lands. We want you to lead our armies against the orcs. You will be in full command. You have taken the rank of captain. We will give you the rank of general. General of the combined armies of the five lands."

"General of the army of Tesnayr," injected Jenel.

"Precisely," said King Edrei.

"This sounds too good to be true," said Tesnayr. "Have you all finally come to your senses?"

"In more ways than one," said King Telinin. "I swear to you upon my life that the army of Belyndril is yours to command, so long as you defeat the orcs."

"Fair enough," Tesnayr said.

"Perhaps you should make him a king," sneered King Slyamal. Nursing his bruised pride, King Slyamal glared at Tesnayr. Something caught his eye. Peering more closely he saw that Tesnayr wore Jenel's pendant. *No!*

"King Edrei, Telinin, Nalim and Shealayr, I will accept command of your armies on one condition: my command supersedes yours for all engagements with the orcs. You must trust me fully and obey my orders. And you swear such oaths before the sorceress."

"Are you mad?" said King Slyamal with a note of fear.

"An oath sworn before the sorceress is not easily broken," said King Telinin.

"Precisely," replied Tesnayr.

"I think it is a wonderful idea," said Ernayn as she moved out of the shadows. "And as you all know, I do not take oaths lightly."

"You have got to quit doing that," King Telinin said to her.

Ernayn eyed the king with one her stern looks.

"Hemíl accepts your offer," said King Edrei stepping forward.

"You have command of the elves," said King Shealayr.

Grunting, King Nalim approached Tesnayr. "MurDair will follow you."

"You have the loyalty of Belyndril," said King Telinin, "We will follow you until the destruction of the orcs."

Everyone glared at King Slyamal. He squirmed and fidgeted uncomfortably. He knew he had done wrong in the past and he knew what was expected of him. He opened his mouth to speak, but Jenel beat him to it. "You have Sym'Dul's loyalty."

"I'm sure he thanks you, my lady, but it is the king who must swear it," Ernayn said calmly, admiring the girl's fortitude.

"Upon my life, you have command over the army of Sym'Dul," King Slyamal grunted to Tesnayr.

"Kneel, Tesnayr," commanded Ernayn.

Tesnayr did so, uncertain of her intent.

"You know what to do," she said to the five kings.

Each of the kings unsheathed their swords placing the tips on Tesnayr's shoulders. "We, the kings of the five lands, declare you, Tesnayr, general of our armies. Now rise," they said together.

Afterward, Tesnayr thanked each of the kings and left. He had work to do. The others filed out as well. "Jenel, a moment please," said King Slyamal. Jenel hung behind. "You dare embarrass your father."

"You have embarrassed yourself," replied Jenel. "I learned the truth while migrating through the mountains. I cannot believe the man who taught me to be honest, betrayed his own conscience."

"I made a mistake."

"A mistake with a huge cost," fired back Jenel. "I do not know if I can trust you anymore."

"Fair enough. One day you will be queen. But until that day I am still the King of Sym'Dul and your father. You will not openly defy me again."

"Is there anything else?"

"Why did you give him your pendant?"

"You know why," said Jenel.

"I beg you to reconsider. He is a soldier and could die at any time."

"I know what you are about to say," Jenel cut her father off, "But I love him. Do not ask me to take it back."

She turned, but before she left the chamber her father spoke one last time. "I heard about what you did for those people, leading them through the mountains and to safety. You showed great courage. A true daughter of kings." Jenel left her father alone. *Just like her mother. Just like her sister. Stubborn.*

Tesnayr rambled through the upper level of the keep. He observed the piles of bricks strewn about for intended construction. He studied the masonry that went into the formation of the already finished walls. The five-foot thick walls were well constructed with sturdy stone. Tesnayr admired the work. King Edrei certainly knew what he was doing.

"Like it?" said King Edrei as he approached from behind.

"It seems well constructed," said Tesnayr. "It should be impressive when finished."

"That it will be. You see those watch towers? When done, they will stretch all the way up to the top of the cliff face."

"A man up there could scout a vast amount of land," said Tesnayr. "I noticed the engraving in the great hall. Pardon me, but it seems a bit extravagant for a fort."

King Edrei smiled. "There is more to that engraving than just the picture. One day it might come into use."

"How's that exactly?"

"Some things are best left a secret," replied King Edrei. "This keep will be more than just a fort. Naturally it is designed to provide protection for the people should we be invaded, but I want it to be a great city. It will be a place where merchants come and trade their wares. A place for socializing. I completed the palace portion on the top level first so that I could live here. As each level is completed there will be places for shops and living space. Too many kings separate themselves from their people. But by living here anyone can come see me if they wish."

Tesnayr listened intently as the king explained his vision for the keep. He could see it himself. A place of protection as well as a place that bustled with life. He hoped that it would come to pass. Right now the only finished sections of the keep were the palace and the outer wall. The rest lay in a rugged pile of rubble.

"My lord," said a messenger as he ran up. He handed a message to the king.

"Thank you," said the king dismissing the messenger. Quickly, King Edrei read the message. His brow furrowed. "The orcs are nearby. They are expected to arrive within a day."

Chapter XI
A Rude Awakening

Tesnayr pored over the map as the flickering candle light caused the lengthy shadows to dance. He released an exasperated sigh. There was little he could do except ride out and meet the orcs head on. He planned to meet them in the valley just outside of Swalya. At this moment Arnin was leading the people of Swalya to the keep. It would provide some protection, but he did not want to fight the battle there. Though the outer walls were fortified, the rest of the keep was incomplete.

The orcs approaching them numbered at least ten thousand. Tesnayr knew he did not have anywhere near that amount even with the addition of Hemíl's army. There was little chance of any of the other kings being able to summon their forces. They were trapped. So it begins, thought Tesnayr.

Tesnayr continued to study the map. There would be little cover where he planned to stage the defense.

"You should sleep." Nigilin stepped into the room.

"I only have hours to plan a battle," replied Tesnayr, groggily. "Blast the heavens I hate this. I do not like being put on the defense. But we've no time to lead them away from the city."

"Then we will do what we can and must," said Nigilin. "You need to sleep. You are little use to us half dead. Besides, with some rest you will be able to think more clearly."

"Perhaps you're right." Tesnayr pulled himself away from the map and stretched out on a nearby cot. "The only way to meet them is head on. But there must be a better strategy."

"I'll wake you before dawn." Nigilin snuffed out the lamp and left.

Idæas concealed himself in the shadows watching as a man snuck through the out buildings that Tesnayr had placed the army in. The elf had never trusted the man since the day he had joined them in the mountains. Something about him did not feel right. His constant sneaking around and evasiveness told the elf all he needed to know. The man darted between the wooden structures taking great pains not to wake anyone. Too great.

Suspicious, Idæas followed him. He kept close to the shadows and outer walls as he crept along. The man paused in front of a structure, the very place where Tesnayr slept. Idæas slipped behind cover as the man looked about him. He peered around a corner watching as the man entered the building. Quickly, Idæas ran for the same room making no sound.

Silently, the man entered the room where Tesnayr slept. Perfect, he thought. He had spent that last few weeks attempting to complete his mission, but that stupid elf kept a close eye on him. But tonight he had been careful.

He listened as the steady breathing of Tesnayr told him the man was asleep. He tiptoed toward the bed. Slowly, he pulled a dagger from his belt. His heart pounded from the excitement, but he steadied it with measured breaths. He towered over the bed and the sleeping man. Raising his dagger high, the assassin brought it down in a perfect stroke.

A clang echoed as the dagger struck another blade in midair. The assassin's arm throbbed as strong hands wrenched the knife from him. Idæas flung the man against the wall pinning him.

Waking from the commotion, Tesnayr jumped from the cot snatching his sword. He had just unsheathed it when he noticed Idæas holding a man against the wall. The man struggled to break free, but the elf's grip held firm. "What is going on here?" demanded Tesnayr as he sheathed his sword.

"This man is an assassin," replied Idæas as guards burst into the room. "I have been watching him for the past few weeks."

"Stupid elf," spat the man, "If I don't kill him someone else will."

"What is your name?" demanded Tesnayr.

"Felznic," replied the man.

Tesnayr took a closer look at the man. "I know you. You came here with King Shealayr."

"Very good, General," sneered Felznic. "I couldn't believe my luck when that stupid elf stumbled upon me and happened to be searching for you."

"Is the man with you also in on this?"

"No. He was just one of the many who fled to the mountains. I simply used him like I used the elf king."

"Why did you want to kill me?" asked Tesnayr. "Why would you work with the orcs?"

"You think you know everything," spat Felznic, "But you know nothing. There are many of us who willingly align ourselves with the orcs. They will conquer this world and we will inherit our just reward for helping them."

"You're right about that," said Tesnayr. "The penalty for betrayal is death. Take him away."

Idæas handed the man to the guards. They hauled him outside with little protest.

"Thank you, Idæas," said Tesnayr. "I don't know how I can repay you."

"Win the battle," replied Idæas. "You go back to sleep. I will stand watch." The elf left the room and stood just outside the door in the shadows once more.

The sun rose that morning but no one really knew it had as a dingy gray light spread across the land. Dark clouds loomed above them as the army awaited the approaching orcs. Thunder rolled in the distance as Tesnayr eyed the gloomy sky. Fitting, he thought, nothing like a thunderstorm to welcome the approach of war.

Clanging metallic armor announced the approach of the orcs. His soldiers squirmed uneasily as they listened to the marching feet and battle cries of the beasts. Gradually, they appeared on the hill opposite them.

"Steady," said Tesnayr as he noticed those near him shift on their feet.

Raucous noise rose up the hill as the orcs beat their chests and roared in an effort to instill terror in their enemy.

"Lock your shields," yelled Tesnayr.

Instantly, hundreds of shields were thrust before the group of soldiers and overlapped. Those holding the shields braced themselves for the attack. Thunder exploded overhead and drowned out the cry of the orcs. Another crack of thunder echoed. Tesnayr felt wet drops of rain land upon his skin. Ignoring it, he kept his eyes fixed upon the orc commander on his larog, the orcs' morbid version of a horse.

A horn blew in the distance. Instantly, the orcs charged down the hill heading straight for Tesnayr and his men. "Brace your selves," he yelled.

Those holding the shields held fast as arrows beat against them. Calmly, Tesnayr watched the oncoming mass of armed orcs. Inwardly, his heart tried to burst out of his chest, but he kept his composure for his men.

"Spears!" he yelled when the orcs were only yards away.

The second row of men lowered their spears just as those with the shields shrank back. Chaos loomed as orcs and their larogs crashed into the shields and spears. Cries of pain echoed across the battlefield as they were skewered. Those behind the first line of orcs attempted to slow down but their momentum caused them to crash into the one before them. They too were struck by the spears.

"Spread out!" ordered Tesnayr.

Obeying his command, the soldiers ditched their formation and ran in every direction placing themselves strategically among the orc army.

"Give the signal," Tesnayr said to Arnin.

Quickly, Arnin raised a bright gold flag and brought it down. Arrows rained down upon the field from those placed on the edges of the valley. Swords clanged as they collided. Tesnayr kicked his horse and rode out onto the field to give his men courage. With expert ease he swung his sword cutting down orcs that charged him. He felt the muscles of the beast as he trampled over those before him.

Suddenly, his horse reared up throwing him off. Tesnayr crashed into the ground. He glanced over to see a larog chomping on his horse's neck. The crunching bones filtered through the mayhem to his ears. Tesnayr and the beast stared at each other. The orc upon the larog flapped the reins and charged toward Tesnayr. Gripping his sword tightly, he felt the surge of power from the blade as it sizzled up his arm. *Believe in the sword.*

The larog's massive paws pounded the mud as it ran for Tesnayr. Just before the creature was upon him, Tesnayr reared up and slashed his blade across the tender flesh of the larog's neck. The animal crashed into the slime as rain continued to pour from the sky. Wasting no time, Tesnayr raced to the orc on the beast and rammed his blade through it. He straightened and spotted Arnin awaiting his command. "Now," he yelled.

Arnin heard Tesnayr's command. He raised the gold flag again and waved it from side to side. An orc appeared behind him. Instantly, Arnin whirled around dodging the killing blow of the orc's weapon. He twisted again skewering the orc with the flag pole before tossing the creature aside. Dropping the flag, Arnin pulled out his sword and charged into the fray.

Nelyn stood on the edge of the trees overlooking the scene. She scanned the battle awaiting the signal from Tesnayr. *There!* Immediately she darted off to where King Edrei was. "The signal has been given," she said as she leaped on her horse.

"Very well," said King Edrei. "Forward!"

The king kicked his horse and raced toward the battle followed by Nelyn and the rest of his cavalry. King Edrei felt the heavy breathing of the horse as it charged toward the turmoil. Focusing intently on the orcs before him he never noticed the arrows heading for him.

An arrow struck his horse in the neck. The horse stumbled and fell. King Edrei slammed into the ground. Pain shot through him as the horse pinned him down. King Edrei struggled under the dead weight of the animal trying desperately to get free. A horse leaped over him and thundered on in its charge. Mud oozed over him as he continued to fight to get out from under his horse.

An orc snuck up behind King Edrei. Slowly, it inched forward with its axe raised. King Edrei noticed the orc too late. He reached for his sword, but could not grab it. Preparing for the end, King Edrei accepted his fate. Suddenly, a lion burst from the trees and tackled the orc. The king watched dazed as the beast clawed relentlessly at the orc. Ferocious roars echoed around him as he watched the lion kill its prey.

"My king," said a man as he knelt by King Edrei. With immense effort the man freed his king from the animal's weight. "Are you all right?"

"Fine, thank you," replied King Edrei. "I need a horse."

"Take mine." The man handed the reins to the king who accepted them without argument. He jumped on the horse and sped off into the battle.

Nelyn plowed through the mass of orcs. She swung her sword with great force and agility. None stood a chance who tried to defy her. She steeled herself for facing the enemy that ravaged her home. A larog attacked her. Quickly, Nelyn turned her horse around with ease and ran off. She pushed her horse onward with the larog behind her. *A little bit further.* Then, she spotted it. Spears stuck out of the ground. Nelyn jammed her heels into the horse forcing it to jump over the javelins. She held her breath as her horse sailed gracefully through the air to land on the other side. A piercing scream echoed behind her. The larog bled profusely as the spikes stuck through its body.

Nelyn kicked her horse again and headed straight for the thick of the fighting. Her breathing matched that of her mount. She pushed the animal harder. Its labored breathing came in snorts. Leaning low in the saddle, Nelyn headed straight for her goal. She trampled over a group of orcs. Nelyn jumped off her steed.

She sliced the air with her blade catching one orc in the middle. Instantly, she whirled around and stabbed another orc in the chest. One attempted to back hand her. Nelyn blocked the swing and punched the orc in the face before cutting her sword across the neck. She dropped to the ground and snatched a sword from the slick surface. Springing back to her feet, Nelyn used both swords to destroy the orcs surrounding her. Block. Cut. Slice. She refused to think about her movements using everything that Idæas had taught. Allowing the swords to dictate her movements, Nelyn became unstoppable.

More orcs approached. She twisted around crossing her blades in an X stopping a killing blow to her heart. With a flick of her wrists she disarmed the orc. Swiftly, Nelyn cut the beast in the leg bringing it to its knees before bringing the point of her weapons to its neck and chopping off its head.

In her focused state, Nelyn never noticed the orc in the distance aiming an arrow straight for her chest. But Jarown did. From his vantage point he watched his daughter and saw an orc take aim with its bow. Wasting no time, he charged across the field to the creature. Slipping on the oozing mud, Jarown fought to maintain his balance and momentum. He scooped a discarded shield from the trampled grass and holding it before him, Jarown rammed into an orc knocking it to the ground. Onward he continued. He swung the shield at another orc's head catching it in the chin before bringing it back and ramming it in the beast's throat.

Jarown continued toward the orc targeting Nelyn. He was almost there. Jarown placed the shield in front of him again bracing himself for the impact. With a loud cry he charged for the orc and crashed into it with all his might sending the beast flying. His arms twinged as they took the impact of the collision.

Quickly, Jarown discarded the shield and unsheathed his sword. He stepped forward bringing his weapon in an upper cut that destroyed the orc's bow. Furious, the beast brought out a knife with a jagged blade. He flung it at Jarown, but the man blocked it. The orc grunted loudly before snatching a javelin from the mud. He lunged. Jarown stepped into the attack twisting his body before striking the beast in the stomach. His sword poked out of the orc's back. Jarown tossed the dead creature to the ground with little remorse.

Jenel stood on the outer wall of the keep overlooking the small canyon that led to the valley and city beyond. Despite the distance from the battle, the rock walls funneled the noise to her ears. She waited in tormented anticipation to know how the battle was going. The waiting drove her insane. She hated it.

"Staring out there will not end the fight any sooner," said King Nalim behind her.

"I can't stand this waiting," replied Jenel.

"You should be below."

"What are you doing here? I thought dwarves hated being left out of a fight."

King Nalim eyed her for a moment. "We do, but someone has to protect the keep. And only fools corner a dwarf."

"I should be out there," said Jenel.

"Your father gave you specific orders."

Jenel snorted.

"And so did Tesnayr," added the dwarf king.

More cries from the battle beyond caught her attention. Jenel huffed in frustration. "I should be out there."

"To what end? Do you know how to use a sword? Are you trained for battle?"

Shamed, Jenel shook her head. Though she had some lessons on the use of a blade, she had never been trained as a soldier. But the waiting for the army to win or lose raked her nerves. What would they do if the orcs reached the keep? "This fort is not finished. How will we protect ourselves if the orcs make it this far?"

"Leave that to me. Now get below," said King Nalim.

Jenel began to leave, but paused. "King Nalim," she said, "I never knew dwarves could be so—"

"Wise?" asked the dwarf when Jenel paused.

"Understanding." Jenel trotted down the stone steps to the area below.

King Nalim looked back out at the gorge. Uneasiness swept over him. He sensed that Jenel planned something. A loud creak echoed as the gates to the keep opened. The dwarf turned toward it about to demand what fool opened the gates, but hesitated. A dark shape on a horse zoomed out onto the canyon road and disappeared into the distance. King Nalim recognized the figure immediately. "Fool of a girl," he shouted.

The dwarf dashed down the steps toward the stables. "You, you, and you," he said pointing at three soldiers standing idle, "Get horses and follow me." He leaped onto a horse and chased after Jenel with the three soldiers behind him.

Jenel paused on the ridge of a hill observing the fight below her. She frowned as she watched. It wasn't going well. Jenel looked about her thinking fast about a way she could help. Desperate, she studied everything. Suddenly, she spotted it. Not far from her stood a catapult manned by ten orcs. She steered her horse in the direction but halted suddenly as King Nalim appeared before her.

"Fool of a girl," he said. "What do you think you are doing? You're coming with me."

"Look," countered Jenel as she pointed to the battle below.

King Nalim followed her gaze and frowned. Instantly, he knew that Tesnayr would lose the battle. There were just too many orcs.

"There is a catapult just over there," said Jenel. "Perhaps we can use it to fire upon the approaching orcs. It may not be much, but it could be just enough."

"Very well, but follow my lead," said King Nalim.

They dismounted and tied the horses up. Carefully, they snuck up on the orcs surrounding the catapult. King Nalim motioned for them to pause. He studied the position of the orcs and their movements. "You three, go around over there and wait for my signal," said King Nalim to the soldiers with them. "You," he turned to Jenel, "Stay here. I mean it."

Jenel clamped her mouth shut and acquiesced.

King Nalim scooped up a rock and left the protection of the bushes. He crept toward the busy orcs. Carefully, he tossed the rock overhead. It landed with a soft thump attracting the attention of the orcs. He pulled out his axe yelling, "Now!" King Nalim planted his axe in the back of one orc while the three men charged in.

The orcs whirled around and met their attackers. The three soldiers dispatched four, while the other six stalked toward King Nalim. The dwarf backed toward the catapult with his axe raised. Jenel watched from her position and soon learned why no one wanted to corner a dwarf.

One orc charged. King Nalim dodged darting between the beast's feet. He jabbed another in the face with his axe before striking a second in the chest with the sharp blade. Turning he lopped off the head of the first. A third attacked. Instantly, King Nalim plowed his weapon into the orc's stomach spilling the creature's insides. Without losing a beat, the dwarf hacked the fourth before crushing the skull of the fifth. The remaining orc wavered.

"Come on you coward," goaded King Nalim.

Angered, the orc ran for the dwarf. King Nalim darted to the side before striking the creature in the neck. The orc stood still, stunned before dropping to the ground.

A twig snapped behind Jenel. Startled, she turned around pulling her knife from her belt. Another orc that they failed to noticed leered at her. Without thinking, she pushed her knife into the beast's windpipe. Warm, thick, black blood oozed over her hand. Stunned, she stood motionless unable to comprehend what had just happened. But Jenel knew that only luck had saved her, not any skill of her own.

"My lady," said King Nalim. "Are you alright?"

"Yes," whispered Jenel. "It's just I've never killed anything before."

"There is a first time for everything," said the dwarf. "You'll be fine. Just remember this: in war, kill or be killed. Now, we have a job to do."

Pulling herself back to reality, Jenel sheathed her knife and went to the catapult. "Help me turn it."

King Nalim snapped his fingers. Each of them grabbed a section of the catapult and pushed. Their feet slid in the greasy mud. Gradually, the catapult moved in the sludge. Sweat dotted their faces despite the cold wind.

"Stop," order King Nalim. "Line it up."

One of the men leaped into the seat on the weapon. Carefully, he aimed it for the middle of the orc forces. "Ready," he said.

King Nalim strode over to the trigger. He gripped his axe tightly, raised it high over his head and sliced through the rope. Instantly, the catapult flung its load. They watched as the boulder slammed into the ground flinging mud everywhere and crushing several orcs. Frightened, many of the orcs below ran away.

"Reload," ordered King Nalim.

They did and released it just like the first. Again, the stone crashed into the ground below them killing more orcs and frightening the others.

Tesnayr watched as the second boulder slammed into the orcs. He looked about him and knew that they could not win this battle the old way. He sounded the retreat. "Fall Back!"

Tesnayr grabbed a nearby horse yelling at the others to retreat. Immediately, his army fled the field. They raced away from the orcs and into the rugged hills of Hemíl. Tesnayr pushed them onward making certain that the orcs did not follow. Once safety was assured, he pulled everyone to a stop.

"Tesnayr," said Nigilin, "Why did we retreat?"

"You know why," replied Tesnayr.

Tesnayr paced the ground agitated. He thought they could have a head on meeting. He was wrong. The orcs were too many. He needed a plan, a trick. And he needed one quick before the orcs regrouped and came after them, or worse, poured into the city itself. An idea struck him. "Sarwyn," he called.

Immediately the fairy appeared before him. "You called?" she said ignoring the battle.

"Can you sneak into the orc camp?" Tesnayr led her away from prying ears.

"Yes."

Quickly, Tesnayr pulled some parchment and a writing utensil from his pocket. He scribbled on it for several seconds. "I want you to take this and get it to the orc commander. Tell him this is a dispatch from Galbrok. Make certain he reads it immediately. Now go!"

Sarwyn disappeared. Tesnayr hoped his plan worked.

"What are you planning?" asked Nigilin.

"We can't win this battle the old fashioned way," replied Tesnayr. "I hope the orcs believe my ruse."

*   *   *

Sarwyn crept into the makeshift camp the orcs had constructed for their commander. Her magic allowed her to pass by like a shadow, but she knew it wasn't enough. She snatched a breastplate and helmet from the ground and she smeared black mud over her skin. That, with her power should do the trick, she thought. Head down, she swerved around passing orcs. Their inhuman grunting made her dislike them even more.

She walked determined not to look any of the beasts in the eye or attract attention. She spotted the command tent up ahead. Sarwyn strode toward it at a fast pace though a guard stood at the entrance. Thinking quickly, Sarwyn tossed a pebble distracting the guard's attention while she swept past him.

The pungent smell within the tent nearly gagged her. Turning her cough into a grunt, she managed to avoid detection. She went to the orc commander who busied himself with his officers. "Commander," she said with a guttural voice placing the fake dispatch in the orc's hand. "This is from Galbrok."

The commander took it. Before the orc could reply Sarwyn snuck out of the tent and disappeared in the mass of orcs preparing for an attack.

The orc leader read the fake dispatch. His expression turned grim. Interesting that this should show up now, thought the orc. He scrunched the parchment into a ball and tossed it to the ground. "Move out," he ordered. "Galbrok has called us back."

Tesnayr watched the orcs in anticipation. Silently, he prayed that his plan worked. If it didn't, he would be forced to attack head on again, a measure he wasn't certain of surviving. An orc horn blew forcefully, reverberating off the surrounding cliffs. Tesnayr held his breath. Slowly, the army of orcs moved off. They looked like ants marching in formation. Another orc horn sounded. It worked. The orcs were leaving. *I bought us some time.* But for how long, Tesnayr did not know.

"We'll set up camp here," ordered Tesnayr.

A nearby soldier saluted and strode off to pass the word.

Chapter XII
A New Ally

Slowly, King Edrei walked across the now silent field with Tesnayr by his side. The rain had stopped. Each step stained his leather boots a brighter shade of red. The king looked out at the valley that had once grown abundantly with fields of crops and farmland. All that remained was mud and rivers of blood. The difference between the two became indistinguishable. The destruction to his home pained him. The once fertile land had become little more than a tomb.

Crows circled above cawing incessantly and waiting to feast upon the dead. King Edrei stepped around the bloodied remains of a horse and its rider. Bodies lay scattered everywhere; an arm here, a leg over there, and a partial torso nearby. Most of the dead had lost any identifying characteristics. The mourning would be great. A particularly gruesome scene greeted him over a small rise. Clasping his hand to his mouth, King Edrei forced himself to keep the contents of his stomach.

Smoke drifting across the valley added to the gloomy atmosphere. Piles of burning wreckage covered what ground wasn't littered with carcasses. Dispersed throughout were soldiers as they solemnly checked for any that still lived. He watched as Tesnayr callously kicked a dead orc with the sharp point of his boot. Despite the roughness of his actions, King Edrei noticed the twisted emotion on Tesnayr's face.

"We need to bury them," said King Edrei.

"We haven't time," said Tesnayr. "My ruse only bought us days. A week at most."

"We can't just leave them here."

"We do not have time to grant every man here an individual funeral. And where would we bury them?"

"I know a place," said King Edrei.

"It will have to be done by nightfall."

King Edrei nodded. "Captain," he called to a passing soldier, "Grab every available man. Search through the field for wounded and cart the dead to Cavern's Den for burial. You have until sunset."

"Yes, my king. And what of the orc remains?"

"Burn them," said Tesnayr.

The man saluted and ran off.

"General," said Nigilin approaching from the side, "We've done the count. There isn't an exact number yet, but at least half of our people our dead. The number of orcs that perished is smaller."

"How many weapons did you obtain?" asked Tesnayr.

"About 200 swords, 96 axes, and 154 shields," replied Nigilin, "Most, however, are too damaged to be of any use."

"Grab some men and go gather supplies: weapons, armor, and food," said Tesnayr, "And take the triplets with you. They seem to be adept at finding what we need."

Nigilin gave a knowing smile and disappeared.

"Triplets?" inquired King Edrei.

"Three brothers who look exactly alike, and have proven to be most useful, while at the same time most annoying," replied Tesnayr. A hint of a smile played across his face.

Soft coughs caught their attention. Not far from them lay a fatally wounded man from Sym'Dul. He clutched his middle as blood squirted between his fingers. Next to the soldier knelt King Slyamal. The king supported the man's head as he tried to speak.

"My king, did we...defeat them?"

"Yes." The sorrow in King Slyamal's voice surprised Tesnayr. "We have won this day. Your courage saved us."

The dying man parted his bloody lips into a grin before going limp.

Gently, King Slyamal picked the dead soldier up. He stopped momentarily when he noticed King Edrei and Tesnayr watching him. Pushing his way past, King Slyamal carried the man off the field.

By sunset all had been prepared for the massive funeral. The bodies had been piled in a cave as directed by King Edrei. Gathered outside stood what remained of the living. Wearied sadness engulfed them all.

Tesnayr stood at the forefront overseeing the entire affair. A part of him envied the dead; their troubles were over. He had wanted King Edrei to give the eulogy, but the king had insisted he do it. "You are our commander now," the king had said.

Clearing his throat, Tesnayr did his best to contain his emotions. *I must be strong.* "We are gathered here to honor those that died this day," he began, "They gave their lives that we might live. These men valiantly fought against the orcs to protect their families and their homes. They have paid the ultimate price.

"Let us not mourn for their loss. They gave it freely. Let us honor them as the brave and courageous men they were. And let us strive to be as honorable as they were."

At the end of Tesnayr's speech, twenty soldiers stepped forward with wreaths made from pine and sage. The sweet aroma of both filled his nostrils blotting out the stench of death. One by one the men placed their wreath within the tomb. Upon Tesnayr's signal, two men rolled a boulder in front of the cave opening.

Silence ensued only to be broken by a strong male voice singing. Gradually, others joined until the mountains of Hemíl echoed with their parting melody.

Oh great voice upon the wind
Hear our plea.

Take these men who died this day
And guide them to the fabled lands.

Do not let them wander, lost souls
Journeying through mountains' mist,
Deep in caverns, a prison with
Endless walking until Time grows old.

Save them from treacherous seas,
Boundless and aimless as can be
Endless lust for far off adventure,
Lost in eternity with no measure.

Take them to bountiful lands
Of flowing rivers with milk and honey.
Spare them from Death's realm
Of tortures and sadness aplenty.

As the final notes of the song ended everyone filed away to tend to their duties. One by one people left the gravesite until all that was left was the silent tomb.

Tesnayr stared at the night sky listening to the men sing again while racking his brains for a new plan. He felt like a failure. Newly appointed general, and the first engagement was a defeat. If it hadn't been for the use of trickery they would have all been killed. Before he had had victories, but not against such a huge army. Besides, it seemed for every engagement won there were three more to fight immediately afterwards. "This isn't working," he said to himself. "Just like the last time."

"Of course it isn't," said Ernayn stepping from the shadows.

Annoyed, Tesnayr stood to greet her. He held his tongue refraining from voicing what he wanted to say to her and her knack for appearing from nowhere. "May I help you?" asked Tesnayr.

"I am here to help you," replied Ernayn.

"Or yourself," muttered Tesnayr.

Ernayn cocked her head at his statement. "It's true that I have my reasons for being here. I like the orcs no more than you do. It is also a fact that your method of fighting is not working, though you have had many victories. I should think that a man who knows the orcs like you do would have discovered where they are most vulnerable."

"Their leader, Galbrok," said Tesnayr, "Is their vulnerability. Kill him and the orcs would be leaderless. They'd scatter."

"Oh, so it is that you know how to beat them."

"Cut the sarcasm," said Tesnayr growing more annoyed. "If you have a reason for being here, state it."

Ernayn pursed her lips. "You would do well to show me more respect."

"You have to earn it first. If you have some advice, please, give it."

"You need a wizard," said Ernayn.

"Wizard," said Tesnayr. "I have seen many strange things since I came here, but people who do magic?"

Fire emanated from Ernayn's hand. "Do not discount it because you have never witnessed it. You are good at fighting the orcs and have had a few victories, but you are no nearer to winning than you were when this war first began. Even you are missing one key element. This wizard has been well placed to overhear rumors. Such insight may prove useful."

"And what is that?" asked Tesnayr.

"You need a wizard," said Ernayn, again, "I know where you can find one."

"Where?"

"In Swalya. There is a tavern there where he spends his time. He has a fondness for drink. The locals will know who you are looking for."

"In a tavern," commented Tesnayr. "He isn't—"

"Oh, I wouldn't worry about that," interrupted Ernayn. "He may be a little inebriated, but no trouble. He may help you where you need it most." Ernayn stalked off into the dark leaving Tesnayr even more perplexed than he was before.

"A wizard," Tesnayr muttered to himself, "Things just keep getting more interesting."

*   *   *

Rybnik carefully stalked his prey in the dim twilight. The deer had not noticed him. Remaining silent, he raised his bow and took aim. A twig snapped. The doe ran off taking supper with it. Rybnik jumped to his feet sword in hand. Two orcs walked toward him.

"Put your weapon down, human," said one.

Rybnik refused.

"We do not wish to fight you," said the orc again. "We have an offer for you."

"Offer?" Rybnik kept his weapon raised in case of an attack.

"We orcs are not unreasonable. As I am certain you humans aren't."

"You are Rybnik," said the second orc.

"How do you know my name?" inquired Rybnik, suspicious.

"Galbrok knows many things. He knows all about you and the failed coup you staged ten years ago. He knows that you have been banished from your home." The first orc circled Rybnik as it spoke. "Let us put all pretense aside. Galbrok has an offer for you. The same one he has made to many of you humans and those who are wise accept."

"What is your offer?" asked Rybnik.

"Your general lost the battle today. We all know it. He could not defeat my master before. He will not defeat him even now."

Rybnik listened intently. He knew that they had not won the battle. It was only chance that made the orcs leave before they had all been killed.

"You are privy to Tesnayr's secrets," said the first orc.

"Hardly," replied Rybnik. "I have only known Tesnayr for a few weeks. And he does not include me in his inner circle."

"But you can acquire that information. You're very good at such things," said the second orc with an oily tone.

"What do you want?"

"Our army is on its way back here," replied the first orc, "We simply want you to ensure that Tesnayr and his forces do not put up much of a fight. If we succeed in killing them all, you will be greatly rewarded. Say the throne of Sym'Dul."

"How do I know you'll keep your word and not kill me after I've delivered my part of the bargain?"

"We could kill you now if we wanted to," said the first orc, "But there is no need. If you refuse our offer you can go freely because no one who stands against Galbrok will survive this war. But if you accept, Galbrok always keeps his word and rewards those who serve him most generously. Think about it. We will be back here tomorrow night for your answer."

The orcs left. Rybnik rested his sword by his side. Unsure of what to do, he stood there for several moments. A bird cawed in the distance. Rybnik went back to camp once he was satisfied that there were no more orcs in the woods.

*   *   *

Tesnayr entered the town of Swalya with Nelyn, Arnin, and Nigilin. They strolled through the winding streets. No one paid attention to them. They appeared to be only another group of soldiers looking to relax. Laughter echoed from a building drawing their attention.

"Where is this wizard?" said Nelyn.

"Ernayn said we would have no trouble finding him," replied Tesnayr.

Nelyn approached a lone man in the street. "Where can we find the wizard?" Immediately, a loud pop sounded from down the street with yells and screams. "Perfect," she said to herself. Nelyn took off for the commotion with the others close behind.

They burst through the grimy doors of the tavern and knew instantly that they had found the right place. In the center of the room sat an old man with stringy brown and white hair hanging around his face. His soiled and torn robes displayed a man with no hygiene.

"Only slightly inebriated," said Nelyn in a sarcastic tone as she watched the wizard swing his mug of ale around. The liquid sloshed and spilt over the side spraying anyone in the way.

"I'm telling you," slurred the wizard, "Women are trouble."

He swung his empty hand around the room. Items exploded where he pointed.

"I was going to get married once," another shake of his hand produced a loud pop. "But she left me." Another loud pop occurred as something else broke. "She wanted to marry a normal person. A normal person! Can you believe that?" This time glasses shattered as the wizard waved his arms around.

Having enough of the side show, Nelyn took the lead and walked up to the wizard. "Wizard," she said, "You're coming with us."

"I'm finishing my drink," slurred the wizard. He pushed his arm out and the fire in the center of the room flared to three times its normal size. The surprised crowd scrambled to avoid the flames, knocking over several tables.

Nelyn snatched the mug from the wizard's hand and slammed it on the table. "Arnin," she said.

Arnin and Tesnayr each took an arm and hauled the wizard from his chair.

"Unhand me," yelled the wizard. "I'll turn you all into pigs." The four stood there waiting for the wizard to carry out his threat. He raised his hands and his face turned red as he concentrated really hard. Nothing happened. "I appear to be out of sorts tonight."

Arnin and Tesnayr grabbed the wizard again and dragged him out of the tavern. His arms flailed and the barrel of mead behind the bar exploded, showering everyone with foamy brown liquid. The patrons dodged out of their way, relieved to have the old man gone.

"Where do we take him?" asked Arnin.

"The river," said Tesnayr trying not to gag from the odor emanating from the wizard. Within minutes they had reached the river. Arnin and Tesnayr unceremoniously tossed him in. The wizard hit the water with a tremendous splash. He burst through the surface gasping and coughing. The cold water seeped through his clothes causing the sensation of needles to surge through his body.

"What is that?" said the wizard as Nelyn waded to him.

"Soap," she replied.

"You wouldn't."

Nelyn seized the wizard and shoved him under the water. She pulled him up and scrubbed his skin raw with the soap. Water splashed everywhere as the wizard struggled to free himself. His flailing caused rocks to fly around them at random. Ignoring his obscenities, Nelyn's hand moved furiously as she scrubbed him down, washing away most of the dirt and grime.

"Apparently she would," whispered Nigilin to the others.

"Enough! Enough," roared the wizard. He twisted and squirmed until he broke free of Nelyn's grasp. "What was all that for?"

"The smell," replied Nelyn, coldly, "You drunken bastard." Water sloshed as she waded to shore.

"I demand to know what is going on."

"Aw, Max, surely a bath will not kill you," said Ernayn, stepping from the shadows into the moonlight.

"Ernayn," spat Max as he crawled out of the water. Slowly, he pulled himself up, his feet slapping the ground as he walked. Puddles formed where he stood on the sand. "I should have known you were behind this."

"Indeed."

"I need to get back to the tavern."

"Your intoxicating friends can wait," said Ernayn.

"Get out of here you witch!"

"I'll leave when I choose."

"Such is always the case. You never do anything for others, always for yourself."

"You're no testament to selflessness and charity," snapped Ernayn.

"Don't you criticize me, you ungrateful ingrate. I'll...I'll—"

"You'll what? You've never been able to best me, wizard, and you know it."

Crunch, rustle, crunch. Watching the argument attentively, Nigilin munched on some nuts from his pocket. Even Tesnayr and Nelyn sat silently as Ernayn's and Max's shouting match intensified.   None of them wished to get between the two as sparks flared from all their fingers.

"You two know each other?" said Arnin, tentatively.

"Know her," thundered Max. He stomped his foot on the ground. A sound resembling an explosion emanated from it and echoed around them.   "Sometimes I think I know nobody, but her. Always showing up unannounced." Bark flew off of a tree sending shards in their direction. "Always getting unsuspecting people to do her bidding. Serving her own interests is more like it."

"Max, you think so ill of me," Ernayn purred.

"My wedding day! You remember that?" A wave of water flared up from the center of the river. "Left there at the altar by my bride because you, you conniving sorceress, had to pop in."

"I didn't receive an invitation," said Ernayn.

"There was a reason for that," replied Max. "I never sent you one. I didn't want you there. I could have married and had children and had a normal life. But, no. You had to show up. The moment she did the guests screamed. They ran away. Couldn't get away fast enough. Then, she drops the fact that I

am a wizard. Not that I was going to be able to hide after that.
And no girl wants to marry a wizard. People who have the ability
of magic are always considered strange and unreliable.

"You scared my bride away," he pointed at Ernayn. "Life has
never been the same since. You old—you old toad!"

"Mind your tongue." A dangerous note entered the sorceress'
voice.

"I ought to blast you into oblivion." Suddenly, blue flames
swirled around the wizard. They built in intensity growing hotter.
The flames fizzled out. "Damn. I need a drink." Nelyn smacked
a flask in the wizard's hand. Greedily, he uncorked it and took a
big swig. Water sprayed everywhere as he spat it out. "What is
this garbage?"

"Water," replied Nelyn.

"Water?" gasped Max, "I need something stronger."

Having enough of Max's attitude Tesnayr stepped in. "Water
is all you are going to get. From this day forward you will not
have any drink."

"What?"

"You know the orcs," said Tesnayr, his tone serious. "They've
swarmed the land."

"I know of those filthy beasts," Max said through gritted teeth.

"We need your help," Tesnayr said, "There are things you
know about them that I do not."

"Tesnayr, the hero of the five lands, who has vanquished the
orcs time and time again does not know how to defeat them,"
said Max, sarcastically.

"Save the snide remarks," replied Tesnayr, "You have spent
months—"

"Years," interrupted Ernayn.

"Spent most of your time," reiterated Tesnayr, "In one tavern
or another. People talk freely around drunks. And you are no
exception. I am certain that you heard rumors, or bits of
information about the orcs from those who support them."

"I might have picked up a detail or two," said Max in a wary voice.

"Unlikely, in your state," said Nelyn.

"My dear girl," Max said, "Even an inebriated wizard is useful. I may not have been able to walk, but I could still observe those around me."

"Will you help us?" asked Tesnayr.

Max glared at Ernayn. "I'm sure this is all her doing."

"Consider it a way to make amends," Ernayn said, calmly.

"Make amends," spat Max. "It wouldn't be necessary if you hadn't butted your nose where it didn't belong."

"I did apologize," said Ernayn.

"Save it," Max shouted.

"Will you help us," interrupted Tesnayr, having grown weary of the two's argument.

"Of course I'll help you," yelled Max. "I don't care for those wretched beasts. Besides I was running out of coins for my habit."

"Really," said Nelyn with slight interest.

"Yes," replied Max, "Even a great wizard like me can run out of theatrical displays of magic that wows the people."

"You mean that they did not care for your parlor tricks," said Nelyn.

Air spurted from the wizard's nose as he huffed in frustration. "One day, dear girl, you will be awed at my magic. One day I will prove to you just how great a wizard I am."

"Perhaps," Nelyn conceded. "Camp is this way, and so is a bath." She stalked off with the others close behind.

Max stood his ground fuming. "I've already had my bath!"

*   *   *

Sing all ye of Hemíl
and of the great King Edrei.
Death tried to take him

but failed against the Great Lion.
So come all enemies
we await your venture
for our king is protected
by the spirit of the lion.

"What is that rubbish they are singing?" asked Max as he stepped away from the opening of the tent.

Tesnayr listened to the new song that one of the soldiers had composed. A small smile crept across his face. "King Edrei's life was saved by a lion the other day. Apparently the men have made a song honoring it."

"What nonsense," said Max. "It was probably pure chance."

"Most likely," agreed Tesnayr. "But let them be. It does them good to be able to sing about their king. Besides, we have other matters to discuss."

"So you need my expertise," said Max as he chewed on his pipe.

"According to Ernayn," said Tesnayr.

"I wouldn't listen to that witch," said the wizard. "The truth is you do not need me."

"Perhaps not," said Tesnayr, "But you have spent most your life in the tavern and men tend to be open mouthed there."

"The orcs have swept over the five lands, this you know," said Max, "They also have men working for them as there are many who are willing to sell their services for a few promises. This you also know. But what you do not know is that the orcs are actively recruiting."

"The orcs have always recruited others," said Tesnayr.

"You misunderstand me," said Max. "The orcs have been seeking people, desperate people. They make offers and even let those who refuse to leave unharmed. They do this by day or night."

"That is a new move for them. I wonder what Galbrok is up to."

"For someone who understands the orcs, you are missing something."

"Don't you start," warned Tesnayr, "If you know something, then tell me. Don't play these games."

"It isn't a game," replied Max, "Merely a statement. I have heard of your exploits, General. Even those who frequent taverns have spoken of you. You have fought the orcs, formed your own army, defied a king, and won many victories. Yet little is known of you. And stranger yet, despite your glorious outcome, you are no nearer to winning. Why?"

"You're the wizard. You tell me."

"Please, General, you don't need me to figure out the obvious."

"So you've said."

"Why Ernayn wanted me out of that inn is anyone's guess. But now that I am out of there I think I will stay away for a while.

"Think, Tesnayr, why did the orcs succeed in conquering your homeland? Why is it that despite your successful exploits that you are no nearer to victory than you were when this first began?"

Tesnayr pondered the question a moment. "There are so many of them. No matter how many orcs we kill, Galbrok always has more. It's as though he grows them in a field. Once more, there are always those willing to serve people like him. Even Blynak has joined his ranks."

"Yes, I remember Blynak. He caused the king of Belyndril a bit of trouble some fifteen years ago. Then he disappeared. And now he is helping the orcs. Most likely he has been promised his own kingdom.

"So, numbers alone will not win the war."

"No," said Tesnayr.

"And this last defeat brought you close to decimation."

"Yes. It was cunning that allowed us to live, but once the orc commander figures out he has been tricked, he will be back. And in a far worse temper."

"And what would it take to truly defeat the orcs?" asked Max.

"Galbrok's death.   The orcs are incapable of truly thinking. They are not intelligent. They think collectively, but are always in need of a leader, of someone telling them what to do. Kill their leader and they will flee in a panic."

"Strike the head of the snake."

"Precisely."

"But if the orcs are not capable of critical thinking, then why is it that Galbrok is?"

"Because Galbrok isn't truly an orc," replied Tesnayr. "Not entirely at least. The orcs like to use people for their pleasure. His father was an orc. His mother was human. She abandoned him when he was born. Many of the orcs who command have a mixed heritage.

"The problem is, Galbrok never fights openly. He stages the battle, but remains in the shadows. He uses fear to conquer. The only way to kill him is to get him out in the open. Or assassinate him. But it has never been done."

"Interesting that you know such intimate details of our enemy," said Max. "So you survived today with cunning. You need Galbrok to show himself so that you can kill him. How do you plan to do this?"

Tesnayr's head ached from all the double talk. Sometimes he just wished someone would tell him what to do instead of forcing him to figure it out. He knew that his current direction would lead to the same end as before.

"It is okay to lose the battle, so long as you win the war," said Max. "You might want to remember that."

Chapter XIII
Discontent

Rybnik stared out at the empty battlefield. *So much death.* He followed Tesnayr only to be led to this moment. The time had come for him to make a choice, a choice he had made long ago.

"I thought I'd find you here," said Jenel.

"You shouldn't have come," replied Rybnik, moodily.

"I'm concerned about you," she said. "You've been distant lately."

"I like my solitude."

"I don't believe that."

"Believe it," said Rybnik.

"Rybnik, what's wrong?" asked Jenel concerned.

"Nothing. It's just, why are we here? We lost the battle yesterday. The orcs have managed to conquer Sym'Dul and Belyndril. Belarnia is destroyed and it is only a matter of time until they take the rest."

"We didn't lose."

"Oh we did. Trust me."

"What has gotten into you?" demanded Jenel.

"Nothing," said Rybnik, "Everything. Why do you trust me?"

"I have no reason not to."

"You do realize that I am responsible for your sister's death?"

"Rybnik," whispered Jenel, "Don't."

"I am," shouted Rybnik. "And what were you doing with that catapult?"

"I merely wanted to help."

"Help? You foolish girl, you could never help us. You're a palace brat who never spent time in the real world." Rybnik drew closer to Jenel. "Foolish, just like your sister. Your father was right not to trust me."

"I-- I don't understand. We have been friends for over ten years," Jenel cried.

"Friends? Did it ever occur to you that I was simply using you for the throne of Sym'Dul, like I used Janine?"

"No! You wouldn't."

"Wake up woman!"

"Why are you telling me this?"

"Because there is a new player in this land, and he is winning," replied Rybnik. "You'd best decide whose side you are on. I've already found mine."

"I don't believe it," said Jenel.

"It's time you realize that the world is full of hurt. Your sister was just collateral damage all those years ago. That little wench meant nothing to me."

A loud clap broke the air as Jenel slapped Rybnik hard across the face. "Get out," she yelled. "Get away from me!"

Rybnik stared at Jenel coldly. His hand whitened on the hilt of his sword as he tightened his grip. "You'll meet the same end." He stalked off leaving Jenel alone with her tears.

It had been five days since the battle. Many within the army were on edge. Tesnayr did not blame them. He knew it was only a matter of time until the orcs showed up again. In the meantime, he ensured that every man busied himself with necessary tasks. The clanking of the blacksmiths' hammers filled the air as they fixed broken shields and sharpened swords. Many set about perfecting their own weapons, while others tried to sleep as best they could.

Food had run low. Tesnayr hoped that Nigilin succeeded in finding some. There wasn't much within the city and the incomplete keep had little to offer. He meandered through the groups of soldiers letting them see him, trusting that his presence would steel their already frayed nerves.

Pounding hooves boomed from behind. Tesnayr turned at the sound. A bunch of horses galloped into the camp led by three men he knew quite well. Nigilin brought up the rear. The triplets pulled the horses to a stop and jumped off their mounts with glee.

"What's this?" asked Tesnayr.

"You wanted supplies, General," said Nular. "And we brought them." He beamed triumphantly.

"Tesnayr," said Nigilin, "You wanted me to use these three to gather supplies and I did. I must say, they found everything we needed rather quickly."

"Where did you get all this?"

"It just so happened that some men were taking these horses to the orcs. They had food and weapons with them as well. These three managed to sneak into the camp and relieve those men of everything," replied Nigilin.

"I'm impressed," said Tesnayr. "How did you three do it?"

The three brothers grinned at one another with glee. "It's quite simple really," said Nular.

"They were just sleeping and had no guard—," said Nular.

"—so we were able to sneak in," said Nedis.

"We clonked them over the head," added Nylin.

"And with a bit of luck—"

"—and finesse—"

"—maybe a bit of both—"

"—we took their horses, food, and weapons," finished Nedis.

"Hardly seems worth it," said a dry voice. Rybnik appeared from behind the group of prancing beasts. "The orcs still outnumber us and they will return soon."

"What's eating you?" asked Nedis.

Rybnik glared at the man.

"You need to lighten up," said Nylin.

"Perhaps we can turn that frown upside down," said Nedis. "Or not," he added when Rybnik glowered at him before walking away.

"Why would the orcs want horses?" asked Nigilin.

"Food," replied Tesnayr. "Good work boys."

The triplets grinned even more as they took the horses and supplies away to be stowed.

"Max?" Nelyn poked her head into the wizard's tent.

"I had a bath earlier this morning and do not need another."

"Might I speak with you?"

"You are speaking," said Max from his cot. Releasing a loud sigh, he sat up. "It appears that a wizard does not need his sleep. Oh very well, what do you want?"

"Arnin and I wish to be married."

"Congratulations."

"And we want you to marry us."

Max gave Nelyn a wary look. "No," he said.

"No? Why no?"

"I mean, I do not do weddings."

"Why not?" demanded Nelyn.

Max whirled on her. "I haven't been to a wedding since—" Calming himself, the wizard started over. "I do not think I am the best one to conduct the ceremony."

Disappointed, Nelyn pursed her lips and headed for the tent opening. "I suppose you're right. Perhaps Ernayn will be willing to perform the ceremony."

"You'd let that witch marry you?" Max's change in tone stopped Nelyn.

"She said that if you refused, then she would be more than happy to."

"Why would you let that pompous, arrogant, manipulating woman marry you?"

Nelyn faced Max with an innocent expression. "We did not wish to disturb the kings and the local elder is ill." Nelyn headed for the opening again. "Do not concern yourself. If you are busy, Ernayn will suffice."

"Wait," said Max stopping her. "There is no way on this green earth that you want that sorceress to perform your wedding. You would be cursed from the start. I will do it. The least I can do is give you two a good beginning by blessing your union. When is the happy day?"

Tomorrow." Nelyn kissed Max on the cheek in appreciation. "Thank you."

The old wizard huffed pushing her away. "There's no need to thank me. No need at all. It will be my pleasure."

Nelyn left with a satisfied smile on her face.

A warm sun rose the next morning lighting up the joyful day and the impending ceremony. People buzzed about administering the last details for the banquet that would follow. The entire town of Swalya attended thankful to have something to celebrate.

Poised in the front of the crowd was Max in fine robes and freshly combed hair. Arnin stood in front of the wizard awaiting his bride. The soft notes of a flute danced through the air.

Slowly, Nelyn walked up the aisle with Jarown by her side. She wore a simple white dress that one of the women from town loaned her. Wildflowers in her hair accentuated its golden color. Jarown placed her hand in Arnin's taking a small glance at her unicorn pendant before stepping aside.

"Today we gather to witness the joining of this man and this woman," said Max. "Who gives this woman to be married?"

"I do," said Jarown.

"And who gives this man to be married."

"I do," replied Tesnayr.

"Nelyn," said Max, "Do you accept this man, knowing only him and to be bound to him for the rest of your days?"

"Yes," Nelyn replied.

"Arnin, do you accept this woman, knowing only her and to be bound to her for the rest of your days?"

"Yes," said Arnin.

Max held a goblet of wine high above his head. "As you have pledged yourselves to each other, drink of this cup and become one."

Nelyn and Arnin each held the goblet taking a sip of the wine.

A child carrying a pillow with two bracelets walked up to Max. He took the gold bracelets placing one on Nelyn's left wrist and the other on Arnin's right. "You may kiss your wife."

Eagerly, Arnin kissed Nelyn almost knocking her off her feet as the entire crowd cheered and clapped. They turned to face everyone. Jarown gave Nelyn a peck on the cheek. "I am so proud of you." He shook Arnin's hand. "And remember what I said about treating her properly."

A table lined with rolls, roast chicken, last season's squash, and a cake stood in the center of the outdoor gathering. The meager wedding meal seemed like a great feast to the attendees.

"Tired?" said Tesnayr to Nelyn as she rubbed her sore feet.

She put her shoe back on, "Not entirely."

"The innkeeper in town has set aside a special room for you and Arnin. Congratulations to you both."

"Thank you, General," said Nelyn.

As night settled on the land people trickled away until only a few stragglers remained.

Chapter XIV
A Dismal Prospect

"I've called you all here to discuss the upcoming battle," said Tesnayr. "As you know the orcs will be here by morning. We will not be facing them on the open field. This time we will fight them in the canyon."

"That is suicide," said King Telinin. "There is no room for maneuverability."

"You asked me to lead your armies. Now I am asking you to trust me," said Tesnayr.

"But we barely survived the last encounter," said King Telinin.

"Every war has its setbacks," interrupted King Edrei.

"But are you certain about the canyon?" asked King Shealayr. "There is no room for maneuvering as Telinin has said. And it puts little distance between the orcs and the people within the keep. And that keep cannot withstand an assault in its current state."

"It's decided," said Tesnayr. "King Nalim is building a barricade across the canyon to stop the orcs. We will place ourselves upon it and in the surrounding cliffs. The point is to group them together."

"Put them in a pen," muttered King Edrei, "A pen for slaughter."

"Exactly," said Tesnayr. "But once they are confined we will need to close their exit. That is where Rybnik comes in."

"Rybnik," said King Slyamal, startled. "I will sooner trust an orc than him."

"Tesnayr, you cannot be serious," said King Telinin, "The man was banished for trying to kill Slyamal. Surely, you can think of a better man than him."

"He's been grumbling an awful lot and sowing discontent among the men," said King Edrei. "Are you certain you want to use him?"

"I know his past and the decision has been made," said Tesnayr, "As for his discontent, it is no different from what some others are voicing. Defeat does that to men. Everything depends upon Rybnik."

"That is what I am afraid of," grumbled King Slyamal.

"You will be dispersed here, here, and here," said Tesnayr as he pointed to his hand drawn map. "Rybnik will close any chance of escape using the cavalry to trap them. Afterwards, we will come out of our hiding places and attack. This tactic has worked in the past and as long as we all do our jobs, it will work again."

"We will do as asked," said King Shealayr.

"Then it is settled," said Tesnayr, "Go prepare your men and may luck be with us all."

Tesnayr looked over the preparations for the battle. He admired the work of the dwarves. They excelled at building things out of nothing. The rock wall that King Nalim and his dwarves built was solid and sound, despite the fact that it had been constructed within hours.

"Will this hold?" asked Tesnayr.

"It will hold," replied King Nalim.

"Protect this ground at all costs. Do not let any orcs get past this wall."

"It will be done."

Tesnayr hiked up the path that took him up the canyon wall where he could await the arrival of the orcs. "They are approaching," he heard the scout yell.

Time to see if all his planning was worth it, he thought. He crouched beside Arnin behind some rocks. The ground thundered from the pounding of the orcs' marching feet. The closer they came, the more Tesnayr's anxiety grew. He eyed Rybnik in the distance. His stern expression masked his thoughts.

The sounds grew louder. The shouts of the orc commander reached the soldier's ears. Tesnayr breathed steadily as he waited for the beasts to take the bait. *Come on.* Slowly, the orcs entered the trap, cornering themselves. For a moment, Tesnayr thought that their numbers seemed smaller. He rejected the thought forcing himself to concentrate on the matter at hand.

With anticipation, he watched as the orcs filled the canyon and stopped at the rock wall that the dwarves hid behind. Perfect, he thought. "Arnin," he whispered, "Give the signal."

Arnin blew on his horn. Instantly, battle cries filled the air as the mix of soldiers under Tesnayr's command burst from their places of concealment and charged into the canyon toward the orcs. The orcs turned to face their opponents as they realized that they had been tricked.

Tesnayr pulled his sword free of its sheath. He gripped it tightly as he felt the power of the blade surge through his arm. He swung at the first orc he met and sliced it clean through the middle. He raced down the rocky hill path and into the thick of the battle. Another orc charged him. Tesnayr swerved missing the deadly blow by inches. Quickly, he whirled around bringing his sword up. The orc blocked.

They locked swords as Tesnayr struggled against his muscular opponent. The orc head butted Tesnayr breaking their standstill. Dazed, he stood still shaking his head to clear it. The orc screamed as it attacked. Clumsily, Tesnayr sidestepped the orc. He finally regained his senses and sliced the orc in the back. Enraged, the orc swung a fist at Tesnayr. He blocked ramming his knee deep into the beast's stomach. As the orc doubled over, Tesnayr brought his sword upward cutting the orc from the groin to the head.

King Nalim waited for the orcs to get closer before springing out from behind the wall. He burst from behind the rock swinging his giant axe. "Come on you filthy scum," he yelled.

Several orcs sneered mistaking his small size as an easy target. King Nalim swung his axe at one cleaving it in two. The other orcs paused momentarily before attacking. King Nalim released a battle cry as he charged the orcs. He smashed one orc in the head with his weapon before lopping off the head of another. With a flurry of movements, the dwarf lined up body after body.

"Protect the wall," he called to his dwarves.

With a ferociousness that matched their king, the dwarves attacked the orcs. No one got past their line.

A group of orcs charged the wall heaving a battering ram. Noticing it, King Nalim leapt off the wall running for them. "Destroy them," he shouted.

Dwarves spilled over the rocky barricade charging the orcs. They hacked with their axes forcing the creatures to drop the battering ram as they feebly tried to defend themselves.

King Nalim snatched a burning piece of wood and set the log aflame. Once it was engulfed, he directed his dwarves back to the wall.

Jenel stood atop the canyon watching the battle rage below. Tesnayr and her father had forbidden her to participate in the midst of it. After repeated protests they relented to let her be the flagman. Her palms were clammy as she gripped the flag pole tightly waiting for the signal. Her heart pounded furiously as she waited in nervous anticipation.

Arnin's horn sounded again. Her ears perked up at its call. It echoed a second time. Recognizing the signal, she released the flag. She waved the gold flag back and forth with all of her strength. An arrow clinked as it landed two hundred feet below her. She smiled inwardly, confident that she was well out of range. The flag flapped noisily as the wind whipped it about. Jenel continued to wave it and hoped Rybnik was watching.

Rybnik ignored the clanging of swords around him. He waited just outside the cave that hid the cavalry he was to lead into battle upon Tesnayr's signal. He saw the gold flag flying in the wind. He remained still as he inhaled deeply.

"Rybnik, sir," said one of the young troops, "There's the signal."

"Yes, son, there it is," replied Rybnik.

Without warning, Rybnik scooped up a rock and flung it at the top of the cave entrance. A low grumble began and rose in intensity as boulders fell sealing the opening. Terrified, the soldiers tried to flee, but were too late. They were locked in the cavern.

Rybnik whistled loudly. Out from the shadows appeared orcs on their mounts of desecrated beasts. "It is time," he said.

"I do not like following human maggots," growled one orc.

"Would you like to tell that to your commander," spat Rybnik.

Uneasy, the orc fell in line.

"Right then," said Rybnik, "Follow me!"

The hooves of their animals echoed on the rock walls as they stormed into the fray.

Tesnayr watched as the gold flag upon the top of the canyon billowed in the wind. He turned toward the canyon entrance knowing that at any moment Rybnik would appear with the cavalry. The pounding hooves of beasts reached his ears. All around him soldiers smiled knowing that the battle would soon be theirs. Their grins turned to somber fear as Rybnik appeared with a band of orcs.

"We've been betrayed," yelled Arnin.

Tesnayr's men fled in all directions frightened for their very lives. The battle had been lost.

"Retreat!" yelled Tesnayr. "Head to the keep!"

Quickly, a mass of men ran for the keep only to be stopped by the very wall Tesnayr had built to trap the orcs. Now they had been trapped by their own plans. The orcs fought with renewed fervor as they realized that their quarry had become easy prey.

Men scrambled over the rock structure in an attempt to break free. They trampled each other in their desperation. King Nalim hopped to the top of the wall and knocked any who tried to climb it back to the ground. "Stand your ground you cowards," he shouted.

Some of the men stopped their panicked frenzy and regained their composure. They turned to face their enemy.

"We will make our stand here," yelled Tesnayr. "King Edrei, archers!"

King Edrei signaled his archers. Instantly, the sky darkened as it filled with hundreds of flying arrows. Each arrow struck its target. Metal against metal rang through the air as swords clashed. Men and orcs alike dropped to the ground as they were killed.

The earth rumbled. The low growl moved through the ground. Suddenly, the earth jerked violently. It shook with such force that the ground broke open shooting cracks through the cliff face. Soldiers lost their balance as the ground rocked back and forth.

Orcs and men panicked. They dropped their weapons and bolted from the ravine. They flattened each other in their attempt to get away from the earthquake. Boulders fell on top of them crushing entire groups as they ran. Their shrieks of terror grew more distant with each passing second.

King Slyamal spotted Rybnik. Rage filled him. He jumped on a horse and chased after the man. He pushed his mount onward ignoring the shaking ground. Anger fueled his movements as he drew closer. Pain gripped King Slyamal as a lance rammed into him knocking him off the horse. The animal galloped away. Panting, King Slyamal rose to his feet making certain that he had not suffered any permanent injuries.

An orc jumped him from behind. King Slyamal flung the creature off. The orc kicked dirt into the king's eyes blinding him momentarily.   Quickly, it swept the man's feet out from underneath him.   King Slyamal heard his sword clatter to the ground as it fell from his grasp. He looked up in time to see the orc leer over him in triumph. Then, the blade of a sword poked out from the beast's stomach. Shock covered its features as it crumpled to the ground.

Tesnayr pulled his weapon free and reached for the king. Reluctantly, King Slyamal grasped the man's hand allowing himself to be pulled to his feet.

Slowly, the ground came to a halt. Silence ensued. Everyone watched as the orcs regrouped with their commander and disappeared over the horizon into the setting sun. Tesnayr stood by King Slyamal's side watching as a lone horseman followed after the orcs.

Rybnik had betrayed them all.

Book Three
Five Made One

Long ago in a faraway place
stood five lands, divided and separate.
They had neither fortitude nor grace

Darkness engulfed them and desperate
they turned to a man named Tesnayr.
For he alone could merit

Willingness and strength to bear
burdens greater than the sun.
So they made him commander and heir.

He did what many thought couldn't be done.
Victory Tesnayr delivered; and peace.
They declared him king: five made one.

Chapter I
Ride East

A somber mood rested upon all within the Keep of Edrei. They had been betrayed. Men grumbled amongst themselves about the wisdom of their general. He had trusted Rybnik. Rybnik had sided with the orcs. Only the sudden earthquake had saved them.

Tesnayr listened to the mutterings of the men from his spot of seclusion. He knew their thoughts. He understood their sentiments. War had dealt their courage a heavy blow by stealing their hope. Hope. Such a thing was difficult to come by. He knew they needed it, but had none to offer.

The phoenix chirruped beside him. Why do you stand here, it seemed to be asking. Tesnayr and the phoenix stared at one another for a moment. Suddenly, he knew what he had to do. He stepped out of the shadows and placed himself among the wearied soldiers.

"The general should never have trusted that Rybnik," grumbled one man, "It was a foolish mistake."

"You're right," said Tesnayr, startling all those present. "Are you surprised to hear me admit such a thing? Why do you all sit here wallowing?"

"We lost the battle," said a young soldier.

"True, but we are not defeated," said Tesnayr aloud. "Galbrok has not won. Even if we lose a hundred battles we are not defeated."

"But if that is so, then how is it possible?" asked the same soldier.

"Battles are not waged on the field alone. If we are defeated here," Tesnayr pointed to his heart, "Then we have lost. But as long as we continue to fight, as long as a single man decides to not accept Galbrok's rule, then we have not truly lost.

"We've suffered a blow, yes, but we are not finished. We shall overcome this challenge. We are men, elves, and dwarves; separated by race, but bound by a common goal. Citizens of the five lands, rise and let it be known that you did not accept defeat, but chose to push onward."

Tesnayr pulled out his sword allowing its power to fill him. With one mighty strike he brought it down upon the stone wall of the keep carving the symbol for his name.

"As long as I breathe, I shall never cease in my quest to bring down Galbrok. As long as I can stand I shall run to meet him head on. As long as I can grasp this blade I shall fight the orcs. What say all of you?"

A chorus of cheers and shouts reverberated throughout the unfinished fort. Above them soared the phoenix screeching in approval of Tesnayr's resolve.

"General Tesnayr," said Idæas as he approached, "The kings wish to speak with you."

"Very well."

Tesnayr climbed up the stone steps to the upper level of the keep. He strode quickly across the courtyard and through the giant doors that led to the great hall where the five kings awaited. Their mood matched that of many of the men. He knew what they wanted. Their expressions hid nothing.

"General Tesnayr," King Telinin said, "We have a problem."

"And you think I am unaware of that?" asked Tesnayr. He knew this was all about Rybnik.

"Come off it, Tesnayr. You put Rybnik in charge of closing this trap you had set for the orcs. And he betrayed us. He betrayed you," said King Telinin.

"What he means is that he thinks that we made a mistake in naming you high commander of all our armies," said King Nalim.

"Do you think so?" asked Tesnayr.

"What I think," replied King Nalim, "Is that with Rybnik's betrayal we are in a lot of trouble."

"Understating the obvious again, dwarf," said King Telinin.

"Gentlemen, please," King Shealayr said. "Rybnik's betrayal is a blow to all of us, but surely you are not implying that Tesnayr knew about this. He had no reason to not trust him."

"He had every reason," said King Telinin, "Slyamal warned you, Tesnayr, about the man."

"Which doesn't mean much," said King Edrei.

"Pardon?" King Telinin replied.

"Telinin, we all know that Slyamal has never liked, or trusted, Tesnayr," King Edrei said. "The issue now isn't Rybnik's betrayal, but what we are to do about it."

"Name a new general," suggested King Telinin.

"Are you mad?" said King Nalim. "One mistake and you want a new commander? Whom did you have in mind?"

"I do not know," replied King Telinin.

"A new commander," said Tesnayr, "What were you all expecting? Surely, you did not expect a quick victory. Traitors have always been among us, so should the fact that I mistakenly trusted one be a surprise? Rybnik helped us cross the mountains. He saved many lives. He gave me every reason to believe that he hated the orcs. One mistake should not scar a man for life."

"What are you suggesting?" asked King Telinin.

"You all named me general knowing that there was the chance of failure. Rybnik's betrayal is a setback, but we are not defeated. I intend to bring down Galbrok. And believe me Rybnik will get what he deserves."

"He's right," said King Slyamal. Everyone turned toward him. The man had sat silently in a corner of the chamber listening.

"Slyamal," said King Edrei. "You've been strangely silent."

"Tesnayr is right," repeated King Slyamal, "There was no reason for him to not trust Rybnik. I on the other hand had every reason to doubt the man's loyalty, but then Tesnayr would know nothing of what happened ten years ago in Sym'Dul."

"But I did know," said Tesnayr, "Your daughter told me."

"And yet you," began King Telinin before being interrupted.

"But she had every reason to believe that he had changed. And I trusted her judgment," said Tesnayr.

"I should have known she'd stay in contact with him," said King Slyamal. "She was only a child when Rybnik tried to usurp my throne. Any lie he fed her she would have believed. He must have been planning to use her against me, but then the orcs came and he found a better offer. No, gentlemen, we cannot replace Tesnayr. We made him our general and despite what happened we are bound to stand behind him."

"But what if he leads us into another defeat?" asked King Telinin.

"Have you forgotten about the oath?" replied King Slyamal.

"Strange that you remember," said King Edrei.

"Strange that you have forgotten," King Slyamal said.

"You seem changed," said King Telinin to King Slyamal.

"Do I? My daughter has spent the last several nights weeping because of Rybnik," said King Slyamal. "Besides, if we admit that Tesnayr is not fit to command, we will be admitting that we made a mistake. Sym'Dul has fallen and Galbrok has made his home in Drynelle. The die is cast. It's time we play our hand." King Slyamal left the room.

"What do you plan to do?" asked King Edrei.

"The orcs will have ridden east back to Drynelle. That is where I propose we go. We'll leave within the week," said Tesnayr.

"Why not now?" asked King Telinin.

"The men need rest," replied Tesnayr. "And it will give the orcs time to think they have won, which will make them cocky."

"But there is one problem," said King Nalim, "Rybnik knows things. He might tell the orcs our secrets."

"That is the risk we will have to take," said Tesnayr.

"Just answer me this," said King Nalim, "If we follow you, will I get the chance to kill these foul beasts?"

"Absolutely," replied Tesnayr.

"Good," said King Nalim, beaming as he stroked his axe.

*   *   *

Those within the keep never noticed the lone figure wandering through the battlefield. She stepped cautiously making certain not to tread upon anyone. In her heart, Nelyn knew that only the dead littered the canyon. Most had been buried, but some remained. She only cared for one. She had not seen Jarown since the beginning of the battle. The more she walked, the more her heart sank with a cold realization: the man she called father was dead.

Her foot brushed against a solid figure. Delicately, Nelyn looked down. Just the remains of an orc. Crows provided the only life in such a desolate place. Something glinted in the moonlight. Nelyn rushed to it recognizing it immediately. She fell to her knees beside Jarown's lifeless corpse. His shield rested by his side. Little good it would do him now.

Gently, Nelyn lifted Jarown's corpse. She cradled it as tears dropped onto his cold skin. *No!* Anguished cries escaped her as she cradled the remains of her father.

Quieting her emotions, Nelyn did what she had to. She laid Jarown delicately on the sand. Carefully, she placed his sword in his hands resting them upon his chest. With great care, she laid his shield beside him. A warrior's pose.

Nelyn searched the empty landscape for brush and wood with which to build a pyre. The people of Belyndril burned their dead; they did not place them in empty tombs. She owed him a proper burial. Hours passed as Nelyn gathered the necessary materials to properly send Jarown's spirit to the afterlife. She skillfully placed the brush around and under Jarown. She made certain that it would burn bright, but slowly. She did not want it to go out before his remains had turned to ash.

"Farewell, father," she whispered, striking her flint. One strike sent sparks to the dried wood. Instantly, it burst into flames.

Nelyn took a few steps back. She stared at the orange flames as they danced around Jarown. Tears streamed down her face as she could no longer hold in her sorrow. Solemnly, she sang a solemn prayer for her departed father.

Hear my plea, voice of wind
Protect this man at his end.
He faced death with valor;
In thy halls grant him honor.
In flaming fire he becomes ash,
Grant him thy honorary sash,
So the world will know his sacrifice;
And that he stood against vice.

Nelyn's voice cracked as she broke down into racking sobs, unable to finish the song. Arnin walked up behind her. He had followed her and noticed the burning pyre. With a solid voice, he finished the melody.

To you a great warrior we send.
Take heed, voice of wind.

Nelyn jerked around. She ran into Arnin's arms. He held her as she wept for the loss of Jarown. They stayed there until the fire burned out, turning into smoldering coals. Nelyn scooped some ash into the palm of her hand. Raising it high above her head, she released it into the wind. The breeze carried the ash away spreading it across the war torn land. Nelyn glanced at Arnin with her puffy eyes before walking back to the keep. He trailed after her in silence.

      *   *   *

Nigilin sat on the cold, wet stone of the wall. Rain drizzled around him soaking him all the way through. He stared out at the canyon beyond where the remains of the battle still stood. The grumblings of the men mostly faded away after Tesnayr's speech. It was a good speech. It even riled him up.

A commotion caught his attention. Nigilin glanced over and saw the triplets dragging another man. Frowning, he walked over to see what they were doing.

"What are you three up to?" he asked.

"Nothing," replied Nedis.

"We were just taking out the garbage," added Nular.

The man in their arms struggled.

"Alright, he was speaking ill of the general," said Nedis.

"I'm certain that we can all handle a few insults," said Nigilin.

The three brothers grunted and headed away.

"Oh, fellas," called Nigilin, "The latrines are the other way."

Smiling broadly, the triplets hauled the man away. Nigilin chuckled to himself. He remembered being that young and doing the same thing to a man that insulted his commander. That should shut the guy up for a while, he thought.

Nigilin looked up and saw a lone light glowing in a window. Jenel's chamber. His heart ached for her. He could only imagine her suffering.

Jenel lay face down on her bed. Her puffy eyes and face told any who saw her that she had been crying. Her tangled hair covered her features. For three days she had refused to see anyone and refused to eat. She hadn't even bothered to bathe or change her clothes. Rybnik's betrayal had cut through her and ripped her heart. She had not only trusted him, but she had loved him the way a child loves a parent.

Soft fur brushed against her and nestled in her lap. Jenel barely registered it. "My lady," said Turyn as he curled in her lap, "The maid is outside with a tray of food."

"I'm not hungry," said Jenel.

'You must eat," said Turyn.

"I can't," whispered Jenel. "I can't believe he turned on us like that."

Turyn put a soft paw on her hand to comfort her.

"He was my mentor, my friend," said Jenel, "And to learn that he had used me for ten years—when he told me that I passed it off as stress. But now I wonder if what he said was true and I foolishly thought he cared about me." More tears streamed down her cheeks.

"Sometimes we don't really know the people we love," said Turyn. "And perhaps, he did care about you in a way, which is why he told you the truth."

"But that doesn't make sense," said Jenel.

"Perhaps it does," said Turyn. "Jenel, I am sorry about all this. But there is little any of us can do about it. Rybnik made his choice. All we can do is choose how we will respond."

"I want him to pay for what he did," Jenel hissed.

"I'm sure he will," said Turyn, "I must go. Take care of yourself."

         *   *   *

"We head for Drynelle," said Tesnayr explaining his plan to the five kings. He had been called into another meeting with them. He understood them wanting to know his agenda, but thought this meeting a waste of time. Politics was not his strong suit.

"Drynelle," said King Slyamal.

"Yes," said Tesnayr, "That is where Galbrok is. He has taken your city and therefore all of Sym'Dul. He plans to head back for Belarnia. He lost it once, but will not lose it again."

"Belarnia has its own measures of protection," said King Shealayr.

"Like it did last time?" asked Tesnayr. He didn't mean to sound rude and regretted his statement. "I'm sorry. The only way to defeat the orcs, is to destroy their master. Galbrok is their master. Orcs think collectively. As such, they need someone capable of independent thought to lead them. Galbrok is half orc, half human and thirsts for conquest."

"A mindless horde then," commented King Telinin.

"Yes," said Tesnayr, "But even a mindless horde is dangerous. He pulled out a map of the five lands and used it to demonstrate his plan. "We will ride southeast first towards Belarnia. After we pass Castille we shall turn northward to Drynelle. It will be easier to ride through the plains instead of hiking through the mountains.

"We are bound to meet some resistance along the way. But it shouldn't be much. Mostly it will be pockets of people spread out."

"How do you know?" asked King Nalim.

"I know Galbrok. He has taken Sym'Dul and Belyndril. Though he has lost Hemíl for now, he knows he has weakened us. He'll take Belarnia next. Then MurDair. After that he can attack Hemíl from both fronts."

"Strange that you know Galbrok so well," murmured King Nalim.

"It's a simple chess game," said Tesnayr.

"A what?" asked King Edrei.

"A game of strategy that I played as a child," said Tesnayr. "The trick is to stop him from taking Belarnia and MurDair. We will win back Belyndril and defeat Galbrok at Drynelle. That is the plan.

"King Telinin, since Belyndril is your kingdom, then you will lead the attack there. Most of your army has hidden just outside of La'nar. You will gather them and take back the city. Once you have done that then we will have won Belyndril. That is the only place the orcs have conquered."

"It was all they needed to," said Telinin. "La'nar is where my castle is. It is the heart of Belyndril."

"Exactly," replied Tesnayr. "Much of the surrounding area has been vacated now that La'nar is in Galbrok's hands. He knows he has won. But he will not expect you to attack.

"King Nalim, I need you go to MurDair and round up your dwarves, any who can fight. You will take them to Drynelle where we will meet you."

"That is no short distance," said King Nalim. "And the time frame you are proposing, we will not be able to meet it."

"Not if you go by foot," said Tesnayr, "You will be riding dragons."

"Dragons!" exclaimed all five kings in unison.

"Yes, dragons," said Tesnayr. "I have their loyalty. They will take you, King Nalim, to MurDair and bring your dwarves to us at Drynelle. Make certain that you are ready to fight when you get there. King Telinin, Selexia will take you to Belyndril."

"Won't that leave MurDair open for attack?" asked King Nalim.

"No," said Tesnayr, "Because when word reaches Galbrok about the fall of Belyndril. He will forget about MurDair. We will keep him busy on this side of the Ársa Mountains.

"Now, we will need someone to stay here at the keep."

"I'll stay," said King Edrei. "It is my keep and these are my people."

"I'll stay as well," said King Slyamal. "Two can protect the people better than one."

"Then it is settled," said Tesnayr. "King Telinin and King Shealayr, we leave in the morning. King Nalim, you fly to MurDair."

"Must I?" said King Nalim, "We dwarves prefer to stay close to the ground."

Tesnayr chuckled to himself. He understood the dwarf's plight. Flying a dragon wasn't on the top of his to-do list either.

The great hall emptied. Only King Edrei and King Slyamal remained behind.

"Edrei," said King Slyamal, "I must ask a favor of you."

King Edrei eyed King Slyamal suspiciously. The two had been locked in war for so long that it seemed strange for them to suddenly be allies. "Name it," he said.

"I need you to watch after my daughter. She cannot go back to Sym'Dul, but she will be safe here. Please."

The note of pleading in King Slyamal's voice caught King Edrei by surprise. The arrogant man was desperate to protect his only child. "I will care for her as though she were my own. She will be safe here."

"Thank you." King Slyamal left the room. He seemed beaten and not as proud as before. A change had taken place in the man. King Edrei pitied him.

The warming sun upon the Keep of Edrei erased the last traces of the battle that took place days before. Tesnayr checked on his men as they saddled up and prepared for the long ride to Drynelle. In a corner of the courtyard, King Slyamal isolated Tesnayr.

"You ride east," said King Slyamal, "Jenel plans to ride with you."

"Your daughter is strong willed," replied Tesnayr.

"She gets it from her mother and her sister," said King Slyamal, "You cannot let her come with you. She is my daughter, a lady of the court of Sym'Dul. She has had many noble suitors and she chooses you, a common soldier."

"Your daughter chooses to come. She takes orders from no one. And she saved all our lives," said Tesnayr.

"None of that matters."

"Give your daughter the respect she deserves."

"No!" King Slyamal caught his breath as he struggled to speak his mind. "Jenel is young and head strong. She possesses a courage that few men have. She would ride into a legion of the enemy to save those she loves. Like her sister, Jenel would sacrifice everything for her people.

"I lost her mother when she was an infant. Her sister died for the love of a man who betrayed her. I do not want to lose Jenel as well. She would follow you into the heart of the orcs if you asked her too. Please do not take her from me."

"You cannot keep her locked away forever," said Tesnayr.

"If you care for her you will leave her here. Do not force me to lose my only daughter," pleaded King Slyamal.

Tesnayr mulled over the king's plea. The desperation in the king's eyes gnawed at him.

"General, it is time to leave," said a soldier.

King Slyamal grabbed Tesnayr's arms and forced him to face him. "Please..." he whispered.

Tesnayr turned and headed for the gate. Jenel waited for him holding the reins to two horses. "General," she greeted him warmly handing him one of the animals.

"Head east," Tesnayr commanded Arnin.

Arnin saluted and gave the order. Thunder rumbled through the ground and dust billowed as the horses took off with their riders.

Tesnayr stole a quick glance at King Slyamal as he hid behind a column watching them. Perhaps the king was right. "Jenel," said Tesnayr, "I left my shield over there. Will you get it for me?"

Jenel gave him the reins to her horse and went to get his shield. Tesnayr seized his chance. He knew it would hurt her, but it had to be done. He smacked the rump of her horse sending it galloping off. Then, he jumped into the saddle of his own and kicked it hard in the sides speeding off after his men.

The sudden pounding of hooves whisked Jenel's attention to where Tesnayr had been. She dropped the shield and chased after him. "Tesnayr!"

"Jenel," screamed King Slyamal as he followed his daughter. "Jenel!"

Jenel ignored him. Focused on Tesnayr's fading form, she continued after him on foot. "Tesnayr! You can't do this! Tesnayr!"

Tears streamed down Jenel's face as her father caught up to her. He folded his arms protectively around her. "Let him go," he whispered to her, "Let him go."

Chapter II
The Council at D'arr

Wind rippled through King Nalim's braids and beard as he clung tightly to the hard scales of the dragon beneath him. He turned his head to the side so as to be able to breathe more easily. The cold air in the sky did not affect him. A dwarf's skin was hardened and tough and could withstand the elements. Nalim's fear of great heights was a different matter. He hated flying, as did most of his race. *Landing can't come soon enough.*

The dragon's massive wings flapped gracefully as she flew toward MurDair. Her steady breathing calmed Nalim some. Ynell was her name. Though a young dragon, she proved quite competent. She soared through the sky in the lead of the group of fire breathing beasts relishing the power of her wings.

"There," said King Nalim pointing to what appeared to be a vacant spot on the ground.

Gradually, Ynell descended. She spread her wings out wide to soar lower to the grassy meadow. Golden grass with specks of green waved in the breeze. Ynell landed with a soft thump. Such gentleness surprised King Nalim who believed that her massive size would not allow it. The remaining dragons set down beside them awaiting their orders.

"Where is this great city?" asked Ynell. The dragon surveyed the surrounding landscape. Nothing resembled a city among the grassland. Pillars of multicolored stone provided the only structure. The misshaped pillars formed a circle around a triangular table covered in runes.

"Beneath you," replied King Nalim.

The dwarf strode to the triangular table. He ran his hand over the markings muttering to himself in his native tongue. "Jôk'lar," he said aloud.

A loud, grinding sound echoed through the air. Slowly, the table turned in a circle as it rose from the ground. The dragons watched in awe as it transformed into a doorway. Dancing torchlight spilled from the dark caverns beneath the earth.

King Nalim beamed with pride. "Welcome to the city of D'arr."

"We will not fit through there," said Ynell.

King Nalim frowned. The dragon was right. The doorway was too narrow for the beasts to slip through. "You must wait out here," he said.

"How are we to assist you if we must stay out here?" asked Ynell.

"You will assist me best by staying here," said King Nalim, "Our previous encounters with dragons did not go well. To prevent bloodshed, you will wait here."

Ynell backed away relenting. Smoke spurted from her giant nostrils as she snorted in response.

"I will be quick," King Nalim assured her.

The dwarf king stepped into the archway and walked down the stone steps. His boots tapped the hard rock with each step he took. Memories flooded him as he entered his home. Familiar smells of roasting pork, potatoes, and beer filled his nostrils. King Nalim inhaled deeply taking pleasure in the aromas. His stomach grumbled reminding him that he had neglected to eat earlier that day.

The stairwell gave way to a vast underground expanse. Smooth, black marble spread out before him covering the cavern floor. Great pillars with the crest of MurDair stretched to the top of the high ceiling. Lit chandeliers dangled from the cavern ceiling shedding light on the entire city. Water trickled down the stream that flowed through the center of the underground city providing a soft melody. Despite the lack of sunlight, patches of grass grew in various places providing splashes of color.

Dwarves strolled across the city center as King Nalim made his way to the council chambers. He trotted across the enormous expanse to the other end. He climbed the winding stairs that led to an upper level courtyard. Panting slightly, King Nalim dashed across the courtyard. On any other day he would have admired the moss covered pillars that lined the foot path he trod on. But he hadn't the time.

A bell stood outside the doors to the council chambers. He grasped the coarse rope. With a huge yank, King Nalim tugged on the rope causing the bell to swing back and forth. A loud clang rang through the city forcing everyone to stop in their tracks. Eyes stared at him as he rang the bell.

After the bell sounded a few more times, King Nalim entered the council chamber and waited. One by one, fifteen dwarves entered and took their respective seats.

"Why have you summoned us?" asked a black bearded dwarf.

"Lord Tyron," greeted King Nalim, "I have called the council because we have need to go to war. You are all aware of the orcs that have ravaged the lands of Sym'Dul and Belyndril. Little is left of them. I have made an alliance with the other kings to defeat this threat."

"Why should we care what happens to the other kingdoms?" asked a dwarf with bright red hair and twin braids in his knee length beard.

"The orcs care little of our quarrels with the other four kingdoms," answered King Nalim, "They only wish to destroy."

"Then let them destroy our enemies," said the red haired dwarf. A series of nods weaved through the group.

King Nalim studied them. He knew he could order them to war, but he wished to have their consent. That is what made dwarves different from the other races. In MurDair, the king was held accountable for his actions. Having the council's approval made going to war easier.

"And if we do, what then?" began King Nalim, "After the other four lands have fallen where will that leave us? The orcs will be here as sure as the sun rises each morning. If we follow your course, Gloniv, we will stand alone. And we will fail.

"An alliance with the other lands is our only chance to defeat this threat. Together we can achieve victory. Together we can make certain that our way of life does not die. The other kings and I have named a man general over our armies. He commands them all.

"He has asked us to meet him in Drynelle where we will crush the orcs once and for all."

"Who is this man?" asked Lord Tyron.

"His name is Tesnayr," replied King Nalim.

The council whispered Tesnayr's name among themselves. King Nalim smiled. He knew that even in MurDair Tesnayr's name was known.

"But it will take us at least a month to cross the mountains," said another dwarf. "And longer still to reach Drynelle. Surely, he cannot wait that long for us to arrive."

A smile crept across King Nalim's face. "He will not have to. Tesnayr commands the dragons. They await us outside the city."

"Dragons," said Lord Tyron. "He commands them? No one commands them."

"General Tesnayr does," said King Nalim, "Selexia herself gave him her horn to summon them. By Tesnayr's orders, they are to carry us to Drynelle.

"I called the council out of respect. We either put our quarrels aside and join with the other kingdoms or wait for the orcs to invade our lands when we are too weak to withstand them."

"And afterwards," said Lord Tyron, "What will happen then?"

"No one can predict the future. I hope and pray that the newly formed alliance between the five lands continues after this war with the orcs. But I do know this. If we do not join them, then we will have sentenced ourselves to death. What say all of you?"

More murmurs rippled through the council as each dwarf made their decision. A female dwarf rose to her feet. "The council has decided," she said, "We stand with you King Nalim and approve of joining our army with those of the other kingdoms to defeat these orcs."

Joy welled up inside King Nalim. He contained his composure instead of letting his emotions spill out of him. "Sound the horn," he ordered.

One of the council members walked over to a gold-covered, narrow tube sticking out of the marble wall. He placed his lips around the end and blew. A deep note reverberated off the walls of the underground city of D'arr. Instantly, dwarves clad in armor dropped their tasks and gathered at the city entrance awaiting their king's orders.

King Nalim watched from the council chambers as dwarves from all around answered the call to battle. He promised Tesnayr soldiers and that was what he would deliver. After the army had gathered, King Nalim left the council chambers walking regally through the city to the head of his fighting force. He surveyed the crowd.

"Dwarves of MurDair," he bellowed over the crowd, "War has come to us. A threat unknown to the five kingdoms has swept over the lands like locust. The great General Tesnayr has asked for our assistance. We will heed that call. Outside these gates are dragons waiting to take us to Drynelle. There we will fight the vile creatures that threaten us. There we will die as dwarves."

A cheer rose through the army as various dwarves raised their weapons in response.

"Ynell," said King Nalim as he walked up to her, "I hope your dragons can carry us all."

"You're late," Ynell said in reply.

The sky blackened as the dragons took to the sky. Each bore four dwarves on their back. They glided over the tallest peaks of the Ársa Mountains toward Sym'Dul and toward their destiny.

Chapter III
A Father's Choice

Slyamal paced impatiently in front of the doors to his daughter's room as he waited for the chambermaid to return.

"I'm sorry, my lord," said the maid as she returned, "But the lady Jenel refuses to see anyone."

Enraged, Slyamal burst through the heavy door nearly knocking the poor girl over. "She will see her own father." He stormed into the room spotting his daughter near a window.

"I wish not to be disturbed," said Jenel calmly.

"Would you deny your own father?"

"Leave us," Jenel commanded the others in the room. "What do you want?"

"You have not left your chamber for days. You take your meals here. No one has seen you. Jenel, I am concerned for your welfare."

"You got what you wanted. Tesnayr is gone and I am locked up here."

"He had to leave, you know that. You could not expect him to stay here when the orcs moved east."

"That is not what I speak of."

"War is no place for a woman."

"Nelyn was allowed to go," said Jenel.

"Nelyn is not my daughter," replied King Slyamal. "Jenel, you are the princess of Sym'Dul. Our station sometimes requires a certain amount of sacrifice."

"At what cost? You once told me that I should choose a man to marry who is selfless, courageous, honest, and has integrity. Tesnayr is all of those things and yet you refuse him."

"He and I have had our differences," said King Slyamal.

"Father I love him!" Jenel immediately covered her mouth after her outburst.

King Slyamal looked in Jenel's tear stained eyes. Just like her sister, he thought. He noticed her fumbling with a ring on her finger. Quickly, he snatched it. "Who gave you this?"

"Tesnayr."

"Is he aware of its significance?"

"Yes, father."

A grim expression crossed King Slyamal's face. He found himself considering the one act he detested, and all for the sake of his daughter. "This is not the fantasy of a young woman." It was a statement, not a question. He left without another word.

"Boy, come here," he said to a passing boy as he entered the corridor. "I want to know where General Tesnayr was headed when he left."

"Yes, my lord." The boy sped off.

King Slyamal marched toward his compartment. He had much packing and planning to do if he was to find Tesnayr.

King Slyamal pulled tightly on the leather strap securing the saddlebag in place. The horse whinnied in the chill air. "Whoa, boy," he soothed. He heaved another saddlebag onto the horse and fastened it. He had a long journey ahead and had no intention of running out of supplies. The damp air seeped through his gloves. He had not even started and already the king felt the cold, winter's final attempt to maintain its hold on the land.

"I thought kings had servants to pack their horses," said a sly voice behind him. Out from the shadows stepped Ernayn.

"I haven't time to waste," replied King Slyamal as he continued his preparations.

"Such urgency," said Ernayn.

"What is your business here, sorceress?"

"I was about to ask you the same," she replied. "Tesnayr left yesterday morn and now here you are preparing to ride. A long journey by the looks of it."

"I have business with Tesnayr," said King Slyamal.

"To kill him?"

"Quite the opposite." King Slyamal finished securing his sword to the horse.

"Interesting. Considering the mark he left you."

King Slyamal rubbed his nose.

"Why must you leave?"

King Slyamal stole a quick glance at the balcony his daughter stood upon. He watched her as she stared into the distance that Tesnayr had ridden in, ignoring the cold. His only reason for doing anything. "I do not do this for myself, but for one I love. I'll not allow her to die of a broken heart, same as her sister."

"Take Quesha with you."

"No," said Slyamal more sternly than he had meant to, "I must do this myself."

"Then allow me to give you a small bit of advice." Ernayn closed the distance between them. "Stay on the high road."

King Slyamal jumped on his horse grasping the reins tightly. "Protect my daughter. I shall return." He kicked his horse and sped off through the canyon and into the valley beyond leaving nothing but clouds of dust.

Chapter IV
Jenel's Decision

Jenel leaned on the rail of the balcony overlooking the keep. She shivered from the chill in the air. She felt alone. Tesnayr had left her behind. Now her father seemed to have disappeared. She wrung the handkerchief in her hands. The tears of sadness that she had shed earlier burned as they turned to anger. She hated Rybnik for betraying her. For betraying them all.

"I thought I'd find you here."

Startled, Jenel whirled around. "Max," she said, "I didn't hear you come in."

"Obviously," said Max.

"Drink," Jenel offered as she lifted a flask of wine and began to pour a goblet full.

Max eyed the ale with longing. Summoning his vestiges of will, he turned it down. "No. I think I should stick with water."

"Why did he do it?" asked Jenel.

Max did not ask about whom she spoke. "I do not have an answer."

Jenel puffed out a lungful of air. "I hope he pays for what he did."

"I'm certain he will," said Max.

"I'm going to kill him," spat Jenel. She swallowed back tears.

"It is natural to want revenge for what he did to you, to all of us," said Max, "But vengeance isn't the answer. Someone very wise told me that it is best to bury your desire for revenge. Such emotions only lead to your destruction. Of course, I thought my mother a fool at the time."

A small smile appeared on Jenel's face. "I cannot just let this go."

"And if you do catch up to him, what then? Will killing Rybnik mend the hurt in your heart?"

Jenel refused to answer the wizard.

"Rybnik made his choice," said Max, "And you have a choice to make as well. Be certain it is the right one."

Jenel looked out at the valley beyond. Dark clouds covered the sky. "It's so cold here. It's so quiet."

"It is the last frost before the coming of spring," said Max. "Soon it will turn warm and the birds will sing. Flowers will grow and life will return to the earth." Max pointed his hand to a tree with buds forming on the branches.

Jenel broke down into another bout of tears. Gently, Max enveloped her in his arms. It had been a long while since he comforted anyone. "There, there," he soothed.

"I loved him," said Jenel, "He was like a father to me."

Max said nothing. He just held her allowing her tears to soak his shoulder.

"Max, where is my father?"

Max pulled away from Jenel. "Your father left yesterday."

"Why did no one tell me?"

"It was his wish that you not know. And that you stay here."

Jenel ran into her room. She tore off her dress and put on her riding clothes. "Where did he go?" she demanded of Max as she strapped on her leather armor.

"Jenel," said Max, "He wanted you to remain here."

"Where did he go?"

Max grunted as he relented. "He rode east after Tesnayr."

Jenel snatched her sword and cloak. She bolted out the door and dashed to the lower level of the keep. She made a quick stop in the kitchen where she packed a bag of food. Max chased after her. Jenel ignored his pleas as she darted to the stable. Quickly, she saddled a horse.

"Lady Jenel," called a voice.

Both Jenel and Max turned. King Edrei ran toward them. A cook had warned him of Jenel's intentions.

"Jenel," said King Edrei. "You are supposed to stay here. I promised your father that I would protect you."

"I am tired of men telling me what to do," said Jenel as she jumped on her horse. "The man I have chosen for my husband rides to his death. My father chases after him. I'll not lose another person I love simply because everyone desires to keep me safe."

"But, Jenel," pleaded King Edrei, "If you leave how am I to keep my oath?"

"My lady," said Max, "If you ride after them, then you go to your death also."

"We all go to our deaths," said Jenel, "I'll not hide here while Sym'Dul is ravaged by the orcs. If you wish to protect me, then come with me."

Jenel kicked her horse. It galloped into the canyon toward the valley beyond. She never looked back as clouds of dust trailed after her. She had made her choice.

King Edrei ran into the stable and grabbed two horses. He brought them out handing one of the reins to Max. "Boy," he called to the stable boy. "Tell the captain of the guard that he is in charge until my return."

He and Max leaped into their saddles. Each dug their heels in their mount and took off after Jenel in fulfillment of a promise.

Chapter V
Battle for La'nar

King Telinin stood on a precipice overlooking the city of La'nar. His home. He barely recognized the castle that he had lived in for the past twenty years. Smoke rose from center of the city. Bits of the palace crumbled from neglect.

Sarwyn stood next to King Telinin. She empathized for him. She knew what she would feel if her home had been taken over by creatures who cared nothing for others. Her long tresses swung in the wind as she waited for Telinin to decide how he wanted to attack.

"Have they come?" asked King Telinin.

"Yes," replied Sarwyn. "All the soldiers I could find have reported."

King Telinin turned away from La'nar and strode down the small hill to where his army awaited him. He had hoped for more men, but what he had would have to suffice.

The generals gathered around him. "General Thomlin, you will attack the front gate. Keep the orcs occupied. No matter what happens, do not retreat.

"General Hiler, you will join me in climbing the wall on the far side of the city. It is not well guarded. They do not expect us to come that way.

"General Jorgin, there is an underground tunnel that has long since been abandoned. It now serves as a drain. You will enter the city through that.

"We take no prisoners. Every orc must be killed."

The three generals stared at their king. What he asked was extremely risky.

"And if we fail?" asked General Thomlin.

"Then I hope you are prepared to meet death," replied King Telinin, "Failure is not an option. We must take back the city. After that, we ride to Drynelle."

"That is quite a distance," said General Jorgin. "How are we to get there in the time you want us to?"

"We will ride nonstop through Knot's Pass. It is clear of snow by now. From there it's a straight path to Drynelle. We must get there within the week. I know I am asking a lot. But everything depends upon this if we are to reclaim our home from this invading force."

"It will be done," said the three generals at once.

"Sarwyn," said the king, "You know where to be."

Sarwyn nodded and disappeared.

"Selexia," said King Telinin, "I need you to help keep the orcs distracted. I want you to fly over the city. Kill as many as you can. If any come near where we are, destroy them."

"With pleasure," said Selexia.

"Selexia," added King Telinin, "I know Tesnayr ordered you to assist us, but will you stay until the end?"

Smoke billowed from the dragon's nostrils as she considered the king's question. "I have vowed myself and my dragons to Tesnayr's service. We are bound by that oath. He has ordered me to help you take back La'nar and to stay with you until we reach Drynelle. Until he commands me otherwise, you have my service King of Belyndril."

King Telinin frowned slightly. That wasn't the most comforting answer. "Very well," he said.

General Thomlin waited outside the city gates for the signal to begin the attack. He hoped the plan worked. He had complete faith in his king, but the sudden swarm of orcs crushed all of their spirits. Too long he had sat by watching people die. No more. He silently vowed to take the city even if it took his last breath.

A small speck of light flew up to him. It swirled around until it landed on his shoulder. He knew what it was.

"It is time," said Sarwyn's voice.

The speck of light darted off and vanished.

"Catapults," yelled General Thomlin, "Fire!"

Immediately, men lit the oil soaked boulders. They pulled the lever releasing the flaming ammunition. Great balls of fire soared through the air crashing into the gates of the city. Instantly, the wood timbers sparked to life as flames licked them, but they held strong.

"Again," ordered General Thomlin.

Flaming boulders flew through the air again bombarding the city entrance.

Projectiles from the castle headed straight for them. "Hold the line!" yelled General Thomlin. The Belyndril soldiers held their ground as massive rocks were flung at them. "First wave!" yelled General Thomlin.

A line of foot soldiers arranged themselves in formation. They held their shields and swords at the ready.

"Attack!" bellowed General Thomlin.

Battle cries erupted from the line of men as they stormed the city walls. A team of six soldiers heaved a battering ram at the burning gates. They carried it with all their might. It jolted their arms with each bang. Still the gates held.

Other soldiers set ladders against the wall of the city. They clambered up them as arrows shot past. More raced to the top of the wall as others fell to their deaths.

The gate rattled violently as the men rammed into it. They heaved the ram into the gates again and again. Sparks flew everywhere with each thud. Suddenly, men screamed as hot oil covered them and melted their skin. Others quickly took their place.

Above the city soared Selexia. She darted downward toward the orcs releasing flames from her mouth. Just as quickly, the dragon shot upward. Her constant darting to and from the ground frightened some of the orcs.

The orcs fired arrows at her that bounced off of her hard scales. Selexia chuckled to herself. She was having fun. One orc climbed to the highest peak of the wall with a lance. He took aim. Quickly, Selexia shot toward him. She clasped her claws around the creature lifting him from the wall. Selexia flew high up. When she reached such a great height that the city looked like a miniature picture below, she released her prey to drop to the earth below.

King Telinin raced quickly to the wall on the far side of the city. The sounds of battle were deadened by the distance. Only one orc stood on sentry duty. The others were too preoccupied by the assault on the front gate. He waved to the archer nearby. The man nocked his arrow, aimed, and fired. The lone orc clutched his throat before collapsing.

Telinin gave the signal. The soldiers behind him ran for the wall. General Hiler waved his men onward. They paused beneath the wall and twirled rope with clawed hooks on the end above their heads. The hooks soared to the top of the wall catching securely on the stone.

"Quickly," ordered General Hiler.

One by one, men scurried up the rope. They heaved themselves over the wall and onto the walkway beneath. Telinin surveyed his surroundings. No one. *Good.* "Take out the watch towers," he said. "General Hiler, help the others at the gate."

The general saluted and sped off with a group of men.

King Telinin snuck through the passage along the wall with five other soldiers. Another group of six headed along the wall in the opposite direction. The king sprinted along the barrier avoiding detection. He dove through archways and ran up some stairs on the ramparts.

Two orcs appeared on the walkway. Stunned at the sight of soldiers, they reacted slowly. Telinin gripped his sword tightly as he plunged it into the belly of one. The other swung at him. The king ducked low to the ground. One of the soldiers with him stabbed the orc in the back. The man clamped his hand over the beast's mouth to prevent it from yelping as he brought his knife up and sliced its throat.

King Telinin continued on to the watchtower followed closely by his men. He reached the bottom of the tower. Telinin's boots echoed on the stone steps as he raced to the top. Breathing heavily, he took the steps two at a time up the winding staircase. He stopped when he reached the trapdoor that led into the tower.

Telinin positioned himself underneath it. The five soldiers circled around him. Nodding to one, he wrapped his hands tightly around the hilt of his sword prepared for what lay beyond. One of the men flung the door open. Telinin burst through snatching the armor of an orc. He pulled with all his strength forcing the beast through the door past him. He heard the creature hit the floor below and groan as it died.

King Telinin somersaulted through the opening and rolled between the legs of another orc. He brought his sword up slicing off the creature's leg. It fell to the ground yowling. Telinin slammed his foot on the orc's hand as it reached for a weapon. He glowered at the creature. All the hatred he felt for it boiled within him. Raising his sword high, Telinin plunged it deep into the orc's torso watching it writhe as it died.

He whirled around as another orc ran toward him. King Telinin pushed his blade into the beast's chest as another soldier struck it in the back. The king looked around at the carnage. He callously kicked the lifeless body of the orc through the trapdoor.

He glanced out at the front gate. General Thomlin still bombarded it with catapults. Some of his men had made it inside the city. Silently, he cursed the strength of the city gates. The only time he would ever do so.

A whistle sounded nearby. Telinin turned in the direction of it. In the other watchtower General Hiler waved at him. Telinin signaled that he understood. "You two stay here," he said pointing at two men, "The rest of you come with me." Telinin hurled himself through the trapdoor and back onto the stairwell. *Time to find the orc commander.*

General Jorgin raced through the tunnels. The eerie silence wore on him. Not even the raucous noise of the battle penetrated below the earth's surface. Only the splashing of their boots as they sprinted through puddles of water broke the silence.

General Jorgin raised his hand signaling his men to stop. They hunkered underneath a manhole. As he listened for the enemy, the pungent smell of the unused tunnel hit his nostrils. He willed himself not to gag.

The general peered through the small opening making certain that no orcs waited nearby. Clear. He squeezed through crouching low once on the surface.

"Hurry," he said.

Quickly, the other soldiers hauled themselves out of the tunnel.

"Head for the gates," said General Jorgin.

"General," said a soldier, "There are unmanned catapults by the armory. We could use those."

Smart lad, thought the general. "Take some men and go get them. Aim them for the orcs."

The young soldier darted off with a group of men. General Jorgin led the others to the front gates. The city was empty except where the siege took place. The orcs weren't too smart, thought the general, they fell for the king's diversion.

They wound their way through the shops and homes along the empty streets. Occasionally they met a stray orc, but disposed of them quickly. The nearer they came to the gate, the louder the battle became. The clanging of steel and the explosions of crashing boulders pierced their ears. General Jorgin thrust himself in the battle.

He plowed into a heavily armed and muscular orc. The beast blocked his initial attack. General Jorgin swung again. The orc knocked the weapon from his hands. It picked the general up as though he weighed nothing and slammed him into the hard ground. Air escaped him as he lay there momentarily stunned. He felt a rib crack as the gigantic orc stomped on him crushing him with its weight.

The orc sneered, sensing victory. He bore down upon General Jorgin. Desperately, the general thrust his dagger into the orc's foot. The beast laughed at such a prospect. Accepting his fate, General Jorgin lay there hoping it would be over quickly.

The orc's head jerked backward as a lance protruded from its throat. The beast teetered, swaying back and forth until it crashed onto the paved ground. General Jorgin wriggled out from under the dead weight. He snatched up his sword. Courageously, the general continued onward into the fray ignoring the pain in his chest.

The young soldier motioned for those with him to stay low. They hugged the ground as they inched toward the idle catapults. One orc stepped in front of him. The beast was oblivious to the soldiers' presence. Gently, the young man freed his knife from its sheath. He held it tightly. Suddenly, the man shot to his feet clamped his hand over the orc's mouth yanking the head back exposing the soft flesh of the neck. In one fluid movement, he dragged the blade across the beast's throat. The orc went limp. The young soldier dumped him as though he were mere trash. Another orc happened upon them. Before the creature could react, the man threw his knife. The orc's eyes opened wide in shock as the knife sunk deep within its throat.

"Grab those barrels of oil and bring them here," ordered the young soldier.

Two men obeyed. They each took a barrel and rolled it to the catapults. After arming them, the men maneuvered the catapults aiming them at the battle in the front of the city.

"Now," said the soldier.

The catapults creaked as they flung the barrels toward the chaos. Each barrel erupted upon impact smothering the area in oil.

"Reload," said the soldier.

Again they loaded barrels of oil on the catapults.

"Fire!"

The catapults sprang to life as their levers were pulled. The barrels of oil sailed through the air reaching their target. The men shot oil drums toward the front gate until none remained.

Silently, Sarwyn crept through the streets of La'nar. She slunk in the shadows of buildings. Her gown matched the background behind her allowing her to blend in. Orcs walked past her. Quickly, Sarwyn uttered a spell allowing her to literally disappear. She waited with baited breath as they passed by unaware of her presence. Once gone, Sarwyn reappeared.

She darted from shadow to shadow as she made her way to the uppermost part of the city. The orc commander was directing the battle from the King's court. The orc's arrogance had made them foolish.

She spotted the stairs leading straight to the court. They narrowed at the top while the bottom spread out. The fairy glanced about her. Alone. She dashed up the steps making no sound. She hid behind some bushes when she reached the top. A group of orcs walked noisily by. Their armor clanked as they passed.

"Soka lar," whispered Sarwyn.

Vines snaked down the trees twisting and turning. They latched themselves around the necks of the orcs. Slowly, the vines squeezed the life from the beasts. The orcs struggled desperately against their assailant as their feet left the ground, but to no avail.

Quickly, Sarwyn raced across the grassy atrium heading for the double doors. She paused listening for movement. Nothing.

Straightening herself, Sarwyn turned into a floating speck of light. She flew through a crack in the door into the king's courtroom.

The orc commander stood in the center of the chamber. His heavily armed demeanor did little to encourage Sarwyn. But she had a job to do.

She floated near a dark corner taking note of the two other orcs in the room. Instantly, she reappeared taking her natural form. The two orcs swung in her direction surprised by her presence. They rushed her. She threw her hands out palms forward. A shower of sparks burst from her hands. The orcs flew backward as a powerful force slammed into them. They crashed into the marble wall of the room.

The orc commander turned toward her. Astounded, he gaped at the fairy for a moment. He unsheathed his crooked sword and charged her. Sarwyn whispered in her native language. Thick, round vines burst through the floor of the chamber wrapping around the beast. The orc leader twisted and turned in an futile attempt to break free. With each movement, the vines clamped tighter around his skin cutting into the flesh.

The orc commander spat curses in his native tongue.

"Silence," commanded Sarwyn. Her cold voice bounced off the walls. In response, the vines placed themselves around the orc's mouth gagging his protests.

A moment later, Telinin burst through the doors. He halted when he saw Sarwyn standing in the center of the courtroom with the orc commander tied up. "How did you--" began the king.

"You told me to bind him and I did," answered Sarwyn. "What do you wish done with him?"

"Bring him," said King Telinin.

The fairy uttered another word. The vines followed outside dragging the struggling orc. They chased after King Telinin as he headed straight for the fight at the city entrance.

"Hurry," ordered King Telinin.

Sarwyn and the other soldiers ran swiftly to keep up. The mesh of vines trailed after them walking along the stone with their prisoner in tow. King Telinin stopped on a balcony that overlooked the rest of the city. It gave a clear view of the gates. He pulled out a horn. Breathing deeply, King Telinin blew on it. The startling cry of the horn reverberated off of every building within La'nar.

Slowly, the fighting stopped. The orcs recognized the cry of the horn as one of theirs. Gradually, all eyes turned toward King Telinin.

"I have your commander," he shouted.

Sarwyn brought the orc leader forth.

"His fate rests with me," said King Telinin.

While the orcs stared aghast at the fate of their commander, the soldiers of Belyndril snuck away from the fray. They ran for the hills or the upper levels of the city. Distracted, the orcs paid no heed.

"This is our city," yelled King Telinin, "This is our land. And we are taking it back." He dragged his knife across the orc commander's throat. Blood ran over his wrist. With a forceful kick, he shoved the lifeless body of the orc over the ledge. It splattered unmoving onto the ground. As Tesnayr predicted, the other orcs did not move. Without a leader they had no direction.

"Now!" yelled King Telinin.

Hundreds of flaming arrows blackened the sky as they arced through the air. They whistled as they flew landing among the still orcs. Instantly, flames burst to life. They leaped and lunged spreading across the oil soaked stone.

Bloodcurdling cries emanated from the orcs as they caught fire. The odor of burning flesh filled the air. They screamed and ran in an effort to flee the inferno. Some orcs managed to escape the flames and headed for the trees.

A dark shape darted through the sky. It hovered a few feet above the ground. Within seconds, Selexia was upon the fleeing orcs. Flames burst from her mouth as she breathed fire on them. Orcs ran in every direction. Their futile efforts did little to save them. Selexia snatched them in her talons squishing their soft bodies.

From his vantage point, King Telinin watched the destruction. He felt no pity for the orcs as they died a painful death.

Chapter VI
Deep in the Orcs' Council

Rybnik sat alone in the shadows as the sun slowly disappeared beneath the horizon. He watched the mixture of men and orcs go about their business. There were no tents, just fires that dotted the landscape. Rats roasting above the flames filled the atmosphere with a stench that nearly gagged him.

Rybnik's cold expression fell upon one man in particular. Blynak. He knew the name. Like him, Blynak tried to overthrow his king. Before execution, he had fled Belyndril finding safety in the farthest reaches of Sym'Dul. He remembered Blynak. The man joined his revolution and even attempted to usurp him. Loathing filled Rybnik's core when he looked upon the man. Hatred, was all he felt. Blynak mirrored the same sentiment.

"Rabok wants to speak with you," croaked an orc.

Rybnik tossed his musing aside and followed the messenger to where Rabok awaited him.

"I am glad that you decided to join us," said Rabok.

Rybnik gave a slight nod of his head in response.

"Rybnik," hissed a sly voice. Blynak stepped into the lamplight. "I know you. You tried, unsuccessfully I might add, to take over Sym'Dul. You nearly succeeded. But the love of a woman stopped you."

"Still trying to feed your ego," spat Rybnik.

"If you had listened to me," sneered Blynak. "Then you would be king of Sym'Dul."

"Listen to a man who betrayed his own friend? If I had followed your advice, I'd be in a grave," shot back Rybnik. "I suggest you leave, before I put you in yours."

"You, who allowed yourself to be blinded by a woman." Blynak leaned close to Rybnik.

"Enough!" snarled Rabok. "Blynak, you have proven useful with your knowledge of La'nar's fortifications. Rybnik is here at my invitation. And he will be meeting Galbrok."

"Galbrok?" said Blynak. "He only just joined us."

"And he helped us greatly in taking Hemíl," replied Rabok. "We would have succeeded if it hadn't been for that earthquake."

"Another near success," grumbled Blynak.

"Can you control the movement of the earth?" demanded Rabok.

Blynak looked away in answer.

"I thought not," continued Rabok, "Rybnik, you were with Tesnayr for some time before you joined us. Can you predict his movements?"

"Yes," replied Rybnik. "Tesnayr was trusting. He told his lieutenants everything, including me."

"Why you?" asked Blynak.

"I gained his trust," said Rybnik. "At the time I needed him to get through the mountains. Act like a hero and he brings you into his fold. Of course, the princess of Sym'Dul assisted me even though she remains unaware of it."

"Really?" said Rabok.

"Yes," said Rybnik, "I spent a number of years pretending to be her friend. When she told Tesnayr that she trusted me, so did he."

"Interesting," said Rabok, "Why did you maintain contact with her even after your banishment?"

Rybnik smiled coldly. "Unlike the convictions of some, I never abandoned my desire to rid Sym'Dul of its current king. Gaining the girl's trust was easy. She was young."

"Clearly, you understand the usefulness of people," said Rabok. "What I want from you now is knowledge of what Tesnayr's next move will be."

"Before the last engagement," said Rybnik, "He planned to go Drynelle. I am certain he is headed there now. Tesnayr believes that if he gathers his army at Drynelle then he will be able to defeat Galbrok. Most likely he will come straight through here. It is the most direct route."

"With King Slyamal with him he will have knowledge of Drynelle's weaknesses," said Blynak.

"You forget, Blynak, that I have the same knowledge," said Rybnik.

"And what of the princess?" mocked Blynak.

"What of her?" said Rybnik without an ounce of concern.

Rabok raised his hand for silence. "You two now serve Galbrok. What he says goes. Now, I think we best leave Tesnayr a parting gift for when he comes through here."

Grudgingly, Blynak and Rybnik saluted in agreement.

"Rybnik," said Rabok, "What happened to the woman you loved?"

Rybnik looked directly into the orc commander's eyes. His face betrayed no emotion. "I killed her," he said.

Rabok grinned pleased at the response. Another useful man had joined their ranks. He knew he could go far with Rybnik.

Chapter VII
To Drynelle

The incessant rumble of hundreds of horses galloping through the canyons of the pass echoed off the rock walls. Warm air escaped the beasts' nostrils as they breathed heavily. King Telinin clung to the reins of his horse as he pushed it hard. The nagging thought that they moved too slowly gnawed at him.

A horse next to him collapsed sending its rider tumbling across the ground. Quickly, King Telinin held up his hand as a signal to stop. Gradually, the roar of their movements ceased.

"Why have we stopped?" asked Sarwyn.

"Look at my men," said King Telinin, "They are exhausted. At this pace, we will die before we reach Drynelle."

Sarwyn surveyed the mass of men as they rested and gave their horses water. Many slumped to the ground barely able to stay awake. Her face scrunched slightly as she thought about a way to ensure that they reached Drynelle alive and in fighting shape.

"Why have we stopped?" Selexia hovered inches above the ground.

An idea struck the fairy. "Selexia, how many dragons are there?"

"We number as many as the stars," replied Selexia.

"What are you planning?" asked King Telinin, tentatively.

Sarwyn grinned at him with a glint in her eyes. "Will your dragons be able to carry a horse and its rider as far as the edges of Drynelle?"

"We can," said Selexia.

"Be carried by dragons," breathed King Telinin.

"I promise we will not eat you," said Selexia, "Or drop you." The dragon arched her head upward releasing a strangled cry the reverberated off the rocky cliffs.

"Tell your men to prepare for departure," said Sarwyn.

Within moments, the sky darkened as dragons filled it. One by one the giant beasts swooped down and gently picked up a rider and his horse. Soon, dragons blackened the sky with their cargo as they headed east.

Chapter VIII
A Village Forsaken

Tesnayr eyed the small village from his vantage point. He did not like the looks of it. The people darted about scared in the faint moonlight. The quickest way to Drynelle was through the village itself. Tesnayr did not wish to frighten them so he decided to go around.

Tesnayr crawled away from the rock he hid behind. It had been awhile since he had scouted terrain, but the skills of a lifetime guided his movements. He made no noise as he stepped on the grass. Unaware that the village had its own scouts, Tesnayr acted as though he were safe.

Rough hands seized him pinning his arms by his side. Another set of hands snatched his sword from his belt. The man gasped in pain as he dropped the blade.

"What's wrong with you," said a gruff voice.

"His sword...zapped me," replied the man who had taken Tesnayr's weapon.

"Grab it and let's go," said the first man.

"He won't be able to," interrupted Tesnayr remembering something the phoenix had told him. *That sword chooses its owner and no one else may touch it.* "Let me handle it."

"You think us fools?" spat the first man.

"Far from it," replied Tesnayr. He refused to struggle. Doing so would lead to his death. "None but me may touch that blade. Try and handle it if you don't believe me."

The leader studied the weapon on the soft ground. Its blade glowed slightly. "Take it then, but no funny business."

The men holding Tesnayr released him. Slowly, he bent down for his weapon. He picked it up by the blade demonstrating that he had no intention of escaping. Carefully, Tesnayr put it back in its sheath. The men seized his arms again.

A commotion arose near them as more men stepped into view. They dragged someone behind them. The man thrashed fiercely, but his hands were effectively tied. Tesnayr recognized him immediately. It was King Slyamal.

"We found this one trailing him," said one of the men holding King Slyamal.

"Bring them both," ordered the leader.

Tesnayr was dragged to the main street of the village along with the King of Sym'Dul. Questions burned within him as to why the king was there. He buried his curiosity. Answers would have to wait.

People gathered around as the strangers were brought into their town. A tall man with greasy hair awaited them at the end of the square where a giant fire blazed. "What have we here?" he demanded.

"Two men skulking about, Seth," answered one of the thugs. "I believe this one is the king," he pointed at King Slyamal.

"How dare you treat your king like this," barked King Slyamal. "Have you no respect?"

"Plenty, but not for you," said Seth. "You are far from your court. And who is the other?"

Tesnayr remained silent.

"Your name," repeated Seth.

"You might try asking nicely," said Tesnayr.

"Sarcasm? What if I kill your friend?"

"He is no friend of mine," said Tesnayr.

"Then it would not grieve you if I killed him," said Seth.

"Kill him if you like," replied Tesnayr, "And I will stick my sword through your heart."

"I thought you said he was no friend," said Seth.

"He isn't," Tesnayr replied, "I just don't like you."

Seth drew closer to Tesnayr. "Your bravery means nothing here. This is my village. The people here do what I will."

"Only because they are too frightened to stand against you," said Tesnayr.

Seth backhanded Tesnayr.

Tesnayr barely flinched. He stared straight into Seth's eyes. "Your bravery means nothing while you are surrounded by your men."

"I know him," said one Seth's thugs. "That crest on his armor, it belongs to one man. A fella they call Tesnayr."

Seth's eyebrows rose. "Tesnayr? Not a day goes by when your name is not uttered. There were some interesting creatures looking for you. I think you know them."

Jenel hunkered behind the wagon with King Edrei and Max by her side. They had followed soon after they noticed that her father and Tesnayr had been captured. Thanks to Max's concealment spell, they avoided capture.

They watched as the firelight illuminated the man called Seth. He railed against Tesnayr and King Slyamal and the supposed tyranny they had spread. "We will rid ourselves of this darkness," he said to the entire village, "By handing these men to the orcs, we can save ourselves."

No one in the crowd cheered. They cowered before the man and his minions.

"Lock them away."

Two muscular guards hauled Tesnayr and King Slyamal away. They threw them into a building and bolted the door.

"I don't understand," said Jenel. "Why would they do this?"

"Some men will do anything for power," said Max.

"It appears that this man has treated this village like his own private kingdom," said King Edrei. "This war has provided him the perfect opportunity."

"And what of the other wars," said Jenel, "I am certain that all of the conflicts my father fought against you provided the same opportunity."

"I'll not deny my part in this," said King Edrei, "If we had not busied ourselves with our petty squabbles, then we both could have spent time bettering our realms."

"We've got to get them out of there," said Jenel.

"Do you have a plan?" asked Max.

Jenel noticed a tankard of mead sitting on the wagon. "As a matter of fact, I do." She picked it up and splashed the contents onto Max's clothing.

"What are—"

Jenel thrust the mug into the wizard's hands. "You remember that day they found you in the tavern," she said, "Act like that."

Max grinned at her, understanding her plan. He left his place behind the wagon and stumbled into the gathered crowd. A shower of sparks flew from his hands striking inches from Seth. He staggered drunkenly waving his mug. "What goes on here?" he slurred.

People backed away from him and his flailing hands. Another set of sparks squirted from them hitting a wagon loaded with weapons. The cart burst into flames lighting up the night even more.

"Someone subdue that man," yelled Seth.

A burly man advanced toward Max. With a flick of his hand, Max launched an invisible force against the man sending him flying. "Oops," said Max, feigning apology. "I appear to be a bit out of sorts."

"You drunken fool," roared Seth.

Pretending to be shocked at such a comment, Max stumbled around some more. "My dear sir, there is no need for anger. Simply point me in the direction of your tavern."

"No friend of yours," mumbled King Slyamal as Tesnayr undid the rope around his wrists. "Go ahead and kill him. And what if he took you up on that offer?"

"He wasn't going to," replied Tesnayr.

"Why didn't you put up a fight?" asked King Slyamal.

"I wanted more information about this place," Tesnayr said, calmly.

"You have a strange way of doing things," said King Slyamal.

Tesnayr searched the empty, one room building they were in. No windows. No weak spots. Not good, he thought. "Why are you here?" asked Tesnayr. "Weren't you staying behind to protect Jenel?"

King Slyamal looked at his feet. Apologies did not come easily to him. "I couldn't spend another day watching her cry herself to sleep. So I set out to find you...to protect you."

"Protect me?"

"I'll not lose another daughter to a broken heart. If I can do anything to keep you from dying in this war, then I shall do it. The king of Hemíl has promised to look after her. Do you love her?"

The last statement by Slyamal startled Tesnayr causing him to stare at the king with a shocked expression.

"Do you love my daughter?" repeated King Slyamal.

"I traveled a path known only in myth and legend, I battled the elements of the Ársa Mountains, all for her," said Tesnayr, "I left her at the Keep of Edrei to spare her from this war. Yes, I love your daughter."

"Then when this is over you will be married straight away."

"Do I not get a choice," laughed Tesnayr.

"Does a woman ever give a man a choice," replied King Slyamal.

Tesnayr nodded at that comment.

"Now, let's find a way out of here," said King Slyamal, "Unless of course you are still studying this town."

"Come on," whispered Jenel to King Edrei, pleased that Max's distraction worked.

She and the King of Hemíl crept along the outer edges of the firelight. They stayed in the shadows taking special care to avoid detection. Jenel spotted three men guarding Tesnayr and King

Slyamal. Splintered wood tugged at her armor. Jenel freed herself. She studied the wood that snagged her. It belonged to a pile of crates. Quickly, she shoved the crates over clattering loudly. Two of the guards rushed over.

"Take care of them," whispered Jenel.

She tiptoed over to the remaining guard in front of the locked building. Quietly, she pulled her dagger from its sheath gripping it tightly in her fist. Silently, Jenel approached the guard from behind.

"Pssst," she whispered.

The man whirled around. She punched him in the face with the hand that held the dagger. In one smooth movement, she brought the blade up and stabbed the man in the throat. He slumped to the ground unmoving. Jenel frantically searched his body for the keys. Her hands touched steel. She ripped the ring of keys from his belt. Jenel jammed key after key into the lock hoping the next one would fit. Click. She yanked the door open.

"Jenel," said King Slyamal in surprise. "What are you doing here?"

"We haven't time," hissed Jenel, "Now come on."

"I thought I left you in Hemíl," said King Slyamal.

"No time to talk," Jenel insisted. "Now let's go." She ran out into the darkness heading straight where she left King Edrei. Tesnayr and King Slyamal followed.

King Edrei stood over the bodies of the two guards that had left their post. They all hid in the shadows watching Max continue his display of fireworks and drunkenness and marveled at how he carried it on for so long.

"We need a plan for getting Max out of there," said Tesnayr.

"I'm certain he can take care of himself," King Edrei replied.

Jenel spotted a saddled horse nibbling on a small patch of grass. A plan formed in her mind. "Wait for my signal," she said. She hopped on the horse and steered it to the road where Max and Seth stood.

"You should stop her," said King Slyamal to Tesnayr.

"She's your daughter," replied Tesnayr.

"She's your fiancé," countered King Slyamal.

"I'd rather face a thousand orcs than try to stop her right at the moment," said Tesnayr.

"Agreed," said King Slyamal.

The three men worked their way toward Seth and his cohorts. Stealthily, they each picked a side to sneak up on, waiting for Jenel's signal.

Jenel galloped into the fray of the gathered townspeople. The horse's hooves echoed on the rocky road as she rode up to the burning flames behind Seth. She tugged the reins pulling the horse to a stop. "What goes on here?" she demanded in a commanding voice.

"Who are you to request such a thing?" asked Seth with an edge to his voice.

"Do you not recognize the princess of Sym'Dul?" replied Jenel. "I am Jenel, the lady and shield maiden of Sym'Dul. You will answer my summons."

Unmoved by her authoritative words, Seth sneered at her. He never noticed Max edging away. "You are not the Lady Jenel. She never leaves the palace of Drynelle." He placed his hand on the reins of her horse.

In a flash Jenel placed the point of her sword at his throat. "Unhand my horse," she growled. "You dare question me?"

Seth released the reins.

"What are you doing here cowering in your homes," continued Jenel, "War is upon us. The orcs pillage and burn our lands while you sit here in groveling fear of a madman. Why do you let this scum tower over you? Are you not men? Are you not the free people of Sym'Dul? Will you not take back your lands?

"I spit upon all of you and the shame you have brought. While others die, you sit here and allow this man to play king."

Jenel glared at Seth. "Your days of enslaving these people are over."

Seth reached for his weapon. Jenel raised her blade high pointing it at the heavens. Instantly, with some help from Max, lightning shot from the point of her weapon arcing to the sky. She swept her sword downward blocking an attack from Seth. Immediately, she backhanded him knocking him to the ground. A muscular man charged her. She jabbed him forcing her blade deep within the upper part of his torso.

The others sprang from concealment. Tesnayr crashed into two of Seth's minions. He elbowed one in the chest while kicking the other in the belly. In a graceful movement, Tesnayr whipped his sword around slashing the man in the side. Instantly, he stabbed the other in the chest.

King Edrei kicked one of the armed men in the middle of the back. The man dropped onto the ground. Wasting no time, he rammed his sword into the soft flesh of the enemy. Another man raced for him. Fluidly, King Edrei dodged out of the way twisting on his feet and bringing his sword down upon his foe's head.

Watching from the sidelines, many of the townsfolk began to burn with a desire to help. Some snatched pitchforks and various farm tools. They charged into the skirmish no longer fearing Seth and his henchmen. In a flash, the entire street filled with the roaring cry of a people fighting for their very freedom.

Tired of being stolen from and tired of their children being used, they fought ferociously. They piled onto Seth's men tearing them to the ground.

King Slyamal noticed a man heading straight for Jenel. He shoved his way through the mass of people. Unaware of the danger, Jenel focused on those in front of her. The man raised his sword. He released a yell as he charged.

King Slyamal flung himself upon the man. They tumbled to the ground rolling through the dirt. King Slyamal sprang to his feet. He smacked the man in the chin with the toe of his boot. "You dare to sell your king," he said as he plunged his sword deep into the man's skull.

Gradually, the fighting diminished to a few bits of tussling. All of Seth's men lay dead. Two farmers held Seth tightly on both arms. Blood oozed from his nose and dripped onto his shirt. They brought the man before King Slyamal.

"We apologize, my king," said a portly man. "What do you want us to do with him?"

King Slyamal glanced at his daughter. Jenel nodded back at him. He understood. "This man has wronged all of you," said the king, "His punishment is in your hands. Do with him what you will."

Yells went up as the mob dragged Seth back to the city square.

"No!" yelled Seth. "No! Don't leave me here!"

A noose was tied around Seth's neck. The people flung the other end of the rope around the branch of a tree. Seth's shoes scraped across the gravel as the townspeople lifted him off the ground.

King Slyamal watched coldly as the man swung in the air dangling. He writhed and wriggled for several minutes until his movements slowly halted.

"And so passes another greedy man," said King Edrei.

"It never should have come to this," whispered King Slyamal. "We need to leave."

The five left the town unnoticed, save by a girl of about six. She paused by Jenel handing her a lily. Jenel accepted it gracefully and thanked the girl.

"What will happen to them, father?" she asked.

"I do not know," replied King Slyamal. "But I hope they choose their next leader more wisely."

Chapter IX
A Trap

Rybnik crept through the forest taking special care to not make a sound. Carefully, he placed his feet on the ground avoiding dried leaves and twigs that would give away his position. He pushed low branches out of his way letting them spring back into their original position. Stealthily, Rybnik moved. He had business in the woods.

Crack!

Rybnik whirled around in the direction of the sound. *Perfect.* He concealed himself against a tree in the darkness. Blynak walked among the trees searching for something, or someone. Leaves crackled beneath his feet. *Noisy bastard.* Rybnik shook his head at the man's clumsiness. Blynak had followed him. Rybnik cursed under his breath. Blynak had proven to be a problem, one that needed solving.

*   *   *

They rode hard pounding the solid earth with the trampling hooves of their horses. Time was of the essence. They had wasted much of it freeing the village from a cruel man. Now they must make up that time. Tesnayr hoped that they would not be too late. They had to reach Drynelle at the same moment that King Telinin did. He wanted to avoid missing him. Alone, their army would be easily defeated. But together they had a chance of victory.

His horse breathed heavily with each mile they covered. Just hold on a bit longer, thought Tesnayr. He did not wish to kill his mount by pushing too hard.

Damp air seeped through his clothing as he rode onward. Thunder roared behind him from the many horses that followed behind.

A black mass crashed into the ground in front of Tesnayr. His horse reared up tossing him to the ground. Instantly, Tesnayr regained his feet. The niht'anda hovered over him. A blast of light slammed into the creature sending it flying.

More niht'andas slammed into the ground surrounding them. Their massive size stood three heads above the tallest man. Tesnayr dove to the ground barely avoiding the five inch claws of one of the monsters. The niht'anda recovered from its miss. Its bat like wings lifted it from the ground. Tesnayr watched his quarry. Suddenly, the creature dove for him. Tesnayr leapt out of the way as it tried to grasp him with the hooked claws on its wings.

"Aim for the small of their back," he yelled at those around him.

Desperately, men tried to kill the massive creatures. Hearing Tesnayr's order, Idæas aimed an arrow for the back of one of the beasts. He released a perfect shot. The arrow struck the center of the niht'anda's back. It went rigid before falling to the ground in a great cloud of dust.

Taking note of how the elf killed the strange creature, others followed suit. Max and some others cornered one of the beasts. It slashed violently with its razor claws. A bloodcurdling cry echoed among the rocks as it screamed in rage.

Max noticed a pointed rock jutting from the ground at just the precise height. He stabbed the ground with his staff. Instantly, the ground shook. Rocks and earth broke the ground as a wave of movement headed for the beast. The violence of the earth knocked the creature off its feet forcing it onto the knife like rock. Surprise filled its eyes as it went limp.

Max glanced about him. All but one remained. "Tesnayr!" he shouted.

The last creature held Tesnayr in a vice like grip. Drool dripped from its fangs as it leered at him. Tesnayr struggled vainly against the claw that held him. He stabbed at the creature. His blade bounced off of the rock hard flesh.

Noticing Tesnayr's plight, King Slyamal gripped his sword tightly. He climbed a small rise that hung just above the niht'anda. Summoning his strength, Slyamal leapt from the rocky ledge to the creature's back. He held tightly to the protruding scales. The beast whirled and twisted violently to knock King Slyamal off.

Despite the violent movements of the creature, Slyamal raised his sword and plunged it into the tender part of its back. Repeatedly, he stabbed the beast. The monster swayed ominously. Slyamal jumped to the ground and rolled out of the path of the dying monster. It plunged into the dirt, dead. Quickly, Slyamal ran to Tesnayr who was still trapped in the monster's grip. He pried the claws open releasing the man.

Tesnayr sucked in some air, thankful to be free. "Are there any more?" he asked.

King Slyamal shook his head in answer. He stared at the dead creature and the splash of red that covered its underside. "These monsters are not from here," said King Slyamal. "They are not from any of the five lands."

"They are the niht'anda," said Tesnayr, regaining his feet.

"And just how would you know that?" asked Max.

"They are from my home world," replied Tesnayr. He noticed people gathering around him wanting answers; answers that he hadn't time to give.

"We must reach Drynelle before nightfall. With any luck, King Telinin will already be there." Tesnayr mounted his horse. "We ride onward!"

Tesnayr spurred his horse and rode into the distance. The rest of the army followed suit. Explanations would have to wait.

*   *   *

Turyn clung tightly to the back of the dragon. He hated flying. *If cats were meant to fly, they would have wings.* The wind rippled through his fur ruffling it to no end. He cringed, thinking about the amount of grooming he would have to do to straighten it out.

His stomach churned as the dragon dipped low and then shot upward again. "Please, don't do that," he yelled over the roar of the wind.

"Shed your fear, little one," answered the dragon, "I will not drop you. Tesnayr commands it."

The dragon's words did little to comfort the black cat. Turyn dug his claws in more deeply. This trip could not end soon enough. *Finally!* A mass of horsemen rode along the land heading north to Drynelle. Tesnayr rode in the lead.

The dragon circled above. He remained high in the sky so that prying eyes from the ground could not see him. He spread his wings out flat and soared, keeping pace with the riders below.

*   *   *

Tesnayr thumped his fist against his thigh. He had promised the kings and Max an explanation about how he knew so much about those creatures. Even Nigilin and Arnin were present. He wished he did not have to tell them a part of his story that he wanted to forget.

"Tell us everything," said King Shealayr. "How do you know those beasts?'

Tesnayr took a deep breath. He twirled the chess piece between his fingers. "Have you ever played chess?" He showed them the piece in his hands. "It is a popular game from where I come from. All children learn to play it. It is a game of strategy and cunning. I taught the game to Galbrok."

The surprised expressions on their faces told Tesnayr that he had just punched them all in the gut. How could he keep this a secret much longer?

"Yes, I knew him quite well," said Tesnayr, "The orcs entered my home fleeing from a terrible monster: the niht'anda. They had destroyed the home of the orcs. The king offered them refuge. When the niht'anda came, we formed an alliance with the orcs. It served our purpose to work together. The niht'anda were stronger than any enemy we had ever faced.

"The war lasted for several years. Gradually, we managed to drive those monsters back. There was one battle that was to end it all. The niht'anda were weak.

"I was in command of the army. Before the battle began that day, Galbrok and I played a friendly game of chess. I thought we were friends. We had fought together throughout the war. He even saved my life a few times. We rode into battle together that day.

"But then things took a turn for the worse. Somehow, Galbrok had gained the niht'andas' loyalty. With the niht'anda behind them, the orcs turned on us. The men under my command were killed within moments and I was taken prisoner. When all was over, Galbrok murdered the king before us to prove that he was our new master.

"While I was held prisoner, I learned the truth about Galbrok. He and the orcs had invaded the realm of the niht'anda. The niht'anda retaliated by vanquishing the lands of the orcs. While we were fighting the niht'anda, Galbrok managed to gain their trust. His lust for conquest matched their own, forming a common bond. Galbrok used the king's good will against him. And you know what the result of that was."

"So this war is really a continuation of the conflict between you and Galbrok," said King Telinin, who had arrived moments before.

"It is much more than that," replied Tesnayr. "The orcs would have come here regardless. That is their way."

"So how do we defeat him?" asked King Edrei.

"By outsmarting him," said Tesnayr. "War is more than a game of strength. It is a game of wits. You must out think your opponent. But now we should rest. We have a long ride ahead of us tomorrow."

"This game you taught Galbrok, did you ever beat him?" asked Nigilin.

"No," answered Tesnayr.

"Why was that?"

"Because I always used the same tactic," said Tesnayr, "Until now."

Nigilin took in what Tesnayr said leaving him alone in the night. A small noise forced Tesnayr to turn around. Turyn silently padded into sight.

"Turyn," said Tesnayr. "What news have you brought me?"

"Plenty," said Turyn.

"Here, have some food," said Tesnayr. "Tell me everything."

Chapter X
Illusions

The night wore on as everyone waited for dawn and the order to attack Drynelle. Frayed nerves plagued everyone. The usual murmur of conversation had been silenced as men sharpened their weapons and checked their armor. Only the occasional clink of a hammer broke the quiet.

Disturbed by the lack of boastfulness, King Edrei racked his brains for an idea. He needed something to feed his men's bravery. Frightened soldiers were of little use in battle. He concentrated on the whetstone that sharpened the blade of his weapon. As he did so, he began to sing of Hemíl.

> Deep in rugged mountains old
> Dwell men of blood so bold.
> Sing ye, of the people of Hemíl.
> Sing ye, of men with iron will.
>
> Far up in mountains' peak
> Is a kingdom of which all speak.
> Majestic lords of valor known;
> Horse lords of great renown.
>
> Dwelling deep in fair mist
> Bring peace to all in our midst.
> Protected by heavens on high.
> Protected as time draws nigh.

King Telinin's head perked up as King Edrei sang. Realizing the intent of the man, Telinin joined singing a song of Belyndril.

O'er mountains ancient and tall
Rests great Belyndril, lord of all.
Great plains and forests deep;
Great warriors with which to keep.

Our fathers came long ago.
Tired of travelling to and fro.
Mighty kings of old have we.
Great tales to share with thee.

Long we've lived in grassy plains.
Staying where freedom reigns.
Proud and just are we;
Standing erect for all to see.

King Nalim joined the song followed by his dwarves.

Far below in caverns dark
Clang hammers strong. Hark!
Royal courage flows thro' our veins.
Abundant honor do we gain.

Tales are sung of MurDair
To people far and near.
Underground rests our city
Of marbled stone, fair and pretty.

Seekers of precious gems;
From us does runic lore stem.
Our courage burns like fire;
A valiance that can mire.

King Shealayr added:

Deep within trees of oak
Lies Belarnia in emerald cloak.
Flowing rivers of white dew
Sing to us old and new.

Ancient and fair are we.
Ne'er ye find truer loyalty.
Possessors of inner strength
We endure to any length.

Pursuers of truth and light,
Enlightenment is our might.
Bound by earthly song;
Sweet melody makes us strong.

Not to be outdone, King Slyamal rose to his feet and joined:

Sym'Dul, vast land of golden grass
And blue seas of crystal glass.
Sweeping gales of olden time
Fill our hearts with their chime.

Olden men of great valor,
Blest with wisdom all o'er.
Protectors of the small an' weak;
Guardians of all the meek.

Great stories told by lyre
Of courageous men with no ire.
Greater still, to others do we endear.
Long shall our men dwell here.

After King Slyamal finished, the chorus of men singing slowly
died. Only the single voice of Arnin broke it.

> Flames entrench five kingdoms old.
> Bonded by fate; a story told.
> Oaths sworn, of loyalties rare.
> An alliance led by Tesnayr.

Together the five kings finished the song:

> Let old quarrels be gone.
> A past buried, as we move on.
> Sing all free people young and old.
> Sing, before the day grows cold.

Tesnayr stood in the crowd watching with admiration the round of singing that the five kings started. He never thought he'd live to see the day when bitter enemies joined in the telling of tales. Quickly, he wiped a tear before it could escape his eye. *Perhaps we can win.* The seeds of doubt flittered away as the soldiers gathered and continued singing, continuing what King Edrei had begun.

He moved away from the group seeking solitude. He needed to think. Everything depended upon what he had planned. If the least little thing went wrong, it could upset their chances. He hoped that this time, he had planned it right.

The cool breeze tickled his skin as it blew past him. It had a touch of warmth to it telling him that spring had reached them. The lack of moonlight shielded Tesnayr as he walked. He sighed.

"Such anxiety," said a voice. Ernayn stepped out of the shadows and strolled with him. "War does that to a man."

"What do you want?" asked Tesnayr. He tired of Ernayn's comings and goings. Her mystique always wore on him.

"Not even a friendly hello? You need to work on your manners."

"And you need to quit sneaking up on people," said Tesnayr.

"I would not be a sorceress if I did," said Ernayn.

"What do you want?"

"Tesnayr: wanderer, warrior, and merciful. Tomorrow shall determine if you are a leader of men. I find it interesting that Max knows about your big plans and I do not."

"You are not a part of them," replied Tesnayr.

"I could make you tell me," said Ernayn with a hint of a threat.

"No, you cannot."

"So certain are you?"

"Powerful you may be, Ernayn, but even you cannot force a man to do anything against his wishes."

"I can be very persuasive." Ernayn closed the distance between her and Tesnayr. She caressed his cheek with her soft hands.

Tesnayr shoved her away. "If you are so interested in my big plans, as you put them, why don't you ask Max?"

The sorceress' face contorted slightly. "That tightlipped wizard will never tell me. And I know that you have included that cat in your schemes. But for some reason magic prevents him from saying a word."

A slight smile crossed Tesnayr's face. He liked having an upper hand on the sorceress. "Then, perhaps you should ask the dragons."

"Who are bound to you. I know that they must keep your secrets for eternity."

"Indeed."

"But you already knew that. You forget, Tesnayr, that I made you what you are."

"On the contrary," said Tesnayr, "You had nothing to do with it. I made myself. These people follow me because they choose to. I do not know why you helped me in the past, but I am not beholden to you."

"You ought to choose your words more carefully," said Ernayn.

"I tire of these games of yours," said Tesnayr. "I thank you for what you have done, but you have given me no reason to trust you. If you wish Galbrok destroyed, then trust in me."

"Trust is not easily come by," said Ernayn.

"Then, maybe you should try it," said Tesnayr. "I have to go." Tesnayr walked away back to the encampment.

Ernayn stared after him.

"Perhaps you should have faith in him, mistress," said Quesha appearing from nowhere.

"And what makes you say so?" asked Ernayn.

"The Stone of Elya," said Quesha.

"You are not ready for the stone," said Ernayn.

"I apologize, mistress, but the stone called to me. I can't explain it, but it pulled me in."

Ernayn eyed her student with curiosity. Rarely did the Stone of Elya call to an individual. "And what did it show you?"

"Tesnayr, at a place. It was a palace, but not one that we know of. He was richly dressed. I do not know what it means. But my intuition tells me to trust the man."

"Strange that it should show you these things," said Ernayn. "We will watch and wait."

*   *   *

Rybnik stood at the table directly across from Galbrok. Blynak stood a few feet away at the same meeting. The irate mood permeated them. Galbrok radiated fear. Even the boastful Blynak remained silent. Rybnik remained impassive with a cold and unreadable expression. He laughed inwardly at the sweat that dotted Blynak's brow.

"I've called you here," began Galbrok, "Because Tesnayr and his army will be here shortly. He seems to be well informed of our defenses."

Blynak began to speak, but cut himself off.

"Something to say, Blynak?" asked Galbrok.

"Yes, we appear to have a traitor in our midst," said Blynak.

Galbrok fiddled with his knife. He used the five inch blade to pick his teeth. "You think I don't know that?"

"Of course not. Naturally, you would already be aware of such things," said Blynak, nervously.

A messenger darted into the room. He whispered in Galbrok's ear and left just as quickly.

A loud bang reverberated through the room as Galbrok jammed his knife into the table. "Belyndril has fallen," yelled Galbrok, his voice bouncing off the walls. "Their army has taken back their city of La'nar. How did this happen?"

"Surely, my lord, you already know," said Rybnik smoothly, "There is only one answer: the traitor."

"And who might that be I wonder," said Blynak.

"Are you accusing me of something," demanded Rybnik.

"Yes," said Blynak, "I am accusing you. Who knows of Drynelle's defenses better than you? And yet Tesnayr knows of them as well."

"Who knows of La'nar's defenses best? I have never been to Belyndril. But you managed to take the city of La'nar once fifteen years ago," said Rybnik. "And you have been here in Drynelle long enough to learn every inch of it."

"And what about your disappearances," said Blynak. He moved closer to Rybnik with a smug grin on his face. "Where do you go in the darkest hours of the night?"

Rybnik glanced about him. All eyes were upon him. Galbrok looked at him expectantly. "You are correct, my Lord Galbrok," said Rybnik in a calm manner, "We do have a traitor in our midst. And he is here in this room. I have been taking nightly strolls, but that is because I have been following that traitor. I have been following Blynak."

"Me?" Blynak backed away. "I am no traitor."

"You are the only person in this room with insight of both La'nar and Drynelle. You have vanished each night to meet with a man from Tesnayr's army. Feeding him information."

"That's preposterous!" roared Blynak.

"I have proof," said Rybnik.

"Show it to me," commanded Galbrok.

"Surely you don't believe this man," pleaded Blynak. Fear clouded his face.

"Show me," yelled Galbrok.

"Check his pockets," said Rybnik.

Two orcs seized Blynak's arms and pulled a scroll from his pocket. They handed it to Galbrok who snatched it and quickly unrolled it. Anger flushed his features. "These are my plans for winning this war," said Galbrok. "How did you get these?"

"They're not mine," screamed Blynak. "It's not mine!"

"He snuck into your chambers this morning," said Rybnik, "I followed him. For weeks now he has acted strangely. I knew eventually I would learn what he was up to."

"And why did you not come to me earlier with this?" asked Galbrok.

"I needed proof," replied Rybnik, "Would you have believed me if I accused him without it?"

"And how do I know that you are telling the truth?" Galbrok asked Rybnik.

Calmly, Rybnik picked the knife off of the table and handed it to the leader of the orcs, handle outward. "If you do not believe me, then pierce my heart with this knife."

Galbrok took the knife from him. He weighed it in his hand attempting in vain to read Rybnik's face. Suddenly, he slashed it across Blynak's throat. To make certain he had killed the man, Galbrok rammed the blade into Blynak's stomach bringing it upward into the ribcage. Galbrok glared at the lifeless body that hit the floor.

"I thank you," he said to Rybnik. "I must commend you. You truly are a man after my own heart. I shall reward you greatly."

"I am here to serve," said Rybnik with a slight bow. He took one last glance at Blynak's dead form. His problem had been eradicated.

Chapter XI
The Burning Plains

The morning sun shone brilliantly on the city of Drynelle. Its walls glittered in the warm light providing a false sense of serenity. Looking upon it, no one would suspect that a battle was about to take place.

Arnin and Tesnayr stood on the great fields before the city eyeing it.

"I do not know if we can win the battle," said Arnin.

"Winning the battle is not important," replied Tesnayr.

"What is?"

"Winning the war. A man can win many battles and still lose the war," said Tesnayr, "Whatever happens, follow the plan."

"As you command," said Arnin.

"I mean it," said Tesnayr, "Follow the plan. The five kingdoms are far more important than me."

Arnin looked at Tesnayr questioningly. He had an uneasy feeling that something was about to happen that he would not like. Tesnayr's words provided little comfort.

"Mount up," said Tesnayr. "It is time."

The piercing sound of an orc horn reached them. So it begins, thought Tesnayr. He watched as Sarwyn and Serein stood poised in front of the city gates. They were yards away but the temptation they offered as targets was clear. An arrow headed straight for them. It soared through the air only to explode inches away from the two fairies. They grinned at each other.

Irked, the orcs along the wall launched a series of arrows in a blackened mass that arced toward the fairies. They pounded the ground creating a prickly carpet on the grass. A wide, clear circle surrounded the fairies as they remained unharmed.

The two began speaking in their own tongue. The ground rumbled as the grass grew rapidly. It twisted and tangled itself as it rose in height stretching out over the land. Tesnayr watched amazed as it slowly formed a catapult.

Giant boulders rolled across the ground to the newly formed catapult. They lined up each waiting to be loaded and fired. Sarwyn snapped her fingers. The catapult instantly flung a boulder toward the city. It sailed over the wall and crashed within the center. Another boulder shot from the catapult smashing into the stone wall. A giant dent remained where the rock hit.

That did it. The heavy gates to the city rumbled as they opened. Out marched a line of orcs. They spread themselves out in front of the gate and stopped awaiting orders. Behind them the gate sealed itself. Banging filled the air as the locks were put into place. The orcs lowered their spears snarling as they eyed the fairies.

"Now!" yelled Tesnayr.

The air filled with the sound of hundreds of pounding hooves as they poured from the trees and small rise heading straight for the city. At the same time the orcs charged heading straight for them.

Sarwyn and Serein stood their ground waiting for the precise moment. Their heads darted from side to side as they watched the cavalry and orcs draw near. At the last second, the two fairies disappeared into two specks of light.

Metal rang out as the two armies clashed. Orcs fell to the ground as horses trampled over them. Other horses reared high as lances pierced them in the chest throwing their riders off.

Arnin held tightly to the reins of his horse as he galloped toward the line of lances. He braced himself as his horse jumped over the beasts and landed hard behind them. Quickly, he turned his mount around striking the orc nearest him.

A massive black shape charged for him. Arnin ducked just in time to avoid being smacked by a niht'anda's wing. His horse neighed in fear as the creature leered toward him exposing its razor fangs that dripped with yellow saliva. The niht'anda's breath nearly choked Arnin. He jabbed his sword at the creature's eye. It dodged. The niht'anda bashed its claw into Arnin knocking him and his horse over.

The niht'anda crept toward him. In one swift movement it sunk its teeth into the flesh of the horse. Arnin cringed when the horse cried out in fear only to be silenced by the crunch of its bones as the dark beast fed on it.

He reached for his weapon. Nothing. The niht'anda's massive claw pinned it to the dirt. Momentarily cursing his luck, Arnin jumped to his feet. He and the niht'anda faced each other for several seconds. Arnin dodged to his left. The creature headed him off. He swerved to his right only to be met by the niht'anda's quick reflexes. A sinking feeling filled his stomach as Arnin realized that the creature was toying with him. Arnin attempted to lunge for his sword. Air burst from his lungs as the niht'anda backhanded him in the stomach. Arnin flew several feet away landing hard on the soil.

The niht'anda leaned on all fours as it moved toward him. Arnin stared at it accepting his grisly fate. Suddenly, shoots of grass shot from the ground latching themselves around the wrists of the niht'anda. Confused, the creature yanked at its bonds. The grass wrapped tighter pulling it to the ground.

Fear filled the niht'anda as more stems of grass wrapped around it covering it. The beast wailed and screamed in fright at its predicament. Its wings viciously smacked the ground in its efforts to break free. Vines burst from the soil grasping the wings of the niht'anda and wrenching them back. A sickening snap filled the air.

Arnin watched mesmerized as the earth pulled the niht'anda into the ground burying it. More grass covered the creature like a blanket until nothing remained except a small mound.

Arnin noticed Sarwyn for the first time. She stood erect among the swarming bodies locked in battle; alone as though ignored by everything and everyone. She pointed at Arnin's sword. Instantly, the earth rolled the weapon to Arnin delivering it to his hand. He picked it up and nodded in her direction as a gesture of gratitude.

A blunt force knocked Tesnayr off of his horse. He crashed into the ground as the wind was knocked out of him. Tesnayr rose with his sword in hand. A niht'anda stood before him. Its massive shape and razor claws sent chills through Tesnayr. The bright red spot on its underside reminded him of blood.

It swiped at him with its claws. Tesnayr ducked just in time. He jumped back to his feet and darted to the rear of the creature. Tesnayr leapt for its back. The niht'anda swung around and flung him to the side. Tesnayr crashed into the ground again.

Desperately, Tesnayr searched the dirt for his sword. It lay feet away from him. He scrambled for it. The niht'anda backhanded him sending him flying again. Stunned, Tesnayr lay still for several seconds. He shook his head slowly to clear it. The niht'anda stamped the ground as it neared. The fangs poking through its lips dripped with sticky drool.

Tesnayr dove for his sword. The niht'anda lunged as well. It reached out with its massive claws and snatched Tesnayr. It squeezed tightly, but its grip remained loose enough to not kill him.

"No!"

Jenel appeared from nowhere. She sprang for Tesnayr plunging her dagger deep into the niht'anda's claw. The creature roared in anger, but its grip held firm. It slammed its fist into Jenel. She gasped and coughed from the impact.

Glancing upward, Jenel watched helplessly as the niht'anda spread its black, leathery wings and lifted into the air with Tesnayr. It rose high above the battle taking its prize to the castle.

Thud! Jenel whirled around. Another niht'anda leered at her. Its foul breath nearly choked her. Jenel's heart raced. She darted to the left. Before she even got a few steps, the beast reached out with its bony claw snatching her from the ground. It brought her to its face. She struggled helplessly. Suddenly, Jenel found herself being hoisted into the air by the creature, heading for the castle as well. The field below her shrank from her view as she was lifted higher and higher.

*   *   *

Quesha leaned on the balcony of the sorceress' palace surveying the lake and the woods beyond it. Ernayn had told her to stay put. She hated being left out and wanted to join her mentor.

A bluish glow formed behind her. Curious, Quesha moved toward it. The Stone of Elya stood before her and seemed to be alive. Cautiously, Quesha stepped toward the magical stone. Pictures formed within the blue marble as she studied it.

The Stone of Elya summoned her, pulling the girl into its clutches. Suddenly, she found herself in a strange place. It was the throne room of a massive palace, but none that she knew of. The place appeared rundown. Jagged cracks shot up the marble stone walls. Bits of the ceiling rested on the floor where they landed when they fell. Quesha looked about her. Clearly, the place had once been beautiful, but had suffered from years of neglect.

A door opened behind her. Its creak echoed around the room. In stepped a young woman of about eighteen. Quesha watched intrigued as she cautiously entered the chamber. The woman walked silently as her eyes darted about. Remaining still, Quesha followed the movements of this stranger as she moved past the young sorceress unaware of her presence.

Then, Quesha noticed it. Tesnayr's sword hung from the woman's waist. *How is that possible?* As the young woman moved, a horn poked out from beneath her cloak. Upon closer inspection Quesha realized it was the same horn that the dragon Selexia had given to Tesnayr. Bewildered, Quesha moved closer.

The stranger turned toward Quesha looking straight through her. A peculiar necklace hung around her neck and it glowed green. The light from the pendant was soft, but enough to be seen clearly in the darkened room. Quesha knew at that moment that this was a vision of future events. She did not know how she knew this, but it was the only explanation.

Instantly, the great chamber vanished in a swirling fog. Quesha steeled her nerves remembering that the Stone of Elya had a will of its own. She waited patiently for the stone to take her back to Ernayn's home. It never did.

When the fog cleared, Quesha found herself in some woods near Drynelle. Beside her was the Stone of Elya. Quesha stared at it. An image of her handing it to Ernayn appeared on the smooth surface. Quesha understood the message. She must hand the stone to her mistress and she must wait there for Ernayn.

Chapter XII
Captured

Clanging chains echoed off the walls as Tesnayr and Jenel were led into the courtroom. Galbrok sat on the throne. Jenel bit her tongue to keep from showing her shock at seeing Galbrok.

Black lines stretched across Galbrok's face from ear to ear. Another set of lines spread from his nose and swirled down his chin to his neck. Every jerk of his head jangled the earrings that lined each ear. Despite his adornment of jewelry and tattoos, rippling, well-defined muscles emerged from beneath his armor. His biceps measured four times the size of Jenel's fist. Now she knew why people feared Galbrok. One look at the barbarian instilled fear.

"Tesnayr," greeted Galbrok, "Nice to see you. I wish it were under better circumstances."

"Say nothing," whispered Tesnayr to Jenel.

"And you have brought a friend," said Galbrok. "She is lovely." He gripped Jenel's chin and stared into her eyes. "Do I frighten you?"

Jenel ripped away from his grasp. "No," she spat.

"Of course I do, darling. It is written all over your face."

Jenel reached into her cloak. She wrapped her fingers around the hilt of the knife their captors missed. When Galbrok turned his back, she pulled it free. Jenel charged for Galbrok bringing her knife to his neck. Galbrok swung his arm knocking her hand away. Her knife clattered on the marble floor.

In retaliation, Jenel reached up and yanked several earrings from Galbrok's ear. Blood poured down his neck streaming past his shoulder. He screamed in pain. Galbrok seized Jenel around the throat and lifted her off the ground.

"You have spirit. I'll give you that," he said. He threw her aside.

Jenel slammed into the floor gasping for air.

"That was foolish of you, Tesnayr," Galbrok continued. "Sending a girl to kill me. I'm surprised at you."

Tesnayr remained silent. He maintained his composure even after Galbrok nearly squeezed the life out of Jenel.

"Has it really come to this? You trying to kill me and failing once again."

"You say I have failed," said Tesnayr, calmly.

"Look around you, Tesnayr. You are my prisoner. Your little army attacks the gate, but they will never break through. And I know about the men in the sewers.

"Is that a flicker of anger? I know you, Tesnayr. We fought side by side. I developed many of the strategies that you know. It should be you by my side. But instead you allowed your overdeveloped sense of morality govern your actions."

"At least I have principles," said Tesnayr.

"Principles? I have principles. All that matters is winning."

"There is more to it than that."

"Ah, yes, the hero that sacrifices everything," scoffed Galbrok. "Tell me, how is it serving you? I destroyed your home. I will destroy this land and every other realm I choose. Nothing can stop me. Not even you with all your knowledge."

"You will be stopped," said Jenel.

"And who will stop me?" asked Galbrok.

"Death," replied Jenel. "No one lives forever."

Galbrok burst out laughing. His roars filled the chamber bouncing off the ceiling, walls, and even the floor. Several minutes ticked by before he stopped. "That may be true," he said, "But until then I will destroy your home, princess. Perhaps I should make you my personal slave."

Jenel grunted in disgust.

"Oh, it won't be that bad," said Galbrok, "You'll find that I can be quite gentle." He brushed a finger down her cheek. "Though my father may have been an orc, my mother was human." Galbrok glanced at Rybnik who stood silently watching the exchange. "And this doesn't bother you in the least?"

"No," said Rybnik, mechanically.

"You," spat Jenel. "How dare you call yourself a soldier of Sym'Dul. Twice you have betrayed my family. I swear upon my sister's grave that you will meet a traitor's death."

Rybnik said nothing. His face betrayed nothing.

"So you know each other," said Galbrok. "I am surprised at you, Tesnayr, allowing a man who betrayed his king into your confidences."

"I believe that some people deserve a second chance," said Tesnayr.

"And look where that belief has gotten you," said Galbrok. "Do you not believe in giving everyone a chance?"

"You certainly deserve none," Tesnayr replied. He noticed a black shadow sweep across the room disappearing behind a corner.

"Come now," said Galbrok, "Call off this little war of yours."

Tesnayr remained still.

"I'll make you a deal," said Galbrok, "A game of chess. If you win, I'll take my forces and leave."

"And if you win?"

"I shall strip the flesh from your bones before I kill you."

Galbrok motioned for the chess board to be brought to him. He sat at one end while Tesnayr took his place at the other. Jenel watched in horror as they calmly moved their pieces across the board ignoring the battle raging outside. The minutes dragged. One by one, Tesnayr lost his pieces. First his pawns were taken, followed by his bishops and rooks. Finally, Galbrok took the queen and knights until the only piece left was the king.

A victorious sneer spread across Galbrok's face. "Only your king remains," he said. "You never were good at this game."

"And you always allowed your arrogance to dictate your moves," said Tesnayr.

"Call the game, Tesnayr. You've lost."

Tesnayr took the king piece and handed it to Galbrok. He pulled the knight piece from his pocket that he had carried for many months. "Sometimes, all you need is one piece to win," he said.

"So you still carry that," said Galbrok. "Take them away to the prison."

Rough hands seized Tesnayr pulling him to his feet. He and Jenel were shoved out of the courtroom and down the familiar steps to the prison chamber.

Turyn scurried from his place of hiding and chased after them. He darted from shadow to shadow staying close. No orc or human paid him any heed. They mistook his black shape as a trick of the mind.

The orcs shoved Jenel and Tesnayr down the moss covered stairwell to the dungeons below the castle. Water dripped into a bucket. The metal door to the cell squealed as they swung it open. Tripping over their feet, Jenel and Tesnayr caught themselves as they were pushed inside. Clang! The door slammed shut with the familiar click of the lock.

The fading clomp of their boots told the prisoners that the orcs had left. Silence ensued. Tesnayr plopped down on a pile of hay.

"Well?" said Jenel, "What are we to do?"

"Nothing," Tesnayr replied.

"Nothing?"

"PSSSST." Turyn's face filled the bottom right corner of the prison door.

Tesnayr jumped up and hurried over to the cat. Hushed whispers filled the cell as they conversed in private. Jenel watched as they ignored her.

"Are you sure?" Tesnayr asked.

"Positive," replied Turyn. "Galbrok has already announced it. Apparently a small part of him still does not—"

"What does he have planned?" interrupted Tesnayr.

"He has ordered Rybnik to murder one of you.   He hasn't specified whom. That is to be a surprise in the morning. It is to be a public execution."

"Rybnik? Why him?" asked Jenel.

"Only Galbrok knows his reasons, my lady," said Turyn. "He probably thinks it will make a very threatening statement by having him kill Tesnayr."

"How do you know it will be me he wants executed?"

"It is most likely. I'm sorry I can't get you out of here."

"Don't worry about it," said Tesnayr. "You know what to do, Turyn."

The black cat bounded off having received his orders.   He squirted around the corner and out of the dungeon.

"What did you mean?" asked Jenel.

"Pardon?"

"Just now.   What do mean by, he knows what to do?   Do what, exactly?"

Tesnayr eyed Jenel for a moment but remained silent.   He moved to the other end of the cell and sat down disregarding her question.

*   *   *

Idæas marched up to Arnin in the moonlight.   "The rumors are true," he said, "Tesnayr and the princess have been captured by Galbrok."

Dismayed, Arnin stared out at the open field momentarily thinking of a rescue. He scratched the idea.

"What are your orders?" asked the elf.

"We carry on as planned," Arnin replied.

"Some of us are willing to attempt a rescue."

"No," said Arnin, "Tesnayr's last orders were to follow the plan. That is what we will do."

Idæas hated the idea of doing nothing, but he knew Tesnayr well enough to not argue with Arnin. "If that was his wish, then so be it. The men are ready when you are."

*   *   *

A mixed crowd of orcs and people gathered in the great hall of the castle eager for the display that Galbrok had planned. Excited murmuring echoed through the room as everyone settled themselves. The orcs were the most anxious, always reveling in a display of blood.

Galbrok sat on the throne at the front holding his staff of steel. He banged it three times on the floor quieting the crowd. "Bring out the prisoners."

Several heavily armed orcs dragged Jenel and Tesnayr into the chamber. Jenel stood defiantly eyeing the mob in an effort to quell her unease. Tesnayr remained unusually calm.

"Rybnik," said Galbrok, "Are you ready?"

Rybnik stepped forward and saluted Galbrok. "Yes, my lord."

"How do you wish to proceed?"

"With a bow."

"Very well," said Galbrok, "Bring him a bow." Nothing happened. "Archer!"

An orc in a far corner jerked awake. He rushed forward with his bow almost tripping over a black cat. The orc handed Rybnik his longbow. He reached toward his quiver for an arrow when he realized that he already had one in his hand. Rybnik took it.

"Bring forth the girl," ordered Galbrok.

Orcs shoved Tesnayr to the sidelines as they pushed Jenel to the center of the room. Tesnayr fought against them and received a blow to the stomach.

"You will kill her," said Galbrok.

Rybnik hesitated from a moment. Aware of all the eyes upon him, he raised his bow, aimed, and fired. The arrow whizzed through the room and struck Jenel just above the heart. She fell to the ground unmoving. Rybnik lowered his arm, his expression unreadable.

A man approached Jenel placing his hand over her mouth. "Dead," he said. Two more came forward and carried her away.

Chapter XIII
Revelations in Stone

King Slyamal stood looking out over the field and the chaos that reigned. He waited patiently for the sun to be in the correct position signaling his time to attack. Steel upon steel filled his ears as men shouted from wrath. Feelings of doubt crept within him. He buried them. Now was not the time to second guess.

"My king," said a messenger.

"It is nearly time," replied King Slyamal.

"My king," said the messenger again. "I'm afraid I have some terrible news."

King Slyamal faced the man. He steeled his features prepared for the worst.

"The princess, I am afraid she is dead."

The words cut through him, twisting and turning an invisible knife until all he had was a gaping wound. "What?"

"It happened early this morning. I only just received word. She was captured yesterday by the orcs. Galbrok had her killed."

King Slyamal gripped his sword until the hilt dug into his skin making him bleed. He wanted to scream. He wanted to lash out. But all he could do was remain still. "Dead?"

"The rumor is, Rybnik killed her upon Galbrok's orders," said the messenger.

A furious rage boiled within King Slyamal as his initial shock at the news transformed. He marched to where his contingent of men waited. Mounting his horse, King Slyamal yanked the reins steering the animal toward the battle. He looked about him studying the faces that watched him. *Orders be damned.*

King Slyamal unsheathed his sword holding it high in the air. "This is the day," he yelled, "When we decide whether we live or

die. This is the day that we destroy those who murdered my
daughter. And I swear to you all that I will not rest until
Galbrok's head rests upon a pike!"

Cheers went up from the men mixed with sadness and
fortitude.

King Slyamal charged toward the battlefield. He rode his
horse hard ignoring the ragged breathing. Whatever anxiety he
had was lost to his anger. The roar of thundering hooves
pounded behind him as hundreds of men raced into the melee.
They trampled the newly sprouted grass. Their yells filled the air
drowning the clamor of the field before them.

The orcs faced their new quarry shoving pikes into the
ground. They braced themselves for the impact. The hammering
of the horses drew nearer instilling fear into them.

King Slyamal jumped his horse over the first row of pikes. He
snatched one from the hands of an orc. Driving his beast
onward, Slyamal thrust the spear into the back of a niht'anda
forcing it to snap in half. Swiftly, he swung the broken handle in
his hand clonking an orc on the head before forcing it into
another's neck.

King Slyamal took his sword and blocked a blow from an orc.
He slashed and sliced mercilessly allowing the fury at losing his
daughter dictate his movements. Tearing through the line of
orcs, King Slyamal left a trail of destruction.

*   *   *

Slowly, Jenel opened her eyes. She yawned a she groggily
sat up. The tent flaps beat against the wind. A figure stood over
her. She recognized the tangled beard of Max.

"How are you feeling?" he asked.

Confused, Jenel stared at the wizard. She touched the place
where the arrow pierced her. It throbbed, but the bleeding had
stopped. "Where am I? And why am I not dead?"

Max handed her a cup of water. Jenel sipped it greedily to alleviate her dry mouth. "I am about to do something that has never been done," said Max, "I am about to break an oath sworn by magic."

"What? Why?"

"Because you need to know the truth. Come with me."

Jenel followed Max to another part of the tent. Before her was the strangest orb. Its blue color filled the area. It was made of smooth marble and floated delicately above a basin of water.

"This is the Stone of Elya," said Max. "Ernayn has allowed me to borrow it."

"What is all this?" asked Jenel.

"Look into the stone," said Max, "It will show you what you need to know."

Jenel eyed him warily.

"Look into it," Max urged.

Jenel regarded the blue stone warily. Suddenly, she found herself being pulled toward it. Before she knew what had happened, the tent changed into one occupied by Tesnayr. He studied maps, oblivious to her presence.

"I need to speak with you alone," said Rybnik as he entered the tent.

"Very well," said Tesnayr, "Come in." He glanced around outside to make certain that they would not be overheard. "What is it you wish to see me about?"

"Two orcs just approached me asking me to join Galbrok," said Rybnik.

"And what was your reply?"

"I told them I'd have to consider the matter."

"How interesting," said Tesnayr, "What made you say that?"

"I thought it best if I did not reply immediately. In fact, they seemed pleased that I was uncertain and gave me a week to consider their request."

"This is most excellent," said Tesnayr, more to himself.

"Excellent?"

Tesnayr ignored Rybnik's question. Unexpectedly, everything that Max had told him made sense. "I understand that you once sought to overthrow King Slyamal."

"Yes, but that was ten years ago. It was because of Janine that I was only exiled instead of executed."

"This is why the orcs approached you. You have a history of betrayal. I mean no disrespect," Tesnayr finished upon noticing the scowl on Rybnik's face. "I want you to accept their offer."

"What?"

"Allow me to explain," said Tesnayr, "This tactic is nothing new with the orcs. They routinely recruit members of their opponent's army to use as spies. Which we can use to our advantage.

"We are not winning this war. Galbrok cares nothing for the loss of a few men within his army. He would murder an entire legion if it gained him dominance over this land. I have gone about this war the wrong way.

"The only way to defeat the orcs is to kill Galbrok. But he never appears in the open. He prefers the shadows. What I need is a man to draw him out. Since you have already been approached, it proves that they trust you, to a degree."

Rybnik listened intently to Tesnayr's words. "What are you asking of me?"

"I want you to join Galbrok."

"If it will win this war," Rybnik said.

"Do not accept this task lightly," said Tesnayr, "If you accept it, understand this, you will be completely alone. Whatever friends you have now will be lost. You can never confide in the orcs nor those who serve them. No one will know the truth, except for myself, the wizard, and Turyn. You will use Turyn to send me messages about the orcs' movements. You will also have to give them some valuable information about this army to make your part convincing. Most importantly, you must do what is necessary to gain Galbrok's trust.

"If you accept this task, you will become the most reviled man in the five kingdoms and you will have to commit the greatest act of betrayal to prove your loyalty to Galbrok. Understand, Rybnik, there is no returning from this."

Rybnik inhaled sharply holding the air in his lungs for a moment before releasing it. "I understand," he said, softly.

Tesnayr poked his head outside the tent. "Turyn. Max."

Moments later, the black cat and the wizard entered the tent. They glanced at Rybnik.

"Max," said Tesnayr, "Make certain that prying ears cannot hear us."

Max uttered a quick spell. He nodded in Tesnayr's direction, indicating that their secrets were safe.

"I have called you in here for an important mission. Rybnik is going to commit treachery so that the orcs will accept him as one of their own. In return, he will spy on the orcs. Turyn, you will carry messages back and forth between us. And you will be traveling on a dragon.

"Max, as I understand it, an oath sworn before a wizard cannot be broken. Therefore, we will swear before you. And you must pretend to think Rybnik a traitor and hate him like the rest of this army will. I swear to you that none of what is said here will be repeated."

Turyn padded forward. "If you wish this Tesnayr, then I will do it. I swear to carry the messages as you command. And I will speak of this to no one."

An orange glow filled the room with each word Turyn spoke.

Rybnik breathed deeply. A part of him wished to back away. But he knew that defeating the orcs was more important than his desires. "I vow to serve you, Tesnayr. I will gain Galbrok's trust by any means. I will pass you the information you need. From this day forth, I am your most loyal servant."

The orange light filled the tent after Rybnik had finished his oath. Max did a quick flip of his hands and the light vanished. "It is done," he said. "None of you can break this vow. But why has the dragon not sworn the same oath?"

Tesnayr smiled a knowing smile. "The dragons answer to me. Selexia vowed their service to me for as long as I shall live. Any command I give them must be obeyed."

"Indeed," said Max, "This is the first that this has ever happened. How did you gain her trust?"

"That is a long story," replied Tesnayr, "And one I shall tell you all when this is over."

Suddenly, Jenel found herself at the exact moment she and Rybnik argued. She found it strange to be watching herself. Tears welled in her eyes as she remembered that fight and how soon after Rybnik had committed his act of treachery. Her mind struggled with the fact that this was all a ruse.

The image faded out before being replaced with that of the battle in front of the Keep of Edrei. She watched once again as Rybnik rode away with the orcs. All the hatred she had felt at that moment rushed back. It boiled within her until she managed to control it. *This was all a trick?* The betrayal had seemed genuine. Many had been killed because of it.

One part of the memory caught Jenel's attention. She remembered how Rybnik's manner had been cold and emotionless. She watched as he lagged behind the fleeing orcs. Rybnik stopped his horse and turned around looking back at what had been, at what he had left behind. A sliver of pain filled his features. In a flash it had gone. Determined, he kicked his horse catching up with the orcs and with what he must do.

Again the image faded away only to be replaced with another. Jenel watched as Rybnik snuck into a room. She recognized the interior of the palace of Drynelle. Rybnik quickly went inside shutting the door silently. He searched the room systematically as he pulled open drawers and inspected the shelves. Finally, he yanked the correct drawer open. Maps spilled out of it. Rybnik scooped up the maps and other bits of parchment. He inspected them making certain that they were what he needed.

A noise startled him. Folding the maps, Rybnik shoved them under his shirt and ran to the door. He carefully opened it peeking out into the corridor. Swiftly, Rybnik darted out of the room shutting the door behind him. He dashed behind a corner just as Blynak appeared.

Blynak glanced about him. Satisfied that no one watched him, he stole into the same room that Rybnik had just vacated. Rybnik stared at the wood door for a moment. Jenel knew he had formulated a plan.

Suddenly, she found herself in another room. Galbrok was there, along with several other orcs, Blynak, and Rybnik. Jenel watched as Rybnik entered the chamber. He strolled past Blynak. Jenel thought he had come too close to the man. She watched carefully, noticing how Rybnik slipped the maps he had taken earlier into Blynak's pocket before settling himself at the table.

The scene changed to a room within the castle of Drynelle. Rybnik paced nervously in front of the fireplace. Sweat glistened on his skin.

"I can't do it, Turyn! I cannot kill him," said Rybnik pacing the floor uncontrollably.

"If Galbrok demands it, you must," said Turyn, "You swore an oath to Tesnayr. You swore before the wizard."

"What if Galbrok puts her up there?"

"You must do what is necessary to remain in Galbrok's confidences. Whomever he chooses, you must kill. And do not betray your emotions."

"I cannot murder Jenel."

"Your love for her will—"

"It is not what you think," said Rybnik, "Long ago I vowed to protect her. To keep her safe."

"Why?" Turyn asked, tenderly.

"I killed her sister."

"Rybnik," soothed Turyn, "Whatever happens you must go through with it. When asked to pick your weapon, choose the bow. And miss the heart."

"But—"

"Trust me," said Turyn.   He vanished into the dancing shadows of the firelight.

Jenel felt the hard earth beneath her feet again.   She breathed deeply regaining her composure after the Stone of Elya released her. She looked about her. The stone remained where it was. Max was near her, studying her.

"Do you understand now?" asked the wizard.

"You mean to tell me that this was a ruse, a plan to gain Galbrok's trust?"

"Yes," said Max.   "Tesnayr realized that there was no other way to defeat him."

"But the men that were killed," said Jenel, "The crushed spirits."

"A calculated risk."

"It could have all gone terribly wrong!"

"Anything can go wrong," said Max, "But you do things hoping that they go the way they should. We needed to get Galbrok into the open. This was the only way to do it, though you almost destroyed Tesnayr's plans."

"Me?"

"There was a reason he left you behind in Hemíl. There was a reason he left you here to protect the rear line. And it wasn't because you are a woman. He didn't want you charging after him and almost ruining what he worked so hard to achieve.

"As it happened, you went charging after him anyway and managed to get yourself captured. You were not supposed to be in the castle. Only Tesnayr was.

"Luckily, Turyn managed to get a message to me in time so that I could ensure you'd be brought back here."

"If I had known—"

"Everything had to appear genuine. Besides, in a plan like this, the less people that know the better," said Max. "I am only telling you now because there is no other way to explain how you are still alive."

Jenel absorbed everything Max had just told her. "Rybnik. How I hated what he had done."

"And now?"

"And now I feel so ashamed."

"You'll get your chance to tell him."

"What do I do now?" asked Jenel.

"That is up to you," replied Max. "I could tell you to remain here, but you'll just go charging off again. Your father has already headed to the city."

"I don't know what to do," said Jenel.

"There is a way into the city. And there are a group of men who have yet to see battle."

"What way?" asked Jenel.

Max led his horse to where Jenel wanted him to meet her. He paused momentarily with that overwhelming sense of not being alone.

"You ought to learn to not sneak up on people," said Max.

Ernayn waltzed into the open. "How do you always know it is me?"

"You project a certain aura," replied Max. "What is it you want?"

"You should learn to have more respect for me," said Ernayn.

Max huffed. "You may be able to scare others with your talk, but not me. I know you, Ernayn, better than you know me."

"Here," said Ernayn handing Max a rowan wood staff.

Max took it carefully. He inspected the wood admiring its soundness. "What is this for?"

"A wizard needs his staff," said Ernayn. "Consider it a peace offering."

Max eyed her suspiciously.

"I assure you it is genuine," said Ernayn.

"Thank you," Max said, slowly.

"Did you make good use of the stone?"

"Yes," said Max. "I thank you for letting me borrow it."

"And what is Jenel planning?"

"I cannot tell you. Do not give me that look. You know full well I would not be able to. But you can make yourself useful."

"Really?" said Ernayn.

"Stop playing these games of appearing when you choose to. You know as well as I that if we lose this day, you lose as well. Nothing will stop the orcs from overrunning your home in Belyndril."

"And what would you have me do?"

"These niht'anda have proven most troublesome. I am certain that you have the power to deal with them. Especially if you were to combine your magic with that of the fairies," said Max.

"Such a thing has never been done before."

"Such creatures have never been here before."

"Why doesn't Tesnayr use the dragons? He commands them," said Ernayn.

"Perhaps you should ask him," Max replied.

"I cannot," said Ernayn, "He asked me to not follow him where he is going. He asked me to trust him."

"Do you not trust him?"

Ernayn circled Max. "I do. I just do not understand his methods."

"You're not supposed to," said Max. "You have shrouded yourself in mystery and separated yourself from the world. Perhaps you should quit trying to influence events and just let them happen."

Max pushed past Ernayn heading for where Jenel awaited him. "Why do you trust him so much?"

"Because I know what the future holds if he wins. And I also know that no one can defeat Galbrok except for Tesnayr."

Ernayn looked at him questioningly.

"You are not the only one whom the Stone of Elya speaks to."

"Perhaps not," said Ernayn.

"I do find it interesting that it chose to speak to Quesha so soon."

"So do I."

Max left Ernayn alone with her thoughts. He found Jenel eagerly awaiting him with a small group of men.

"You'll leave your horse here," she said.

Without question, Max took his weapons from the saddle and strapped them to himself. He slapped the animal's rump to make it run away.

Chapter XIV
An End to all Things

King Shealayr held his sword above his head as he trekked up the flowing stream in the aqueduct. Elves and men trailed after him. The strong current impeded their efforts as they waded through the waist deep water.

His arms tingled as they tired from holding his sword. King Shealayr ignored it. Focused on his goal, he trudged onward against the liquid force. His soaked clothes weighed him down forcing him to summon his reserve strength to move onward.

Slowly, they moved up the aqueduct and across the city. Above them orcs were unaware of their presence. They trod carefully making certain to not slosh the water and give away their position. Everything depended upon the element of surprise.

Jenel and her group crept to the abandoned wall. Satisfied no sentry stood guard, she ordered the ladders set up. Men rushed forward leaning the ladders against the stone without making any sound.

"Quickly," said Jenel.

One by one, men climbed the wooden ladders heaving themselves over the top of the wall. Jenel glanced about her keeping careful watch. "Go," she told Max when he paused momentarily. Once everyone had gone, Jenel pushed her way up the ladder and into the city. She scrambled over the rough stone and looked about her.

The city seemed strangely quiet despite the chaos at the front gate. *Where are the people?* Before she had time to dwell on the matter a group of orcs burst from hiding. Jenel lunged to the ground just in time to avoid being struck by an arrow. She rolled over on her back and sat up quickly plunging her sword into the belly of an orc. Mercilessly, she pushed him over the wall.

Another came straight for her. Jenel readied herself. She sidestepped to her left clipping the orc in the back. The beast whirled around as though it felt no pain. Its red eyes bore into her instilling fear. She stood, frozen. Its red eyes continued to overpower her will as the orc crept toward her.

Jenel desperately tried to move her limbs. They disobeyed. Closer the red eyed orc came. A wicked sneer crossed its lips as it sensed victory.

A whoosh swept past Jenel's ear as a brown blur whapped the orc on the shoulder. Another brown blur struck the beast in the neck. The spell broken, Jenel jumped from her spot in time to see Max whip the orc with his staff again. Repeatedly, the wizard jabbed the beast in the stomach before knocking it to the ground.

Another red eyed orc approached. It stared into Max's eyes, but its magic had no effect on the wizard. With a flurry of movement, Max rammed his staff into the creature's face.

Another orc charged Jenel from behind. A soldier grasped her and pushed her out of the way before the beast could strike. The man sliced with his blade before thrusting a dagger into the orc's neck.

A bloodcurdling cry rose up from below. They looked about them. A swarm of red eyed orcs surrounded them and rushed toward them in a frenzy.

"Everyone jump!" yelled Max.

Without question Jenel and her cadre of men plunged the fifteen feet from the top of the wall to the ground below. Pebbles dug into her skin as she crashed onto the hard earth. Max jammed his staff into the ground. A dazzling silver light burst from it spreading over their area of the city destroying everything in its path.

The light slowly dissipated. Max stood alone surrounded by a pile of dead orcs. "Not bad for an old drunk," he said.

Disbelieving what had just happened, Jenel stared at the wizard. She had never witnessed such power. "What were those things?" asked Jenel.

"The Nŏk'ta," replied Max. "Tesnayr told me about them before this battle began. They are Galbrok's reserve forces. They can overpower you by instilling fear. According to Tesnayr, if he is using them, then he must be desperate."

"Princess," said a soldier.

Jenel turned toward the man.

"They have locked many of our people in the town hall. The orcs plan to burn them alive."

"Follow me," ordered Jenel as she ran off toward the city square where the town hall was.

The clinking and clanking of metal tools beat against the stone exterior of the city walls as the dwarves picked the stones apart. The slippery mud made the process difficult. They worked steadily. Bit by bit the bricks came loose.

"Hurry," urged King Nalim as the hole in the wall slowly grew.

They froze as the stamping of feet above them walked past. They watched as a lone man crossed the wall. Nalim nodded his head. A dwarf took careful aim and flung a knife at the guard. The dagger struck the man in the chest.

"Quickly," said King Nalim.

His dwarves returned to their work scraping away the mortar that held the bricks. The more they picked at it, the more easily the stones broke away. Pleased that the hole was wide enough, King Nalim ushered his dwarves through.

"You know where to go," he told them.

Turyn slunk through the dimly lit corridor, his belly gently brushing the floor. He found the door to the prison cell slightly ajar. The cat slipped through the narrow crack squirting under the table. The orc standing guard noticed nothing. Carefully,

Turyn crept to a broom in the room. He jumped at it pushing it over before darting back under the table.

The loud clatter attracted the guard's attention. Grunting, the orc went over to it. He stooped down and picked up the broom eyeing it with curiosity.

Seizing his chance, Turyn floated to the top of the table and snatched the key. He pushed himself with his powerful hind legs soaring across the room. Turyn landed with a soft thump. Quickly, the cat ran for the cell Tesnayr was locked in. He pushed the key through uttering a short *mrrrp* before darting away. Turyn found the guard seated at the table again. He stayed in the shadows as he moved toward the door and into the abandoned hallway.

Tesnayr heard the *mrrrp*. He glanced over smiling broadly as his eyes rested upon the key. Silently, he praised Turyn's ingenuity. Tesnayr scooped up the key. He reached for the pile of lard that sat upon an abandoned plate. Galbrok's idea of a last meal. Tesnayr rubbed the fat onto the hinges of the cell door. Quietly, he inserted the key into the lock and turned.

Click!

Tesnayr pushed the door open and slunk against the wall. Cautiously, he stepped toward the orc standing guard. Tesnayr peeked around the corner. The orc sat in a chair facing him, but had not noticed him. Tesnayr rushed toward the orc tackling him. They rolled across the floor as they struggled.

Tesnayr landed several punches on the orc's bloodied face. He hauled the orc to his feet and thrust the beast into the slimy wall. Without wasting a moment, Tesnayr bashed the orc's face into the stone before finally twisting its neck. The familiar crunch signaled that the orc was dead. He let the body flop to the ground.

Quickly, Tesnayr snatched his weapons and the horn. He darted into the corridor heading for the stairs. *Time to deal with Galbrok.*

Ernayn and the two fairies strode onto the field. They placed themselves in front of the gate ignoring the fighting mass behind them and spread themselves evenly. Ernayn stood in the middle with Serein on one side and Sarwyn on another.

They chanted in an ancient language. The ground vibrated under their feet as the intensity of their chant grew in volume. With each word they spoke the ground trembled even more violently. Wind swirled around the three women whipping their hair and clothes in every direction. More and more they chanted until the roar of the wind practically hurt their ears.

All went still. Suddenly, a violent force shot from the three women crashing into front gate of Drynelle. The impact silenced those on the battlefield as they all turned in the direction of the blast.

Ernayn, Serein, and Sarwyn remained where they were taking stock at what they had done. The gate was gone, disintegrated. Much of the city walls had disappeared. Bits and pieces crumbled to the ground.

Silence reigned over the field. Men and orcs alike stared at the sorceress and the two fairies with wonderment and fear.

"I'm sure that got Galbrok's attention," said Ernayn.

From his vantage point, Arnin studied the newly made hole in the city wall. He viewed it as an opportunity. "Retreat," he yelled, remembering the plan.

A roar went up on the field. It grew with each passing minute. Men ran away from the city entrance over a small rise. They scrambled over the hill as the orcs and niht'anda chased after them sensing victory. The beasts cheered as they crested the small hill only to have their victory ripped away. A line of dragons awaited them.

Arnin gave the signal. Instantly, his men hugged the ground as waves of flame soared above them slamming into the orcs. Agonized screams filled the area as the orcs floundered helplessly, burning alive. More fire from the dragons caught the orcs in the second charge.

"Fire!" yelled one orc.

Spears and arrows flew toward the dragons bouncing off of their bodies. One by one the dragons spread their massive wings. Winds pounded the ground as they beat their strong wings and ascended into the air.

Hoards of niht'anda escaped to the sky. Selexia was ready for them. She released a deafening cry. Instantly, her dragons shot toward the escaping niht'anda plucking them from the sky with ease.

"To the city," yelled Arnin.

His men jumped to their feet and charged for the gaping hole in the wall. They dashed over the field with renewed fervor. Within minutes they had closed the distance and joined King Telinin and his men as they swarmed into Drynelle.

King Telinin had watched from his place of concealment as Arnin gave the signal. He hadn't expected Ernayn or the fairies to do what they did, but did not question it. As the field emptied over the hill, Telinin gave the order. "Now!"

He and his men burst from their hiding place and raced to the opening. Orcs poured out of the hole toward them. King Telinin had expected this. He snatched a pike from the earth and threw it with all its strength. It poked through an orc's neck.

Sarwyn sent an orc flying through the air with the force of her power. Suddenly, a stabbing pain pierced through her back. She reached behind her and felt a wet spot forming. Blood dripped from her hand. Sarwyn collapsed to the ground as her strength left her.

Serein immediately knelt by her side. Gently, the fairy lifted her sister cradling her. Fear etched her face as the realization that Sarwyn was dying filled her. A shadow surrounded Serein as a change took place within her.

"Serein," said Sarwyn, "No." The fairy's last words barely escaped her lips before she died.

The shadow around Serein intensified. Her face changed to a hardened expression as her skin darkened. Within moments, the anger at losing her sister took over. He skin turned grey as her clothes turned black.

Instantly, Serein leapt to her feet. She forced her hand before her as an immense blast escaped from it tearing through anything in its path. Determinedly, Serein stomped through the fighting mass of people. She grabbed an orc by the neck and twisted its head off. The fairy snatched another and chucked him over the city wall.

The darkened fairy no longer cared who was friend or foe. Another forceful blast from her hand ripped men and orcs to pieces. One of Telinin's men tried to stop her. Serein snatched a sword from the ground and rammed it into his middle. She spotted King Telinin. Serein headed straight for him disposing any who got in her way.

A gold blur raced through the crowd toward the fairy. It stopped directly in front of her spreading its wings wide forcing Serein to stop. She stared at the phoenix blankly as she returned to herself. Slowly, her skin returned to its normal color.

Serein glanced about at what she had done. She spotted Sarwyn's dead form on the ground. Stretching her hand toward her sister, Serein uttered words in her language as grass covered Sarwyn's body. It grew tall, twisting and stretching until it formed a giant tree with luscious green leaves.

Jenel peeked around a corner to make sure the way was open. Her face bumped into King Nalim who was doing the same thing. "Nalim," she said startled. "What are you doing here?"

"Following orders," said the dwarf king. "Tesnayr knew that Galbrok would have the people rounded up and executed. It is our job to save them."

"Good," said Jenel, "Then you can follow us. That is where we are headed."

"I should have known," muttered King Nalim. He motioned for his dwarves to follow.

Quietly and swiftly, the combined cadre of men and dwarves raced through the city streets to the town hall. Their boots made barely a sound on the cobbled streets. Jenel held up her hand halting everyone. They hunkered low behind crates of food and half full wagons.

Orcs stood guard outside the locked building. Jenel spied several of the red eyed orcs as well. She silently cursed. Only Max was able to withstand their hypnotizing magic. "Max," she said, "They have more of those red eyed creatures."

Max peeked around her. He took a quick note of how many there were. Quickly, Max took a cloak from one of the soldiers and wrapped it around himself. "Wait here," he said.

The wizard walked toward the building and the orcs guarding it. They allowed him to approach thinking him to be nothing more than an old man. One of them said something in their harsh language. Max hunched over in response. A red eyed orc approached him staring straight into Max's eyes. It soon became apparent that their magic had no effect on him.

Max cast off the cloak and jabbed his staff into one of the orcs. He swung around as lighting shot from its ends and sent a red eyed orc flying. He threw his hand in the direction of another. White light escaped his hand destroying the beast.

Jenel signaled for the others to follow her. She blocked an attack from an orc disarming it quickly before dispatching the creature. Jenel tore through the chaos heading straight for the door of the building.

"Quickly," she said.

King Nalim grasped the timber across the locked door, pried it away, and flung it aside. Jenel opened the doors to revel a mass of frightened people. She stepped through the opening and wasted no time. "Out! All of You!"

Quickly, the terrified people within the building scrambled over each other to escape their prison. They rushed out into the daylight overwhelming their orc captors. Scattering in all directions, they ran away from their nightmare.

Jenel plunged her weapon into an orc that tried to sneak up on Max. She looked up and immediately found herself facing a red eyed orc. She felt its magic overpower her will. Max saw her plight. He whacked the beast with his staff before slicing its throat open.

Gradually, the excitement died down as all of the orcs were killed. Jenel surveyed the carnage. "To the castle," she said, "All of you."

An orc on the watchtower took careful aim with his bow targeting Jenel. He pulled the bowstring back preparing for its release. Suddenly, Quesha appeared before him. She snatched the bow from the orc's hands and shoved him over the side. Quesha noticed another orc in the second tower aiming at Jenel. She raised the bow, aimed, and fired. Her arrow struck the orc in the neck. She watched dispassionately as the orc clutched its wound and tumbled over the side.

Galbrok rushed down the corridor with Rybnik by his side. The battle continued to draw closer to where he was. His assured victory had been ripped from him as flying reptilian beasts swooped through the city streets. *How did he get such creatures?* Disbelief filled Galbrok.

"Galbrok," said a messenger running toward him, "They have taken the city."

"They are only at the front gate you fool," spat Galbrok.

"No," said the messenger, "They are within the city. Some broke through the wall near the mudflats. Others snuck in through the aqueducts."

Galbrok glared at Rybnik. They eyed each other for a moment. A flurry of movement followed as Galbrok ripped out his crooked blade and plunged it into Rybnik's side before he could react. Rybnik crumpled to the ground.

"You told me no one could come through there."

"I lied," spat Rybnik.

"Galbrok," began the messenger.

Galbrok silenced him by stabbing the man in the chest. "Out of my way, filth," he hissed.

Galbrok tore into the throne room of the castle. Fury guided his movements. *How could it have come to this?* He stared out the window as the forces of Tesnayr poured into Drynelle destroying his orcs. They even managed to overcome his Nŏk'ta. *How could I lose?* Tesnayr had never once managed to beat him. And Rybnik. The betrayal cut deep within Galbrok. Never had anyone dared such an act against him.

He whirled around and stopped cold. A single chess piece sat upon the armrest of the throne; the black knight. Galbrok walked over to it. Carefully, he picked it up studying it. Only one man in the world would put it here. He touched the nick within the chess piece.

"Maybe I underestimated your understanding of the game," said Galbrok. He placed the chess piece back on the throne. "It never occurred to me that you meant to be captured."

Tesnayr stepped out from behind the tapestry, "Are you admitting a weakness?"

Galbrok laughed. "You, Tesnayr, were always interesting to me. I killed your family and yet you never succumbed to the grief. Even when I had your brother killed, you managed to escape. I must admit that I was surprised to find you here and fighting for these people."

Tesnayr circled Galbrok maintaining his distance.

"This land is diverse and has proven a challenge to conquer."

"Has it now?"

"You humans are easily taken," Galbrok continued, "You're easily swayed. One little whisper casts doubt within your minds.

That is why your home is nothing more than a blackened and barren wasteland."

"The niht'anda," said Tesnayr, "How is it you control them?"

"They are mine," said Galbrok.

"They never ravaged your lands?"

"Oh they did," replied Galbrok, "But I managed to work out a deal with them. They were created from darkness, and their hearts are as black as my own. They love destruction. As do I. How do you think I managed to destroy your homeland?"

Tesnayr's grip tightened on his sword.

"Did you really think that you and your king were helping me? The land of the orcs has always been dark and barren. I simply used the niht'anda to start a panic in your land. A simple plea from me and your human compassion did the rest."

Tesnayr's face flushed red.

"Did I anger you? All those times we drank together. All those times we played the game of chess. Not once did you or your king realize that you were being backed into a corner.

"And now here we are again. Your little rebellion will soon be squashed. You cannot defeat my army. We are too many."

"You remember what the first rule of chess is?" Tesnayr eyed Galbrok betraying no emotion. "Dismiss your pride. It is the same in war. The second rule is to never underestimate your opponent. The third: do not become predictable. You have failed on all counts."

Galbrok's smug expression faded.

"All this," said Tesnayr, signaling the battle raging outside, "Had nothing to do with taking the city. It was merely my way of getting to you. Despite all your knowledge, you still failed to realize that it was you being backed into a corner."

"You have not defeated me."

"Where are your guards, Galbrok? Where is the man you trusted most?"

Enraged, Galbrok charged Tesnayr. Tesnayr dodged. He whirled around in time to block an attack by Galbrok. Sparks flew from their swords as they locked. Galbrok head butted Tesnayr. Momentarily stunned, Tesnayr stepped back losing his grip on his weapon.

Galbrok seized his chance and stabbed at Tesnayr. His sword sliced through the man's armor, but did not pierce the skin. Tesnayr grasped Galbrok's sword arm and bent the wrist backwards while jamming his elbow into Galbrok's throat. Galbrok staggered backward gasping for air as he clutched his throat.

Tesnayr charged. He raised his fist and punched Galbrok repeatedly until blood poured from his nose. Tesnayr grabbed his sword again and swung with all his might. Galbrok blocked, punching him in the stomach. Doubled over, Tesnayr dropped his weapon once more. Galbrok kicked it across the room.

"Did you honestly think that you could beat me," sneered Galbrok.

He swung at Tesnayr. Tesnayr caught Galbrok's hand and flipped him over onto the hard floor. Instantly, he rammed his foot into Galbrok's armpit and twisted it until he felt Galbrok's shoulder pop out of its socket. Galbrok roared in agony. He swiped his sword at Tesnayr nicking him in the leg.

Galbrok pulled himself to his feet as Tesnayr clutched his bleeding leg. "You have no weapon," spat Galbrok.

He attacked. Tesnayr dodged. They moved around the chamber as Galbrok chased Tesnayr with his sword. With his mind darting around, Tesnayr found it difficult to think of a plan. Galbrok pounced from behind. He kicked Tesnayr's feet out from under him. Pain seared through Tesnayr as he hit the stone floor with a thud. His stomach burned as Galbrok kicked him.

Why do you fight him?

The words flowed through Tesnayr's mind as he remembered his first meeting with the phoenix. His mind jumped to memories of the people he led across the Ársa Mountains. He thought of Jenel. He remembered Jarown and Nelyn. Even the triplets, Nedis, Nylin, and Nular popped into his mind. In that second of clarity Tesnayr realized that he had gone beyond wanting Galbrok's head. He longed to help those affected by the orcs' destruction and no longer used them as an excuse for revenge.

Galbrok rammed his foot into Tesnayr's stomach again. He leered over the man poised for the killing stroke. Suddenly, a scream of pain escaped Galbrok as Rybnik plunged a knife into his back. Galbrok backhanded the wounded man sending him sprawling on the floor.

Tesnayr noticed a ray of light shining upon him. His sword lay several feet away from him, glowing. Summoning his resolve, Tesnayr hauled himself to his feet. He stared determinedly into Galbrok's eyes.

Galbrok charged. Tesnayr snatched a dagger from his belt ducking low as he rammed it into Galbrok's hip. Quickly, Tesnayr rolled across the floor toward his weapon.

He wrapped his fingers around the hilt of his sword. His arm tingled as the power of his weapon flowed through it. Warmth encompassed his body as he allowed the magic to possess him. The light of his sword shone brightly filling the entire room.

Galbrok gaped at him disbelieving. "That blade. Where did you get it?"

Curiosity got the better of Tesnayr. "What do you mean?"

"I've dreamt of it," replied Galbrok. "All my life. It's just a dream. And you...how did you come by it?"

Taken aback, Tesnayr replied, "It was given to me."

"Never," shouted Galbrok. "Never!"

A crazed look crossed Galbrok's face as he charged toward Tesnayr. Tesnayr strengthened his grip on his sword. He sidestepped allowing the weapon to dictate his movements. In a swift move, Tesnayr brought his sword down and cleaved Galbrok's weapon in two. A loud clatter echoed off the walls as the broken blade hit the stone floor.

Galbrok stared at his sword blankly before raising his eyes toward Tesnayr. Tesnayr lifted his weapon and plunged the cool steel into Galbrok's chest until it poked through his back.

"How?" whispered Galbrok with his last breath.

Tesnayr shoved him off of his sword allowing Galbrok's body to thump on the cold floor. Blood pooled around the dead leader of the orcs.

Running footsteps forced Tesnayr to turn around. Jenel stood in the entrance way with King Nalim. She looked at Galbrok's dead form and then back at Tesnayr. A cough drew her attention and for the first time Jenel noticed Rybnik. She ran to him.

Chapter XV
Amends

Rybnik lay in a pool of his blood clutching his mortal wound. Jenel knelt beside him as Rybnik's short breaths barely registered. Gently, she lifted his head into her lap. Tears streamed from her eyes and down her cheeks landing delicately on Rybnik. Despite weeks of hating the man who had betrayed her, all she felt now was sorrow. She still loved him, her mentor.

"Jenel," whispered Rybnik, "Forgive me."

"Shh," soothed Jenel. "Rest. I'm going to save you."

"You saved me a long time ago. Forgive me."

"You always have my forgiveness," said Jenel. "The healers will be here soon."

"It's too late for that," said Rybnik. "I only wanted to save Sym'Dul, and you."

Jenel swallowed back a sob. She must remain strong. "I know."

King Slyamal sprinted into the throne room. His eyes lit up when he saw Jenel. He stopped himself from running to her when he noticed Rybnik's unmoving form. King Slyamal stepped into the shadows and watched from a distance.

Rybnik placed a bloodied hand on Jenel's cheek. He looked into her hazel eyes. "You have your sister's heart, your mother's strength, and your father's stubbornness."

"And your courage," said Jenel.

Rybnik smiled weakly. "I have shamed all of you."

"No," Jenel whispered, "The halls of your ancestors sing joyously of the honor you have brought. Now rest. Tomorrow there will be another letter in the stone."

Rybnik's hand flopped to his side as his last breath escaped his lips. A great man had died that day. Jenel hugged him close. She berated herself for loathing him. Great sobs racked her body as she pleaded in vain for death not to take her friend.

"My lady," said a soldier next to her, "Why do you cry? He is only a traitor."

Jenel placed Rybnik's head back on the cold, stone floor and covered him with her cloak. Calmly, she rose to her feet. "How dare you! How dare any of you! This man deserves to be honored. You are to carry him high on your shoulders. He will be buried with all the grandeur of any king."

"But, he is just a traitor," said the man.

Jenel slapped the soldier across the face.

"Why you little," the soldier raised his hand in response.

"You dare strike my daughter," roared King Slyamal stepping away from his hiding place.

Instantly, the soldier lowered his hand and bowed before the king. "No, my lord."

"This man," said King Slyamal, "Is the reason why Galbrok is dead. By Tesnayr's orders, he sacrificed everything to bring the demise of the orcs. You will do as my daughter commands."

The soldier saluted. He waved three others over. Together they lifted Rybnik's body high upon their shoulders and carried him proudly into the rays of the sun.

Jenel ran into the arms of her father. "Father," she cried.

"I know," soothed King Slyamal stroking her hair. "He did what we were unwilling to do."

"I hated him when he betrayed us that day," wailed Jenel, "If only I had known. If only—"

"Do not waste your tears on such sentiment," said King Slyamal. "He loved you and protected you. He did what I did not. Sym'Dul lost a great man today, but has gained an even greater hero." He held his daughter tightly comforting her. "Cry my child. You father has you."

From a distance Tesnayr watched the pair. He wiped away a single tear. Inwardly, he wept for Jenel's grief.

Stifling his emotions, Tesnayr turned his attention to more pressing matters. "What news of the battle?" he asked another soldier.

Before the man could answer, the giant window shattered as a black form crashed into the chamber. The niht'anda swiped its immense claw across a nearby soldier sending him flying to the courtyard below. A low growl escaped its throat as it stalked Tesnayr.

Instantly, men attacked the niht'anda with spears jabbing and poking it in the face. The creature smashed one man with its giant wing. It whirled around snatching another in its sharp teeth.

Tesnayr charged it. He struck it with a stake hitting it squarely in the throat. The niht'anda yanked the spear out tossing it aside. In one swift movement, Tesnayr jumped onto the creature's back, holding tightly to its protruding spine. He stabbed it in the small of its back. Stunned, the niht'anda stood erect on its hind feet before tumbling over the rail of the balcony and to the ground below.

King Slyamal rushed over to the rail. Tesnayr clung to a jagged stone a few feet below. "Take my hand," said Kung Slyamal leaning far over the rail and reaching out for Tesnayr.

Tesnayr reached for the king's outstretched hand. They barely touched.

"Take it!"

"It's too far."

Quickly, King Slyamal glanced about him searching for anything he could use as a rope. The drawstring to a curtain caught his eye. He cut it loose. Desperately, he lowered the tassel to Tesnayr. "Take it!"

Tesnayr reached for the makeshift rope unaware of another niht'anda that had noticed his plight. The beast flew toward him, jaws open. Its leathery wings flapped noisily in the wind as it charged its prey. Instantly, a dragon swooped out of the sky snatching the niht'anda in its jaws.

Snatching that line, Tesnayr clung to it as King Slyamal hauled him up. He heaved Tesnayr over the rail. "You're not getting out of marrying my daughter that easily."

Tesnayr grinned at the king and clapped him on the shoulder.

"General Tesnayr." Selexia hovered outside the window. "The orcs have fled into the hills. They are scattered and confused. I have sent my dragons after them."

"Good. I don't want any left alive," said Tesnayr.

"We will do our best." Selexia flew off.

Nelyn sprawled on the mushy ground as a niht'anda hit her from behind. She rolled onto her back and stared at it defiantly. Scrambling, she reached for her weapon. The niht'anda blocked her attempt as it slammed a claw into the dirt flinging pebbles everywhere. It leered over her savoring its victorious moment. Accepting her fate, Nelyn closed her eyes.

An agonized scream erupted from the niht'anda as it crumpled to the ground. Cautiously, Nelyn opened her eyes. Banis stood before her, his horn covered in black blood.

"How—," began Nelyn.

"When you need me most," said Banis. "Many of the orcs have escaped, but a few lag behind. Come with me."

Three more unicorns appeared behind Banis as smoke drifted past them.

"Alone?"

"You may choose three."

Nelyn looked about her. "Nedis! Nular! Nylin! Come with me!"

The triplets stopped what they were doing at Nelyn's command. They eyed the unicorns with interest as Nelyn climbed aboard Banis. Smiling at one another, they darted for the other unicorns before galloping off with Nelyn after the orcs.

Slowly, the battle sounds died away as the orcs bolted with the niht'anda close behind. As the catapults and the ringing of steel lessened, silence reigned once again over the plains.

Chapter XVI
Five Lords

Two weeks had passed since the siege of Drynelle. King Edrei paced in front of the gnarled trees away from everyone. He did not wish to be overheard and felt the seclusion in the woods was best for the meeting he had in mind. With the castle overrun by people celebrating the great victory, he knew there was no chance of having the discussion he wished in private.

A sound attracted his attention. King Nalim walked up. He gave a cursory nod in Edrei's direction before leaning on his ever present axe.

Kings Telinin and Slyamal arrived as well.

"You wished to speak with us," said King Shealayr as he melted away from the surrounding trees. Leave it to an elf to always approach silently.

"Yes, I did," replied King Edrei. He figured it best to get down to business. "I wanted to discuss what happens now."

"What happens now?" questioned King Telinin. "What do you mean?"

"Surely it has come to your attention that now that the five lands are free from the danger of the orcs, we must decide what we wish to do next. My point, gentlemen, is we need to end our constant war with each other.

"We formed a temporary alliance out of convenience. Now I propose that we make that alliance permanent."

"Permanent?" said King Nalim.

"Yes," replied King Edrei, "Permanent. I tire of war. My people have suffered enough. And after this latest mess, all I want is to salvage what is left. Continue your disputes if you wish, but the people of Hemíl are going back to the mountains."

"We need more than just an alliance," said King Shealayr.

"What are you suggesting?" asked King Telinin.

"A High King," replied the elf, "Someone who will mediate our disputes."

"MurDair will never surrender its sovereignty," grumbled King Nalim. "Nor will it be governed by anyone but its king."

"You misunderstand me," said King Shealayr. "Each of the five lands will retain their own independence. However, in matters that affect all of us, we will adhere to the authority of the High King."

"But what is to keep this High King from overstepping his bounds?" asked King Telinin.

"The dwarves have a council," said King Nalim. "Whenever the king of MurDair wishes to negotiate a treaty or go to war he must acquire the consent of the council."

"And each one of us may chose whom we send to sit on the council," said King Edrei.

"So the king's authority will be tempered by us," added King Nalim.

"But who will be the High King?" asked King Telinin.

"Tesnayr," said King Slyamal, ending his silence.

The others noticed him for the first time.

"Strange that you would choose him," said King Nalim. "I thought you didn't like the man."

"Like has nothing to do with it," replied King Slyamal. "Tesnayr bows down before none of us. He has no loyalty to any one of the five lands. But he does genuinely care for their people. He has demonstrated that time and again.

"It is because of him that the orcs have fled. The people cheer his name in the streets. He is the proper choice if he chooses to accept it."

"That is a big if," said King Shealayr. "I am certain he wishes to return home. As we all do."

"Then I suggest we ask him," said King Edrei.

"Ask me what?" Tesnayr stepped from the shadows. He looked at each of the five kings in turn.

"What are you doing here?" asked King Edrei.

"Turyn caught wind of your summons and he told me about it," replied Tesnayr. Turyn shrank behind him wrapping his tail around his paws.

"Tesnayr," said King Edrei, "We wish to do something that has never been done before. We want to not only end our disputes, but name you High King of the five lands. We would adhere to your authority so long as we retain governance of our own kingdoms. A formal treaty will need to be written and signed, but this is the gist of our plan.

"Do you accept our offer?"

Tesnayr fingered the hilt of his sword. Its magic flowed through him. He only wanted to return home. But since that day he found the dead orc on the beach with Nigilin, Tesnayr knew he would never have a quiet life. "Yes," he said.

"Excellent," exclaimed Max, appearing from nowhere.

"Is nothing sacred?" said King Edrei with frustration.

"I might have accidently told the wizard," squeaked Turyn.

"However, a treaty such as this will have to be done in front of witnesses," said Max, "And, I can't believe I'm about to say this, but I am going to need Ernayn's help." Max cringed at the thought of needing the sorceress. He shuddered a moment before returning to his regal self.

The next morning the five kings gathered in an isolated chamber of the castle. Joining them was Tesnayr, Max, and Ernayn. The talks started off civil, but portions of it became heated as time progressed. They spent an entire month debating the amount of independence the five lands would retain as well as the amount of authority the High King would have. They had nearly finished their drafted document until Max almost put an end to it.

"The king needs an advisor and who would be better than a wizard?" asked King Edrei. "Besides, some oaths must be sealed by magic."

"I'll not live in a stone cage," said Max.

The kings and Max stared at one another for a long while until Ernayn broke the stillness. "What if you only have to be present when the king needs you," she said.

Max crossed his arms before grunting in agreement.

"Very well," said King Shealayr, "We are in agreement." He picked up the document from one of the elven scribes. Quickly, the elf king looked it over before handing it back to the scribe.

"Are we ready to sign?" asked King Edrei.

Each of the kings signed their name to the document. Tesnayr signed his next followed by Max and Ernayn. Afterward, a golden light swept up and down the parchment sealing it.

Max picked it up. "There you are," he said, "Here is your new beginning. The coronation ceremony will be within the week in the town of Norlyk."

"Why Norlyk?" asked King Telinin.

"Because I like it there," retorted Max.

*   *   *

Jenel rubbed her fingers across the weathered stone as she searched for one in particular. She felt it. Carefully, Jenel removed the loose stone. Bits of dust fell as she revealed the hole behind it. She reached into it. Empty. She hadn't expected there to be anything in there, but a part of her had hoped for one last letter from Rybnik.

Jenel pulled a folded piece of parchment out of her pocket. Sorrowfully, she placed it in the empty space and replaced the stone. "Thank you, Rybnik. Take care of Janine."

She noticed Serein hovering near the tree where Sarwyn had died. The fairy's solemn demeanor tugged at her heart. *Poor Serein.*

Jenel left her place as she went over to the fairy to offer comfort.

*   *   *

"Max," said Tesnayr, "I was hoping to catch you."

Max faced Tesnayr with curiosity. "Something on your mind?"

Tesnayr pulled a gold feather from his pocket. "I need a favor." Hours before he had woken suddenly remembering the feather the phoenix had given and knowing what to do with it.

Max gingerly took the feather awed by its beauty. "Is this—"

"Yes," said Tesnayr. "I need it to be taken to a place far away for safekeeping. No one must know of its existence."

"May I ask why?"

Tesnayr shook his head. "It was entrusted to me momentarily, but now must be hidden until it is needed. But it won't be needed by us."

"Understood." Max twirled the feather in his fingers admiring it. "I think I know just what to do with it. A place no one will think to look."

"Thank you," said Tesnayr.

Chapter XVII
High King

The week passed quickly as people came from afar to see their new king crowned. Some had even traveled from the western edge of Belyndril. They had the help of Ernayn to thank for the ease of their journey.

Tables lined the valley overflowing with food for the grand banquet. The enticing smell tantalized all who came near.

On a stage built by the townsfolk, Max waited with Ernayn off to the side. Quesha was beside her. Tesnayr stood in front of Max with the five kings behind him. His white tunic with the golden crest of the phoenix stood out allowing all gathered to see him.

"Do you, Tesnayr, vow to protect the people of the five lands and to follow the law as prescribed in this document?" asked Max in a booming voice.

"I so swear it," answered Tesnayr.

Max held his hand out to Ernayn. She gracefully walked to him with a shimmering crown made by the elves. "I, the sorceress of these lands, declare you High King of the five lands: MurDair, Belyndril, Hemíl, Belarnia, and Sym'Dul." She gave the crown to Max.

Max held it high above Tesnayr's head. "I, the Great Wizard of these lands declare you High King of the five lands: MurDair, Belyndril, Hemíl, Belarnia, and Sym'Dul." Max gently placed the golden crown upon Tesnayr's bowed head. "Long may you and your descents govern justly, and bring us peace and prosperity."

Tesnayr rose to his feet and looked out over the massive crowd.

"Or I shall haunt you from my grave," added Max, under his breath.

Grinning slightly, Tesnayr contained his laugh.

"Is there any other business to be conducted here?" asked Max.

"Yes," said King Slyamal. He strode over to his daughter taking her hand. Jenel allowed herself to be led to where Tesnayr stood. King Slyamal placed his daughter's hand into Tesnayr's. "I propose a wedding."

Speechless, neither Tesnayr nor Jenel said anything.

"A wedding?" said Max. He had not expected this. "Do you two agree to this?"

Both Jenel and Tesnayr nodded eagerly.

"Very well. Who gives this woman to be wedded this day?"

"I do," said King Slyamal.

"And who gives this man to be wedded this day?"

"I do," said Nigilin, stepping away from the crowd.

"Jenel," said Max wrapping their clasped hands with a purple cloth, "Do you accept this man as your husband, to know only him and to be bound to him for the rest of your days?"

"Yes," Jenel replied.

"Tesnayr, do you accept this woman, knowing only her and to be bound to her for the rest of your days?"

Tesnayr's tongue swelled in his throat. A discreet nudge from Nigilin worked it loose. "Yes."

Someone handed Max a goblet full of mulled wine. He handed it to Jenel, and then Tesnayr, who each took a sip. "As you have pledged yourselves to each other, drink of this cup and become one."

Max pulled two gold bracelets from his pocket. He looked at everyone sheepishly. "Well, you never know," he muttered. He placed one on Jenel's left wrist and the other on Tesnayr's right.

"Then, I pronounce you two husband and wife. Now kiss your bride before I do it myself."

Tesnayr didn't need to be told twice.

The wedding feast went far into the night as music traveled across the valley to accompany all the dancers. Wine flowed freely and with the help of Max, it never ran out. People ate until they could eat no more and the cake reminded Tesnayr of Hana's cake.

Jenel and Tesnayr strolled amongst the guests thanking everyone for coming. Many wanted to shake the hand of the first High King.

A smack stung the back of Tesnayr's head. He whirled around wondering who had hit him. Hana stared at him with her hands on her rounded hips. "Over a year ago you left and not one letter."

"I was...busy," stammered Tesnayr. He never thought he would see Hana again.

"Uh-huh," said Hana. "So, I see you found yourself a wife. Such a lovely woman." Hana hugged Jenel beaming with pride. "You got yourself a fine husband. I should give you the recipe for my three layer cake. Tesnayr loved it."

Jenel smiled at the old woman instantly liking her.

"And you," she slapped Tesnayr in the stomach, "Visit me sometime. Or I shall storm the gates of your home."

"It will be an honor to visit your home," said Jenel, graciously.

Nigilin walked up to them, saw Hana, and immediately turned away.

"Oh no you don't," said Hana chasing after him. "Just where do you think you're going?"

"I like her," said Jenel, "She's sweet."

"Not one word!" echoed Hana's voice from a distance.

Tesnayr chuckled. "As long as you're on her good side."

A boisterous tune caught their attention as one man belted out the song of unity between the five kings. Jenel paused to listen to the tenor voice. "Who is that man?" she asked a passerby.

The man paused and glanced in the direction she pointed. "Bastyon. A great hero."

"Great hero?"

"Yes, my lady. He saved my life."

Jenel thanked the man and took one last look at Bastyon before walking away with Tesnayr.

A fluffy bite of cake hovered before the wizard's mouth as his licked his lips. He had spent the last twenty minutes waiting for this cake and his mouth watered at the thought of tasting it. Without warning, a black paw swiped the piece off of the fork.

Frustrated, Max looked around. Turyn sat beside him munching happily. He glanced up at the wizard with an innocent expression.

"That was my cake," grumbled Max.

"And it was very tasty," said Turyn.

"Why you blasted feline," Max chucked his plate at the cat as he pranced away with his tail up. Huffing, Max meandered back to the table hoping there would be more cake. Nothing. *Just my luck.*

Max noticed a juicy leg of roast chicken. Settling for what he could get, he reached for it. Instantly, two bowls of punch launched into the air smothering Max in their sticky liquid. Fuming, Max stared at the table of food. Three figures sneaking away caught his attention. "Hold it you three," he yelled.

The triplets stopped in their tracks. Slowly, they faced the wizard.

"Well, what do you have to say for yourselves?" roared Max.

"We—" began Nular.

"—didn't mean—" said Nylin.

"—it," finished Nedis.

Max glowered at them. "I want a nice piece of cake. Get one for me and I might forget about this incident." Punch dripped from his robes onto the ground.

"But there isn't any," Nedis said.

"Then I suggest you learn how to cook," said Max.

The three brothers darted off before Max could do anything to them.

"Congratulations," said King Shealayr as he walked up to Jenel and Tesnayr with Idæas by his side. "I have something for you. A wedding present."

He waved an elf over who approached with a sealed box. King Shealayr opened it pulling out two pendants. One he placed around Jenel's neck. She admired the phoenix shaped necklace and its brilliant shine.

King Shealayr placed the other around Tesnayr's neck. Tesnayr studied the medallion with a hole in its center that matched Jenel's pendant.

"Let these be a symbol of your love and union. May they also serve as a reminder of a new beginning of hope."

"I don't know what to say," said Tesnayr.

"You've already said it." The king clasped both their hands before turning away.

Tesnayr eyed the medallion a moment. "I get the feeling there is more to this than just a gift."

"With elves it always is," said Jenel. "Come, we have more guests to receive."

Far above them the phoenix soared through the evening air. The majestic bird landed on the roof of a building and folded its wings as it watched the celebration with a smile. The phoenix faced the sun as it hung low in the purple sky. Most would have been awed by the beautiful sunset, but to the phoenix it was a sunrise.

Epilogue

Bastyon rode along the lonely road to where the sorceress awaited him. Birds chirped merrily unaware of the sacrifice he was about to make. Clop. Clop. His horse trudged on steadily, content with its long journey. As Bastyon rode, he thought back to when King Tesnayr had given him his assignment.

He remembered walking in on Tesnayr as he leaned on a balcony overlooking the ocean. The newly constructed palace just outside the small village of Norlyk was a wonder to behold. The dwarves had worked efficiently when they chose to construct the citadel at Norlyk.

"My lord," Bastyon had said when he entered the room.

"Bastyon," greeted Tesnayr. "It is good of you to come. I suppose the situation has been explained?"

"Yes, Idæas told me what it is you wish to do." Bastyon did not understand the order, but he would do anything for his king.

Tesnayr unhooked the sword from around his waist and solemnly handed it to Bastyon. He took it admiring its markings. "But, my king, your sword. Surely, you must—"

"Part with it," interrupted Tesnayr. Sorrow filled his face momentarily before he regained his composure. "The sword served me well, but I no longer need it and must let it go. I do not ask for you to understand. Only that you heed my command."

"I will do as you ask."

"Do not take this job lightly, Bastyon. I am entrusting you to guard this sword from any who dare steal it for their own purposes. One day, its rightful heir will find it. When that day comes you will know. But know this: it may be a very long time. You could be locked away from the world for centuries."

"You have my word."

"Very well. You will travel to the edges of MurDair. There is a place just outside the town of Samara. It is a deep cave, you can't miss it. Ernayn will be waiting for you there."

"The sorceress," said Bastyon.

"She will not harm you," assured Tesnayr. "But you must do as she commands."

"Yes, my king." Bastyon turned to leave.

"One other thing," said Tesnayr. He picked up a large book and wrapped it in a velvet cloth before handing it to Bastyon. "You will need this. Guard the sword with your life. Only when the world has need of it again will it resurface. On that day, your mission will end. Good luck."

"On my honor, I will not let you down." Bastyon left barely hearing the last words Tesnayr spoke to him.

"I know you won't."

I know you won't. Such trust. Determined, Bastyon touched the sword making certain he still possessed it.

"You made it." Ernayn, the sorceress, pulled him from his reverie.

Bastyon halted his horse and dismounted. "Was there any doubt?"

"This way," said Ernayn in answer. She moved into the dark hole of the earth. Bastyon followed.

"Wait a moment." Ernayn sealed the cave opening with a spell. "This way." She walked deep underground until the gravelly corridor led into a chamber. The well-lit area revealed a pedestal and a tapestry.

Bastyon marveled at the chamber that had been prepared for him.

"Put the book on the pedestal."

Bastyon did as he was told. Gingerly, he placed it on the table and unwrapped it.

"I will leave it up to you to decide where to place the sword within the chamber. The book contains a history of the five lands. It even contains records of Tesnayr's feats against the orcs."

"But why—"

"None of your concern," interrupted Ernayn, "When Tesnayr's heir arrives he will have to be able to read from the book. It is written in the ancient language. You have studied it I presume."

Bastyon nodded in answer.

"This is your last chance to turn around and head home."

"I have no intention of leaving. I gave my word to King Tesnayr." Bastyon understood the cost.

"Very well," said Ernayn. "I am going to perform a simple spell. It will transfer the long years I, as a sorceress, possess to you. This will enable you to not age at all. You will have no need of food and drink."

Bastyon absorbed the sorceress' words. "What will become of you?"

"My death."

The simple statement shocked Bastyon. The sorceress was going to die?

"It is necessary," said Ernayn, "I have lived long enough. The only way I can ensure your success on this assignment is to die. Do not look so sad." She touched his cheek. "You will be alone down here."

"Yes, sorceress. I just did not expect you to have to die."

"Every person has an end. This is mine. Now, give me your hand."

Bastyon stretched out his hand. She took it firmly. Her soft skin surprised him.

"Dolsè ac n'him," said Ernayn is a strong voice that echoed through the cave.

A blue light spread from her hand stretching up Bastyon's arm. Tendrils of light spilled from her encompassing them. More light spilled from Ernayn filling the chamber with its powerful glow. Brighter and brighter it grew until suddenly, it disappeared.

A pile of rock and ash remained where Ernayn had been. Bastyon reached down and touched what was left of the powerful sorceress. He looked at his hand. It looked the same, but he felt different. Flexing his fingers, Bastyon studied himself. He felt powerful and strong as though time could not touch him.

Bastyon pulled out Tesnayr's sword from beneath his cloak. He held it in the sheath knowing full well what would happen if he touched the blade. He studied the markings on the scabbard. The tapestry caught his attention. An idea struck him. Whomever was meant for the sword should be able to solve a simple riddle.

Centuries passed and in all that time no one knew of Bastyon, the cavern near Samara, nor the treasure he guarded. And so Bastyon remained. Alone, in the dark.

Glossary

Arnin	are-nin	Nelyn	nell-lynn
Banis	bane-is	Nigilin	ni-gell-lynn
Bastyon	bast-e-on		
Belarnia	ba-lar-knee-a	Ninspíríl	nin-spear-ul
Belyndril	ba-lynn-drill	Nular	new-lar
Blynak	bly-knack	Nylin	nigh-lynn
Drinylle	dry-knell	Quesha	k-sha
Edrei	eh-dree	Rybnik	rib-nik
Ernayn	er-nay-in	Sarwyn	sar-win
Galbrok	gal-brock	Selexia	se-lex-e-uh
Hemíl	heh-mill		
Idæas	e-day-us	Serein	ser-rene
		Shealayr	sha-lar
Jarown	ja-roun	Slyamal	sla-mall
Jenel	je-knell	Sym'Dul	sim-dull
MurDair	myrr-dare	Telinin	tell-i-nin
Nalim	na-lem	Tesnayr	tez-nay-air
Nedis	neh-diss	Turyn	tur-in

Coming 2013:
Legends Lost Galdin

Sneak Peek inside.

Captain Dylan burst through the chamber doors. "We must leave, my lady," he urged. The sounds of battle echoed throughout the grounds. *Betrayed.* The king was dead. Killed by his most trusted general. Captain Dylan had an oath to fulfill. But it was more than that. To Captain Dylan the king was like a brother. He viewed the king's family as his own. This would be his final act of loyalty to his king.

"So it has begun," said Kylana.

"General Vasagius has staged a coup. His soldiers have overrun the palace. You and your children are in danger. He has come for them."

"He wouldn't dare."

"My lady, I watched as he stabbed the king not once, but three times."

"Where are the others? Are you the last in which loyalty still resides?"

The castle rumbled beneath their feet as catapults bombarded it. Captain Dylan raced to the balcony and watched in anguish as Vasagius' army stormed the gates; filling the castle grounds with their slaughtering thirst. Vasagius himself issued orders from atop his horse in the courtyard. Captain Dylan knew time did not favor them. "My lady, please," he begged with a note of urgency in his voice. The screams of the dying came closer as death's grasp tightened over the castle. The vile taste of fear crept from his chest to his throat, desperate for escape. Captain Dylan's military rigor refused to let it through.

Kylana remained reserved. The cries of the soldiers grew louder. "Nylana, grab the child," she said to her daughter.

"Yes, mother." Nylana walked to the cradle and gently lifted the baby boy from it. She handed him to her mother.

Kylana rose to her feet. She held her baby close and placed a reassuring hand on her daughter. "Lead the way, Captain."

Captain Dylan saluted and led them into the corridor where two of his men stood guard. "This way." They walked quickly. The battle cries resonated from the stone walls, drowning everything else. The rioting soldiers drew closer. Captain Dylan's heart ached. He longed to be with his men. A soldier belonged on the battlefield, not creeping through dark hallways. Yet, he had sworn an oath. That oath placed him with the queen and in charge of her safety. He stopped them in front of a giant statue. The two guards pushed it aside revealing a dark and damp tunnel.

Kylana approached the tunnel warily. With a glance at Captain Dylan she entered, followed quickly by Nylana. Captain Dylan followed the ladies while the two guards sealed the entrance. Captain Dylan's heart pounded as they moved through the dank tunnel, carefully treading on the slimy floor. If caught, they'd be slaughtered. Perhaps this is what death feels like, he thought, endless anticipation of the inevitable. The baby whimpered. He looked back. Kylana skidded on the slime and fell. Captain Dylan hurried to help her up. Vasagius may have succeeded in taking the throne today, but Captain Dylan vowed to protect the true heir so that one day the rightful king would reign. These tunnels would not become their tomb.

Thunderous explosions rumbled above them shaking the tunnel walls. Rock fell over them. They were thrown into the slimy muck on the floor. As the dust cleared Captain Dylan looked around. "Anyone hurt?" he asked. The baby wailed in reply.

Captain Dylan scanned the pile of rock. He saw a small hole near the bottom right of the newly formed rock wall. *Too small.* Captain Dylan and his men set feverishly to work widening the hole. Their efforts and slow progress reminded them of time whittling away. Coughing and wheezing filled the air. A distant crash in the tunnel sounded behind them. Wide enough or not, they had to go through the hole.

"Go." Captain Dylan shoved Kylana and her baby through first. Next, went the two guards. "Come on," he said holding his hand out to Nylana. Nylana stared at him with saucer sized eyes. She was terrified. Can't blame her, he thought, her entire world had just been ripped away. Marching footsteps echoed through the passageway. "Come," urged Captain Dylan once more. Nylana pulled away from him as he snatched her and shoved her through the hole.

Once on the other side, Captain Dylan plugged the hole. He pushed the queen onward. He did not like being rough with her, but their survival was imperative. A sliver of light lay ahead. They were close to the tunnel's end. Air brushed their flushed cheeks as they finally escaped the dark underground and greeted the sun's rays. Celebrations would have to wait, however, as they were still far from safety.

Captain Dylan commandeered a hay wagon. He put the queen and her children onto the wagon covering them with hay. One guard secured the driver's seat while the other rounded up horses. "We must cross the river," he yelled climbing up. He turned his horse and charged for the bridge. It wasn't far. Once across, they could escape in the woods beyond.

A horn sounded in the distance alerting others of their escape. Soldiers lined up on the castle wall. Others on horseback raced out of the gates chasing after them. Arrows rained down on them. Captain Dylan watched powerlessly as they pierced the hay in the wagon. He turned back pulling out a dagger. He flung it at the approaching soldiers striking one of them in the chest. More followed.

He followed the wagon. His heart lurched as he watched it bounce a foot into the air upon reaching the threshold of the bridge. Such a wagon was not meant to be driven so hard, or so fast. He hoped it held together long enough to get them to safety. He would not falter now. The wagon lurched again as one of the wheels broke off. A woman's scream pierced his ears. Kylana sat bolt upright as the wagon swerved from side to side before coming to a screeching halt. "My baby," she screamed. Captain Dylan stared in disbelief as the river's current carried the baby away. There was nothing her could do. Vasagius' soldiers approached and the baby had reached the waterfall. As Kylana ran to the edge of the bridge, he kicked his horse and rushed to his queen before she could jump in after the child. He grabbed her arm and yanked her onto his horse. She struggled to break free. He punched her in the jaw rendering her unconscious. "Let's move," he yelled as one of his men grabbed Nylana.

As he reached the rivers' edge and rode to the safety of the trees sorrow swept over him. He choked it down. The child was lost. Only the queen and her daughter remained. I have failed you my king, he wept inside. "Captain," yelled one of his soldiers, yanking him from his self-pity. He steeled his heart for the moment. Grief and second thoughts had to wait. For now, they remained in the vast emptiness of the unknown.

Farther up the river, in the northern reaches of Sym'Dul, a woman lay by a fresh mound of dirt. Tears streaked her soiled face as she wept for the child she would never know. Her sorrow blocked the chill seeping from the wet earth. A flutter of wings sounded overhead. She looked up and stared at the grave next to the one she laid upon, the one of her husband. Two losses within five months weighed heavily upon her.

Cold steel pricked her fingers. She pulled out the dagger she always carried with her. She turned it in her hands. It glinted slightly in the dimming twilight. My salvation, she thought. Not wanting to bear the pain within her broken heart, she lifted the dagger. The sharp point settled on her left breast. Taking a deep breath, she tightened her grip and—

CAW!

The harsh screech of a bird stayed her hand. The woman glared into the sad eyes of a strange bird on the edge of the river. Its brilliant feathers glowed brightly despite the oncoming of night. "Who are you that disturbs me in my grief," said the woman.

The bird glanced down at a bundle before it. For the first time, the woman noticed it and the tiny hand the stuck out. An infant's cry filled the air. Forgetting her grief, the woman dropped her dagger and rushed to the child. *He's beautiful.* Gently, she lifted the baby cradling him in her arms. Her vision blurred as tears filled her eyes. A small smile crossed her face.

An inscription on the infant's cloth diverted her attention. Galdin, it read. "Well, Galdin, let's go home," she said soothingly to the child.

The woman sang to the infant as she carried him to her home. Her previous sadness remained buried with the fresh mound of dirt. Now, she had a son to care for.

About the Author

Janet McNulty (aka Nova Rose) began writing the Legends Lost Trilogy ten years ago. Tesnayr is the second book; Amborese is the first. She will finish the trilogy in Galdin which is to be released in the summer of 2013.

She has also written a mystery series, *The Mellow Summers Series*, and two nonfiction books: *Illogical Nonsense* and *Politics and Insights from History (An Anthology of Blog Entries from April 2009-June 2012)*.

Ms. McNulty has always enjoyed writing, penning stories since the age of eight. After years of public education and college enlightenment, she decided to make a career of it.

Follow on Twitter: JMRUL
Follow her blogs: Books and Legends

If you liked Tesnayr, you'll enjoy:

Amborese thought she was a peasant's daughter until one night dark creatures murdered her parents and pursued her into the forest. Saved by a talking cat and her friend Zolo, she fled for her life only to learn that she had a bigger destiny than she once believed. Pursued across the five lands of Tesnayr by an evil wizard's army, Amborese must overcome her doubts and unite the dragons, elves, dwarves, and the five lands themselves. But will they follow a mere girl?

Available at Amazon and barnesandnoble.com.

Visit www.legendslosttrilogy.com to learn more about the Legends Lost Trilogy.

Other young adult fiction by this writer under Janet McNulty

The *Mellow Summers Series*.

Mellow Summers moves to Vermont to attend college, accompanied by her friend Jackie. They soon find themselves running into ghosts and one mystery after another.

Get the Latest Trilogy by Janet McNulty

Available Now

Imagine living in a world where everything you do is controlled.

www.ingramcontent.com/pod-product-compliance
Lightning Source LLC
Chambersburg PA
CBHW030753260626
47169CB00001B/24